His movements were grace and brutality;
his body a testament of his convictions.

TWISTED LOYALTIES

Cora Reilly

Book design by Inkstain Design Studio
Cover design by Romantic Book Affairs Designs

Subscribe to Cora's newsletter to find out more about her next books,
bonus content and giveaways: http://corareillyauthor.blogspot.de/p/newsletter.html

TWISTED LOYALTIES

PROLOGUE

NEW YORK - FAMIGLIA TERRITORY

Luca had been Capo for more than ten years, but things had never been this fucked up. Perched on the edge of the wide mahogany desk, Luca scanned the crinkled map showing the borders of their territory. His Famiglia still controlled the entire length of the East Coast, from Maine to Georgia. Nothing had changed in decades. The Camorra, however, had extended their territory far beyond Las Vegas into the east, having acquired Kansas City from the Russians only recently. Their Capo, Remo Falcone, was starting to get too confident. Luca had a fucking inkling that his next move would be attack either Outfit or Famiglia territory. Luca had to make sure Falcone set his sights on Dante Cavallaro's cities and not his own. Enough of his men had already died in the war between the Famiglia and the Outfit. Another war with the Camorra would tear them apart.

"I know you don't like the idea," he muttered to his soldier.

Growl nodded. "I don't, but I'm in no position to tell you what to do. You are Capo. I can only tell you what I know about the Camorra, and it's not good."

"So what?" Matteo, Luca's brother and right hand man, said with a shrug, spinning his knife between his fingers. "We can handle them."

A knock sounded and Aria entered the office, which was in the basement of Luca's club, the Sphere. She curiously raised her blond eyebrows, wondering why her husband had called her. He usually handled business on his own. Matteo and Growl were already inside. Luca was leaning against the desk and unfolded his tall frame from when she stepped into the room. She went over to him and kissed his lips lovingly then asked, "What's wrong?"

"Nothing," Luca said matter-of-factly, his lips set tight, his eyes holding a wary glint. Something was off. "But we've contacted the Camorra for negotiations."

Aria glanced at Growl. He had fled Las Vegas six years ago after he'd killed the Camorra's Capo, Benedetto Falcone. From what he'd told them, the Camorra was much worse than the Outfit or the Famiglia. Besides the usual business of drugs, casinos, and prostitution, they also dealt in sex slavery and kidnapping. In the mafia world, the Camorra was considered bad news. "You did?"

"The fight with the Outfit is weakening us. With the Bratva already breaching our territory, we have to be careful. We can't risk the Outfit forging a deal with the Camorra before we get the chance. If they fight us together, we'll be in trouble."

Guilt filled Aria. She and her sisters were the reason why the truce between the Chicago Outfit and the New York Famiglia had dissolved. Her marriage to Luca was supposed to create a bond between the two families, but when her youngest sister, Liliana, fled Chicago to marry Luca's soldier, Romero, the Outfit's boss, Dante Cavallaro, declared war on them; he couldn't have reacted any other way.

"Do you think they will even consider talking to us?" Aria asked. She still wasn't sure why she was here in the first place. She didn't have any useful information about the Camorra.

Luca nodded. "They sent one of their own to talk to us. He'll be here soon." Something in his voice, an undercurrent of tension and worry, raised the little hairs on her neck.

"They're taking a huge risk by sending someone. They can't know if he's going to return alive," Aria said in surprise.

"One life is nothing to them," Growl murmured. "And the Capo didn't send one of his brothers. He sent his new Enforcer."

Aria didn't like the way Luca, Matteo, and Growl were looking at her.

"They think he'll be safe," Luca said and after a long pause added, "because it's your brother."

The ground dropped away from Aria's feet, and she gripped the edge of the desk. "Fabi?" she whispered.

She hadn't seen or talked to him in many years. Since they declared war, she wasn't allowed to contact her brother. Her father, the Consigliere of the Outfit, had made sure of it.

She paused in her thoughts. "What's Fabi doing with the Camorra? He is a member of the Outfit. He was supposed to follow my father as Consigliere one day."

"He was supposed to, yes," Luca said, exchanging a look with the other men. "But your father's got two younger sons with his new wife, and apparently one of them will become Consigliere. We don't know what went down, but for some reason Fabiano defected to the Camorra, and for some reason they took him in. It's difficult to get accurate information on the matter."

"I can't believe it. I'm going to see my brother again. When?" she asked eagerly. Fabiano was almost nine years younger than Aria, and she'd practically raised him until she had to leave Chicago to marry Luca.

Growl shook his head with a frown.

Luca touched Aria's shoulder. "Aria, your brother is the new Enforcer of the Camorra."

It took a few seconds for the information to sink in. Aria's eyes darted over to Growl. His tattoos and scars, and the darkness lingering in his eyes, scared her. And being married to Luca, she wasn't easily scared anymore.

Growl had been the Enforcer of the Camorra when Benettone Falcone had been Capo. And now that Falcone's son had seized power, Fabi had taken over the role. She swallowed. *Enforcer.* They did the dirty work. The bloody work. They made sure people obeyed, and if they didn't obey, Enforcers made sure their fate was a warning to anyone considering the same.

"No," she said softly. "Not Fabi. He's not capable of that kind of thing." He had been a caring, gentle boy and had always tried to protect his sisters.

Matteo gave her a look that told her she was being naïve. She didn't care as long as it kept the memory of her kind, funny little brother alive. She didn't want to imagine him as anything else.

"The brother you knew won't be the brother you'll see today. He'll be someone completely different. That boy you knew … he's dead. He has to be. Enforcement isn't a job for the kindhearted. It's cruel and dirty work. And the Camorra doesn't show mercy toward women like is habit for New York or Chicago. I doubt that's changed. Remo Falcone is a twisted fucker like his father," Growl said in his raspy voice.

Aria looked at Luca, hoping he'd contradict his soldier. He didn't. Something in Aria cracked. "I can't believe it. I don't want to," she said. "How could he have changed so much?"

"He's here," one of Luca's men informed them, walking into the office. "But he refuses to hand over his weapons."

Luca nodded. "It doesn't matter. We outnumber him. Let him through."

Then he turned to Aria. "Perhaps we'll find out today."

Aria tensed with the sound of steps approaching. A tall man stepped through the open office door. He was almost as tall as Luca. Not quite as broad, but muscled. A Tattoo peeked out under his rolled-up shirtsleeves. His dark blond hair was buzzed on the sides and slightly longer on top, and his ice-blue eyes . . .

Cold. Calculating. Cautious.

Aria wasn't sure she would have recognized him in the street. No longer a boy, he was a man—and not just judging by his age. His eyes settled on her. The smile of the past didn't come, even though recognition flashed in his eyes. God, there really was nothing left of the lighthearted boy she remembered. But he was still her brother. He would always be. It was foolish, but she rushed toward him, ignoring Luca's growled warning.

Her brother grew tense as she threw her arms around him. She could feel the knives strapped to his back, the guns in his chest holster. She was confident there were more weapons on his body. He didn't hug her back, but one of his hands cupped her neck. Aria looked up at him then. She hadn't expected to see the anger in his eyes as he returned his focus to Luca and the other men in the room.

"No need for drawn weapons," he said with a hint of cold amusement. "I haven't traveled all the way to hurt my sister."

His touch on her neck seemed more like a threat and less like a gesture of familiarity.

Luca's fingers closed around her upper arm, and he pulled her back. Fabiano followed the scene with dark humor in his eyes, remaining stock-still didn't move an inch.

"My god," Aria whispered in a voice thick with tears. "What happened to you, Fabi?"

A predator grin curled his lips.

Not Fabi anymore, she thought. That man in front of her . . . he was someone to be afraid of.

Fabiano Scuderi.

Enforcer of the Camorra.

CHAPTER 1

THE PAST - FABIANO

I curled into myself and didn't fight back. I never did.

Father grunted from the effort of beating me. Punch after punch—my back, my head, my stomach—creating new bruises and awakening old bruises. I gasped when he shoved the toe of his shoe into my stomach, swallowing down bile. If I threw up, he'd only beat me worse. Or use the knife. I shuddered.

Then the hits stopped, and I dared to look up, blinking to clear my vision. Sweat and blood dripped down my face.

Breathing hard, Father glowered at me. He wiped his hands on a towel that his soldier, Alfonso, had handed him. Perhaps this was the last test to prove my worth. Maybe I'd finally become an official part of the Outfit. A Made Man.

"Do I get my tattoo?" I rasped.

Father's lip curled. "Your tattoo? You won't be part of the Outfit."

"But—" He kicked me again, and I fell back to my side. I pressed on, not

caring about the consequences. "But I will be Consigliere when you retire."
When you die.

He gripped my collar and pulled me to my feet. My legs ached as I tried to stand. "You are a fucking waste of my blood. You and your sisters share your mother's tainted genes. One disappointment after another. All of you. Your sisters are whores, and you are weak. I'm done with you. Your brother will become Consigliere."

"But he's a baby. I'm your oldest son." Since Father had married his second wife, he'd treated me like dirt. I thought it was to make me strong for my future tasks, so I'd done everything I could to prove my worth to him.

"You are a disappointment like your sisters. I won't allow you to bring shame down on me." He let go of me and my legs finally gave out.

More pain.

"But, Father," I whispered. "It's tradition."

Rage twisted his facial features. "Then, we'll just have to make sure that your brother is my oldest son." He nodded at Alfonso, who rolled up his sleeves.

Alfonso landed the first punch in my stomach then my ribs. My eyes remained on my father as blow after blow shook my body, until my vision finally turned black. My own father would have me killed.

"Make sure he won't be found, Alfonso."

Pain. Bone deep.

I groaned. Vibrations sent a twinge through my ribs. I tried to open my eyes and sit up, but my lids were crusted shut. I groaned again.

I wasn't dead.

Why wasn't I dead?

Hope flared up inside me.

"Father?" I croaked.

"Shut up and sleep, boy. We'll arrive soon."

That was Alfonso's voice.

I struggled into a sitting position and peeled my eyes open. Through blurry vision, I could see I was sitting in the back of a car.

Alfonso turned to me. "You're stronger than I thought. Good for you."

"Where?" I coughed then winced. "Where are we?"

"Kansas City." Alfonso steered the car onto an empty parking lot. "Final stop."

He got out, opened the back door, and pulled me out. I gasped in pain, holding my ribs, then staggered against the car. Alfonso flipped open his wallet and handed me a twenty-dollar note. I took it, confused.

"Perhaps you'll survive. Perhaps you won't. I suppose it's up to fate now. But I won't kill a fourteen-year-old kid." He grasped my throat, forcing me to meet his eyes. "Your father thinks you're dead, boy, so make sure you stay away from our territory."

Their territory? It was my territory. The Outfit was my destiny. I didn't have anything else.

"Please," I whispered.

He shook his head then walked around the car and got in. I took a step back when he drove off, sinking down to my knees. My clothes were covered in blood. I clutched the money in my hand. This was all I had. Slowly, I stretched out on the cool asphalt. Pressure against my calf reminded me of my favorite knife, strapped to a holster there. Twenty dollars and a knife. My body ached. I never wanted to get up again. There was no sense in doing anything. I was nothing. I wished Alfonso had done as my father ordered and just killed me.

I coughed and tasted blood. I'll probably die anyway. My eyes flitted around. Graffiti covered the wall of a building to my right: a snarling wolf in front of swords.

The sign of the Bratva.

Alfonso couldn't kill me himself.

This place surely would. Kansas City belonged to the Russians.

Fear urged me to get to my feet and leave. I wasn't sure where to go or what to do. I hurt all over. At least it wasn't too cold. I began walking, looking for a place to spend the night. Eventually, I settled for the entrance of a coffee shop. I'd never been alone, never had to live on the streets. I pulled my legs against my chest and swallowed a whimper. My ribs. They hurt fiercely. I couldn't return to the Outfit. Father would make sure I was dead this time. Perhaps I could try to contact Dante Cavallaro. He and Father had worked together for a long time, and I'd look like a fucking rat. A coward and weakling.

Aria would help. My stomach clenched. Her helping Lily and Gianna was the reason why Father hated me in the first place. Running to New York with my tail between my legs, begging Luca to make me part of the Famiglia, wasn't going to happen. Everyone would know I had been taken in out of pity, not because I was a worthy asset.

Worthless.

This was it. I was alone.

Four days later. Only four days. I was out of money and hope. Every night I returned to the parking lot, hoping, wishing that Alfonso would return, that Father had changed his mind, that his last pitiless, hateful look had been my imagination. I was a fucking idiot. And hungry.

No food in two days. I'd wasted the whole twenty bucks on burgers, fries, and Dr. Pepper the first day.

I held my ribs. The pain had gotten worse. I'd tried to get money by pickpocketing today. Chose the wrong guy and he beat up. I didn't know how to survive on the street. I wasn't sure I wanted to keep trying.

What was I going to do? No Outfit. No future. No honor.

I sank down on the ground of the parking lot, in plain view of the Bratva graffiti. I lay back. The door opened as men left the building, walking away. Bratva territory.

I was so fucking tired.

My death wouldn't be slow. They would take their time. The pain in my limbs and hopelessness kept me in place. I stared up at the night sky and began reciting the oath I'd memorized months ago, in preparation for the day of my induction. The Italian words flowing from my mouth filled me with loss and despair. I repeated the oath over and over again. It had been my destiny to become a made man.

There were voices to my right. Male voices in a foreign language.

Suddenly a black-haired guy stared down at me. He was bruised, though not as badly as me, and dressed in fight shorts. "They say there's a crazy Italian fucker outside, spouting Omertá. I guess they meant you."

I fell silent. He'd said 'Omertá' like I would say it, like it meant something. He was covered in scars. Probably a few years older than me. Eighteen, perhaps.

"Talking that kind of shit in this area means you've got a death wish or are bat-shit crazy. Probably both."

"That oath was my life," I said.

He shrugged then looked over his shoulder before turning back with a twisted smile. "Now it's going to be your death."

I sat up. Three men in fight shorts, bodies covered in tattoos of wolves and Kalashnikovs and heads clean shaven, stepped out of a door beside the Bratva building.

I considered lying back and letting them finish what Alfonso couldn't.

"What family?" The black-haired guy asked.

"Outfit," I replied, even as the word ripped a hole in my heart.

He nodded. "Suppose they got rid of you. No balls to do what it takes to be a made man?"

Who was he? "I got what it takes," I hissed. "But my father wants me dead."

"Then prove it. Get the fuck up from the ground and fight." He narrowed his eyes when I didn't move. "Get. The. Fuck. Up."

And I did, even though my world spun and I had to hold on to my ribs. His black eyes took in my injuries. "Suppose I will have to do most of the fighting. Got any weapons?"

I pulled my Karambit knife from the holster around my calf.

"I hope you can handle that thing."

Then the Russians were upon us. The guy began some martial arts shit that kept two of the Russians busy. The third headed my way. I swiped my knife at him and missed. He landed a few hits that had my chest screaming with agony, and I dropped to my knees. With my body battered and bruised, I had no chance against a trained fighter like him. His fists rained down on me, hard, fast, merciless. *Pain.*

The black-haired guy lunged at my attacker, ramming his knee into his stomach. The Russian fell forward, and I raised my knife, which buried itself in his abdomen. Blood trickled down my fingers, and I released the handle like it burned me as the Russian toppled to his side, dead.

I stared at my knife sticking out of his belly. The black-haired guy pulled it out, cleaned the blade on the dead man's shorts, then handed it to me. "First kill?"

I nodded, my fingers shaking as I took it from him.

"There will be more."

The two other Russians were dead as well. Their necks had been broken. He held out his hand, which I grabbed as he pulled me to my feet. "We should leave. More Russian fuckers will be here soon. Come on."

He led me toward a beat-up truck. "Noticed you slinking around the parking lot the last two nights when I was here to fight."

"Why did you help me?"

There was that twisted smile again. "Because I like to fight ... and kill. Because I hate the fucking Bratva. Because my family wants me dead too. But most importantly, because I need loyal soldiers who will help me take back what's mine."

"Who are you?"

"Remo Falcone. And I will be Capo of the Camorra soon." He opened the door to his truck and was halfway in when he added, "You can help me or you can wait for the Bratva to get you."

I got in. Not because of the Bratva.

Because Remo had shown me a new purpose, a new destiny.

A new family.

CHAPTER 2

LEONA

The window of the Greyhound bus felt sticky hot, or maybe it was my face. The infant in the row behind me had stopped wailing ten minutes ago—finally, after almost two hours. I peeled my cheek from the glass, feeling sluggish and tired. Squeezed into the stuffy seat for hours, I couldn't wait to get out. Las Vegas' posh suburbs rolled past me, their immaculate landscaping sufficiently watered by sprinklers. Surrounded by desert, that must be the ultimate showcase of having money. Elaborate Christmas decorations adorned the porches and the fronts of freshly painted houses.

Despite how beautiful, that wouldn't be my stop.

The bus trudged on, the floor vibrating under my bare feet, until finally it arrived in that part of town where no tourist ever dared set foot in. The all-you-can-eat buffets cost only $9.99 around here, not $59; I could afford neither. Not that I minded. I'd grown up in areas like these. In Phoenix, Houston, Dallas,

Austin, and more other places than I cared to count. I slipped into my flip-flops, swung my backpack over my shoulder, getting ready to depart the bus.

Out of habit, I reached into my pocket for a cell phone that was no longer there. Mother had sold it for her last dose of crystal meth. The twenty dollars she got for it had been out of pity, no doubt.

I waited until most of the other people had left before I stepped off the bus, releasing a long breath as I stood under the sun. The air was drier than in Austin, and it was a few degrees colder, but still not wintery cold. Somehow, I already felt freer being away from my mother. This was her last shot at therapy. She needed to make it a success. I was stupid for hoping she could.

"Leona?" came a deep voice from somewhere to the right.

I turned, surprised. My father stood a few feet from me, with about thirty more pounds on his hips and less hair on his head. I hadn't expected him to pick me up. He'd promised to do it, but I knew what promises from him and my mother were worth. Less than the dirt under my shoes. Perhaps he'd really changed like he'd claimed.

He quickly stubbed out his cigarette under his worn loafers. The short-sleeved shirt stretched over his paunch. There was an disheveled air about him that had me worried.

I smiled. "The one and only."

I wasn't surprised he'd had to ask. The last time I'd seen him had been on my fourteenth birthday, more than five years ago. I hadn't exactly missed him. I'd missed the idea of having a father—one he could never be. Still, it was nice to see him again. Maybe we could start anew.

He came over and pulled me into an awkward hug. I wrapped my arms around him despite the lingering stench of sweat and smoke. It had been a while since someone had hugged me. Standing back, he scanned me from head to toe. "You've grown." His eyes paused on my smile. "And your pimples are gone."

Have been for three years. "Thank god," I said instead.

My father pushed his hands into his pockets, as if he was suddenly unsure of what to do with me. "I was surprised when you called."

I tucked a strand of hair behind my ear, unsure where he was going with this. "You never did," I said before soon regretting it. I hadn't come to Vegas to dish out guilt. Dad had never been a good father, but he'd tried occasionally . . . even if he always failed. Mom and him . . . They were both fucked up in their own ways. Addiction had always been the thing that got in the way of caring for me the way they should have.

He gave me an appraising look. "Are you sure you want to stay with me?"

My smile wavered. Was that what his hesitation was all about? He didn't want me around? I really wished he mentioned that before I'd paid for a bus ticket that took me through half the states. He'd said he beat his addiction, that he had a decent job and a normal life. I wanted to believe him.

"It's not that I'm not happy to have you with me. I missed you," he said quickly. Too quickly. Lies.

"Then what?" I asked, trying but failing to hide my hurt.

"It's not a good place for a nice girl like you, Leona."

I laughed. "I've never exactly lived in the nice parts of town," I told him. "I can handle myself."

"No. It's different here. Believe me."

"Don't worry. I'm good at staying out of trouble." I'd had years of practice. With a meth-addicted mother who sold anything, even her body, for her next fix, you had to learn to duck your head and mind your own business.

"Sometimes trouble finds you. It happens around here more often than you'd believe." The way he said it, I worried that trouble was a constant guest in his life.

I sighed. "Honestly, Dad, I've lived with a mother who spent most of her days in a drug haze. You never worried enough to take me away from her. Now that I'm grown up, you're worried I can't handle living in the City of Sin?"

He looked at me as if he was going to say more but then finally took my backpack from me before I could tighten my hold on the strap. "You're right."

"And I'm only going to stay here until I've earned enough money for college. There are enough places around here where I can make decent money with tips."

He looked relieved that I wanted to work. Had he thought I was going to live off him?

"There are more than enough places, but few that are fit for a girl like you."

I shook my head, smiling. "Don't worry. I can handle drunkards."

"I'm not worried about them," he said nervously.

FABIANO

"Are you really thinking about working with the Famiglia?" I managed to pant as I dodged a kick aimed at my head. "I told you how they fucked with the Outfit."

I thrust my bandaged fist into Remo's side then tried a kick at his legs, but he landed a fist into my stomach instead. I jumped back, out of Remo's reach, and feigned an attack to the left and instead kicked with my right leg. Remo's arm shot up, protecting his head, taking the full force of my kick. He didn't fall. "I don't want to work with them. Not with Luca fucking Vitiello nor with Dante fucking Cavallaro. We don't need them."

"Then why send me to New York?" I asked.

Remo got two quick blows to my left side. I sucked in a breath and rammed my elbow down on his shoulder. He hissed and darted away, but I got him. His arm was hanging low. I'd dislocated his shoulder. My favorite move.

"Open refusal?" he asked half in jest, giving no indication that he was in agony.

"You wish."

Remo liked to break things. There wasn't anything he liked better. Sometimes I thought he wanted me to revolt so he could try breaking me because I'd be his biggest challenge. I had no intention of giving him the chance. Not that he'd succeed.

He glared and lunged at me. I barely dodged his first two kicks; the third hit my chest. I was thrown into the boxing ring and almost lost my balance but caught myself by gripping the rope. I quickly straightened and raised my fists.

"Oh fuck this shit," Remo snarled. He grabbed his arm and tried to reposition his shoulder. "I can't fight with this fucking useless limb."

I lowered my hands. "So you give up?"

"No," he said. "Tie."

"Tie," I agreed. There had never been anything but ties in our fights, except for the very first year when I'd been a scrawny kid without a clue how to fight. We were both strong fighters, used to pain and indifferent about whether we lived or died. If we ever fought it out till the end, we'd both end up in body bags. No doubt about it.

I snatched a towel from the floor and wiped the blood and sweat from my chest and arms.

With a grunt, Remo finally managed to set his arm. It would have been quicker and less painful if I'd help, but he'd never let me. Pain meant nothing to him. Nor to me.

I threw a clean towel at him. He caught it with his injured arm just to prove a point. Attempting to dry his hair, he only managed to spread the blood from a cut on his head all over his black hair. He dropped the towel unceremoniously. The scar running from his left temple down to his left cheek was an angry red from fighting.

"So why?" I asked, removing the red-tinged bandages around my fingers and wrist.

"I want to see how things are going over there. I'm curious. That's all. And I like to know my enemies. You will be able to gather more information than any of us just by watching them interact. Most of all, I want to send them a clear message." His dark eyes became hard. "You aren't thinking about playing happy family with your sisters and becoming one of Vitiello's lapdogs, are you?"

I cocked one eyebrow. More than five years and he really had to ask? I swung myself over the boxing ring and light on my feet, I landed on the floor on the other side with close to no sound. "I belong to the Camorra. When they all abandoned me, you took me in. You made me who I am today, Remo. You should know better than to accuse me of being a traitor. I will put my life down for you. And if I must, I will take the Outfit and the Famiglia to Hell with me."

"One day you will get your chance," he said.

To lay down my life for him or to take down the other families?

"I have another task for you."

I nodded, expecting it. He held my eyes. "You are the only one who can get close to Aria. She is Vitiello's weakness."

I kept my expression impassive.

"Bring her to me, Fabiano."

"Dead or alive?"

He smiled. "Alive. If you kill her, Vitiello will go on a rampage, but if we have his wife, he'll be our puppet."

I didn't have to ask why he had an interest in tearing down the Famiglia. We didn't need their territory, and it wasn't worth much as long as Dante owned everything in the middle. We were making enough money in the west as it was. Remo was out for revenge. Luca had made a mistake when he'd taken in the former Enforcer of the Camorra, and he'd made an even bigger mistake when he'd sent the man back to kill many high-ranking Camorrista while Las Vegas was without a strong Capo to lead the city. Before Remo, that is.

"Consider it done."

Remo inclined his head. "Your father was a fucking fool for overlooking your worth. But that's how fathers are. Mine would have never allowed me to become Capo. It's a pity I didn't get to kill him myself."

Remo envied me for that. I could still kill my father, and one day I would.

It had been years since I'd last treaded New York ground. I'd never liked the city much. It represented nothing but loss to me.

The bouncer in front of the Sphere gave me the once-over as I approached. I detected another guard on the roof. The street was deserted except for us. That wasn't going to change until much later when the first partygoers would try to get into the popular club.

I stopped in front of the bouncer. He rested his hand on the gun at his hip. He wouldn't be quick enough. "Fabiano Scuderi," I said simply. Of course he knew. They all knew. Without a word, he let me walk into the waiting room. Two men barred my way.

"Weapons," one of them ordered, pointing at a table.

"No," I said.

The taller of the two, several inches shorter than me, brought his face close to mine. "What was that?"

"That was a no. If you're too deaf or stupid to understand me, get someone who can. I'm losing my patience."

The man's face turned red. It would take three moves to severe his head from his body. "Tell the Capo he's here and refuses to put down his weapons."

If he thought he could intimidate me mentioning Luca, he was mistaken.

The times when I'd feared and admired him had long since passed. He was dangerous, no doubt, but so was I.

Eventually, he returned and I was finally allowed to pass through the blue-lit lobby and dance floor then down to the basement. It was a good place if someone wanted to stop outsiders from hearing the screaming. That didn't manage to unnerve me either. The Famiglia didn't know the Camorra very well. They didn't know me very well. We'd never been worth their attention until our power had grown too strong for them to ignore.

The moment I stepped into the office, I scanned my surroundings. Growl stood off to the left side. *Traitor.* Remo would love to have his head delivered to him in a plastic bag. Not because the man had killed his father, but because he'd betrayed the Camorra. That was a crime worthy of a painful death.

Luca and Matteo, were in the middle of the room, both tall and dark. My sister, Aria, with her blond hair was like a beacon of light.

I remembered her to be taller, but then again, I was a kid when I'd last seen her. The shock on her face was obvious. She still wore her emotions on the sleeve. Even her marriage to Luca hadn't changed that. You'd think he'd have broken her spirit by now. Strange that she was the same as I remembered though I had become someone new.

She rushed toward me. Luca reached for her, but she was too quick. He and his men drew their weapons the moment Aria collided with me. My hand came up to her neck momentarily. She hugged me, her hands splayed out on my back where I had my knives. She was too trusting. I could have killed her in a heartbeat. Breaking her neck would have taken little effort. I'd killed like that before, in fights to the death. Luca's bullet would have been too late. She looked up at me hopefully. Then, slowly, realization and fear set in. Yes, Aria. I'm not a little boy anymore.

I looked back at the men. "No need for drawn weapons," I said to Luca.

His cautious gaze flitted between my fingers positioned perfectly on her neck and my eyes. He recognized the danger his little wife was in, even if she didn't. "I haven't traveled all the way to hurt my sister."

It was the truth. I had no intention of hurting her, even though I could have. What Remo had in mind for her, I couldn't say. I slipped a note into the pocket of her jeans.

Luca lunged toward us and pulled her away from me, warning clear in his eyes.

"My God," Aria whispered, tears filling her eyes. "What happened to you?"

Did she really have to ask? Had she been so busy saving my sisters that she hadn't considered what that would mean for me?

"You, Gianna, and Liliana happened."

Confusion filled her face. She really didn't get it. Cold fury shot through me, but I pushed it down. Every horror of my past had made me into who I was today.

"I don't understand."

"After Liliana ran off as well, Father decided that something must be wrong with all of us. That perhaps Mother's blood running through our veins was the problem. He thought I was another mistake in the making. He tried to beat it out of me. Maybe he thought if I bled often enough, I'd be rid of any trace of that weakness. The moment his whore of a second wife gave birth to a boy, he decided I was no longer of use. He ordered one of his men to kill me. The man took pity on me and drove me to some shithole in Kansas City so the Bratva could kill me instead. I had twenty dollars and a knife." I paused. "And I put that knife to good use."

I could see the words sink in. She shook her head. "We didn't want to hurt you. We just wanted to save Liliana from a horrible marriage. We didn't think you'd need saving. You were a boy. You were on your way to becoming a soldier for the Outfit. We would have saved you if you'd asked."

"I saved myself," I said simply.

"You could still … leave Las Vegas," Aria said carefully. Luca sent her a glare.

I laughed darkly. "Are you suggesting I'll leave the Camorra and join the Famiglia?"

Wincing, she seemed taken aback by the harshness of my tone. "It's an option."

I turned my gaze toward Luca. "Is she Capo or you? I came here to talk to the man leading the show, but now I think it might be a woman after all."

Luca didn't seem fazed by my words, at least not openly. "She is your sister. She does the talking because I allowed her to do so. Don't worry, Fabi, if I had anything to say to you, I'd say it."

Fabi. The nickname didn't provoke me the way it was supposed to. I'd grown out of it. Nobody knew me by that name in Vegas, and even if they did, they wouldn't dare use it.

"We are not your enemy, Fabi," Aria said. And I knew she meant it. She was the Capo's vice, and yet she knew nothing. Her husband saw me as I saw him: an opponent to watch. A predator intruding on his territory.

"I'm a member of the Camorra. You *are* my enemies." If this journey had been good for anything, it proved to myself that there was truly nothing left of that stupid, weak boy I'd been. That had been beaten out of me, first by my father, and later in the street and in the fighting cages as I fought for a place in this world.

Aria shook her head, refusing to believe it. She hadn't abandoned me on purpose, hadn't sealed my fate by helping my sisters run away, but sometimes the things we caused by accident were the worst.

"I have a message from Remo for you," I told Luca, ignoring my sister. I'd deal with her later. She wasn't the only reason why I had come to New York. "You have nothing to offer Remo or the Camorra, unless perhaps you send him your wife for a joy ride." The words left a bitter taste in my mouth, if only because she was my sister.

Luca was halfway across the room before Aria stepped in his way. I had my gun out and one of my knives. "Calm down, Luca," Aria begged.

He glared at me. Oh, he wanted to rip me to shreds, and I wanted to see him try. He'd be a challenging opponent. Instead, he let my sister talk him down, but his eyes held a promise: *You are dead.*

Remo would have never listened to a woman, would have never shown that kind of weakness in front of anyone. Neither would I. The Outfit and the Famiglia both had grown weak over the years. They weren't a threat to us. If we handled the situation with cleverness, soon their territories would be ours.

I performed a mock bow. "I assume that's all."

"Don't you want to know how Lilly and Gianna are doing?" Aria asked hopefully, still looking for a sign of the boy she used to know. I wondered when she'd realize that he was gone for good. Perhaps when the Camorra took over someday, I'd ram my knife into her husband's heart.

"They mean nothing to me. The day you left for your pampered life in New York, you ceased existing for me."

I turned. Presenting my back to the enemy wasn't something I usually did, but I knew Aria, with her puppy dog eyes, would stop Luca from killing me. I wanted to show him and his brother, Matteo, that I didn't fear them. I hadn't feared anyone in a long time.

It was almost two o'clock in the morning. It had begun snowing a while ago, and a fine layer of white powder covered my jacket and the ground. I'd been waiting for more than one hour. Perhaps Aria had more sense than I gave her credit for.

Soft steps crunched near my right. I pushed off the wall, drawing my gun but lowering it when Aria, wrapped in a thick wool coat and scarf, came into view. She stopped across from me. "Hello, Fabi." She held out the paper that I'd shoved into her pocket. "You said you wanted to talk to me alone because you needed my help?"

Her need to help others—first Gianna, then Lily, and now me—was her greatest weakness. I really wished she'd stayed home. I moved closer.

She regarded me with sad eyes. "But you were lying, weren't you?" she whispered. If we weren't standing so close, I wouldn't have understood her. "You were trying to get me alone."

If she knew, why had she come?

Did she hope for mercy? Then, I realized why she'd whispered. I tightened my hold on my gun. My eyes searched the darkness until I found Luca leaning against a wall to the far left, his gun pointed at my head.

I smiled because I'd underestimated her. A small, weak part of me was relieved. "Finally being sensible, Aria."

"I know a thing or two about mob life."

Only the things Luca allowed her to see, no doubt.

"Aren't you worried for your life?" she asked curiously.

"Why would I be?"

She sighed. "Did the Camorra want to kidnap me?" Again, a whisper, obviously not meant for Luca's ears. Was she trying to save me from his wrath? She shouldn't.

I didn't say anything. Unlike Luca, I didn't divulge information because she batted her eyelashes at me. The time when she'd held power over me as my older sister had long since passed. My silence seemed all the answer she needed.

She lifted one arm and I followed the movement cautiously. With her other hand, she removed a piece of jewelry from her wrist and held it out to me.

"It was Mother's. She gave it to me shortly before her death. I want you to have it."

"Why?" I asked as I peered down at the gold bracelet with sapphires. I didn't remember our mother wearing it, but I was twelve when she'd died and on the brink of starting the induction process to the Outfit. I had other things on my mind than expensive jewelry.

"Because I want you to remember."

"The family that abandoned me?"

"No, the boy you used to be and the man you can still become."

"Who says I want to remember?" I said in a low voice, leaning down to her so she could look into my eyes despite the darkness surrounding us. I heard the soft click of Luca releasing the safety of his gun. I smirked. "You want me to be a better man. Why don't you start with the man who's pointing a gun at my head?"

She pushed the bracelet against my chest, and I took it reluctantly.

"Perhaps one day you'll find someone who will love you despite what you've become, and she will make you want to be better." She stepped away. "Goodbye, Fabiano. Luca wants you to know that next time you come to New York, you will pay with your life."

My fingers tightened around the bracelet. I had no intention of returning to this godforsaken city for any other reason than to rip New York from Luca's bleeding hands.

CHAPTER 3

FABIANO

Returning to Vegas always felt like returning home. I'd been in Nevada for almost five years. When I first arrived, I didn't think I'd last that long. Five years. So much had changed since Father had wanted me dead. The past was the past, but sometimes the memories came back. They were a good reminder why I owed Remo my loyalty and my life. Without him, I'd be dead.

Perhaps I should have seen it coming after I messed up my first job as an initiate of the Chicago Outfit. I'd been honored with the task of patrolling the corridors on the wedding day of my youngest sister, Liliana. I was excited … until I came across my sisters, Aria and Gianna, with their husbands, Matteo and Luca, as well as Liliana and someone who *definitely* wasn't the man she'd married.

I knew immediately that they were taking Liliana to New York with them, and I also knew that as a member of the Outfit, I was supposed to stop them. I didn't have my tattoo yet, since my initiation wasn't completed, but I'd already been sworn into the Outfit. I was only thirteen. I was weak and stupid back then and had allowed Aria to talk me into letting them go. I'd even let them shoot me in my arm so it would look convincing to everyone. To make it look as if I'd *tried* to stop them. Dante Cavallaro didn't punished me. He believed my story, but Father wrote me off that day like he'd written off the daughters he couldn't control. And that's when it all started. Things were set in motion that led to a member of the Outfit becoming part of the Camorra.

After my messed up first job, I was only allowed to watch from the sidelines, deemed too young to be a real part of the Outfit. I was still eager to please Dante and my father but failing miserably.

I should have died after Alfonso had left me in Bratva territory. The Russians would have beaten me to death; if not them, then someone else. I had no clue how to survive on the street or on my own. But Remo knew. He had been born a fighter. It was in his blood, and he showed me how to fight, how to survive, how to kill.

He let me live in the shabby apartment he shared with his three brothers. He put food on our table with money he won in the fighting cages, and I paid him back with loyalty and the fierce determination to become the soldier he needed at his side to help him kill the fuckers laying claim on a territory that was rightfully his.

Almost four months later, I wasn't the pampered Outfit boy anymore when we arrived in Reno, part of the Camorra territory. Remo and Nino had beaten it out of me in training fights and had taught me how to fight dirty. More importantly, Remo had showed me my worth. I didn't need the Outfit, didn't need a position handed to me on a silver platter. Remo and I, we had to fight for what we wanted. That was all I needed: a purpose and someone who saw my worth when no one else could.

When we first set foot on Camorra ground, they were still in turmoil since their Capo had been killed by a man called Growl. Without a new Capo, there was a lot of fighting over the position.

Remo, Nino, and I spent the next few months in Reno, earning money by fighting and eventually winning every match until even the newest Capo in Las Vegas started to notice. We went there together to kill everyone who was against Remo. And when he finally took over as Capo, I became his Enforcer, a rank I hadn't inherited—a rank I'd paid in blood and scars for. A rank I was proud of and would defend till my death, just like I would defend Remo.

The tattoo on my forearm marking me as a made man of the Las Vegas Camorra went deeper than my skin. Nothing and nobody would ever make me break the oath I'd given to my Capo.

I drew in a deep breath. The smell of tar and burnt rubber hung in the air. Familiar. Exhilarating. The flashy lights of Las Vegas burned in the distance. A sight I'd grown used to. *Home.*

The glamor of the Strip was missing in this part of town, just off Sierra Vista Drive. Violence, my favorite language, was spoken fluently around here.

A long row of race cars lined the parking lot of the closed Boulevard Mall. It was the starting point of the illegal street race going down tonight. Some of the drivers nodded a greeting in my direction, while others pretended not to notice me. Most of them still had debts to pay, but tonight I hadn't come for them. They didn't have to worry.

I headed toward Cane, one of the organizers of the race. He hadn't yet paid what he owed us. It was a sum that couldn't be ignored, even though he was a profitable asset.

Most of the money we made with illegal street races came from bets. We had a camera team that filmed the races and put them in a locked forum on the Darknet; everyone with the log-in code could watch. This part of the business was pretty new. Remo had established the races when he seized power. He didn't hang on to the old fashioned rules that bound the Outfit and the Famiglia—rules that made them slow to adapt. He was always on the lookout for new ways to make the Camorra more money, and he was successful in his endeavors.

A few engines roared, saturating the air with gasoline vapors. The start was only a couple of minutes away, but I hadn't come to watch the race. I was here on business.

I spotted my target next to our bookie, Griffin, who was a short guy, almost wider than he was tall. Cane's pockmarked face twisted when he saw me coming his way. His eyes searched the parking lot and it looked like he considered running.

"Cane," I said pleasantly as I stopped before him. "Remo is missing some money."

He took a step back and raised his hands. "I will pay him soon. I promise."

I promise. I swear. Tomorrow. Please. Words I'd heard too often.

"Hmm," I murmured. "Soon wasn't your due date."

Griffin shut off his iPad and excused himself. The dirty work in our business drove him away. He was only interested in the financial aspects.

I took Cane by the collar of his shirt and dragged him off to the side, farther away from the starting line. Not that I cared if anyone watched what I was doing, but I wasn't keen on eating smoke and dirt once the cars raced off.

I pushed Cane away from me. He lost his balance and fell on his backside. His eyes darted left and right, as if he was searching for something to defend himself with. I grabbed his hand, twisted it all the way back, and broke his wrist. He howled, cradling his injured hand against his chest. Nobody came to help him. They knew how things worked. People who didn't pay their debts got a visit from me. A broken wrist was one of the kinder outcomes.

"Tomorrow, I'll be back," I told him. I pointed at his knee. He knew what I meant.

Over to the left side, near the starting line, I noticed a familiar face with black curls. Adamo, Remo's youngest brother. This was definitely not where he was supposed to be at this time of the night. He was only thirteen and had been caught racing before. Apparently, Remo losing his shit on him hadn't made him see reason. I jogged over to him and the two older guys beside him, who looked like they were up to no good. The moment they spotted me, they dashed off, but Adamo knew better than to try that.

"What are you doing here? Shouldn't you be in bed? You've got school in the morning."

He gave a bored shrug. Too cool for a proper reply.

I grabbed his collar, forcing his eyes to finally meet mine. "It's not like I need an education. I'll become a made man and earn money with illegal shit."

I released him. "Can't hurt to use your brain so the illegal shit won't send you to jail." I nodded toward my car. "I'll take you to Remo."

"You didn't finish school. And Remo and Nino didn't either. Why do I have to do this shit?"

I slapped the back of his head lightly. "Because we were busy taking Las Vegas back. You are only busy getting yourself in trouble. Now move."

He grimaced, rubbing the back of his head. "I can go home by myself. I don't need a ride."

"So you can try to sneak in without him noticing?" I nodded toward my car again. "Not going to happen. Now move. I have better things to do than to babysit you."

"Like what? Beating up other debtors?"

"Among other things."

He trudged toward the car and practically flung himself into the passenger seat then closed the door with so much force I feared he'd damaged the soft close mechanism. Since he'd hit puberty, he was completely intolerable, and he had been difficult even before that.

The moment I set foot in the gaming room of the abandoned casino that functioned as our gym, I heard the gasps. I placed my palm against Adamo's chest, stopping him. I should have known Remo wasn't alone. Bad news always drove him to the gym.

"You will wait here."

Adamo crossed his arms. "It's not the first time I've seen Remo beating someone up."

The youngest Falcone brother had witnessed violence over the years. It was impossible to shelter him from the cruel realities of it all, but Remo didn't want Adamo to start the induction process before his fourteenth birthday. Until then, he wouldn't see the worst of our business.

"You will wait." I said firmly before I walked over to Remo. Adamo skulked over to the broken Champagne bar and began smashing a few glasses.

When I stepped into the second gaming room that we used for kickboxing training, Remo was kicking the living daylights out of some poor fucker I didn't know. He was probably still furious with me because I hadn't been successful in bringing Aria back to him. Or maybe he was mad because of my earlier phone call telling him about his brother being out in the middle of the night. Again.

He stopped when he spotted me, wiping some sweat and blood from his forehead with the back of his hand. He hadn't even bothered wrapping his hands with tape, too eager to let off some steam.

"I took that one off your hands. Sometimes I need to get down to business myself," he said. He looked back down at the bloody heap of a man curled into himself, moaning, his gray hair matted with blood.

I chuckled as I jumped up onto the platform of the kickboxing ring. "I don't mind."

"Where is he?"

"I made him wait in the entry."

He nodded. "And?" Remo came toward me, letting his victim lie in his own blood. The scar over Remo's eye was slightly redder than usual, as it always was when he overexerted himself. "How did it go in New York? Your message wasn't very enlightening."

"I failed, as you can see. Luca didn't let Aria out of his sight."

"I figured as much. How did he react to my message?"

"He wanted to tear out my throat."

An excited gleam filled his eyes. "I wish I could have seen Vitiello's face." One of Remo's wet dreams included a cage fight against Luca. Tearing apart the Capo of the Famiglia will be his ultimate triumph. Remo was a cruel, ruthless, deadly fighter. He could beat almost anyone, but Luca Vitiello was a giant with hands built to crush a man's throat. No doubt, it would be a fight that made history.

"He was pissed. He wanted to kill me," I told him.

Remo gave me the once-over. "And yet there isn't a scratch on you."

"My sister held him back. She's got him in the palm of her hand."

Remo's lips curled in disgust. "To think that people on the East Coast still fear him like he's the Devil."

"He's a huge, brutal fucker when my sister isn't around to keep him in check."

"I'd really love to meet her. Vitiello would lose his fucking mind."

Luca would tear down Las Vegas for Aria—or at least he'd try. I was uneasy discussing the topic of Aria. Despite my indifference toward her, I didn't like the idea of her being in Remo's hands.

Remo looked down at my hand. I followed his gaze and realized I was twirling the bracelet around my fingers.

"When I told you to bring me Luca's treasure, I meant something else," he said darkly.

33

I shoved the bracelet back into my pocket. "Aria thought she could soften my heart with it because it belonged to our mother."

"And did she?" Remo asked, something dangerous lurking in his dark eyes.

I laughed. "I've been your Enforcer for years now. Do you really think I still have a heart?"

Remo chuckled. "Black as tar."

"What about that guy?" I nodded toward the whimpering man, wanting to distract Remo. "Are you done with him?"

Remo seemed to consider the man for a moment, and the man quieted immediately. Finally, Remo nodded. "It's no fun if they're already broken and weak. It's only fun to break the strong." He jumped over the ropes of the ring and landed beside me. Clapping my shoulder, he said, "Let's grab something to eat. I have organized some entertainment for us. Nino and Savio will join us too." Then he sighed. "But first I'll have to have a talk with Adamo. Why does that kid have to get in trouble all the time?"

Adamo was lucky his oldest brother was Capo or he would have ended up dead in a dark alley by now. Remo and I went back into the entry area. Adamo was leaning against the bar counter, typing something on his phone. When he spotted us, he quickly slipped it into his back pocket.

Remo held out his hand. "Mobile."

Adamo jutted out his chin. "I have a right to some privacy."

Few people dared to disobey Remo. Even fewer survived when they did.

"One of these days, I'll lose my fucking patience with you." He grabbed Adamo's arm and turned him around, motioning for me to grab the mobile and I did.

"Hey," Adamo protested, trying to reach for it. I blocked him, and Remo pushed him against the wall.

"What's the fucking matter with you? I'll tell you again, don't test my fucking patience," Remo muttered.

"I'm sick of you telling me to go to school and be home by ten when you, Fabiano, Nino, and Savio spend the night doing all kind of fun stuff."

Fun stuff. He'd see how fun most of the things were once he was inducted next year.

"So you want to play with the big boys?"

Adamo nodded.

"Then why don't you stay here? A few girls are coming over in a bit. I'm sure we'll find one who will make you a fucking man."

Adamo flushed red then shook his head.

"Yeah, that's what I thought," Remo said grimly. "Now wait here while I call Don to pick you up and take you home."

"What about my phone?"

"That's mine for now."

Adamo glowered but didn't say anything. Ten minutes later, Don, one of the oldest soldiers in Remo's service, picked up the youngest Falcone.

Remo sighed. "When I was his age, I didn't say no to a free piece of ass."

"Your father set you up with your first hooker when you were twelve. Adamo probably hasn't even gotten to second base yet."

"Perhaps I should push him more."

"He'll be like us soon enough." This life wouldn't leave him with a choice.

Soon, the first girls from one of Remo's strip clubs arrived. They were eager to please, as always. Not that I minded, I'd had a long day and could use a good blowjob to get rid of some of the tension. I watched through half-closed eyes as one of the girls got down on her knees in front of me. I leaned back in the chair. This was why the Camorra would overrun the Outfit first and then the Famiglia. We didn't let women meddle in our business. We only used them for our needs. And that was something that would never change. Remo would never allow it. And I didn't give a fuck. I jerked my hips toward the willing mouth. Feelings had no place in my life.

CHAPTER 4

LEONA

D ad lived in a small, run-down apartment in a desolate corner of the city. The Strip seemed far away—and so did the beautiful hotels with their generous customers. He showed me to a small room. It smelled of cat piss, like the rest of the apartment, even though I hadn't seen one. The only furniture was a mattress on the ground. One wall was packed almost to the ceiling with old moving boxes stuffed with God knew what. He hadn't even put sheets on the mattress, nor did I see any kind of bedding.

"It's not much, I know," he said, rubbing the back of his head. "I don't have a second set of bed linen. Perhaps you can go out and buy some today?"

My mouth almost fell to the floor. I had to pause to compose myself. I'd spent almost all of my money on the bus ticket. What I had left was supposed to buy me a nice dress for potential job interviews in decent restaurants and cocktail bars near the Strip, but I could hardly sleep on an old mattress that had sweat stains on it ... or worse.

"Do you at least have a pillow and a spare blanket?"

He placed my backpack beside the mattress, grimacing. "I think I have an old wool blanket somewhere. Let me check." He hurried off to who knew where.

Slowly, I sank down on the mattress. It was saggy and a plume of dust rose into the stale air. My eyes traveled over to the mountain of boxes threatening to crush me beneath them. The window hadn't been cleaned in a while, if ever, and only let dim light in. There wasn't even a dresser where I could put my clothes. I dragged my backpack over to me. Good thing I hardly owned anything. I didn't need much. Everything I ever held dear, my mother had sold at some point for her next hit of crystal meth. That taught me not to cling to physical things.

Dad returned with a heap of black rags. Could that be the source of the cat smell? He handed the pile over to me, and I realized that it was the wool blanket he'd mentioned. It was moth eaten and smelled of smoke and something else I couldn't place—but definitely not cat. I set it down on the mattress. I had no choice but to buy bed linen. I stared down at my flip-flops. Right now they were my only shoes. The soles of my favorite pair of Converse sneakers had fallen off two days ago. I thought I'd be able to get new shoes as soon as I arrived in Vegas.

I pulled thirty dollars from my backpack. Dad eyed the money in a strange way. Desperate and hungry.

"I don't suppose you have some spare change for me? Business is slow right now, and I need to buy some food for us."

I hadn't asked what exactly his business was; I learned that asking too many questions often led to unpleasant answers.

I handed him ten dollars. "I need the rest for bedding."

He looked disappointed but then nodded. "Sure. I'll go get us something to eat for tonight. Why don't you go to Target and see if you can get a comforter and some sheets?"

It almost seemed as if he wanted to get me out of the apartment. I nodded. I really wanted to get out of my sweaty pair of jeans and T-shirt, but I grabbed my backpack and got ready to leave.

"You can leave that here."

I smiled. "Oh … no. I'll need it to carry whatever I buy," I lied. I learned to never leave my stuff lying around with my mother or she would pawn it. Not that I had anything of worth, but I hated people rummaging through my underwear. And I knew that look Dad had when he'd seen my money. I was fairly certain he'd been lying when he said his addiction was a thing of the past. There was nothing I could do about that. I couldn't fight that battle for him.

I trudged out of the apartment, Las Vegas' dry air hitting me once again. Despite the cold, a few guys were swimming in the community pool, doing dives and shouting. The pool area looked like it could use a good cleaning as well. One of the guys spotted me and let out a whistle. I picked up my pace to avoid a confrontation.

Sheets, a comforter, and a pillow cost me $19.99, leaving me with exactly one cent. No pretty dress or shoes for me. I doubted a restaurant would hire me in my secondhand clothes.

When I returned home, Dad wasn't there … and neither was any food. I searched the fridge but found only a few cans of beer and a jar of mayonnaise. I sank down on the chair, resigning myself to wait for my father.

When he came home, it was dark outside. I'd fallen asleep at the table, my forehead pressed up against my forearms. I scanned his empty arms and miserable expression.

"No food?" I asked.

He froze, his eyes flitting around nervously, searching for a good lie.

I didn't give him the chance to lie to me and rose to my feet. "It's okay. I'm not hungry. I'm going to bed."

I was starving. I hadn't had a morsel to eat since the donut I'd treated myself to in the morning. I kissed Dad's cheek, smelling alcohol and smoke on his breath. He avoided my eyes. As I headed out of the kitchen with my backpack, I saw him taking a beer out of the fridge—his dinner, I assumed.

I put the new sheets on the mattress then dropped the comforter and pillow on top. I didn't even have nightclothes. Instead, I took out a t-shirt and a fresh pair of panties before lying down on the mattress. The new linen, with its chemical scent, masked the stale stench of the mattress. I hadn't seen a washing machine in the apartment, so I'd have to earn some money before I could have my stuff washed in a laundromat.

I closed my eyes, hoping I could fall asleep despite the rumbling of my stomach.

When I got up the next morning, I showered, trying not to look at anything too closely. I would have to give the bathroom and the rest of the apartment a good clean once I found a job. That had to be my top priority for now. I changed into the nicest things I owned, a flowery summer dress that reached my knees. Then I slipped on my flip-flops. It wasn't an outfit that would get me any bonus points at a job interview, but I didn't have a choice. Dad was sleeping on the sofa, in yesterday's clothes. When I tried sneaking past him, he sat up.

"Where are you going?"

"To look for a job."

He shook his head, not looking very hungover. Alcohol was the least of his problems. "There aren't any respectable places around here."

I didn't bother telling him no respectable places would ever hire me looking the way I did.

"If you get the chance, maybe you can buy some food?" Dad said after a moment.

I nodded without saying a word. Swinging my backpack over my shoulder, I left the apartment. Unfortunately, Las Vegas' winter decided to rear its ugly head today. In my summer clothes, it was bitterly cold, and the promise of rain lay in the air. Dark clouds hung heavy in the sky.

I strode through the neighborhood for a while, taking in the shabby exteriors and homeless people. I walked for ten minutes, heading toward downtown Las Vegas, when the first bar came into view. I quickly realized that for a girl to work there, she had to be willing to get rid of her clothes. The next two bars hadn't even opened yet and looked so run down that I doubted there was any money to be made working there. A wave of resentment washed over me. If Dad hadn't made me spend all my money on bedding, I could have bought nice clothes and gone looking for a job closer to the Strip and not around here, where the worth of a woman was linked to the way she could dance on a pole.

I knew strippers earned good money. My mom had been friends with dancers, before she'd started selling her body to truck drivers and worse for a quick buck.

Losing hope, my head started to swim from lack of food. The cold air wasn't helping either. It was already one in the afternoon and things didn't look good. Then the sky opened up and it began raining. One fat drop after another plopped down on me. Of course, the one day in December it rained in Nevada I was wearing sandals. I closed my eyes for a moment. I didn't really believe in a higher power, but if someone or something was up there, it didn't think too fondly of me.

The cold became more prominent as my dress stuck to my body. I shivered and rubbed my arms. I wasn't sure how far from home I was, but I had a feeling that I'd be down for the count with a cold tomorrow, if I didn't find shelter soon. The low hum of an engine drew my attention back to the street and to the car coming my way. It was an expensive German car, a Mercedes of some sort, with tinted windows and matte black varnish. It was sleek and almost daunting.

My mother hadn't been the kind of mother that warned me of getting into strangers' cars. She was the kind of mother who brought creepy strangers home because they paid her for sex. I was cold and hungry and just over this city already. I wanted to get back into the warmth. I hesitated then held out my arm and raised my thumb. The car slowed and came to a stop beside me. The way I looked, I assumed he would have driven right past me.

Surprise rushed through me when I saw who sat behind the wheel. A guy, early twenties maybe, dressed in a black suit and black shirt. No tie. His blue eyes settled on me and heat crawled up my neck from the intensity of his gaze. Strong jaw, dark blond hair, shaved on the sides but longer on top. He was immaculate, except for a small scar on his chin—and I looked like I'd crawled out of the gutter. Wonderful.

FABIANO

The girl, dressed for anything but this weather, caught my attention from afar. Her wet dress was plastered to her thin body and her hair to her face. She had her arms wrapped around her stomach and an ugly backpack hanging off her right shoulder. I slowed considerably as I approached her, curious. She didn't look like one of our girls, nor did she strike me as someone who knew the first thing about selling her body. Maybe she'd only just arrived in Vegas and didn't know that these streets belonged to us and she would have to ask if she wanted to hit them.

I expected her to scuttle off when I came closer. My car was easily recognizable. She surprised me when she held out her hand for me to pick her up. I pulled up beside her. If she tried to offer me her body, she was in for a nasty surprise. And if this was some insane robbery scheme, with her accomplices waiting to catch me by surprise, they'd be in for an even nastier surprise. I put my hand down on my gun before I slid my window down. She bent over to look inside my car.

She smiled in embarrassment. "I got lost. Can you take me home perhaps?"

Not a hooker.

I leaned over and pushed the door open. She slipped in then closed the door. She put her backpack on her lap and rubbed her arms. My eyes fell to her feet. She was wearing only sandals and dripping water on my seats and the floor.

She noticed my gaze and blushed. "I didn't expect rain."

I nodded, still curious. She definitely didn't know me. She was pale and trembled ... but not from fear. "Where do you need to go?"

She hesitated before letting out an embarrassed laugh. "I don't know the address."

I raised my eyebrows.

"I only arrived yesterday. I live with my father."

"How old are you?"

She blinked. "Nineteen?"

"Is that the answer or a question?"

"Sorry. I'm out of it today. It's the answer." Again with the embarrassed, shy smile.

I nodded. "But you know the direction to your father's place?"

"There was a sort of campground nearby. It isn't very nice there."

I pulled away from the curb then sped up. She clutched her backpack.

"Are there any markers you remember?"

"There was strip club nearby," she said, a deep blush tingeing her wet cheeks. Definitely not a hooker.

I humored her and drove in the general direction she'd described. It wasn't like I needed to be anywhere else. Her ignorance of my position was almost amusing. She looked like a drowned cat with her dark hair plastered to her head and her dress clinging to her shivering body. I could hear her stomach rumble.

"I wish I knew the name of the club, but I was only paying attention to bars I could work in … and that definitely wasn't one of them," she said quickly.

"Work?" I echoed, cautious again. "What kind of work?"

"As a waitress. I need to earn money for college," she said then fell silent, biting her lip.

I considered her again. "About a mile from here is a bar called Roger's Arena. I know the owner. He's looking for a new waitress. The tips are good … from what I hear."

"Roger's Arena," she echoed. "Strange name for a bar."

"It's a strange place," I told her. It was an understatement, of course. "But they don't have high standards when it comes to their personnel."

Her eyes widened then she flushed with embarrassment. "Do I look that bad?"

My gaze traveled from her slender calves over her narrow waist up to her fine-boned face. She didn't look bad, quite the opposite. But her clothes and wet hair and those worn sandals … they didn't really help matters. "No."

She didn't seem to believe me and tightened her grip on her backpack. Why was she clinging to it so tightly? Did she have a weapon inside? That would explain why she'd risked getting into a stranger's car. Maybe she thought she'd be able to defend herself. Her stomach growled again.

"You're hungry."

She tensed, which was more than the simple question called for. "I'm okay." Determined and stubborn, her eyes remained glued to the windshield.

"When was the last time you've eaten?"

A quick glance my way then her eyes fell down to her backpack.

"When?" I pressed.

She looked out the passenger window. "Yesterday."

I narrowed my eyes at her. "You should consider eating every day."

"We had no food in the fridge."

Didn't she say she lived with her father? What kind of parent was he? From the way she looked, probably as caring as my own father had been.

I steered the car toward a KFC drive-in.

She shook her head. "No, don't. I forgot to take money with me."

I could tell she was lying.

I ordered a box of wings and fries and then handed them to her.

"I can't accept this," she said quietly.

"It's chicken and fries, not a Rolex."

Her eyes darted to the watch on my wrist. Not a Rolex, but not any less expensive. She didn't put up much of a fight, her resolve quickly dissipating. Soon, she tore into the food as if her last decent meal had been a lot longer than just yesterday. I watched her from the corner of my eye as my car glided through traffic. Her nails were cut short, not the long red fake nails I was used to.

"What do you do? You look young for a businessman or lawyer," she said when she was done eating.

"Businessman? Lawyer?"

She shrugged. "Because of the suit and the car."

"Nothing like that ... no."

Her eyes lingered on the scars covering my knuckles, and she didn't say anything anymore. She sat up suddenly. "I recognize the street. Turn left here."

I did and slowed when she pointed at an apartment complex. The place seemed distantly familiar. She opened the door then turned to me. "Thank you for the ride. I doubt anyone else would have picked me up with the way I look. They probably would have thought I wanted to rob them. Good thing you aren't scared of girls in flip-flops."

My lips twitched at her joke. "No. I'm not scared of anything."

She laughed then quieted as her blue eyes traced my face. "I should go."

She got out and closed the door, quickly running for cover. I watched her fumble with the keys for a while before she disappeared from view. Strange girl.

LEONA

I glanced back out the window as the Mercedes sped off. I couldn't believe I let a total stranger drive me home. And I couldn't believe I let him buy me food. I thought I'd outgrown that kind of thing. Back when I was a little girl, strangers had occasionally bought me food because they pitied me. But this guy ... he hadn't showed any signs of pity. He didn't watch me open-mouthed, only to tear his eyes away the moment I noticed his gaze and he definitely didn't look ashamed for his own wealth. And the suit ... somehow it seemed out of place on him.

He hadn't revealed what he did for a living. Not a lawyer or businessman, then what? Maybe his parents were rich ... but he didn't seem like the trust fund type.

Not that it mattered. I'd never see him again. A man like him, with a car like that, he must spend his days on golf courses and in fancy restaurants, not in the places where I could work.

Dad wasn't home. Considering the force of the rainfall, I'd be stuck in the apartment for a while. I walked into the kitchen, checked the fridge, but found it as empty as it was this morning. Then I sank into a chair. I was cold and tired. If I wanted to wear these clothes tomorrow, I'd have to hang them so they could dry. The dress was the nicest piece of clothing I owned. If I had any chance securing a job at this arena, I needed to wear it.

So far, this new beginning wasn't very promising.

The next day I went in search for Roger's Arena. It took me a while, and eventually I had to ask passersby for the way. They looked at me like I had lost my mind, asking for a place like that. What kind of place had Mercedes guy suggested to me?

When I finally found Roger's Arena, a nondescript building with a small red neon sign with its name beside the steel entrance door, I stepped inside. Now I understood why people had reacted the way they had.

The bar wasn't exactly a cocktail bar or night club; it was a huge hall that looked like it had once been a storage facility. There was a bar on the right side, but my eyes were drawn to the huge fighting cage in the center of the large room. Tables were arranged all around it with a few red leather booths against the walls for the VIP customers.

The floor was cement and so were the walls, but they were covered with wire mesh fence. Woven into the wire were neon tubes that formed words like honor, pain, blood, victory, and strength.

I hesitated in the front, half a mind to turn around and leave, but then a black-haired woman headed my way. She must have been thirty, thirty-one. Her eyes were heavily lined and her lips were a bright pink. It clashed with the red glow of the neon lights. She didn't smile but didn't exactly look unfriendly either.

"Are you new? You're late. In thirty minutes, the first customers will be here, and I haven't even cleaned the tables or the changing rooms yet."

"I'm not really working here," I said slowly. And I wasn't sure it was a place I should consider working.

"You aren't?" Her shoulders slumped, one of the thin spaghetti straps sliding off and giving me a glimpse of the strapless pink bra beneath her top. "Oh damn. I can't do this alone tonight. Mel called in sick, and I ..." She trailed off. "You could work here, you know?"

"That's why I'm here," I said, even though the fighting cage freaked me out. *Beggars can't be choosers, Leona.*

"Perfect. Then come on. Let's find Roger. I'm Cheryl, by the way."

She gripped my forearm and pulled me along. "Is the pay bad? Is that why are you having trouble finding staff?" I asked as I hurried after her, my sandals smacking against the concrete floor.

"Oh, it's the fighting. Most girls are squeamish," she said offhandedly, but I had a feeling there was more she wasn't telling me.

We walked through a black swinging door behind the bar counter, along a narrow corridor with bare walls and more doors, toward another massive wooden door at the end. She knocked.

"Come in," said a deep voice. Cheryl opened the door to a large office that was foggy from cigarette smoke. Inside, a middle-aged man, built like a bull, sat behind a desk. He flashed his teeth at Cheryl, his double chin becoming more prominent. Then his eyes settled on me.

"I got us a new waitress," Cheryl said, the hint of flirtation in her voice.

"Roger," the man introduced himself, stubbing out a cigarette on the ketchup-smeared plate in front of him. "You can start working right away."

I opened my mouth in surprise.

"That's why you're here, right? Five dollars an hour, plus everything you make from tips."

"Okay?" I said uncertainly.

"Dressed like that you won't earn many tips." He picked up his cell phone and gestured for us to leave. "Get something that shows off your ass or tits. This isn't a nunnery."

When the door had closed, I gave Cheryl a questioning look. "Does it always go like that?"

She shrugged, but again I got the impression that she was keeping something from me. "He's just really desperate right now. Tonight's an important fight, and he doesn't want things to get messy because we're low on staff."

"Why does it matter how I'm dressed?" Worry overcame me. "We don't have to do anything with guests, right?"

She shook her head. "We don't have to, no, but we have a few rich customers that spend good money ... especially if you give them some special attention."

I shook my head. "No, no. That's not going to happen."

She nodded, leading me out back. "It's up to you. You can leave your backpack here." She pointed toward the floor behind the bar. I reluctantly set it down. I couldn't keep it on me when I worked. She rummaged through a small closet to the left of the bar and appeared with a mop and a bucket. "You can start by cleaning the changing room. The first fighters arrive in about two hours, until then clean everything."

I hesitated and she frowned. "What? Too good for cleaning?"

"No," I said quickly. I wasn't too good for anything. And I'd cleaned up every possible disgusting thing in my life. "It's just that I haven't eaten anything since last night and I feel a bit faint."

The fridge was still empty, and I was still out of money. Dad didn't seem concerned about food at all. Either he ate wherever he was at night or he lived on air alone. Pity crossed her face, making me regret my words. Pity had been something I had been subjected to far too often, and it had always made me feel small and worthless. Having a mother who sold her body on the street, my teachers and social workers had showered me with their pity—but never with a way out of the mess. When the guy from yesterday bought me food, it hadn't felt like an act of charity.

Cheryl set down the mop and bucket and grabbed something from a fridge behind the bar. She set down a coke in front of me then turned and went back through the swinging door. She showed up a minute later with a grilled cheese sandwich and fries, both cold.

"They're from last night. The kitchen isn't open yet."

I didn't care. I scarfed everything within a few minutes and washed it down with the cold coke. "Thanks," I said with a big smile.

She searched my face then shook her head. "I probably shouldn't ask, but how old are you?"

"I'm old enough to work here," I said. I knew I needed to be twenty-one to work in a place like this, so I didn't mention that I'd just finished high school this year.

She looked doubtful. "Be careful, chick," she said simply and pushed the mop into my arms. I took it, picked up the bucket, and headed for the door with the red neon sign reading, "Changing Room." I wedged it open with my elbow and slipped in.

There were several open shower stalls, a wall of lockers, and a few benches inside. The white-tiled floor was covered with bloodstains and dirty towels. Great. They'd probably been there for days. The smell of beer and sweat hung in the air. Good thing I learned to deal with stuff like that, thanks to my mother. I began mopping and was still at it when the door opened again. Two middle-aged men tattooed from head to toe stepped inside. I paused.

Their eyes wandered over me, settling on my flip-flops and dress. I smiled anyway. I'd quickly learned that it was easier to disarm people with a smile than with anger or fear, especially if you were a small woman. They nodded at me, disinterested. When the first began to tug at his shirt, I quickly excused myself and headed out of the room. I didn't want to watch them undressing. They might get the wrong idea.

A few guests were already mingling around the now red-lit bar, obviously impatient for drinks. Cheryl was nowhere in sight. I set down the bucket and the mop and hurried toward the counter. Once behind it, I faced the group of thirsty men, smiling.

"So what can I get you?"

Relief flooded me as beer seemed to be the only thing they wanted. That request was one I could handle. If they asked for cocktails, I'd be lost. Half of them wanted draft beer. I handed them their full glasses and the other half got bottles. I quickly scanned the fridge. There were only three bottles of beer left, and I doubted they would last long. These guys looked like a case of beer would be a good appetizer.

Where was Cheryl?

When I was starting to get nervous, she finally walked through the door, looking slightly disheveled. Her skirt was askew, her top put on the wrong way, and her lipstick was gone. I didn't say anything. Had she already earned some extra money with a customer? I glanced around toward the few men gathered at the tables and the bar. Some of them were throwing me curious glances, but none of them looked like they were about to offer me money for having sex. I relaxed slightly. It was a touchy subject for me because of my mom. The moment one of them put money in front of me for sex, whether I was desperate for money or not, I'd be out of this bar so fast. There was a strange atmosphere in the bar; people exchanged money, talking in hushed voices. Someone sat in the corner, typing into his iPad, as customers approached him and handed him money. He was a very round, very short man with a mousy face. He must be taking bets. I didn't know anything about the laws in Nevada, but this didn't look legal.

None of my business.

"Doll? Give me a beer, would you?" a man in his sixties said.

I flushed then quickly reached for a glass. It started to feel like this place might be prone to trouble.

CHAPTER 5

FABIANO

I pulled up into the parking lot of Roger's Arena, killing the engine. My muscles were already taut with eagerness. The thrill of fighting still got me after all these years. In the cage, it didn't matter if your father was Consigliere or construction worker. It didn't matter what people thought of you. All that mattered was the moment, your fighting skills, and your ability to read the enemy. It was one against one. Life was seldom as fair as that.

I stepped into Roger's Arena. It was already crowded. The stench of old sweat and smoke clung to the air. It wasn't an inviting place. People didn't come here for the atmosphere or good food. They came for money and blood.

The first fight was about to start. The two opponents were already facing each other in the cage in the center. They weren't the main attraction. All eyes turned to me then quickly avoided my steely glare as I strode past the rows of tables filled with spectators. My fight was last. I'd fight the poor sucker who had proven to be the best over the last few weeks. Remo thought it was good to have me beat the strongest fighters to a bloody pulp in a cage to show everyone what kind of Enforcer the Camorra had. And I didn't mind. It helped me remember the beginning, helped me stay grounded and vicious. Once you allowed yourself to get used to the easy life, you set yourself up for attack and for failure.

My eyes were drawn to the bar. It took me a moment to recognize her, since she wasn't shivering and dripping wet like yesterday. She had long amber curls, sharp yet elegant features. She was serving drinks to the men gathered at the bar, men with eyes like hungry wolves. She was focused on the task, oblivious to their staring. Taking too long pouring a simple beer, it was clear she did not have any experience working in a bar. To be honest, I hadn't expected her to start working here. That she had taken the job after seeing the cage told me one of two things: she was desperate or she'd seen worse in her life.

She glanced up, noticing my attention. I waited for her inevitable reaction, but it didn't come. She smiled shyly, her eyes lingering on my clothes. No suit today. Black jeans and a black long sleeved shirt, my preferred style, but sometimes the suit was necessary. She hesitated then quickly returned to the task of serving beer to an old fucker.

Who was this girl? And why wasn't she scared?

Tearing my eyes away from her, I headed toward Roger, who was talking to our bookie, Griffin. I shook hands with both men. Then I nodded toward the bar. "New girl?"

Roger shrugged. "She showed up in my office today, looking for a job. I need new staff." He narrowed his eyes, regarding me with uncertainty. "Do you want me to alert Stefano?"

Stefano was our romancer. He preyed on women, pretended to be in love with them, and eventually forced them to work in one of the Camorra's whorehouses.

I didn't get along with him and gruffly shook my head. "She doesn't fit the profile."

I didn't know how Stefano chose the girls he pursued, and I didn't give a fuck.

"So how's it going?" I nodded toward Griffin's iPad, where he managed all of the incoming bets.

"Good. The few idiots who have bet against you will bring us a lot of money."

I nodded, but my eyes found the bar counter again. I wasn't even sure why. I had driven the girl home last night on a whim and that was it. "I'm grabbing something to drink."

Not waiting for either of them to reply, I made my way toward the bar. People chanced looks at me before sheepishly averting their gazes. It was annoying as fuck, but I'd worked hard to earn their fear.

I stopped in front of the counter and put my gym bag down beside me then sat on a stool. The men at the other end of the bar threw uneasy glances my way. I recognized one of them as someone I'd recently paid a visit to over three grand. His arm was still in a cast.

The girl I'd picked up on the street came over to me. Her skin was slightly tanned but didn't have the unnatural orange tinge of someone who went to the tanning beds like most of the women who worked in our establishments.

"I didn't expect to see you so soon," she said, smiling that shy smile that reminded me of days long gone. Days I wanted to forget most of the time. She had a light sprinkle of freckles on her nose and cheeks and cornflower blue eyes with a darker ring around the irises. Now that her hair wasn't dripping wet, I noticed it wasn't black but a dark auburn with natural golden highlights.

I rested my forearms on the counter, glad my long sleeves covered my tattoo. There would be time for the big reveal later. "I told you I frequented this place."

"No suit but still all black. I take it you like it dark," she teased.

I smirked. "You have no idea."

Her brows drew together then the smile returned. "What can I do for you?"

"A glass of water."

"Water," she repeated doubtfully, the corners of her mouth twitching. "That's a first." She let out a soft laugh.

I hadn't changed into my fighting trunks yet. I didn't tell her that I had a fight scheduled that evening, which was one reason why I couldn't drink or that I had to break some legs in the morning, which was the other.

She handed me a glass of water. "There you go," she said, walking around the bar and wiping a table next to me. I let my eyes trail over her body. Yesterday I hadn't paid nearly enough attention to the details. She was thin and small, like someone who never knew if there would be food on the table. But she managed to carry herself with a certain air of grace, despite her baggy clothes that hid the shape of her body. She wore the same dress from yesterday and those horrible flip-flops ... still completely wrong for the temperatures.

"What brought you here?" I asked.

Her father lived in a bad part of town. I couldn't believe that she didn't have anywhere else she could stay. Anything would have been an improvement. With her freckles, shy smile, and elegant features, she belonged in a nice suburb, not a fucked-up neighborhood, and definitely not working at a fight club in mob territory. The latter was my fault of course.

"I had to move in with my father because my mother is back in rehab," she said without hesitation. There was no reservation, no caution. Easy prey in this world.

"Do I know your father?" I asked.

Her brows puckered. "Why would you?"

"I know a lot of people. And even more people know me," I said with a shrug.

"If you're famous, you should tell me so I don't embarrass myself with my ignorance," she joked easily.

"Not famous," I told her. Notorious was more like it.

She waved a hand at me. "You don't look like a lawyer or businessman today, by the way."

"What do I look like, then?"

A light blush traveled up her throat. She gave a delicate shrug before she headed back behind the bar, hesitating again as she eyed my arms that I had propped up on the bar.

"Could you help me get a few beer cases from the basement? I doubt Roger wants to do it, and I don't think I'm strong enough. You look like you can carry two or three without breaking a sweat."

She turned and walked over to the swinging door leading to the back then looked over her shoulder to see if I was following.

I set down my glass on the counter and stood from the barstool, curious. She seemed completely unaware of *what* I was. And I didn't mean my rank in the mob. People were usually uneasy around me, even without seeing my tattoo. She wasn't a good actress, and I would have sensed fear had she harbored any. I followed her to the back and then down the long staircase into the storage area. I knew exactly where we were. I'd used it for a couple intense conversations with debtors. The door shut behind us. A flicker of suspicion shot through me. Nobody could be that trusting. Was this a setup? That would have been equally stupid.

She searched the back of the room, never once looking over her shoulder to see what I was doing. Too trusting. Too innocent.

"Ah, here they are," she said, pointing at a couple of beer cases. She looked over at me then frowned. "Is something wrong?"

She sounded concerned. For fuck's sake, she sounded concerned *for me*. Every other girl in Vegas, and every man as well, would have shit themselves if they were in a soundproof basement ... alone with me. I wanted to shake some sense into her.

I strode toward her and picked up three cases. As I straightened, I caught a whiff of her sweet scent. *Fuck.*

She smiled up at me. She wore close to no makeup, only enough to highlight her natural beauty. Touching the soft dusting of freckles on her cheek, she sheepishly asked, "Do I have something on my face?" finishing with an embarrassed laugh. I could tell she was self-conscious about her freckles, but fuck me, I liked them.

"No," I said.

"Oh, okay." She searched my eyes, her brows drawing together. *Don't try to look behind that mask, girl. You won't like it.* "We should probably go back upstairs. I'm not supposed to leave the bar unattended for too long."

Had she seen something in my gaze that finally gave her a healthy dose of fear? The way she held the door open for me with that same unsuspecting expression, I guessed not.

I nodded toward the stairs. "Go ahead."

She hesitated then walked in front of me. Maybe she thought I wanted to get a good look at her ass, but her dress made that impossible. The truth was I hated having people behind me.

We strode through the narrow corridor, when the door to the main area opened revealing Roger and Stefano.

Both of them looked dismayed, seeing me with the girl. Her face shifted into one of unease at the sight of Stefano, which made me curious. He looked like any mother-in-law's dream, and his charm was the Camorra's best weapon when it came to luring women into our whorehouses.

"Fabiano, can I have a word with you?" Roger asked, his eyes scanning the girl, probably looking for a sign that I'd assaulted her in the storage room. Stefano, too, gave me a contemplating look. "Go back to work, Leona."

Leona. So that was her name. She hadn't struck me as a lioness as her namesake insinuated. Perhaps there was more to her.

She hadn't moved, despite Roger's order. Her eyes were on me. I nodded. "Go ahead," I told her. "I'll be there in a minute."

She left and to my utter annoyance, Stefano decided to go after her. *Back off, fucker.*

He'd definitely set his sights on her. Why was he even considering her for one of our whorehouses? She really didn't look the type.

"I know you handle things however you want, but recently I've lost too many waitresses to the Camorra's whorehouses ... or unfortunate accidents."

Those accidents were mostly related to Remo's soldiers acting out of turn.

"I'm glad to have that new girl. The customers seem to like her, and she actually knows how to behave herself. I'd appreciate it if she could stay in my service for more than a couple of weeks."

"We handle things however we want. You just said it, Roger," I said in warning. "If we decide to put her to use in one of our other establishments, we don't ask you."

He nodded, but a vein in his forehead swelled with suppressed anger. He didn't like it. That made two of us.

I walked past him and pushed the door open with my elbow then stepped behind the bar.

Leona was busy chatting to two ancient customers, laughing at something they had said. Stefano sat at the other end of the bar, watching her like a hawk. His brown hair was immaculately slicked back. I bet the asshole spent hours in front of the mirror. As Leona continued to chat with the older men, it seemed she was determined to ignore Stefano. I set down the cases, and Leona shot me a grateful look with those baby blues. When the men at the bar saw me, they quickly focused on their beer.

I walked around the bar and picked up my gym bag where I'd left it, stopping beside Stefano. He glanced up at me from his sitting position. He was below me in ranks, so the challenging glint in his eyes made me consider sticking my knife into them. "You think about making a move on her?"

"I'm considering it," he said. "She looks like she would respond well to the slightest sign of kindness. Makes her easy to manipulate." Would that sick as fuck leer still be on his face if I cut his throat?

"She doesn't seem interested in your advances."

"That'll change," he said smugly.

"Has Remo seen her?" That was the only thing that mattered.

"No. I only just found her, but I'm sure he'll approve."

I had a feeling Stefano was right. "Don't waste your time. She's already taken."

"By whom?"

"Me," I growled.

He frowned at me but then shrugged, emptied his beer, and left. I watched his back as he disappeared through the door. Stefano was someone to watch. He and I had never gotten along, and I had a feeling that wouldn't change anytime soon. Stefano knew better than to make a move on someone I wanted.

My eyes found Leona again. She'd been watching my exchange with Stefano with a confused expression. With the background noise of the bar, there was no way she could have heard anything. She was so different from the women that usually frequented the places I spent time in. There were women who were unable to hide their fear and then ones that hoped to gain something from being close to me. She didn't know who I was. It was strange being treated like someone … normal. I'd fought hard to receive the respect and fear everyone showed me, but it hadn't bothered me that she was unaware of my status. I wondered how long it would be before someone told her and how she'd look at me then.

"I know that look," Remo said, sneaking up beside me. I should have realized he'd entered the scene. People were even more uneasy than they were when it was only me in the room. He nodded toward Leona. "Take her if you want. She's yours. She's nobody. It's not like we need her anyway. She doesn't look like much entertainment, though."

I glanced over to Leona. She was wiping the counter, unaware of the lewd looks she was drawing from some of the men around her.

"I don't want to take her," I said then amended when I saw Remo's bewildered expression. "I won't."

"Why not?" Remo asked curiously.

Danger. "You said it yourself, she doesn't look like much entertainment."

"Perhaps she's more exciting when she's trying to fight you off. Might be worth a try. Some women turn into feral cats when they're cornered." He clapped my shoulder.

I didn't say anything.

Remo shrugged. "But if you don't want her …"

"I do," I said quickly. "I'd appreciate if word got around that I have my eyes set on her. Just in case. I don't want Stefano messing with her."

Remo chuckled. "Sure. Put your claim on her, Fabiano."

That was the advantage of being on his good side. Remo allowed me things his other soldiers couldn't even dream of. With that, he left and went to a table with some of the high rollers from one of our premium casinos. I returned to the bar. There would be time to change into my fighting trunks later.

The other men excused themselves, and Leona came over to me, her brows drawn together. "Am I missing something?"

I shrugged. "I'm the reason why some of them lost money." *And limbs.*

She opened her mouth to say something, but the sound of a body smashing against the cage silenced her, followed by a round of ecstatic applause. She clapped a hand over her lips, eyes widened with shock. I glanced over my shoulder. One of the fighters was lying on the ground, unconscious. The other was standing over him, arms raised, doing some sort of weak-ass victory dance. Perhaps he'd be my next opponent in a couple of weeks … if he won a few more times. I'd have to break his knees to prevent future dancing.

"It's horrible," Leona whispered, her voice clogged with compassion, as if she could feel their pain.

I turned to her.

"Why does anyone want to watch something that brutal?"

Brutal? She hadn't seen brutal yet. If she was lucky, she never would. "It's in our nature," I said. "Survival of the fittest. Power struggles. Blood thirst. That's all still ingrained in our DNA."

"I don't think that's true," she argued. "I think we've moved on, but sometimes we fall back into old habits."

"Then why do people still look up to the strong? Why do women prefer the alpha males?"

She snorted. "That's a myth."

I cocked one eyebrow and leaned closer, catching a glimpse down her dress. White cotton. Of course. "Is it?" I asked.

She scanned my face, red creeping up her throat and settling on cheeks.

I stifled a laugh and got up before she could say anything. It was time to change. "I'll be back in a moment," I told her.

When I entered the changing room, the other fighters fell silent. A couple of them returned my stare; one openly challenged me with his eyes. I assumed he'd be my opponent tonight. He was around six-four, one inch taller than me. Good. Maybe this would be a longer fight.

I got undressed then pulled up my shorts. Hopefully they saw all my scars. They knew nothing of pain. I smirked at my opponent. Maybe he'd live to see tomorrow.

I left the changing room and walked back to the bar. Leona was frozen as her eyes trailed from my bare feet up to my shorts and my naked chest. The glass she was cleaning fell from her hands and landed with a plop into the dishwater. A myriad of emotions flashed across her face. Shock. Confusion. Fascination. Appreciation. That last one I could feel in my dick. I'd worked hard for my body.

I grabbed my glass sitting on the bar and downed the rest of my water. Then I took the tape out of my bag and began wrapping my hands, feeling her curious gaze on me the entire time.

"You're one of them?"

I tilted my head, not sure what she was referring to. A fighter? A member of the Camorra? A killer? Yes, yes, and yes.

There was no fear in her eyes, so I said, "A cage fighter? Yes."

She licked her lips. Those damn pink lips gave my cock ideas I didn't need before a fight.

"I hope I didn't offend you earlier."

"Because you think it's too brutal? No. It's what it is."

Her eyes kept tracing my tattoo and the scars—and occasionally my six pack. I leaned over the bar, bringing our faces closer. I knew everyone was watching us, even if they tried to be discreet.

"Are you still certain women aren't into alpha males?" I murmured.

She swallowed but didn't say anything. I took a step back. Everyone in the room should have got the message. My balls tightened with the look she gave me. Something about that girl drew me in. I couldn't say what it was, but I'd figure it out.

"It's my turn," I told her when I was done taping my hands.

"Don't get hurt," she said simply.

The men near the bar exchanged looks, snickering, but Leona was unaware of their reaction.

"I won't," I said then turned and made my way past the tables, toward the fighting cage.

I stepped into the cage under the yowling and thunderous applause of the crowd. How many had bet against me? If I lost, they'd be rich. Unfortunately for them, I never lose.

I caught Leona watching me from behind the bar counter, eyes still wide in surprise. Yes, I was a fighter, and that was the least dangerous part of me. She stopped what she was doing and came around the counter. She climbed on a barstool, shook off her flip-flops, and brought her legs up until she sat cross-legged, the skirt of her dress carefully draped over her thighs. This girl. She didn't belong here.

My opponent entered the cage. He called himself Snake. He even had snakes tattooed to his throat; they rose up over his ears and bared their fangs on both sides of his head. Snake. What a fucking stupid name to give yourself. I didn't know why people thought a scary name would make them seem scary. I'd never had to call myself anything but Fabiano. It was enough.

The ref closed the door and explained the rules to us. There were none—except that this wasn't a fight to the death, so Snake would likely live.

Snake hit his chest with his flat hands, letting out a battle cry. Whatever got his courage up.

I lifted a hand and beckoned him forward. I wanted to get this fight going. With a roar, he charged at me like a bull. I dodged him, grabbed his shoulder, and rammed my knee into his left side three times in quick succession. The air left his lungs, but he didn't fall. He swung a fist at me and got my chin. I jumped back, aimed a hard kick at his head, and despite his quick reaction, my heel caught his ear. He staggered into the cage, shook his head, and attacked again. This would be fun.

He lasted longer than the last, but eventually my kicks to his head got him. His eyes went out of focus more and more. I grabbed him by the back of his head, brought up my knee at the same time I thrust it into his face. I could feel the crunch of his nose and cheekbone as they broke against my knee. He yowled hoarsely and toppled backwards. I went after him. I jump-kicked him into the cage, and when he hit the ground with a resounding thud, I crouched over him and rammed my elbow into his stomach. Once. Twice. He weakly patted the floor, face swollen, breathing labored. Giving up.

"Surrender!" cried the ref.

I never understood men like him. I'd die before I surrendered. There was honor in death but not in begging for mercy. I rose to my feet. The crowd cheered.

Remo gave me the thumbs-up from his spot at the table with the high rollers. I could tell from the excited gleam in his eyes that he wanted to get into the cage again and soon. Schmoozing the high rollers was high up on his hate list, but someone had to do it. Nino was eloquent and sophisticated, but after a while, he forgot to plaster emotions on his face; once people realized he didn't have any, they ran as fast they could. Savio was a teen and capricious, and Adamo ... Adamo was a kid.

I turned around. Leona was still sitting on the stool in front of the bar, watching me, horrified. That was a look that was closer to the ones I was used to getting from people. Seeing me like this, covered in blood and sweat, maybe she finally understood why she should be terrified of me.

She untangled her legs from her dress, hopped down from the stool, and disappeared through the swinging door.

I climbed out of the cage, dripping blood and sweat on the floor. I'd need to stitch myself up.

I occasionally heard, "Good fight," from someone as I walked by. I shook a few congratulating hands then retreated into the changing room. Seeing that my fight had been the last of the night, and my opponent was on his way to the hospital, the room was empty. I opened my locker when a knock sounded. I grabbed one of my guns and held it behind my back as I turned. "Come in."

The door opened a crack before Leona poked her head in, her eyes closed. "Are you decent?"

I put my gun back into my gym bag. "I'm the least decent guy in this city." Except for Remo and his brothers, perhaps.

She opened her eyes cautiously, searching the room until they settled on me. Relief flooded her face, and she slipped into the room before closing the door behind her.

My eyebrows shot up. "Are you here to give me a victory present?" I asked, leaning against the lockers. My cock thought of all kind of presents she could give. And all of them involved her perfect mouth and her undoubtedly perfect pussy.

"Oh ... I only have a bottle of water and clean towels." She showed me what she held in her hands, smiling apologetically.

I shook my head, chuckling. God, this girl.

Realization flooded her face. "Oh, you meant ..." She gestured in the general direction of her body. "Oh, no. No. Sorry."

I closed my eyes, fighting the urge to laugh. It had been a while since a woman had made me laugh. Most of the time, they just made me fuck them senseless.

"I hope you can live with a bottle of cold water," she said in a teasing voice.

When I opened my eyes, she was in front of me, holding out the bottle. She was more than a head shorter than me and less than an arm's length away. Stupid girl. She needed to learn self-preservation. I took the bottle and emptied it in a few gulps.

She scanned my body. "There's so much blood."

I chanced a look. There was a small cut over my ribs where the sharp edge of the cage had grazed me. Bruises were forming over my left kidney and on my right thigh. The majority of blood wasn't mine. "It's nothing. I've had worse."

Her eyes lingered on my forehead. "You've got a cut that needs to be treated. Is there a doctor around I should get?"

"No. I don't need a doctor."

She opened her mouth to argue but then seemed to think better of it. She paused.

"You looked so …" She shook her head, her nose puckering in the most fucking adorable way possible. Fuck, those damn freckles. "I don't know how to describe it. *Fierce.*"

I straightened, surprised. She sounded almost fascinated. "You weren't disgusted? I thought it's too 'brutal.'"

She shrugged, one delicate motion. "I was disgusted. It's such a savage sport. I don't even know if you can call it that. It's all about beating each other up."

"It's also about reading your opponent, about seeing his weaknesses and using them against him. It's about speed and control." I scanned her again, reading her like I did all my opponents. It wasn't difficult to guess why Stefano would have chosen her if allowed. It was obvious that she'd had a difficult life, that that there was nobody to take care of her. It was obvious that she wanted more, that she wanted someone to take care of her, someone who was kind to her, someone to love. Stefano was good at pretending he was someone like that. Soon she'd learn that it was best to rely only on yourself. Love and kindness were rare, not only in the mob world.

"I don't understand why people watch others hurt each other for sport. Why do people enjoy inflicting pain on somebody?"

I was the last person she should ask. She had never seen me hurt people. That fight was a joke in comparison to my jobs as an Enforcer of the Camorra. I liked to hurt people. I was good at it and had learned to be good at it.

CHAPTER 6

LEONA

His eyes were unreadable. What was he thinking? It dawned on me that I was starting to annoy him with my constant talk about the brutality of fighting.

Cage fighting was obviously important to him. I was still trying to understand the three sides of him I'd seen so far: the businessman, the guy next door, and the fighter. Though, I now realized that only the latter had seemed natural ... like it was the only one where he didn't feel he was pretending.

"I should probably leave," I said. It wasn't the best idea to be in the changing room with him. People might get ideas and start talking, and that was something I really didn't want.

He nodded. The way he was watching me sent a shiver down my spine. His eyes, always so keen and cautious, and blue like the sky over Texas in spring, kept me frozen in place. *Get a grip.* I turned and strode toward the door. Before I walked out, I risked one more glance over my shoulder. "I don't even know your name," I said.

"Fabiano," he said. The name seemed too normal, too gentle for a man like him, who was now covered in blood.

"I'm Leona," I told him. I wasn't even sure why, but for some reason he made me curious.

He hooked his fingers in his shorts, and I quickly left, but before I closed the door, I caught a glimpse of his backside as he headed for the shower. His muscles flexed with every step. Oh hell. I tore my gaze from his perfect butt. There were scars all over his back, but they didn't look like flaws on him. Heat shot straight to my head, and I quickly turned around, only to stare at Cheryl's face. "Hon, don't play with the big boys. They don't play nicely," she said cryptically.

"I'm not playing with anyone," I said, embarrassed that she had caught me spying on Fabiano.

She patted my shoulder. "Just stay away from the likes of him."

I didn't get the chance to ask her what she meant. Roger shouted for her to come into his office. She thrust the mop at me. "Here, you have to clean the cage." Then she rushed off.

It was already two in the morning, and I was incredibly tired. Only a few guests remained scattered around tables, drinking their last beer. Most people had left after Fabiano's fight. I shuddered when my eyes took in the bloody mess that was the fighting cage. I'd never had trouble with blood, but this was more than I'd seen in a long time. The last time I'd had to clean up such a mess was when my mother had hit her head on the bathtub in a crystal meth rage.

I sighed. There was no use in postponing the inevitable. I climbed through the cage doors and began mopping. The last guests gathered their things, and I waved at them when they called out to me, wishing me a good night.

I kept my eyes open for Roger, hoping he'd give me some cash for today's work. I really needed a few bucks to buy food and perhaps another pair of shoes. I grimaced when I saw a few drops of blood had gotten on my naked toes. Sandals definitely weren't a wise shoe choice for a job like this.

Occasionally, I allowed myself to glance in the direction of the changing room door, but Fabiano seemed to be taking his time showering. An image of him naked under a water stream came to my mind. I quickly wiped the last bloodstain away and got out of the cage. I was too tired to think straight. I needed to get home, though the idea of walking home in the dark for over a mile didn't sit well with me. I wasn't easily scared, but I had a healthy sense of self-preservation.

After I'd put the mop and bucket away, I continued into the corridor that led to Roger's office, but I hesitated halfway through it. A woman was screaming. I shivered. Then I heard Roger's voice. "Yes, you like it up your ass, you slut. Yes, just like that."

Cheryl was the one who'd screamed, but apparently it was in pleasure. This was too disturbing. I desperately needed the money Roger owed me, but there was no way I was going to interrupt whatever they had going on. I backed away and straight into a strong body. Opening my mouth, I was about the release a startled scream when a hand clamped down over my lips. Fear shot through me and instinct took over. I shoved my elbow back as hard as I could and collided with a rock-hard stomach. My opponent didn't even wince, but he tightened his fingers around my waist.

"Shhh. It's me."

I relaxed, and he dropped his hand from my lips. I twisted in his hold, tilting my head back. Fabiano. He was dressed in his black shirt and jeans, and he was clean. The wound at his hairline was stitched up. So that was what had taken so long! I couldn't imagine fixing myself with a needle, but as a cage fighter he probably had to suffer through worse pain than a few needle pokes.

"You scared me."

There was a hint of amusement in his eyes.

FABIANO

I scared her? If this was the first time I'd scared her, then she was as crazy as she was beautiful.

"I didn't want you to interrupt Roger with your scream," I said. Nobody wanted to see Roger with his pants down.

Her eyes skittered to the door and she shuddered. "I didn't know they were a couple. They didn't act like one."

"They aren't," I said. "They fuck."

"Oh." A tantalizing blush colored her cheeks. "I should be going."

"Do you want me to drive you?" I wasn't sure why the hell I was offering her a ride again. After all, she didn't exactly live around the corner from my apartment.

She paused, conflict dancing in her eyes. Finally some distrust. Perhaps seeing me fight had made her realize that she should have never gotten in my car in the first place. It was funny how differently people reacted to someone, depending on the outfit they wore. Suit? Trustworthy.

"I can't let you do that again."

"Then call a taxi. You shouldn't be walking in this area alone at night." I could name all the reasons why she shouldn't.

"I don't have any money," she said then looked like she wanted to swallow her tongue.

I reached into my bag and pulled out a roll of fifty-dollar bills.

Leona's eyes grew wide. "Where do you get so much money?"

She didn't look impressed, only wary. Good. There was nothing worse than women who decided you were only worth their attention after they saw you had money.

"Money for winning my fight." Which was almost the truth.

I untangled a fifty-dollar bill and held it out to her.

She shook her head vehemently. "No. I really can't take it."

"You can give it back when Roger's paid you."

She shook her head again but with less conviction this time. She was tired. I could tell. "Take it," I ordered.

She blinked up at me, stunned by the command but unable to resist, so she finally took the note. "Thank you. I'll pay you back soon."

People always said that to me.

She hoisted her backpack up on her shoulder. "I need to go," she said apologetically.

I walked her outside. My car was right in front of the door. She glanced at it. "Do you earn that much money cage fighting?"

"It's not my job. It's a hobby."

More curiosity on her part. No questions. A girl who had learned that curiosity killed the cat.

"Call a taxi," I told her.

She smiled. "Don't worry, I will. You don't have to wait."

She wouldn't call a taxi. I could tell. I waited patiently. If she thought she could drive me off like that, she was mistaken.

"I don't have a phone," she reluctantly admitted.

No money, no phone. I reached for mine in the pocket of my jeans when she sighed and shook her head.

"No, don't. I really want to walk. I can't afford to waste money on a taxi," she said with blatant discomfort.

It was obvious she was poor, so it was futile of her to try to hide it from me. Stefano wouldn't have seen her as the perfect prey if she wasn't an easy target. And hell, with this shabby dress, shabbier sandals, and the fucking shabbiest backpack on the planet, it took no fucking genius to see how poor she was.

"Then let me at least walk with you," I told her to my own surprise.

I didn't want Stefano to give her another go or have one of the thugs put a hand on her. Something about her trustful innocence drew me in like a moth to the flame. It was the thrill of the hunt, no doubt. I'd never hunted someone like that.

"But you could drive. You don't have to walk."

"You can't walk alone at night, believe me."

Her shoulders slumped and her eyes darted to my car. "Then I'll ride with you. I can't let you walk with me and then back to the bar again to get your car."

I held the door open for her, and she slipped in. Too trusting. I slid into the seat beside her. She sank into the leather seat, yawning, her arms wrapping tightly around her old backpack.

I doubted she had any treasures hidden in its depths. Perhaps she really had some sort of weapon inside to defend herself.

Knife? Pepper spray? Gun?

Nothing would have saved her if I had any intention of having my way with her. I started the engine, which came to life with a roar, and pulled out of the parking lot. In a confined space like this, she wouldn't be able to get in a good shot. I would have no trouble disarming her, and then she'd be defenseless. Women often carried weapons because they thought they would protect them, but without the knowledge of how to use them, they were only an additional risk.

She told me her address again.

"I remember, don't worry."

She ran her fingertips along the black leather of her seat. "Are you from a rich family?"

I was, but that wasn't why I had the car and everything else. "No," I told her.

She fell silent. She was brimming with more questions. It was written all over her face.

When I pulled up in front of the apartment complex, the door on the second floor opened. I immediately recognized the man—moderately tall, half bald, paunch drooping over his belt, all over pathetic—as one of the gambling addicts who frequented one of our casinos. I hadn't handled him yet. He wasn't important enough and had never owed us enough money to warrant my attention. Soto had dealt with him once. He took care of the lowlife scum our business attracted. After that one time, he'd always been on time with his payments. He was a looser who always chased the next dollar to spend it on gambling.

"That's my dad," Leona said. There was a hint of tenderness in her voice. Tenderness that he sure as hell didn't deserve. "Thanks for the ride."

Her father was heading down the walkway toward us then froze when he recognized me behind the steering wheel. Leona and I got out.

"Leona!" he croaked. His eyes did a quick scan of her body. "Are you okay? Did he …?" He cleared his throat at the look I gave him. I hadn't expected that kind of worry from him. From what I'd seen of him so far, he only gave a fuck about himself. People like him always did. That was why I enjoyed dealing with them.

Leona blinked. "What's going on? I'm fine. Why are you acting so strange?"

"Are you okay?" he asked again.

I strode over to them. Immediately, the smell of cheap spirits wafted into my nose. Gambling and alcohol were a thunderous combination, one that eventually led to an early grave. Either by the Camorra, or by Mother Nature.

She nodded, then gestured toward me. "Fabiano was nice enough to drive me home."

I was many things, but nice wasn't one of them. Her father looked like he was going to blow a gasket. "Haven't I told you to be careful around here? You can't just go around talking to …" He fell silent, saving his own sorry ass.

I gave him a cold smile. "I really enjoyed *talking* to your daughter."

He nervously rubbed his palms over his faded jeans.

"Leona, go ahead. I need to have a talk with your father," I said.

Leona's eyes darted between her father and me. "You know each other?"

"We have a mutual friend."

"Okay." She gave me an uncertain smile. "See you soon?" It was half a question, half a statement.

"You bet," I said quietly.

Her father clutched my arm the moment she was gone.

"Please," he begged. "Is this because of the money I haven't paid? I will pay it soon. Just don't—"

I let my gaze fall to his fingers grabbing my arm, and he let go like he'd been burned. "Don't what?" I asked dangerously.

He stepped back, shaking his head. He was worried for himself. He'd thought I had come to deal with him.

"I would be sad to see her leave," I said casually. "I suppose she's going to stay for a while?"

He stared at me.

"I'd really hate for her to hear the wrong things about me. Understood?"

Slowly he nodded.

I returned to my car. His fearful gaze followed me as I drove off. I wasn't even sure what exactly made me want to make her mine. Her father knew there was nothing he could do to stop me, not that he was the type to try. The only thing that could have stopped me from pursuing her, now that my interest had been stirred, was Remo, and he had no reason to interfere.

CHAPTER 7

LEONA

I slept late the next day. I didn't have to work until three in the afternoon and needed to get some rest. When I walked into the kitchen, a box of donuts sat on the table. Dad was clutching a coffee cup.

"Morning," I said, even though it was almost twelve o'clock. I poured some coffee for myself before I sank down into the chair across from him.

"You got us breakfast," I said, and helped myself to a donut. I knew better than to expect pleasant surprises to occur on a daily basis.

"I asked a neighbor for some money until I get paid tomorrow." He was some sort of courier, from what I'd gathered. I wondered how he could keep the job, considering that his breath always stunk of alcohol.

"I could give you fifty dollars," I said, pulling out the money from the waistband of my shorts. I'd learned to hide money close to my body. "Then you could pay him back and get us food for the next few days."

He eyed the money as if it was something dirty. "Where did you get it?"

"I found a job," I said with a smile.

He didn't look happy. "And they paid you fifty dollars on your first day?"

He made it sound like I had been doing something forbidden, *something dirty.*

"No, not yet. I will get paid today, though." That was what I hoped at least. I wasn't sure how Roger handled things, but since he didn't ask for my social security number or any other relevant information, I assumed that it wasn't a regular paycheck.

"Then where did you get that money?"

He looked angry. What was the matter with him? He and Mom had definitely never asked many questions when it came to money. "Fabiano gave it to me."

He jumped up, his chair toppling to the ground with a bang. I flinched in my seat. Distant memories of him fighting with my mother as he raised his fist and she clawed at him filled my mind.

"You borrowed money from … him?"

"What's wrong?" I asked.

"You can't go around borrowing money from people like him. We don't need any more attention from him."

"People like him," I repeated. "What kind of people exactly?"

He looked torn. I wasn't sure who or what he was trying to protect, but it certainly wasn't me. He had never been the protective father figure.

"I know he's a cage fighter, Dad. I saw him fight, okay? So please mind your own business." Like you've done the last five years.

"You did? Why?" Then something seemed to click in his mind, and he closed his eyes. "Don't tell me you're working in Roger's Arena."

"I do."

He picked up the chair and straightened it before falling into it, as if his legs were too weak to carry him. "You should have never come here. I shouldn't have let you. You're going to get us both in trouble. I really can't use this kind of baggage right now."

I frowned at my coffee. "I'm a grown up. I can handle myself. I can't be picky with the jobs I get. It's not like I have much of a choice."

"Give him that money back today. Don't use it for anything. And—"

"Stay away from him?" I interrupted. It was too late for Dad talk.

"No," he said quietly. "Be careful. I don't need you to mess things up. It's too late for me to tell you to stay away."

I got the feeling that he meant it in a different way than I had. "I could stay away. It's not like I'm bound to him."

Dad shook his head. "No, you can't stay away, because that's no longer up to you. He'll decide from now on, and he won't let you stay away until he gets whatever it is that he wants from you." His lips curled, like he knew exactly what that was.

I hated how he could make me feel dirty with that one expression. Like he had any right to judge me when he gladly let my mom sell her body so he could pay his gambling debt.

"We're not living in the Middle Ages, Dad. It's not like he holds any power over me." I wasn't even sure why we were discussing this. Fabiano and I had done nothing but talk, and so far he'd been the perfect gentleman. Perhaps Dad's drinking problem was worse than I thought. Or maybe he was into harder drugs. Mom had been paranoid too.

He pulled a cigarette—his last one—from a battered packet before lighting it and taking a deep pull. "The Camorra owns the city and its people. And now *he* owns you." He released the smoke from his lungs, cloaking us in it. I coughed.

"Camorra?" I had heard the term in a report about Italy on television a while back. They were a branch of the mob, but this was Las Vegas not Naples.

"You mean the mob?"

Dad got up. "I said too much already," he said regretfully, taking another drag. His fingers that held the cigarette shook. "I can't help you. You're in too deep already."

In too deep? I'd been in Las Vegas for three days and worked at Roger's bar for only one day. How could I be in too deep? And what exactly did that mean?

Dad didn't give me the chance to ask more questions. He rushed out of the kitchen, and a few seconds later, I heard the entrance door slam shut.

If he insisted on beating around the bush, I'd have to pepper Cheryl with questions. If her cryptic warnings from yesterday were any indication, she definitely knew more. I wasn't going to ask Fabiano directly about it unless I had no other option. He'd probably laugh in my face if I asked him about the mafia.

Cheryl was putting glasses onto the shelves attached to the wall behind the bar when I walked in. The red neon lamps were still off, and without their glow, the area looked dull. There was also another woman wiping the leather of the booths. She nodded in my direction when she caught me staring. Her hair was a nice shade of light brown, but her face looked long in the tooth, used up. Hard drugs. It made her age difficult to guess. She could have been forty or thirty. There was no telling.

I headed straight toward Cheryl and put my backpack down behind the bar. When our eyes met, my cheeks grew hot at the memory of what I'd overheard her do with Roger last night. Luckily, she didn't seem to notice.

"You're late," she said, a bit on edge.

I glanced at the clock on the wall. Actually, I was right on time, but I decided not to say anything. After all, I needed to pump Cheryl for information.

"Sorry," I said as I grabbed two glasses and helped her fill the shelves.

"You could clean up the changing room or Roger's office. I've got this."

Roger's office was the last place I wanted to clean. "I'll clean the changing rooms," I said, turning to her.

She returned my gaze questioningly. "What's up?"

"You know I'm new in town, so I'm not in on what's going on around here," I began and could see her defenses on alert. Perhaps getting answers from her wouldn't be as easy as I'd hoped.

"But people are acting strange around Fabiano ... You know, the guy who fought the last battle?"

She laughed bitterly. "Oh, I know him."

I was taken aback. "Oh, okay. So what's the matter with him? My father freaked out when Fabiano gave a ride home last night."

"*He* gave you a ride home?"

Okay. This was really starting to grate on my nerves. Why couldn't she just spill it?

"He did. It was late and he didn't want me to walk by myself. He seemed worried." I decided not to mention that he'd picked me up the night before too.

Cheryl gave me a look like I'd completely lost my mind. "Trust me, he wasn't. I don't know why he took you home, but it sure as hell wasn't out of the kindness of his heart. You are lucky nothing happened."

I moved closer to her until we were almost touching. "Cheryl, just tell me what's going on. This bar, Fabiano ... everything is off."

"This is Camorra territory, chick. Everything belongs to them—and your Fabiano—to some degree."

He wasn't my Fabiano, but I didn't want to interrupt her, fearing she would change her mind about giving me an honest answer.

"He's Falcone's right hand."

"Falcone?"

The name didn't ring a bell, but it sounded Italian. She cursed under her breath. "It's not my business. I don't want to get in trouble."

"So is Falcone some kind of mobster?" I'd seen movies about the mafia, and I knew they were the bad guys, but was that even reality? This was the twenty-first century. The mafia seemed like something out of the roaring twenties, old men smoking cigars in fedoras. Fabiano was someone who instilled respect in others, I could see that, but did that stem from him being a mobster or the fact that he looked intimidating? Anyone who'd seen him in the fighting cages would think twice about a confrontation with him.

"Some kind of mobster," she murmured like I had committed blasphemy. "You say it like it's a normal job, chick. It's not, trust me. The things the Camorra does, the things your Fabiano does, they …" Her eyes went to something behind me, and she fell silent.

"Go clean the changing rooms," she muttered.

I turned, spotting Roger a few feet from us, a disapproving expression on his face. He wasn't looking at me, only Cheryl, and a silent conversation I wasn't privy to seemed to take place between them.

Taking the mop and bucket, I hurried past him. I was used to being the new girl in town. I'd moved about a dozen times in the last ten years and had always felt like I was on the sidelines of life because of it. I never got the inside jokes.

I knew being a mobster wasn't a normal job. These people were bad news. But Fabiano hadn't seemed bad. Something about him made me curious, made me want to catch a glimpse behind that cautious mask he wore. Who knew why he'd become a mobster? Sometimes life just left you with no choice.

I was glad that cleaning the changing room required no concentration at all, because my mind was occupied processing the news. I wasn't sure what to think because I didn't know enough. The Camorra, Falcone, mobsters … the words held no meaning for me. But for my father and Cheryl, they did. For them, they instilled fear.

My train of thought was interrupted when the first fighters entered the changing room. Apparently, there were fights scheduled every evening. I wondered where Roger found all these guys eager to beat each other up. Many of them had as little choice as I did when it came to finding a job.

One of them, the youngest of the lot—around my age—sauntered closer. I lifted the bucket from the white-tiled floor, ready to leave them alone. He gave me a flirtatious smile, which died when one of the other guys whispered something in his ear. After that, I might as well have been invisible. Confused, I left the room. Was I some kind of pariah? The untouchable cleaning lady?

Not that I had any interest in flirting with that guy, but his change in demeanor was a slight blow to my confidence. I didn't kid myself into thinking I was a stunner like some other girls, certainly not wearing the same flowery dress as I did yesterday.

At least I didn't smell. Yet.

I faltered in my steps when I saw a familiar face enter the bar. Fabiano was dressed in black slacks and a white dress shirt with the sleeves rolled up. The white contrasted nicely with his tan. He was a sight to behold. Tall and handsome, aloof and cool, he exuded power and control. He held himself with natural grace that mesmerized me. It was like watching a lion on the prowl. There was almost too much of him to take in. His words about alpha males flashed through my mind, followed by the fact that he was a member of the Camorra. People had warned me to stay away from him.

My mother had always said I was a fixer. I needed something broken so I could see if I was capable of mending it. Injured animals, sick people, broken-down cars. *Her*. She'd said it would get me in trouble one day. Because people couldn't be fixed, and one day I'd find someone so broken, he'd break me before

I could mend him.

Was that what had drawn me to Fabiano from that very first second? Had I sensed that something about him was broken and I needed to fix it?

FABIANO

Something in her expression was different. She was a bit more hesitant than before. I watched her carry the bucket and mop behind the bar then busy herself taking stock of the fridge, with her back turned to me.

I had a feeling she didn't want me to see her face. Perhaps she thought she could disguise her emotions from me. *Like that was going to work.* A look at her body told me everything I needed to know. She was tense and her breathing was too controlled, as if she was trying to appear unaffected but failing miserably.

I leaned against the counter, resting on my elbows, watching her silently. She wore the same dress again and the same sandals. It was starting to drive me crazy. Couldn't her father stop gambling for one fucking day so she could buy herself some decent clothes? Rage rose up inside me at the obvious neglect she'd probably been suffering all her life. Neglect was something I knew all too well. It came in different shapes and forms.

I waited patiently until she could no longer pretend that there was anything remotely interesting inside the fridge. She squared her shoulders and turned to face me. Her smile was all wrong. Tense and unsure. On the verge of being fake. There was a flicker of caution in her eyes but still no fear.

"Water?" she guessed, already reaching for a glass.

I shook my head. "No fight tonight. Give me a Scotch."

"Right," she said. "Are you going out? You look nice."

"Nice, hmm . . ." She didn't need to know that Remo and I would be checking out one of our strip clubs tonight. There had been some inconsistencies with the books, which we needed to investigate. And after that, we'd have a long talk with the sluts working there.

A blush spread over her cheeks, making me want to reach over the bar and brush my fingers over them to feel her heated skin and those damn freckles. The innocent act usually wasn't something that got to me, because it usually was just that ... an act. With Leona I could tell she wasn't acting.

"All business, no fun," I told her.

Her smile faltered again. She reached for the cheapest bottle of Scotch. I shook my head. "Not that one. Give me the Johnnie Walker Blue Label over there." It was the most expensive Scotch Roger's Arena offered. It wasn't really an establishment for fine tastes. The guys around here liked their drinks how they liked their women: cheap.

"That's thirty dollars a glass," she said.

"I know," I said when she slid the glass over to me. I downed a long sip of the amber liquid, enjoying the burn. I didn't drink often and had only been drunk twice in my life. There were other ways to get a high ... fucking and fighting, my favorites.

I pushed a fifty-dollar note over to her. "Keep the rest."

Her eyes grew wide, and she gave a small shake of her head. "That's too much."

She fumbled in the cash register and pushed the twenty dollars over to me. Then she bent down for a moment to retrieve another fifty-dollar bill and put that down in front of me as well.

"I told you I don't want that money back, and that twenty dollars is your tip."

"I can't accept either. It's not right."

"Who told you?" I asked.

She blinked, then averted her eyes. "Who told me what?" She was a horrible liar and an even worse actress.

"Don't lie to me," I said, a hint of impatience creeping into my tone.

Her blue eyes met mine. She hesitated. "I overheard a few people talking."

I didn't believe that shit for a second.

She scanned my face. "So is it true?"

"Is what true?" I challenged.

"That you are part of the Camorra?"

She said it like the word meant nothing to her. She didn't know what we stood for, didn't know how powerful we were. For most people, the mere word fostered fear, but not for her. I hoped it would stay that way, but I knew it couldn't. Living in this part of town, working for Roger, she'd soon see or hear things that would make her realize just who the Camorra was and what they did.

"I am," I said, emptying the rest of my Scotch.

Her eyes widened in surprise. "Aren't you supposed to keep it a secret?"

"It's difficult to keep a secret that isn't one." The Camorra was Las Vegas. We controlled the night clubs and bars, restaurants and casinos. We organized the cage fights and street races. We gave the poor fuckers bread and games, and they greedily accepted any distraction from their miserable lives. People knew of us, recognized us. There was no sense in trying to pretend we were something else.

"But what about the police?" she asked.

A few other customers tossed glances her way, their glasses empty, but none of them would dare come over to interrupt us.

"Don't worry," I said simply. I couldn't tell her about our association with the sheriff of Clark County or even our connection to some of the judges. That wasn't something she needed to know.

Seventy dollars sat on the bar between us. I picked it up and stalked around the bar. Leona's gaze was a mixture of caution and curiosity. I took her wrist. She didn't resist, only watched me intently. I fought the urge to back her up against the wall and get a taste of her. Fuck, I really wanted that taste.

I turned her hand and put the money into her palm. She opened her mouth, but I shook my head. "I don't want that money back. You will buy yourself a nice dress and wear it tomorrow. And do me a favor, get rid of those fucking sandals. Then our debt is settled."

Embarrassment filled her face as she looked down at herself. "Do I look that bad that you feel the need to buy me clothes?"

"I'm not buying you anything. I'm just giving you the money."

"I'm sure it's a big no-no to take money from someone like you," she said quietly. I still held her hand, and I could feel her pulse speeding up under my fingertips.

I leaned down to her ear. "It's an even bigger no-no to refuse a gift from someone like me."

She shuddered but still didn't pull back. When I released her, she stayed close to me. "Then I have no choice, I suppose," she said.

"You don't," I agreed.

People were watching our exchange with poorly hidden curiosity. A glance at the clock revealed I needed to get going. I didn't want to make Remo wait.

"Tomorrow I expect to see you in your new clothes," I told her.

She nodded then finally took a step back. Her expression was torn.

"So you'll be back tomorrow?" she asked.

I walked back around the bar then turned to her once more. "Yes."

LEONA

I watched Fabiano's retreating back. Now that he wasn't there to distract me anymore, I realized how many customers were sitting in front of empty glasses. Cheryl and the waitress of unidentifiable age were at the other end of the room and only now began to make their way over to me. I quickly hid the money in my backpack before I rushed toward the first table to take their orders. I could tell that people were eyeing me curiously. The conversation with Fabiano had drawn more attention to me than I enjoyed.

I could still feel the remnants of shame when I thought of his demand. I needed to buy a new dress for myself. I knew my clothes had seen better days. And my flip-flops … I stifled a sigh.

Perhaps I should have stood my ground and refused the money. Owing the mafia money was bad news, but Fabiano had gifted me the money not as a mobster but as a … what exactly? We weren't friends. Barely knew each other. Was I in his debt … or worse in the Camorra's? Did he expect something in return?

The idea was terrifying and exciting all at the same time. Not that I would ever give him any kind of physical closeness in return for money, but the idea that he might be interested in me filled me with a giddy kind of excitement.

"So staying away from him isn't going so well, huh?" Cheryl said as she came to a stop beside me, carrying a tray stacked with beer bottles.

"I can't stop him from having a drink in the bar," I said with a small shrug.

"He isn't coming for the drinks. Before you started working here, he was hardly around, and to be honest, I preferred it that way." She sauntered off, her hips swaying from side to side as she expertly maneuvered past tables on her high heels.

I sighed. My mother's knack for troublesome men had obviously been handed down to me. Perhaps there was a way for me to shirk Fabiano's attention. The problem was part of me didn't want him to lose interest in me. Some twisted, idiotic part was eager for his attention. That a man like him had even a flicker of interest in me boosted my meager self-esteem. Back in school, boys had only showed me attention because they thought I'd give it up easy being the daughter of a whore. They weren't interested in me because I was pretty or clever but because they thought I was easy. Fabiano didn't know about my mother, and with the way he looked, he certainly had no trouble finding willing women.

Cheryl shot me a glare across the room. I'd been lost in my thoughts and ceased working again. I pushed Fabiano out of my head. If I didn't want to lose this job, I'd have to get a grip.

That night after work, Fabiano wasn't there to drive me home. And I realized I'd been secretly hoping that he'd come in after he handled business ... whatever that meant.

I swung my backpack over my shoulder and gripped the straps tightly as I began my walk home. Few people were around at this time, and those that were made me want to run. I quickened my pace, checking my surroundings. Nobody was following me, and yet I felt as if I was being hunted. All this talk about the Camorra had been fuel for my imagination.

It was ridiculous. I was used to walking on my own. My mom had never picked me up from anywhere back home, not that we even had a car. I had been the one who had to search for her on more than one occasion when she didn't return home. Often, I'd find her passed out in one of her favorite bars or in an alley.

When I finally made it to my dad's, I released a relieved breath. The lights were still on in the living room.

"Leona? Is that you?"

Dad sounded drunk. I hesitated. I remembered the last time I'd seen him drunk when I was twelve. He'd had a huge fight with my mother and hit her so hard she lost consciousness. She left him after that. Not that the men got better. For my mom, life was a downward spiral that never stopped. Perhaps she'd put a stop to it now, her last chance rehab.

I stopped in the doorway of the living room. Dad was sitting on the sofa, the table in front of him covered with beer bottles and papers. They looked like betting slips. I doubted he was celebrating his luck.

"You are late," he said, a slight slur in his voice.

"I had to work. The bar is open late," I said, wanting nothing more than to go into my bedroom and let him sleep off his intoxication. He pushed off the sofa and came around it, closer to me.

"I thought you weren't drinking anymore."

"I'm not," he said. "Most of the time. Today wasn't a good day."

I had a feeling the good days were few and far between. "I'm sorry," I said automatically.

He waved it off, taking another step in my direction, almost losing his balance. Memories of all the fights between him and my mother that I'd witnessed resurfaced, one after the other. I didn't have the energy for them now. "I should probably go to bed. Tomorrow will be another long day."

I turned when I heard his uncoordinated steps and then his hand clamped around my wrist. I jumped in surprise.

"Wait," he slurred. "You have to give me some money, Leona. Roger must have paid you by now."

I tried to slip out of his grip, but it was too tight—and painful. "You're hurting me," I said through gritted teeth.

He didn't seem to listen. "I need money. I need to pay off my betting debts or we'll be in trouble."

Why would *we* be in trouble if he didn't pay *his* betting debts?

"How much do you need?" I asked.

"Just give me all you have," he said, his fingers on my wrist as much a way to keep me from leaving as it was to keep himself upright.

I knew how it was going to go; Mom was the same way with her addiction. She stole every penny she found in my room, until I had no choice but to carry it on my body at all times. Not that I was able to fend her off on her more desperate days.

"I need to save money for college and we need food." I didn't hold much hope that he'd use his own money for grocery shopping. The donuts had been a one-time exception.

"Stop thinking about college. Girls like you don't go to college."

I finally managed to free myself of his crushing grip. Rubbing my wrist, I took a step back from him.

"Leona, this is serious. I need money," he said.

The despair on his face made me reach into my backpack. I took the fifty-dollar note and handed it to him. That left me with a little over one hundred dollars after Roger had paid me today. Tips were decent in the arena.

"That's all?"

I didn't get the chance to reply. He staggered forward, catching me by surprise. He ripped my backpack out of my hand, shoved his arm inside, and began rummaging through my belongings. I tried to get it back, but he pushed me away. I collided with the wall. When he found the rest of the money, he dropped the backpack and pushed the notes into his jeans pocket.

"A good daughter wouldn't lie to her father," he said angrily.

And a good father wouldn't steel from his daughter. I picked my backpack off the ground. One of the straps had now ripped. Fighting tears, I rushed into the bedroom and closed the door.

Tired and shaken, I sank down onto the mattress. Of course, nothing had changed. I'd lost count of the times my mother had promised me she'd start anew. The drugs had been stronger than her willpower and her love for me. And here I was with my father, who battled his own addiction, and I was stuck with him. Why did people in my life always break their promises?

I had no money to leave Las Vegas, and even if I did, where would I go? I couldn't afford an apartment anywhere, and I had no friends or family I could turn to.

I undressed, putting the dress carefully on the ground. Without money, I wouldn't be able to buy new clothes, but there was no way I could wear my dress again. It smelled of sweat and had a ketchup stain on the skirt. I took jeans shorts and a plain white shirt out of my backpack. They were crumpled from Dad rummaging through my bag, but they'd have to do.

Tired, I lay back on the mattress.

College isn't for girls like you.

Perhaps I was silly for dreaming about it, but my dreams were the only thing that kept me going. I wanted to get a law degree. Help people who couldn't afford a good lawyer. I closed my eyes. An image of Fabiano popped into my head. Nobody would ever take money from him. He was strong. He knew how to get what he wanted. I wished I were like that. Strong. Respected.

Early the next morning, I washed my summer dress then hung it over the shower stall to dry. Even though I still had a few hours until work, I left the apartment. I didn't feel comfortable there after the incident with Dad yesterday. He hadn't scared me. Too often, I had been confronted with the same blatant despair from my mother.

Luckily, I'd found a few dollars in coins that I'd gotten as tips yesterday at the bottom of my backpack. I wanted to grab breakfast for myself.

With my coffee to-go and a Danish, I strode through the streets without any real purpose. When I noticed the bus, which was heading toward the Strip, I used the last of my money to buy a ticket. I wasn't even sure why. It wasn't as if I could ask for a job anywhere there. They would laugh in my face.

I got off near the Venetian and just kept walking, marveling at the splendor of the hotels, at the lightheartedness of the tourists. This was a different Las

Vegas than the one I'd experienced so far. I eventually stopped in front of the fountains of the Bellagio. I closed my eyes. How was I ever going to get a good job around here when I couldn't even buy myself a decent dress?

I had seen the security guards keep an eye on me when I'd wandered through the hotels. They had me pegged as a thief from just one look.

Dad would keep taking my money, unless he suddenly stopped losing his bets, which was highly unlikely. The house always won.

I asked a passerby for the time since I had no watch or phone. I had only thirty minutes until I had to be at work. There was no way I was going to be on time, considering that I'd given my last cent for the bus ticket to the Strip and would have to walk back. That would take at least one hour, probably longer. With my luck, it would probably start raining again.

Walking away from the luxury of the Bellagio, I felt more and more out of place on the Strip, with my wrinkly white shirt and secondhand jeans shorts. To top it off, I was freezing my butt off. Perhaps Dad had been right and I didn't belong in college; I'd still be working in Roger's bar when I was old and bitter. I almost laughed then shook my head. If I stopped believing in my future, it was lost, but days like yesterday made it hard to stay hopeful.

FABIANO

I spotted Leona the moment I stepped out of the Bellagio. The doorman handed me the key to my car, and I slipped in, never taking my eyes off the girl. The engine came to life with its familiar roar, and I pulled out of the driveway, heading down the street toward Leona.

She didn't notice me until I pulled up beside her and rolled down the window. My eyes traveled down to her fucking flip-flops. "Shouldn't you be wearing your new dress today?" I shouted over the noise of the engine and the traffic driving past us as I leaned over the passenger seat to get a good look at her.

Leona was dressed in a wrinkly white shirt that was stuffed into old jeans shorts. Though I appreciated the first glimpse of her lean, toned thighs, I was annoyed that she hadn't bought a new dress for herself. I wasn't used to people ignoring my wishes like that.

She shrugged, though looked obviously uncomfortable. I pushed the passenger door open. "Get in," I ordered, trying to rein in my annoyance.

For a moment, I was sure she'd say no, but then she dropped her backpack from her shoulder and sank down on the seat. She closed the door and put the seat belt on before finally meeting my gaze, almost defiantly.

I let my eyes wander over her body, coming to rest on the faint bruises on her left wrist. I took her hand and inspected the bruise. She pulled away and hid her wrist beneath her other hand.

"I lost my balance in the shower this morning," she lied easily.

"Are you sure you didn't fall down the stairs?" I asked in a low voice. Anger began to simmer under my skin. I knew bruises. And I knew the lies women told to hide they were being abused. My father had hit my sisters and me almost every day, especially Gianna and myself. We were the ones he couldn't control, the ones always doing wrong in his eyes. I'd lost count of the times I'd seen my mother cover up her bruises with makeup.

The bruise around Leona's wrist was from a grip that was too tight.

She gave me a look, but her expression faltered and she shook her head. "It's nothing."

"Who did this?"

"It's nothing. It doesn't hurt or anything."

"Your father."

"What makes you think that?" she asked, her voice a bit higher than before.

"Because he's the only one you have reason to protect."

She licked her lips. "He didn't mean to hurt me. He was drunk. He didn't notice how tightly he was holding me."

Did she really believe that? Or was she scared of what I'd do to him? And by God, I wanted to tear into him like a starved bloodhound.

It wasn't like it was my business what her father did to her. It shouldn't be. But the mere idea that he was hurting her made me want to pay him a visit and give him a taste of what I was capable of.

"Is that why you're dressed like that?" I asked with a wave at her clothes. I pulled the car away from the curb, crossed four lanes to reach the turning lane, then did a U-turn, which was followed by a cacophony of car horns and raised middle fingers from drivers on both sides of the street.

"What are you doing?" Leona asked, gripping the sides of the seat. "That's the wrong way."

"It's not. We're buying you a dress and fucking new shoes. If I have to see you in those fucking flip-flops one more time, I'll go on a rampage."

"What?" Her eyes widened. "Don't be ridiculous. I need to get to work. I don't have time to go shopping."

"Don't worry. Roger will understand."

"Fabiano," she said pleadingly. "Why are you doing this? If you expect anything in return, I'm not that kind of girl. I'm poor, but that doesn't mean I can be bought."

"I have no intention of buying you," I told her. And it was true. Something about Leona made me want to protect her. It was a new experience for me. Not that I didn't want her in my bed, but I wanted to make her want it too. I'd never had to pay for sex, and never would. The whores in Vegas were on the Camorra's payroll anyway.

She watched me for a long time. "Then why?"

"Because I can and because I want to."

The answer didn't seem to satisfy her, but I focused on the street, and she didn't ask more questions, which was a fucking good thing, because I really didn't want to analyze my fascination with her. She reminded me of my sisters. Not in a kinky way. More like she reminded me of a longing I'd buried deep in my chest. Fuck me.

"So your father stole the money I gave you?" I asked eventually, my fingers bearing down on the wheel wishing it were his fucking throat.

She nodded. "He seems to be in trouble."

If he were in real trouble, I'd know it. The money he owed us, it couldn't be much. If Soto still handled him, he was a lucky man.

"Men like him are always in trouble," I told her. "You should get away from him."

"He's my father."

"Sometimes we have to let go of our family if we want to amount to anything in life."

Surprise and curiosity registered on her face. I gritted my teeth, annoyed at myself for my words.

I parked at the curb in front of one of the high-class boutiques that the It-Girls I occasionally fucked—when they felt they needed to add a thrill to their pampered life—frequented.

Leona looked toward the storefront then back at me, her lips parting in disbelief. A small crease formed between her brows. "Don't tell me you want me to go in there. They won't even let me inside looking the way I do. They'll just think that I've come to steal their clothes."

Would they? We'd see about that. I got out of the car, walked around the hood, and opened the door for her. She stepped out then reached for her backpack. I stopped her. "You can leave it in my car."

She hesitated but stepped back so I could shut the door. She looked around nervously, feeling fucking uncomfortable. I held out my hand for her. "Come," I said firmly.

She put her palm in mine, and I closed my fingers around her hand. That Leona trusted me despite what she knew about me made me want to be good to her, which was surprising. I rarely wanted to be good to anyone. I had enough money so one dress wasn't going to kill me. And new shoes were really more for my own sanity than anything else. These flip-flops had to go.

I led her toward the store. The shop window was decorated with silver and golden Christmas decorations. The security guard, a tall, dark-skinned fucker, gave her the once-over but let us enter when he registered my face. The saleswoman couldn't hide her disdain at Leona's appearance. Her red painted lips twisted, and Leona's hand in mine tensed. My eyes slanted to Leona. Her free hand fidgeted with her wrinkly white shirt; shame washed over her face and her freckles disappeared among her blush.

Leona shifted closer to me, seeking safety. She sought fucking safety with a man like me. I doubted Leona noticed, *but I had*—so I raised my eyes to the saleswoman's face, letting her glimpse behind the mask I wore so she could see why I was the Enforcer of the Camorra. Why some people begged me before my knife was ever against their skin. She stiffened and recoiled.

I smiled coldly. "I assume you can help us."

She nodded quickly. "What is it you're looking for?" she asked me.

"You should ask her," I said in a low voice, nodding toward Leona.

"A dress," Leona said quickly then added, "And shoes."

The saleswoman took in Leona's flip-flops, but this time her expression didn't betray her disdain. Good for her.

"What kind of dress?"

Leona sought my gaze, helpless. I gestured for the woman to give us a

95

moment. She scurried off to the back of the store, where another saleswoman stood behind the cash register.

"I never got to choose. I don't know anything about dresses or shoes. I got whatever fit me from Goodwill."

"You never had a new piece of clothing?" I asked.

She looked away. "Clothing wasn't a priority. I had to put food on the table." Her eyes were drawn to the rack of dresses to our right.

"Try on whatever catches your eye."

It became obvious pretty quickly that she wasn't going to touch any of the dresses, so I pulled out a dark green dress with long sleeves and held it out to her. She took it and followed the saleswoman toward the changing rooms in back. I leaned against the wall, keeping my eyes on the curtain hiding Leona from view. It was taking longer than it should for her to get changed.

"You okay in there?"

She came out, grimacing. I straightened. The dress hugged her body in all the right places and flared out until it reached her knees. The back dipped low, revealing her delicate shoulder blades and spine. She looked completely different. She regarded herself in the mirror and shook her head, her lips setting in a tight line. "This feels like a costume," she said quietly. "As if I'm pretending to be someone I'm not."

I moved closer. "And who is it you're pretending to be?"

She glared. "More than *white trash*."

"White trash," I repeated in as calm a voice as my anger allowed. "Who called you that?"

"I'm the daughter of a junkie and a gambling addict. I am white trash. I'm not this." She gestured at her reflection.

"Nobody will ever call you white trash again, you hear? And if they do, you will tell me and I will rip their throats out. How about that?"

She tilted her head, again trying to read me ... to understand. "You can't change my past. You can't change who I am."

"No," I said with a shrug, my finger trailing down her throat. She wasn't breathing, and I, too, held my breath at the feel of her soft skin. "But you can. I can only force people to treat you as you want to be treated."

She tore her gaze away from mine and took a step back. I dropped my hand then went back out and selected another dress. She took it without a word and slipped back into the dressing room.

I sank down onto one of the armchairs that was way too soft. Leona looked fucking good in every dress she tried on. Nobody would take her for white trash dressed like that. Nobody should take her for white trash dressed in her fucking secondhand clothes either. "Buy them all," I told her, but she shook her head firmly.

"One," she said, raising a single finger. "I'll get one because I promised you, but no more." She lifted her chin and straightened her spine. Stubborn and brave, despite what she knew of me.

"Then take that one." I pointed at the dark green dress that she'd put on first.

"Isn't it too revealing?" she whispered.

"You have the body for it."

A pleased blush spread across her freckled cheeks, but she still hesitated. "I don't want people to get the wrong impression."

I tilted my head. "What kind of impression?"

She looked away, fumbling with the fabric of the dress. When the saleswoman was out of sight, she said quietly, "That I'm selling more than drinks. Cheryl mentioned that a few customers pay her to do *other things*."

I rose from the armchair and moved closer. She peered up at me. "Nobody will try anything, Leona. They know you are off limits."

Her brows drew together. "Why?"

"Take the dress," I ordered.

She stiffened her spine again. Stubborn. I softened my next words. "You promised."

She nodded slowly. "Okay."

I turned to the saleswoman, who was hovering outside the changing rooms. "She's going to put it on right away. We still need shoes."

She hurried off and came back with matching flats in dark green leather. I'd hoped for stilettos but doubted Leona could walk in them anyway. I nodded my approval, and she handed them to Leona. Her eyes met mine, filled with question, before she disappeared behind the curtain once more.

Leona came back out of the changing room, dressed in her new dress and shoes, looking fucking amazing. I let my eyes wander over her slender shoulders, her narrow waist, and lean legs. The dress ended a couple of inches above her knees and dipped low on her back, revealing inch by inch of immaculate skin.

She carried her old clothes. I wanted to tell her to throw them away, but I had a feeling she didn't have any clothes to spare. Instead, I went over to the cashier and paid for the dress and shoes.

Leona's eyes grew wide when she saw the sum.

"I can't believe how much you paid! I could have bought ten dresses at Walmart for that much money," she whispered as I led her out of the shop.

I pressed my palm against the naked skin between her shoulder blades, relishing in her small shiver and the way goose bumps rose on her skin. The familiar blush spread over her cheeks. Before I opened the door, I leaned down to her, my lips brushing her ear. "It's worth every penny, trust me."

She released a small, shaky breath and quickly got into my Mercedes, as if she needed to put some space between us. There was no way I'd let her get away from me.

CHAPTER 8

LEONA

I smoothed my fingers down the soft material of the dress. It was made from silk and cotton, something I'd never worn before. It felt almost too good for me. I never could have afforded this kind of dress, nor would I have ever paid that much money for a piece of clothing. And the shoes. I didn't know leather this soft existed. For Fabiano, it was nothing.

"Thank you," I said eventually. We'd been driving in silence for a while. The surroundings that flew past us were becoming shabbier. It wouldn't be long before we arrived at Roger's Arena.

Fabiano nodded his head as he drove. I wished I knew what was going on in there, why he was really doing this. My eyes lingered on his strong jaw, the dark blond stubble, the way his mouth was set in a determined line. He always seemed in control. Even during his fight, he never gave up control. He had dominated his opponent with little effort. Was there a time when he ever lost it?

As I watched him drive, I got my first good look at the tattoo on the inside of his right forearm. It was a long knife with an eye on the top of the blade, near the hilt, with words written in intricate letters. It looked like Italian and was too small for me to read.

Fabiano pulled into the parking lot of Roger's Arena and turned off the engine. He purposely held out his forearm so I could take a closer look. Had I been staring that openly?

"What does it say?" I touched my fingertip to his skin, tracing every single letter and marveling at how soft his skin felt. He was all hard lines and muscle, power and danger, but his skin betrayed that when I touched him, he was only human.

"Temere me, perché sono l'occhio e la spada," Fabiano said in flawless Italian, from what I could tell. He caressed the words with his tongue, almost as if he was their lover. A shiver raced down my back. I couldn't help but wonder how it would feel if he whispered words of passion into my ear in that same voice. "What…" I cleared my throat, hoping he couldn't tell how his closeness and voice affected me "…what does it mean?"

"Fear me cause I'm the eye and the blade."

A lover's voice delivering such harsh words. "Do all mobsters have this tattoo?" I asked.

He smirked. "Made men or Camorrista, as we like to call ourselves, but yes, members of the Camorra all have the same tattoo. It's a way to recognize each other."

"The eye and the blade," I repeated. "What does it mean? What do you have to do to bear that tattoo?"

He leaned over and for a moment, I was sure he would kiss me—and worse that I would have let him. Instead, he ran a finger down the length of my arm, a dark look in his eyes. "That's something you don't want to know," he murmured.

I nodded. With him being so close, it was hard to concentrate. I needed to get out of this car.

"Go out with me."

"I have to work," came my dumb reply.

He smiled a knowing smile. "Not every day. When's your next day off?"

I hadn't talked to Roger about that, and with the way my financial situation was, I couldn't afford to take a day off.

"It doesn't matter. Let's say Wednesday."

That was only two days away. I didn't come to Vegas for a date. I swore to myself that I'd keep my head down and stay out of trouble. Going on a date with a member of the mob wasn't exactly doing that.

"I can't. I ..." I couldn't come up with an excuse, and Fabiano's eyes spoke a clear meaning. Any answer other than yes was unacceptable.

"I don't know if I can get that day off."

"You will."

Did the bar belong to the Camorra? Or was Roger too scared to refuse Fabiano's request?

All my life people had trampled over me. Nothing had ever come easy. I'd had to fight for everything I had, and suddenly here was Fabiano, who got what he wanted and could handle things for me with a few simple words. It shouldn't have felt good, but I'd always been on my own. My mother hadn't been in any state to take care of me, and my father was hundreds of miles away and just as incapable. Now there was someone taking care of me, and I liked it, liked handing over some of the burden of always having to fend for myself, having to make every decision. I liked it too much.

Men like Fabiano were used to controlling others. If I let him, he'd take total control of my life, *of me*: body and soul. I needed to be careful.

I tore my gaze away from his face. A trickle of sweat trailed down my back. The air was too stuffy in his car. I got out, glad for more space between me and Fabiano.

He followed me, of course. *More like prowled after me.*

"Are you coming in for a drink?" I asked, torn between wanting him to and wanting him to leave.

"Not today, but I'll have a quick talk with Roger about Wednesday."

His hand touched my back as he led me inside. The heat of his palm on my skin was way more distracting than it should have been.

The moment we entered the bar, Cheryl's angry eyes zoomed in on me, then on Fabiano, before she whirled around and headed through the door behind the bar. Most of the tables were still empty. The first fight hadn't begun yet, but a look at the clock revealed I was almost one hour late. Guilt overcame me. I hated disappointing people who relied on me. Roger was certainly furious.

His reddened face as he stalked into the bar confirmed my worry. He stopped in his tracks when he saw me standing beside Fabiano.

Fabiona stroked my skin lightly with his thumb. I had to resist leaning into his touch. Instead, I gave him a quick smile then rushed off toward the bar. Roger didn't spare me a glance, but I could tell that he was seething. I watched as Roger walked toward Fabiano and listened to him, eventually nodding, but he didn't look happy about it.

Cheryl slid up to my side. "New dress?" she asked suggestively.

I flushed, though I had nothing to be embarrassed about. I removed a few of the empty bottles lined up next to the sink and stashed them in the crates below the bar.

"Chick, I know you're new here, but don't think he's buying you stuff because he feels sorry for you. That man isn't capable of feeling sorry."

Annoyance rushed through me. She pretended like she knew all about him. How could she say that he had no feelings? Just because he didn't show them didn't mean he didn't have them.

"Cheryl, I know what I'm doing. There's nothing to worry about, trust me."

She pointed at my bruised wrist. "That's only the beginning."

"He didn't do that." Cheryl rolled her eyes. Men sitting at a table had tried to catch our attention, so I went over to them. This conversation with Cheryl was leading nowhere.

Fabiano came over to me. The men at the table fell silent as he stopped beside me. He touched my naked back again, and I saw the look he gave the other men. Was he being possessive? He leaned down. "Wednesday, I'll pick you up at six on your street." He straightened and stalked off, leaving me with the searing imprint of his touch on my back.

"So, two lagers and three pale ales?" I repeated their order.

They nodded but didn't say another word.

When I returned home that night, the apartment was dark and quiet. The door to Dad's bedroom was ajar. He wasn't there. I really hoped he wasn't gambling again.

I slipped out of the dress and carefully laid it on one of the moving boxes. Tomorrow I'd wash it so I could wear it again for my date with Fabiano on Wednesday. My stomach tightened with nerves and excitement. When I finally lay down and closed my eyes, I could feel his hand on my back again and smell his musky scent. My hand found its way between my legs, remembering the way he looked half-naked, the lithe way he'd moved during his fight, the strength he oozed so easily. I'd never felt so drawn to someone before. I moved my fingers at a quick pace, imagining it was Fabiano.

After I finished, I felt even more nervous about our date. I never had trouble refusing guys; none were ever remotely interesting enough for me to risk my reputation. But refusing Fabiano ... that would prove to be more difficult.

FABIANO

Remo was lounging on the sofa, watching the latest race on his enormous TV. The races were getting more and more popular by the day. If we could operate the races in all of the states and Canada, we'd be swimming in money. With the Outfit and the Famiglia in the U.S. and the fucking Corsican Union in Canada in our way, that wasn't going to happen any time soon. Not to mention the Bratva and the Cartel. Everyone wanted to have a fat piece of the cake.

"What's going on between you and that new girl at Roger's?" Remo asked, sending my body into high alert.

My face remained blank as I took a sip from my drink then leaned back on the couch.

Remo seemed focused on the race, but that could easily have been a way to make me lower my guard.

"Nothing's going on," I told him offhandedly.

His eyes met mine. "You're buying her things and you're taking her out. That's nothing?"

I let out a dark laugh. "Are you spying on me, Remo? Since when do you care about the girls I'm fucking?"

"I don't. She seems a strange choice. Not your usual style. And I don't need to spy on you. You know how it is."

Oh, I knew. People were always eager to talk shit about me behind my back, hoping they could rat me out to Remo and earn a reward. If they thought he'd be impressed by them acting like a stinking rat, they didn't know shit about him. Remo would remember their names, but definitely not in a way they'd appreciate.

"She's a welcome distraction. The other girls ... they're all the same. They are starting to bore me."

The women laughed because they had to, smiled their fake smiles. They regarded me like an opportunity. And I never cared. They were good for fucking and sucking.

"The thrill of the chase," Remo mused.

I smirked. "Perhaps. Let me have some fun. It won't interfere with my duties."

Remo nodded, but there was a look in his eyes I didn't like. "Have fun." He returned his attention to the bar. "She might be more skilled than she looks. Her mother is a cheap street hooker in Austin."

What the fuck? I tensed. Her mother was a whore? Was he fucking shitting me? That Remo had done a background check on Leona unsettled me even more. It was never a good thing when something caught Remo's attention. I shrugged, trying to appear nonchalant, though I had a feeling Remo had picked up on my shock. He was too damn observant. That was why he was Capo.

"I don't give a fuck who her mother is."

Remo's eyes bored a hole into my fucking skull, never halting his relentless stare. I stood from the sofa. "I'm going to work out for a while."

I needed to blow off some steam before I went to get Leona. I was *on edge*. I'd have to spend the next hour kicking the hell out of a heavy bag if I wanted to keep my cool with her.

LEONA

Dad had avoided me since the incident. I heard him return home early in the morning, bump against walls, and smash his door shut in a drunken stupor. He was still hidden away in his room when I left for work.

On Wednesday I had my day off, and he couldn't avoid me. When he stepped out of his bedroom and shuffled into the kitchen, dressed in only faded gray boxers and a yellowed wife beater, he froze in the doorway after spotting me. He obviously expected me to be at work.

"Did they fire you?" he asked uncertainly. It almost looked like there was guilt on his face. The bruises on my wrist were already faded, so he was probably feeling guilty about the money he had taken from me.

I shook my head as I sipped my coffee. I had hardly eaten anything so far, even though the fridge was stashed with food for once after I'd gone to the grocery store. "No, it's my day off."

"On a day of a big fight?" he asked. "One of the Falcone brothers is in the cage tonight."

Surprise filled me. "I can't work all the time."

Dad sat down across from me. Under his eyes were dark circles, and he looked like he could use a long shower.

I waited for him to ask me for more money. He must have been thinking about it. He stared down at his hands then sighed. "I never wanted this kind of life for you. When you were born, I thought everything would change. I thought I could give you a good life."

"I know," I said simply. Mom and Dad both had wanted to be good parents, and for a while they had tried.

"Are you going to be home tonight?" he asked. "You could watch the cage fight with me. They're showing it on the big screen at a bar around the corner from here."

I wasn't really in the mood to watch another cage fight, but I was touched that he wanted to spend time with me, even if part of me couldn't help but be wary. And I hated it, hated that I had to be cautious when my parents showed any interest in me.

"I'm already going out," I said carefully.

"You are?" Curiosity flashed in his eyes.

I nodded and stood quickly. I placed my cup in the sink, deciding to clean it later when Dad wasn't breathing down my neck. "I should probably start to get ready." It was still two hours until Fabiano would pick me up, but I wanted to avoid a confrontation with my father.

I'd be rattled me even more, and I was already on edge because of my date. It seemed less and less like a good idea, but I couldn't back out now. Perhaps Fabiano would lose interest after tonight. It wasn't like I had anything remotely interesting to say, and I definitely wasn't going to talk about my mother. If he knew about her, he'd look at me in a different way.

I dressed in the dark green dress again. I shouldn't have let Fabiano buy me anything. All my life, I'd had to work hard for what I wanted. Having something gifted to me like that had felt amazing. Now I couldn't help but think of Fabiano's intentions. Nothing in life was for free. That was a lesson I learned early.

I checked my reflection in the mirror. It was finally possible to get a good look, after I'd cleaned the thing and the rest of the apartment yesterday. I was never into heavy makeup, even for the date, so I decided to keep it to a minimum. I didn't want it to look like I was making a huge effort, so I put on some foundation with just a hint of blush and then brushed my eyelashes with mascara. I reached for my only lipstick, a berry tone that complimented my hair color and complexion perfectly. With it almost touching my lips, I paused. What if Fabiano tried to kiss me tonight? Would lipstick get in the way?

I flushed. No kissing. I had no intention of kissing anyone, least of all Fabiano. But a treacherous part of my body tingled with excitement at the idea. Sighing, I lowered the lipstick and tossed it aside.

When six rolled around, I was nearly trembling with nerves. Luckily, Dad had left the apartment ten minutes ago, so I didn't have to worry about a confrontation between Fabiano and him.

I risked a peek out the window when I heard the sound of a car pulling up. Fabiano was already getting out and a lump formed in my throat at the sight of him. He looked marvelous, not like someone who would date white trash like me. I didn't kid myself into thinking I was anything else. A dress and nice shoes wouldn't change that.

Grabbing my backpack, I quickly left the apartment. I didn't want him to glimpse inside and see how little we had. I closed the door. Fabiano was already waiting at the bottom of the stairs, intense blue eyes scanning my body.

I descended the stairs slowly, my hand on the rail like an anchor. He was dressed in a white button down shirt that hugged his muscular form. His sleeves were rolled up again, revealing strong, tanned forearms and the tattoo of the Camorra. He'd left the upper two buttons of his shirt unbuttoned, showing off a hint of his perfect chest. Somehow knowing what was beneath his shirt, how he looked wearing only his fighting gear made this even harder. When I reached the second to last step and was eyelevel with him, a shiver ripped through my body. He looked like he wanted to devour me. I thought of something sophisticated to say, anything that would stop him from giving me that hungry look.

"Hi," was all I got out, and even that one word sounded hushed.

His mouth twitched, and he slid his hand behind my back, his palm finding the same spot of naked skin where it had rested the last time. My body came alive with a tingling, but I didn't let it show. I needed to stay in control of this evening, and most of all myself.

He led me toward his car and then we were off. It was hard not to fidget as we drove in silence. He looked perfectly at ease, as usual, long fingers curled loosely around the wheel. The tiny hairs on his hand glistened and I wondered if he was possibly still wet from a shower? *Don't go there, Leona.*

My nerves grew as the city lights thinned out and we left them behind completely. "Where are we going?"

I tried to mask the apprehension in my voice. The stupid stories I'd read about the mafia came uninvited into my mind, and I envisioned myself being buried under the desert sand. Not that the mafia had any interest in me.

He steered the car up a steep road then stopped it on a plateau. "Here."

I followed his gaze out the windshield and released a surprised breath, leaning forward for a better view. We overlooked Las Vegas from our spot. It was an incredible sight. Against the night sky, the colored flashing lights seemed even brighter. A promise of excitement and money. Despite the miles between the Strip and me, I could almost taste the endless opportunities. I wished that only once in my life I would be offered the same opportunities so many people had.

It seemed like such a romantic location for a first date. I hadn't pegged Fabiano as the romantic type, and perhaps he wasn't. Perhaps he wanted to take me somewhere remote so we could be alone. My heart thumped in my throat at the idea. His warm, musky scent filled the car, and my body reacted to it in a way I'd never experienced. He was watching me intently as I watched the Las Vegas skyline. I wished there was something I could say to break the tension, but my mind drew a blank. He reached up and stroked a finger down my neck, further down along my spine, leaving goose bumps on his way. The sensation tingled all the way down to my toes. I marveled at the gentleness of his touch, still remembering how these same hands had broken his opponent's bones with little effort. I wondered how the same hands would feel on other parts of my body. *Stop it, Leona.* If I started thinking like that, it was only a small leap before I acted upon it.

"Let's get out," he said in a low voice that left my mouth dry and my nerves on edge. When he exited the car and closed the door, my breath whooshed out of me. I tried to steal myself for his closeness, but I knew the moment I got near him again, my body would be a melting pot of conflicting feelings.

CHAPTER 9

FABIANO

The cool night air filled my lungs. I was glad for the reprieve from Leona's tantalizing scent. I wanted to bend her over the hood of my car and bury myself to the hilt inside of her. Fuck, I wanted to do it over and over again. I wasn't sure why these damn freckles and cornflower blue eyes got to me, but they fucking did. She must have seen it in my expression, because I'd never seen her more uneasy in my company than in that car.

I ran a hand through my hair, which was still damp from my earlier shower. I'd pummeled the fucking heavy bag for too long and was almost late for our date. In the last couple of years, I mainly dealt with whores or pole dancers. Their intentions were always clear from the start. They either wanted money, drugs, or a favor. They weren't shy. They wanted something *from me*, so they showed me what they could offer. The sex had been a satisfying joyride, but Leona was different. Her shyness irritated and fascinated me at the same time.

She was a challenge like I'd never had, and my body was eager to conquer it. Too fucking eager.

Leona stepped out of the car, looking almost flustered. She kept her eyes trained on the sight below us as she came around to meet me. Her hands clutched that tacky, old backpack.

"You are obsessed with that thing," I said, feeling the irritating urge to lighten the mood and set her at ease.

She let out a small laugh, her eyes crinkling. "I thought it went well with my shoes." She lifted her foot a couple of inches.

My gaze went to her dark green leather flats then up to the backpack of an unidentifiable color. Perhaps it had been beige a long time ago. She was definitely the first woman that came on a date with me, holding a fucking backpack. I chuckled.

"Remind me next time we go shopping to buy you one of those fancy purses girls go crazy over."

Her eyebrows shot up then knit together. "You can't keep buying things for me."

I swiveled my body around so we were standing even closer, leveling my gaze on her. She didn't back off, but I could see goose bumps form along her slender arms. "Who's going to stop me?"

Remo couldn't care less if I spent my money on women, cars, or property, as long as I didn't start betting or gambling or worse ... neglect my duties.

"I will ...?" It sounded more a question than a statement.

"Are you asking me or telling me?"

Her frown deepened, and she sighed. "I'm no good at playing these power games."

"Who said this is a power game?"

"Isn't it always? With men, it's always about exerting dominance. And you ...'"

She shook her head.

"And I …?"

"Everything you do is a sign of dominance. When I saw you in the fighting cage that was perhaps the most relaxed I've ever seen you act. Outside of it you act like a hunter, always looking for someone who might dare to challenge your status."

I smiled. She seemed to think she knew me. I got that she'd seen a lot in her life, but the world I grew up in was a very different kind of shark tank. "In our world, you are either hunter or prey, Leona. I know what I am. What are *you*?"

Pressing my palms against her bare shoulders, I started to slide them lower, watching her reaction. She shivered but didn't push me away, though I could tell that she was thinking about it.

"Prey," she admitted reluctantly. "I will always be." She gazed past me, toward Las Vegas, looking lost and resigned.

My hands stilled on her back. This unguarded admission did something strange to me. It unleashed a protective, fierce side I hadn't experienced toward a woman since I'd been a scrawny kid and tried to defend my sisters. The soft breeze tugged at her brown curls as she lost herself in the sight of the city.

I bent down and kissed her ear. She released a shuddering breath. "Perhaps you need a protector so you stop being easy prey."

"Am I easy prey?" she asked quietly.

I didn't bother replying. We both knew how it was. And in a city like this, a city ruled by us, a girl like her was lost. "Do you want a protector?"

She closed her eyes as I kissed the skin below her ear. For once it was hard to read her. "And you think you can be my protector?"

I could protect her against almost any threat. Not against the Camorra. And not against myself. But that wasn't something I wanted to consider. "You saw me fight. Do you doubt it?"

She opened her eyes and tilted her head up toward me, blue eyes soft and probing. "No," she said. "But I think you and your way of life are threats too."

I didn't deny it.

"Why do you even want to protect me?"

To be honest, I didn't know. Perhaps Aria had somehow managed to get through to me. It made me fucking furious to think about it. That fucking bracelet. I shouldn't have accepted it.

"There's nothing I could give you in return." Her expression became more determined. "I don't have any money to spare, but I don't think you'd want it. You certainly don't need it. If there's something else you want, I'm not that kind of girl."

Not that kind of girl. Remo's words about her mother flashed through my mind. Was this an act after all?

There was an easy way to find out, of course. I gripped her hips. Her lips parted in surprise, but I didn't give her the chance to voice her protest.

I kissed her and after a moment of hesitation she kissed me back.

I could tell she didn't have much experience kissing. Fuck. That knowledge was the last straw. I had to have her. Every little inch of her. Every goose bump. Every freckle. Every fucking shy smile. All for myself.

And I had to protect her from all the wolves she believed were sheep. My fingers tangled in her curls, angling her head to the side to give me better access to that sweet mouth of hers.

I slid my hands from her waist to her bare back again then lower. Her hands came up against my chest. I savored the taste of her for a few seconds more before I allowed her to push me away.

Her dark lashes fluttered as her eyes found mine. In the dim light, I couldn't see if her cheeks were as flushed as I expected them to be. I brought my hand up and brushed my knuckles along her high cheekbones. Her skin was practically burning up with embarrassment and want. My cock twitched in my pants.

She tore herself away from me, walked to the edge of the hill we were on, and looked out toward the bright city lights.

I let my eyes take in her silhouette for a couple of moments, allowing her to gather herself before I approached. I came to a stop right behind her. She didn't acknowledge my presence, except for the slight tensing of her shoulders. Her sweet, flowery perfume drifted into my nose. I traced the line of her spine with my knuckles, needing to feel her silky skin.

LEONA

That touch ignited desires I'd suppressed for a long time. Fabiano always touched me in a way that never gave me any real relief. Did he know the effect he had on me?

"Why did you bring me here?" I asked.

"Because I thought you'd appreciate the sight. You haven't been in Las Vegas for very long."

"Wouldn't the Strip be a better place to show someone the city?"

Fabiano stepped up to my side, and I was glad to be able to see him again. Having him so close behind me, his fingers running down my spine, was too distracting.

He pushed his hands into the pockets of his slacks, his blue eyes scanning over the city below us. And for the first time I caught the briefest glimpse behind his mask. This was a place he came often. I could tell. This city, it was important to him. It was his home.

I'd never had a place to call home. How would it be to look at something or someone and feel at home?

"There are too many people around who don't get the city. Up here, I have the city to myself."

"So you don't like to share?" I said teasingly.

He turned his gaze to me. "Never. Not even my city."

I shivered. Nodding, I quickly looked back to the skyline. "Were you born here?"

I wasn't very perceptive but the stiffening of his shoulders told me he didn't like where our conversation was heading.

"No. Not in the sense that you mean," he said quietly. "But I was reborn here."

I searched his face, but he wasn't giving anything away. It was all hard lines as the silence stretched between us.

"I thought this could be a new start for me as well," I said eventually.

"Why would you need a new start?"

"All my life I've been judged by the actions of my mother. I want to be judged for my own doing."

"Being in the shadow of your family isn't easy," he said, meeting my gaze. Another small crack in his mask. "But being judged for your own wrongdoings can be hard as well."

"Do you think I've done too many wrong things?"

He smirked. "You are here with me. I'd say you have a strong penchant for doing wrong things."

I feared he was right. "Because you're in the mafia."

"Because I am part of the *Camorra*." I loved the way he rolled the r's when he said the word. I could almost feel the vibrations all the way in the pit of my stomach. I wondered why he insisted there was a difference between the Camorra and the mafia.

"Because I am their *Enforcer*."

"Enforcer," I said, furrowing my brows. I'd never heard that term before. "So you're enforcing their laws like some kind of mob police."

He chuckled. "Something like that," he said darkly. My gut tightened at the dark undercurrent in his voice.

I waited for him to elaborate, but he seemed content to leave me guessing, so I decided to ask Cheryl about it later. If I had a cell phone, or if my Dad had a working computer, I would have Googled the term. As it was, I needed to rely on old-fashioned channels to get information. Fabiano was obviously unwilling to reveal any more about what his mafia title entailed.

"I thought you'd be eager to see tonight's fight. I hear it's a big one."

Fabiano shrugged. "It is, but I have watched thousands of fights in my life and have fought hundreds. I don't care if I miss one." His eyes settled on me. "And I wanted you for myself."

Was he embarrassed of being seen with me? The poor little waitress and the big deal mobster.

I rubbed my arms, the night's cold air catching up with me. Fabiano pressed up behind me and began stroking my arms through the thin fabric of my dress. Always close, always touching. His spicy aftershave engulfed me like his arms did.

"What do you want from me?" I whispered.

"Everything."

Everything.

That word still made my breathing hitch as I lay awake later that night after our date. There was no way I could fall asleep.

I don't like to share.

Everything.

I was attracted to Fabiano and was curious, but curiosity killed the cat. I feared that being close to Fabiano would put an end to all the plans I'd so carefully made for my future, but I wanted to see him again. I wanted to kiss him again. I knew it wasn't a good idea, and I wasn't sure what to do.

Just let it happen.

Being with him made me feel good. Very few things in my life did. Why not allow myself this small sin? Because that's what he was ... sin.

The next day I made sure to be at work early so I would have time for a conversation with Cheryl. That other waitress, who I still didn't know how old she was, was there as well. Her name was Mel. I had to wait until she was finally out of earshot, off cleaning the changing rooms, before I could confront Cheryl. A few of our regular customers were already sitting at their favorite table, but they could wait a couple of minutes. The bar wasn't even officially open yet. It wasn't like they came here for the extraordinary service.

"You had the evening off," was the first thing out of Cheryl's mouth when Mel had disappeared through the back door. "On the night of a big fight."

"I had a date with Fabiano."

She shook her head, her mouth puckering. "God, chick, don't you know what's good for you?"

"What's an Enforcer?"

She sighed, nodding toward the table with the early customers. "See Eddie over there?"

I nodded.

"His arm is in a cast because of your Fabiano. First warning as they call it."

My eyes grew wide. Fabiano beat people up? "First warning," I said carefully. "What's the second and third warning?"

She smiled sympathetically. "That depends how much money you owe and what kind of mood Falcone and Fabiano are in. Smashed knee cap? Cut off finger? Having the living daylights beaten out of you?" She paused for effect, gauging my reaction. "Third warning will make you wish for death."

"And if people still don't pay?" What if people weren't ever able to pay? It could happen. I lost count of the number of times my mother had been broke. A beating wouldn't have changed that. And even if she came into money, she would probably have used it for meth.

Cheryl ran a finger over her throat.

I looked down at my hands clutching the bar counter. It would have been a lie if I'd said I couldn't imagine Fabiano capable of something like that. I'd seen him fight, had seen the darkness in his eyes.

"Now you're having second thoughts," she said. "Maybe you'll get lucky and he'll lose interest in you soon. It's not like these men would ever consider having a serious relationship with someone like us."

I stiffened. "What do you mean?"

"They are Italian mobsters. They like to play with normal women, but they'll marry Italian virgins from noble upbringing. It's always been like that. I don't think a new Capo will change that."

"This is the twenty-first century, and we're not in Italy."

"Might as well be because their traditions and rules are from there."

Everything.

In my silly mind I'd construed the word to mean body and mind, but now I wondered if Fabiano was on the lookout for a few nights of fun before he moved on to the next woman. This was all too much baggage for me to handle: Fabiano being an Enforcer and the mafia with their old-fashioned rules. My life had always been a mess—and was still messed up enough without him adding any fuel to the fire. Even if my body ached for his touch, and even if some stupid part of me wanted to get to know him—the real him—I had to stay away from him. Maybe I was a fixer, but I had to fix my own life before I could consider fixing someone else.

Business was slow that evening. Most customers had lost considerable amounts of money the night before, during the big fight, and stayed away from the bar. I wouldn't have minded a busy day; it would have distracted me from my wandering thoughts. When I walked past a table occupied with two older men, who'd been drinking the same beer for almost one hour, I overheard a snippet of their conversation that caught my attention.

"Killed him. Just like that. Twisted his head, broke his neck. But the old guy knew what was coming. Shouldn't have tried to run away without paying his debt. Falcone don't like that. I always pay. Even if it means no food for days. Better hungry than dead."

"You got it," rasped the other man, who then fell into a coughing fit. I busied myself wiping the table next to them, hoping to find out who had broken someone's neck. The mere idea sent a shiver down my back. Sadly, the men seemed to have caught on to my presence and switched their conversation to the upcoming fights. Had Fabiano been the one to kill a man?

When I left the bar at quarter after two that night, Fabiano's car was parked in front of the entrance.

I froze mid-step, half hoping it was a coincidence. He shoved open the passenger door. "Get in. Can't let you walk on your own at night."

One look at his handsome face, I wasn't sure I could end things between us. I wasn't even sure I wanted to anymore. People had seldom kept their promises to me. I learned to expect disappointment, but here he was, keeping his promise to protect me. For the first time in my life, there was someone who could protect me. My mother had never been capable of protecting me from her mood swings or the beatings of her disgusting boyfriends. And she certainly could not protect me from the insults other kids hurled at me.

Fabiano was dangerous. He wasn't someone to be close to, but having someone in my life that could keep me safe was too enticing.

FABIANO

I caught her hesitation when she'd spotted me. Like a mouse in front of the trap, torn between tasting the cheese and running off.

"What are you doing here?" she asked, arms wrapped around her old backpack, like she needed another barrier between us.

"I told you I would protect you, and that's what I'm doing. I don't want you to walk around alone at night."

She stared out of the passenger window, hiding her face in the shadows. My grip on the steering wheel tightened. "You can't drive me home every night. I'm sure you've got *work* to do."

Her lips pinched together and her fingers dug into her backpack. What had she heard? There were always rumors about me. The worst were usually true.

"Don't worry. I can make time for important things."

The Camorra was important. Remo and his brothers were important. She wasn't supposed to be.

She turned, brows furrowing. "Important? Am I?"

She wasn't. She was … I wasn't sure what she was to me. I kept thinking about her when she wasn't around. About those damn freckles and her shy smiles. About how she was alone, had been alone even when she'd still lived with her mother. I knew how it was to be alone while living in a house with other people. My father. His second wife. The maids.

I ignored her question. "If I'm not in the parking lot after work, then wait in the bar for me until I pick you up."

"I'm not in kindergarten. I don't need someone to pick me up. Not even you, Fabiano. There's no reason for you to do this. I can protect myself."

I pulled up to her street.

Once I'd shut off the engine, I turned to face her. "How?"

"I just can," she said defensively.

I nodded toward her backpack. "With what's in there."

"How do you ..." Her eyes widened a fraction before she caught herself. "It's my problem, isn't it?"

"It was before. Now it is mine. I don't like the idea of someone getting their filthy hands on you."

She shook her head. "We're not together, are we? I can't see how it's your business."

I leaned over but she backed up against the passenger door. So that's how it was going to be? "The kiss we shared means it is my business."

"We won't kiss again," she said firmly, determined.

I smirked. "We'll see." I knew she was attracted to me. I'd sensed how strongly the kiss had affected her, how her eyes had dilated with lust. Perhaps her mind was telling her to stay away, but her body wanted to get much closer, and I would make her give in to that desire. Even now, as I leaned close to her, I could see the conflict in her body language, the way her eyes darted to my lips and her fingers clutched her backpack at the same time.

"You can't force me," she said then bit her lip, reconsidering.

"I could," I said with a shrug, leaning back in my seat to give her space. "But I won't." There was no fun in using my power to get what I wanted. Not with Leona. I wanted to conquer her. I wanted many things.

She gripped the door handle, but I put a hand down on her knee. She shivered under my touch but didn't pull away. Her skin was warm and soft, and I had to suppress the urge to trail my hand up under her skirt and between her legs. "What do you have to defend yourself?"

She hesitated.

"Believe me, Leona, it doesn't matter if it's a knife, gun, or Taser. Against me, it won't do any good."

"A butterfly knife."

I'd have guessed Taser. Women usually preferred them or pepper spray because it was less personal than having to ram a blade into someone's flesh. "Have you ever used it?"

"You mean on someone?"

"Of course. I don't care if you can make a sandwich with it."

Anger flared in her blue eyes, and I had to admit I enjoyed seeing that kind of fire in them, especially when she'd seemed so docile and sweet the first time I talked to her. It was promise she was more fun in other areas too.

"*Of course not.* Unlike you and your mob friends, I don't enjoy killing people."

Friends? The mob wasn't about friendship. It was about dedication and loyalty. It was about honor and commitment. I didn't have friends. Remo and his brothers were the closest thing to friends I had, but what connected us was stronger. They were family. My chosen family. I didn't bother explaining all this to Leona. She wouldn't have understood. For an outsider, this world wasn't easy to understand.

"You don't have to enjoy killing to be good at it. But I doubt that you'll ever get the chance to kill someone. You'd be disarmed in no time and probably get a taste of your own blade. You have to learn how to handle a knife, how to hold it and where to aim."

"You didn't deny it," she whispered.

"Deny what?"

"That you've killed people ... that you enjoyed it."

I didn't tell her that with some people there had been quite a bit of joy ending their fucking lives. And I knew that killing my father one day would outshine every other kill so far. Leona looked honestly puzzled by my reaction. Had she still not grasped the concept of being a made man?

Instead of replying, I tapped the tattoo on my forearm.

She reached out, fingertips gracing the black lines of ink. Her touch was always so careful. I had never been touched like that by a woman. They usually raked their fake fingernails over my back, clutching and stroking. Nothing careful about these encounters. I enjoyed it, but this … Fuck, this I enjoyed more.

"Could you get it removed? Could you stop being what you are?"

I didn't know any other life. The few days when I hadn't been part of the Outfit and not yet part of the Camorra, before I'd found Remo or rather before he'd found me, I had been like driftwood caught up in the tide, no destination to my journey. Days that had felt like eternity. I'd been adrift. "I could. But I won't." Remo, of course, wouldn't allow me to quit. This wasn't a fucking job where you could give two-weeks' notice. This was for life. "You said it … it's who I am."

She nodded. Perhaps it had finally sunk in.

"I will teach you how to use that knife and how to defend yourself."

She looked tired, which was probably why she didn't try to argue even if I could tell that she wanted to. She opened the door and got out but turned to me. "Sleep tight, Fabiano … if your conscience lets you." She closed the door and headed toward the apartment building.

When I'd started my induction process in the Outfit, I felt guilt over what I'd seen others doing. And even later, when I first started to fight at Remo's side, I felt bad for some of the things I'd done. But now …? Not anymore. After being an Enforcer for years, I didn't feel anything anymore. No regret or guilt. People knew what they were getting into when they owed us money. No one got into this without a fault of their own. And most of these guys would sell their own mother if it meant money to gamble or bet or buy shit.

I'd never had to kill an innocent person. There were no innocents that frequented our bars and casinos. They were lost souls. Stupid fuckers who lost their family's home because they spent their nights gambling.

Leona was innocent. Despair had driven her to work at Roger's bar. I hoped she'd never get caught in the crossfire. I didn't like the idea of having to hurt her.

CHAPTER 10

LEONA

There had been many sleepless nights because of the noise coming from my mother's room. Either because she was at it with a john or because she was having a drug-induced fit. Now it was the noise in my head that kept me awake.

Fabiano's blue eyes flashed before me. Cold and calculating. Attentive and alert. Seldom anything else, except for when we'd kissed. There had been a warmer emotion in them. Perhaps only desire or lust, but I wanted to think it could have been something else as well.

I pressed my palms against my face. *Stop it.*

I needed to stop imagining there was something in him. I needed to stop wanting his touch when the same hands did horrible things to others. Things I couldn't even imagine. Things I didn't even want to know.

There was a sick fascination I couldn't deny nor suppress. The mafia had always been something mysterious. I just thought it only existed in the movies. But this was real life, not a Hollywood movie with a happy ending. In real life, mobsters weren't misunderstood antiheroes. They were the bad guys, the ones you didn't want to encounter.

Bad. It was such a difficult term to quantify. What was bad? I was trying to sugarcoat this whole situation, something I had a lot of practice doing. I twisted and turned then eventually sat up on my mattress and reached for my backpack in the dark.

I shoved my hand in the bag and found my knife. I yanked it out then pressed the button that made the blade shoot out with a soft click. The steel of the blade gleamed in the dim moonlight streaming in through the dust-covered windows. I'd never used it, not really. I pointed it at someone once, the same guy I'd stolen it from. He was one of my mother's johns, the worse kind. The kind that liked to beat and insult women like my mother. The kind that enjoyed making them feel even more like crap than they already did. The kind that liked to haggle over the price after the deed was done and often refused to pay. If my mother hadn't been desperate, she probably wouldn't have done him more than once, not after he barely paid her for sucking his disgusting dick and doing other disgusting things.

I was locked in my room when I heard them argue. Despite my mother's warnings to keep my room locked at all times when she had clients, the fight drew me out.

His trousers were on the couch, so I decided to check them for money. Instead, I found the knife. I hid it behind my back when he and my mother stormed out of her bedroom. Mom had been half naked, and he was wearing only his socks and underpants.

"You're not worth thirty bucks."

"You asshole, I let you come in my mouth without a condom."

"As if your dirty mouth is worth anything."

He stopped when he spotted me. A sick grin curled his lips. "For her ... I'd pay thirty."

I was only fifteen.

He took a step in my direction. My mother's gaze had darted from me to him. Her eyes had been hazy and unfocused. She needed a fix.

I jerked the knife forward and released the blade.

"That little shit stole my knife," he snarled.

"Don't move ... or I'll stab you."

I'd wanted to, and I probably would have without remorse, if my mother hadn't started pummeling him with her fists, shrieking. "Get out! Get out, you sick fuck! Get away from us!"

He'd left without his pants, muttering curses and leaving us with sixty bucks and a knife.

I moved the knife from side to side, considering it in the moonlight. I knew I was capable of using it if need be. I wasn't as innocent as Fabiano perhaps thought I was. I knew there were people out there who deserved to die. I slid the blade back in place then shoved it under my pillow. Fabiano called to a side of me I didn't like, a side that survived under the harsh years of growing up with a whore for a mother and a gambling, addict father. Maybe that was why Fabiano's closeness scared me.

I worried he'd bring out my dark parts. I was my parents' daughter, after all, and they both were not good people. I went out of my way to be nice and not to suspect the worst in people. Over the years, I learned to smile ... even when it was hard.

I wasn't sure where this thing between Fabiano and me was going, but fighting it cost too much energy and head space, both of which I needed if I wanted to build a new life. If I kept my focus on working and finding a new job, I'd be leaving Vegas in a couple of months, and then Fabiano would be a thing of the past.

The banging on my door startled me. I looked around with bleary eyes. The sun was low in the sky. As the door swung open, Dad stumbled into my room.

I sat up sleepily. "What's wrong? What time is it?"

"You need to give me some money. I know you must have gotten paid for working this week."

I had gotten money, but apart from getting us food, I set the rest aside to finally buy another less expensive dress. I rubbed my eyes, trying to get rid of the brain fog. "I thought you were working too."

He didn't say anything for a while. "They fired me."

"Before I came here?"

He sighed then nodded. So he'd lied to me. "Leona, I really need that money."

"Who is it you owe money to? The Camorra?"

"It doesn't matter."

"It does. I could talk to Fabiano—"

"Are you stupid? Just because he's fucking you doesn't mean he's going to listen to anything you say."

I screwed my lips shut, suddenly wide awake. Had he really said that?

"Don't give me that look. People are talking. You've been seen riding around in his car. They call you his whore."

My stomach tightened at the insult. I fought so hard so that label would never be put on me, and now, far away from my mother in Las Vegas, people actually called me whore.

"That's none of your business," I gritted out, anger filling my veins. I didn't want to lash out at him, even if he deserved it for lying to me constantly. "I don't have money for you."

"I let you live here and this is what I get for it?"

He was drunk. It became more and more obvious. "I pay for our food. I clean the apartment, and you already took money from me."

Even though he'd hurt me with his insults, I still felt guilty for refusing him.

Without a word, he barged in and grabbed my backpack. He rifled through it, but I'd learned from last time. He made me jump when he grabbed my wrist, dragging me to my feet. "Tell me where it is."

I smelled tequila on his breath. It had always been his favorite and my mother's.

His grip was even harder than last time. Tears burned in my eyes as I ground out, "Let me go. You're hurting me."

"Tell. Me. Where. It. Is." He shook me with every word he said.

Fury, hot and blinding, burned through me. "That's why mom left you. Because you always lost it and beat her. You haven't changed a bit. You disgust me."

He shoved me away, and I fell back on the mattress. He whirled around to leave the room, and I heard another male voice. I stiffened as steps came closer. I quickly got to my feet and pulled my jeans short over my panties.

Dad came back in, saying, "She's nice to look at. Have a go at her. That should pay my debt."

I sucked in a breath. Addiction turned even the kindest people into ruthless criminals, and my father wasn't even all that kind. Still, I never thought he'd do something like this to me. I'd always suspected he was the reason why my mother had sold her body in the first place.

Dad pointed in my direction. A man with dark hair with gray streaks came into my room. He seemed distantly familiar. One glance at his forearm showed me that he was part of the Camorra. My chest constricted with terror. I squared my shoulders, my eyes darting to my backpack that was on the ground between them and me. I wished Fabiano was here and that realization scared me shitless.

The dark eyes of the man scanned my face. Then he shook his head. "No can do, Greg. She belongs to Scuderi."

What? I stopped myself from contradicting him. If being Fabiano's meant I was safe from my father selling me off like cattle, then I was gladly his ... for the time being.

Dad sputtered and opened his mouth to argue, but the mobster turned on him and smashed his fist into Dad's face. Blood shot out of his nose, and he dropped to his knees. "Soto," Dad gasped.

Soto hit him again and again. I jumped over the mattress and grabbed the man's arm, trying to pull him off my father. Maybe Dad deserved it, but I couldn't bear seeing it. I couldn't stand back and watch him be beaten to death.

Soto pushed me aside, so I stumbled backwards and landed with my butt on the mattress. He finally let up. "Two hours," he told Dad. "Then I'll be back."

"No wait," I called when he was halfway out the door. Dad sat with his head between his knees, blood dripping onto the floor from his nose and lip. I went over to the moving boxes stacked up against the wall and reached behind the one on the ground, pulling out all my money. Two hundred dollars. I handed it to Soto. He counted the money without a word. He gave a nod and just disappeared.

"How much did you owe him?" I asked.

"150," Dad rasped.

"But he took two hundred."

"That's for his trouble of paying me a visit," Dad said bitterly. He pushed himself to his feet, one bloody palm against the wall. "If you'd given me the money right away, this wouldn't have happened. It's your fault."

He stumbled out of my room, leaving only the bloody imprint of his palm on the gray wall. I sank down on the mattress, completely drained—of my money and fight.

FABIANO

I kicked the heavy bag once again. I really needed another fight soon.

Soto strode through the training hall toward me. His expression was a bit too triumphant for my taste. That was never a good thing with the idiot. "Hall offered me his daughter as a way to pay off his debt," Soto said, stopping beside me.

"Hall?" I asked. The name was ringing a bell somewhere. He wasn't someone who owed us big money or else I'd have to take care of him. Not important.

"Leona Hall."

He didn't get the chance to say another word. I thrust him against the wall and dug my elbow into his throat. His head was turning red, then purple, before I let up slightly. "If you touched as much as a hair on her body, I'll rip you to shreds."

He coughed, glaring daggers at me. "What the fuck? I didn't do anything."

Remo strode in, glancing between me and Soto, still pressed up against the wall. I released Soto and took a step back. He rubbed his throat. "Next time I won't tell you shit about that girl of yours." He reached into his pocket and tossed a heap of bills to the ground. "There. That's what she gave me." With a nod toward Remo, he staggered off.

Remo perched on the edge of the boxing ring, elbows on his thighs, dark eyes watchful. "What was that about?"

"Nothing important."

Remo tilted his head to the side, studying me. I hated when he did that. "I don't suppose it had something to do with *that girl of yours*."

How long had he been listening to the conversation? Damn it.

"I don't like to share my spoils," I said angrily.

"Who does?" Remo said. "If she's gets your blood pumping like that, perhaps I should have given her a try before I allowed you to claim her for yourself."

131

My blood boiled, but I kept my mask of indifference in place. Remo was baiting me. He would never take a woman from me nor I from him. That would be the ultimate betrayal.

"You missed a spectacular fight. Savio destroyed his opponent."

"Good for him. People will stop thinking you favor him because he's your brother. They'll see he can handle himself."

Remo nodded. "You worked a lot with him."

I was glad he didn't press the matter with Leona.

We kept discussing the upcoming fights as well as Remo's plans for an expansion of the illegal races, but my mind kept returning to what Soto had said. I needed to have a word with Leona's father.

He reminded me of my own bastard of a father, who would have sold me off too if it had meant gaining an advantage. After all, he basically sold off my sisters to their husbands. Long buried anger resurfaced. It caught me off guard.

After I left the abandoned casino, I went to Leona's apartment, but nobody was home. I hadn't ever dealt with her father. After questioning a few of my contacts, I found out where he usually spent his day, losing money and drinking himself into a stupor.

It was one of the smaller and definitely dingier casinos we owned. The navy blue carpet had faded to a worn slate blue in many places, and the cigarette burns and unidentifiable stains just added to the overall filth of the joint. I let my gaze stray through the long room with a low ceiling that was filled with slot machines as well as machines for black jack, poker and roulette. This place wasn't profitable enough to invest in actual roulette or poker tables. The guys frequenting this casino didn't have high standards anyway. Savio's fight, as well as the latest street race, was shown on the television screens in the back. I had to admit that Savio had shaped up nicely. At only sixteen, he had taken out a much older and more experienced opponent. Arrogant as he was, he didn't shy away from hard work.

Dick, the casino manager, rushed toward me the moment he noticed me. I hadn't been here before. This was usually a casino one of the low soldiers handled if there was a problem.

"Mr. Scuderi," he said with a small tilt of his dead. "What can I do for you?"

That name always reminded me of my father. Being compared to him was the last thing I wanted. My mood faltered, but I kept my anger in check. Dick wasn't the target of my anger.

"You can tell me where Greg Hall is," I said.

He didn't ask why, just pointed to the far right.

Leona's father was sitting at a black jack machine. He just forced his daughter to pay his debts and he was already gambling away money he probably borrowed from one of our loan sharks. If I killed him now, I'd be doing Leona a favor, but she probably wouldn't see it that way.

I tilted my head in acknowledgement, leaving him standing there as I made my way toward the despicable coward.

I was still a few steps away when Leona's father spotted me. He dropped the plastic cup holding chips and leaped off the stool, making a beeline for the exit. I gave a sign to the security guard at the door, who body-checked Hall. I wasn't going to run after that fucker. He wasn't even worth that much effort. Hall tried to get back to his feet but the guard shoved him back down and kept him in place until I arrived at their side.

"I'll take it from here," I told him then grabbed Hall by the collar of his shirt and dragged him outside toward the parking lot, around the corner to where the dumpsters were. He was making choked sounds, which I enjoyed very fucking much.

I let go of him and he scrambled back. "I paid!"

"Do you think I'm making my way over to this shithole because of a few fucking hundred dollars?"

That silenced him. His dull blue eyes were nothing like Leona's. That someone like him could have ever fathered someone like her, it didn't seem possible.

"And your debt isn't settled. Soto may have accepted your daughter's money, but I won't. That money, you owe it to me now, and I won't be very patient with you."

"But ..." he sputtered.

"But?" I snarled and punched him hard in the stomach. "And how dare you try to sell off something that's mine?"

Hall's eyes were wide like saucers.

"Your daughter. She belongs to me. So you think you can offer her to other men?"

He shook his head. "It was a misunderstanding. I didn't know she was yours."

My lip curled in disgust at his fucking cowardice. I grabbed him and rolled him over so he was sprawled out on his stomach. Then I lifted his sweaty shirt and pulled my knife from the sheath at my leg. He began fighting against my hold, but I didn't ease up. I dug the tip of the knife into his skin. Blood welled to the surface. A fucking marvelous sight. He screamed like a little girl as I cut a C into his skin. "C stands for coward. Next time I'll finish the word. Got it?"

He nodded weakly against the asphalt, panting.

I pushed to my feet. He peed his fucking pants. Fucking waste of air and space. With one last glance at the pathetic man on the ground, I got into my car. I needed to see Leona.

CHAPTER 11

LEONA

Despite my lack of sleep after my father's rude awakening, I was full of energy all day. My pulse still thumped with anger and disappointment over what had happened. I wasn't sure why it still threw me off balance when one of my parents messed up. They had a habit of doing so … but offering me to his debtor like a whore …? That was low, even for my father. Desperation wasn't an excuse for everything.

"You've been cleaning the same glass for fifteen minutes. I think it's as clean as it's gonna get," Fabiano drawled.

I jumped, my eyes zeroing in on him. He leaned against the bar, elbows propped up on the smooth wood, a piercing look on his face. It was only eight o'clock. I still had almost six hours of work ahead of me. What was he doing here now?

I put the glass aside and Fabiano snatched my forearm to pull me closer.

He scanned the new fingerprint-shaped bruises on my wrist. I had forgotten about them.

His eyes narrowed, his mouth setting in a hard line. He stroked his thumb lightly over the bruise before he let go. "Tomorrow I'll pick you up at home around ten o'clock. I'll teach you how to defend yourself."

It surprised me that he didn't ask who had hurt me. Unless of course he somehow found out what had happened. He confirmed my suspicions when he slid two hundred dollars over to me. I quickly glanced around to make sure no one was watching. I didn't need people to speculate the reason for the money exchange. "Here's your money back."

"My father . . ." I swallowed. "Is he okay?" I couldn't believe I even had to ask. "He's fine."

I nodded and glanced at the money. "But I paid his debt. If you give me the money back, he'll be in trouble."

"That's not your fight, Leona," Fabiano muttered. "Your father will keep losing money, and eventually he'll die because of it. Don't let him drag you down with him. I won't allow it."

I knew he was right. Dad was probably already losing money he didn't have right as we spoke. He couldn't act any other way. He let his addiction rule his life. I doubted he even considered going to rehab. Rehab wouldn't save you if you didn't have the willpower to go through with it.

"Take your money..." Fabiano pushed the notes farther in my direction "...and use it for yourself, for fuck's sake."

I picked up the money and stashed it in my backpack. "Do you want something to drink while you're here?" I grabbed the Johnie Walker Blue Label from the shelf.

"You remember," he said with a smirk.

"Of course," I said simply. I remembered every moment of our encounters.

They were the bright light of my time in Las Vegas so far, as ridiculous as it may sound. I poured him a generous amount. It wasn't as if Roger would care. The Camorra owned everything anyway.

Fabiano took a large gulp then held the glass in my direction. "Want a taste?"

It sounded dirty the way he said it. "No. I don't drink. Ever."

He nodded as if he understood. Then he downed the rest of his scotch and pushed back from the bar. "I still need to do some business. See you in a few hours."

So he really intended to drive me home every night. I watched his broad back as he made his way through the hall, his gait elegant and lithe like that of a predator.

Sometimes I wondered if I was his prey, if this was an amusing chase for him that he'd soon get bored with. I wasn't sure if that was something I should be hoping for.

He didn't try to kiss me again when he drove me home that night and hadn't since our first kiss. Maybe he sensed that I would have pushed him away.

"Tomorrow morning, I'll pick you up. Dress in something you can work out with."

I got out of the car. Fabiano waited until I was inside before he drove off.

The lights were out in the apartment when I entered. I turned one on and was heading to my room when I noticed movement on the couch in the living room. Dad was sitting with his head bowed, moaning. I approached him slowly.

First I noticed the empty beer bottles on the table. If he stopped throwing away money on alcohol, he'd be better off. Then my eyes focused on his naked back and a glaring red mark.

I turned on the lights in the living room. Someone had cut a C into his back. Blood had dried around the wound. It didn't look as if Dad had treated it in any way, except for numbing the pain with alcohol, of course.

Dad didn't acknowledge my presence. He kept his face buried in his palms and let out a low moan.

"Dad?"

He grunted.

"Who did this?" I knew the answer of course.

Dad didn't reply. He was probably too drunk, considering the number of empty bottles that littered the ground. I turned and headed for the bathroom to grab a washcloth. I soaked it with cold water then searched the cabinets for something to put on the wound. Except for expired Tylenol and a few dirty Band-Aids, the shelves were empty.

I returned to the living room and touched Dad's shoulder to alert him of my presence. "I'm going to clean up your wound," I warned him. When he didn't react, I gently pressed the cold washcloth to the cut.

He hissed and lashed out at me. I avoided being hit by his elbow. "Shhh. I'm trying to help you, Dad."

"You've done enough. Leave me alone!"

His bloodshot eyes flashed with anger when he looked up at me.

"You should go to a doctor," I said quietly then put the wet washcloth down on the table in front of him in case he decided to clean his wound on his own.

He returned to his bowed position, ignoring me.

I went to my bedroom and closed the door, bone tired from a long day at work and what I'd seen. Fabiano had cut my father as punishment for what he'd done. I didn't kid myself into thinking that this small wound was the full extent of what Fabiano would do to my father if he messed up again.

I wasn't sure if I could stop Fabiano, and I wasn't sure I had the energy to try. I was sick of solving other people's problems, when I had enough of my own.

I was dressed in my jeans shorts and a loose T-shirt when Fabiano picked me up at ten o'clock.

His eyebrows climbed high along his forehead when he saw my clothes. "That's not what I meant when I told you to wear comfortable clothes."

"I don't own any workout clothes. And to be honest, this is one of three outfits I own in total, including the dress you bought for me," I said snidely.

Fabiano looked at me for a long time before he set the car in motion.

"I saw what you did to my father," I told him.

No sign of guilt on his face. "He got what he deserved. If he wasn't your father, he would have gotten worse."

"This is you being lenient?" I asked incredulously.

"If that's what you want to call it."

It wasn't the first time my father got into trouble like that. When I was around ten and lived with my parents in Dallas, he owed money to some biker group. The guys had almost beaten him and my mother to death over it. It didn't stop my father from borrowing money again.

I leaned back against the seat, my head tilted toward Fabiano. He was steering the car with one hand, the other resting on the center console. I wondered if his cool demeanor reflected his insides. Could he really be that at ease with his life?

My eyes lingered on the dark blond five-o'clock shadow. It was the first time I saw him with anything but a perfectly shaved face, and it made me want to rake my fingers over the short stubble.

Sin. That was what he was.

He glanced at me, his lips curling up, and I tore my gaze away. Playing with fire had never been part of my plan. Then why couldn't I stop thinking about the man beside me?

He pulled up in front of an opulent white concrete building, at least ten stories high with a curved driveway, shielded by a long roof with thousands of light bulbs in multiple colors, most of them broken. An abandoned Casino building, I realized as we stepped through the glass revolving door into the game room. Silence had replaced the sound of the roulette wheels and slot machines. The red and gold chandelier was covered in dust. An air of forlornness lay over the empty poker tables and Champagne bar. Broken Champagne flutes littered the black countertop. This was where we would train?

"Come on," Fabiano said and continued past the deserted cashier booth.

The red and blue carpet was worn out from thousands of feet. I followed him, breathing in the old, musty smell. Fabiano wasn't impressed by our surroundings. He was in his zone. I could already see a change in his demeanor, as if he was eager for the fight. Perhaps the thrill of it was his addiction. Perhaps everyone had an addiction.

We left the first game room and stepped into the next, this one even more splendid than the first. Crystal chandeliers hung from high-arched ceilings above our heads, and the fluffy carpet softened our steps as my eyes took in the black marble columns and gold ornamental wallpaper. Most of the roulette tables had been removed, but a few remained. They were no longer the main attraction.

A fighting cage and a boxing ring dominated the center of the room, their stark brutality a shocking contrast to the luxury from the past. Randomly positioned among the remaining roulette tables were bench presses, punching bags, and other weightlifting equipment. Heavy burgundy drapes covered the shell-shaped windows. The sun shone bright, through the gap between them. Fabiano flipped a switch, and the chandeliers cast us in their splintered golden glow. This wasn't what I'd expected.

"So this is where you come to fight?"

Fabiano smirked. "This is where I come to train and occasionally fight … yes."

"Is it always this empty?"

"Depends. It's mainly for my boss, his brothers, and me. Few other people ever come here."

"And I'm allowed here?" I asked.

He didn't say anything, only led me to a dark mahogany door, then along a hallway with peeling paint and torn carpet, around a corner and through another door. Suddenly, we were in a pool area. This room had been renovated recently. I didn't get the chance to register more than the large swimming pool made from stainless steel and the Jacuzzi sitting on an elevated platform to the right.

"We need to find you some decent training shorts," Fabiano said as he pulled me into the adjoining locker room.

It was functional like the pool area, nothing fancy or splendid.

"Why this place?"

Fabiano shrugged as he rummaged in a basket with clothes. "Remo wanted it, so he got it."

"But isn't it expensive to keep the place from falling apart? It's a huge building."

"Parts of it are falling apart, yes, but it costs us more money than a standard gym would. Still … what's life without the occasional irrational decision?"

His blue eyes held mine, and the nerves I'd managed to calm returned full force. Fabiano yanked red shorts out of the basket. "The youngest brother of my Capo uses these. Maybe they will fit you."

I took them from him. "Capo?" I asked curiously. I had heard the term, of course, but Fabiano had said it with so much respect it surprised me.

"Remo Falcone, he is my Capo. My boss if you will."

"You think highly of him."

He nodded once. "Of course."

I had a feeling he wasn't just saying it because he had to. Cheryl had sounded terrified when she'd uttered Falcone's name, but there was no fear in Fabiano's voice.

"We didn't come here to chitchat, remember?" he said with a grin. "Now let's get changed."

Without a warning, he unbuckled his belt.

I turned around with a surprised gasp. "You could have warned me."

"I could have, but I didn't want to. I intend for you to see much more of me."

I glanced around for some privacy, but the room didn't provide any. There weren't any stalls, only lockers and an open shower area. Oh, damn it. I pulled down my jeans shorts and quickly slipped on the boxing shorts then faced him. Fabiano's full attention was on me as he leaned against the wall with his arms crossed over his bare chest. I'd forgotten about that little detail; he didn't wear a shirt when he was in the cage. My eyes trailed down to his dark blue boxers that hugged his narrow hips with the delicious V disappearing in his waistband.

"And?" he asked.

I blinked at him, tearing my eyes away from his chest. "And?" I repeated.

"Does it fit?"

How could anything not fit that body?

I realized he meant *me*. "Oh, the shorts, you mean? They are a bit loose, but it should be fine."

"You look sexy in them," he said in a low voice.

My face blazed with heat.

"Don't forget your knife. I want to see you use it."

I bent over my backpack, glad my hair hid my blush, but he probably already saw it. I grabbed the knife and straightened. He opened the door and waited for me to go through. His warm scent wafted into my nose as I passed him. I had to get a grip. We headed back to the beautiful game room, and I continued toward the boxing ring, glad to focus on something other than the dangerous, muscled man behind me.

"Not that way," Fabiano said, a smirk in his voice. I turned, and he pointed at the fighting cage to the right.

"In the cage?" I asked, horrified.

142

He jumped up on the elevated platform of the cage, grinning like a shark. "Of course. I want to see how you deal with stress."

"Great," I muttered. "As if fighting with you wasn't stressful enough."

He held out a hand to me. I slipped mine into his, and his fingers closed around me, warm and strong. He pulled me up. I bumped against his chest, and he held me there for a moment. I peered up at his face. The glow of the chandelier above our heads making his hair appear golden.

But a golden boy? No, he definitely wasn't that.

"I thought we were going to fight," I whispered.

His lip curled. "Just seeing how much more uncomfortable I can make you," he said.

I glared. "What makes you think this makes me uncomfortable?"

His smile widened. "It doesn't?"

I untangled myself from his hold and pointed at the cage door. "How does this thing open?"

He pressed down the handle, looking way too full of himself.

I stepped inside and goose bumps formed on my skin. I could smell stale blood beneath the prominent smell of disinfectant and steel. Fabiano closed the cage with a quiet click.

"I don't get the appeal," I said, looking around the cage. "Why do people enjoy being locked in a cage like animals?"

"It's the added thrill of not having an escape. The cage is unrelenting."

I nodded, fumbling with the knife in my hand. The biggest chandelier dangling from the ceiling right above my head was more daunting than decorative.

"I want to see you handle it."

I pressed the button that released the blade. It gleamed in the golden light. I held the knife out.

Fabiano hooked his finger, invitingly. "Do what you would do to an attacker."

143

I held the knife a bit higher, my palm closing tightly around the handle.

Fabiano stifled a smile. For him this was probably more than a little entertaining. "Attack."

I took a step forward but he bridged the remaining distance between us and feigned an attack. "Try not to lose your knife."

I tightened my hold further, even though it seemed impossible. Before I knew it, Fabiano was there in front of me, tall and imposing and muscled and so at ease with what he was doing. With painful pressure to my wrist, the knife clattered to the ground. I reached for it, but Fabiano was quicker. He twisted the knife in his hand, admiring the blade.

I glared. "It's not fair. You are much stronger and more experienced." I rubbed my wrist. I hadn't even seen what Fabiano had done.

Fabiano shook his head. "Life isn't fair, Leona. You should know. Your attacker won't be a one-hundred pound female with delicate feelings. He will be a two-hundred pound fucker who likes to hurt females with delicate feelings." And then he towered over me again, and I wanted to kiss him, not fight him.

"That knife," he said in a low, threatening voice as he held out the blade between us, "it can be your salvation or your downfall." He gripped my arm and whirled me around. My back collided with his chest as he pressed me against him. I was frozen with shock. He touched the tip of the blade to the skin between my breasts then slowly trailed it down to my stomach. The pressure wasn't enough to leave a mark but my stomach turned at the thought of how it would feel if it were. "That knife can give your opponent another advantage over you. If you can't handle the knife, you shouldn't use it." He let go of me, and I staggered forward, out of his embrace. My heart pounded in my chest as I looked down at myself. I could still feel the steel on my skin. I closed my eyes, trying to stop my rising panic and worse ... arousal.

Fabiano was right. If my attacker got hold of my knife, he'd use it against me. The knife had given me a sense of security, but now even that was gone. I faced Fabiano, who was watching me intently. He held the knife out to me, and I approached him slowly and took it.

"Cut me," he said.

"Excuse me?" I asked.

"Cut me. I want to see if you have what it takes to hurt someone. Cut me."

I shook my head, taking a step back. "I won't. This is stupid."

Fabiano shook his head in obvious annoyance then snatched the knife from my grip. His eyes held mine as he pressed the blade against his palm and slashed. I staggered back, not from the sight of blood, but from his actions. He dropped the knife to the ground. Blood dripped down onto the gray flooring. He squeezed his bleeding hand into a fist and more blood coated his knuckles.

"I can see that you are scared. Fear is never a good companion in a fight," Fabiano said, looking completely at ease in the fighting cage. No sign of pain either.

This was familiar ground for him, a place he felt at home in. For me, the cage seemed to tower over me menacingly. Even its luxurious surroundings couldn't change that. And it wasn't really helping that I was supposed to fight Fabiano. With his rock-hard stomach, muscled arms, and keen eyes, he already looked like a fighter. I had seen him fight. There was nothing I could compare it to. His speed. His strength. His determination.

I, however, felt out of place.

Fabiano opened his arms, palms outward. My eyes lingered on the gash in his palm. "Hit me. That's something you can do, right?"

I took a step toward him.

"Curl your hands into fists. Don't even think about hitting me with your open palm. You're not swatting at a fly."

He was making fun of me. I clenched my fists just as he ordered and took another step toward him. I wasn't even sure where to hit him. He took a sudden step toward me, startling me, and I backed off.

"Hit me," he ordered again.

I propelled my fist forward and rammed it into his stomach. A second before impact, his six pack became an eight pack as he tightened his muscles.

My knuckles collided with his hard stomach, and I winced. I pulled back immediately.

"Was that your hardest hit?" he asked.

I frowned. "Yes. Was it that bad?"

His expression gave me an unmistakable answer. "Now kick me as hard as you can and aim as high as possible."

Hitting had already felt strange, but kicking someone was completely out of my comfort zone. I swung my leg and landed a kick against his ribs. He shook his head. I might as well have batted at him with a feather boa.

"That's not good. I'm not even moving and your aim and force are already bad."

Did he have anything nice to say? I was starting to get annoyed.

He got into a fighting stance and turned away from me. Then he did a high kick against the cage. The crash made me jump and the ground vibrated under my bare feet from the force of Fabiano's kick. It was still hard to believe how high he could raise his leg and how hard he could kick with it. My leg would have fallen off if I tried to get it that high.

"Perhaps you don't have the right incentive. Most women only ever dare to hit hard when they're cornered. Let's pretend I'm attacking you."

The thought thrilled and terrified me. I nodded, trying to look like I was ready for this.

His blue eyes slid over my body. "Do what you must to escape my grip. Hurt me."

As if there was the slightest chance that I could. Without a warning he lunged forward, grabbed my shoulders, and pressed me up against the cage.

Caught between the cold metal and his warm muscled chest, there was no way I could hit him. I twisted, but his hold on me didn't waver.

"Fight, Leona. Imagine I was out to hurt you, to rape you, to kill you," he said in a dark whisper that raised the hairs on my neck.

I tried to push away from the cage again, but there was no way Fabiano was budging. He was as unmovable as the steel of the cage.

"You need to do better than that," he murmured against my ear then licked a trickle of sweat from my throat. It sent a tingle down my spine. Without warning, he released me, and I quickly faced him, hoping he couldn't see what the gesture had done to my body.

He pushed his hair back, a self-satisfied smile on his face. "Brace yourself. I expect you to do better this time."

I was on the verge of protesting when he jumped forward. Before I knew what was happening, he kicked my legs out under me. I gasped as I fell backward, bracing myself for the impact. But it never came. Instead, Fabiano's arm snaked around my waist and he lowered me to the ground. Of course that wasn't the end of it. He knelt over me and pressed my wrists into the floor above my head. His palm was slippery against my skin. Blood. One of his knees wedged between my legs, forcing them apart.

My heart galloped in my chest as I stared up at his face. Was this still a game? He looked so focused and ... eager. But then a slow smile spread across his face and breathing became easier. "I hope this wasn't you really trying," he said. "An attacker could have his way with you now. It wouldn't be very difficult to rip your clothes off and force myself on you."

"You would kill anyone who did," I said. It was a horrible thing to say. And I didn't know why I had said it. I didn't know if Fabiano would go that far.

He lowered himself completely on top of me, and somehow his warm weight felt perfect. "You think?" he murmured. "Why would I do such a thing?"

His eyes immobilized me. I couldn't say anything for a while.

Suddenly I felt foolishly daring. "Because you don't like to share."

Possessiveness filled his face. He bucked his hips against my crotch, and my eyes shot open. He was hard. Heat flooded me. I should have pushed him away, but I was too surprised and fascinated.

He bent down and licked my collarbone. "I want nothing more than to fuck you right here, in the middle of this cage."

My muscles tensed. This was too fast. I still wasn't sure if I should keep this thing going between me and Fabiano. And I definitely didn't want to be fucked in a cage like an animal, even if a tiny part of my body disagreed.

I didn't get the chance to push him away, though, because he shoved himself off the ground and landed on his feet in one graceful move.

FABIANO

I crouched in front of her, taking in the sight of her widened eyes and disheveled locks. She propped herself up on her elbows but made no move to stand.

Her eyes went to my boxer before she quickly looked away. I knew she'd be blushing if her face weren't already red from exertion. A thrill went through me, as it always did when her innocence shone through. I straightened, and slowly she stumbled to her feet as well.

She was a horrible fighter. It wasn't in her nature to hurt people. Perhaps I could have pushed her into hitting harder if I actually hurt her. Pain was a strong catalyst, but hurting her wasn't something I had in mind. I wanted to make her scream but not from agony.

She balled her hands into fists. Her wrists were covered in bloody fingerprints, but the gash in my palm was only a dull throb.

"Are we going to try again?"

I smirked. She was trying to escape the situation. I inclined my head then feigned an attack. She raised her arms protectively and closed her eyes. "Don't ever close your eyes in front of an enemy."

She glared at me and tried to land a hit against my stomach. I sidestepped her futile attempt and grabbed her from behind. I locked her arms under mine and pressed my hips against her butt. I moved her forward until she was pressed up against the cage and my erection was pressed up against her firm ass. She made a sound of protest.

"Fabiano," she wheezed, anger seeping through. "Stop it."

"Make me," I challenged then lightly bit the crook of her neck, sucking the skin into my mouth. She let out a moan, stilled, and began squirming. When I released her soft skin, I'd left my mark. She tried a backwards kick but only lightly grazed my shin. "You can do better," I said.

She tried to push back, but again had no chance against me. Perhaps it was unfair. Even the best fighters didn't last long in a fight against me. What I was doing with Leona didn't even come close to fighting. Playing was more like it.

Suddenly she became slack under my touch and pressed her butt against my erection. If she thought that would throw me off, she was sorely mistaken. Unlike her, I had more than enough experience and wasn't unnerved by an ass against my cock. The only bothersome thing was the clothes separating her from my cock.

"Playing with fire?" I asked quietly.

"You started it," she muttered, indignation flashing in her eyes. There was finally some fight in them.

"And I'm willing to play it to the end," I said suggestively. "Are you?" I ground my erection against her butt once more.

She became still. "No. I'm not." Her voice was no longer playful or angry.

I peered down at the soft freckles of her nose and cheek. Her eyes met mine. She was uneasy and nervous, but not scared. She trusted me to respect her boundaries. Leona might be my undoing. I loosened my hold on her arms, allowing her to turn around. She tilted her head up, searching my face. I wondered when she'd stop looking for something that wasn't there. I pressed my palms into the cage beside her head, letting my head fall forward until our lips were less than an inch apart. Her eyes darted down, and she surprised me when she rose on her tiptoes and closed the gap. Her kiss was soft and restrained. My body screamed for something else. I deepened the kiss then grabbed her ass and lifted her until her legs wrapped around my waist. Her back pressed up against the cage, I ravished her mouth. She clung to my shoulders, her nails digging into my skin and her heels into my butt. When she pulled back, she was breathless and dazed.

"You're not good at setting boundaries," I told her.

She leaned her head back against the cage. "I know," she said guiltily.

"So that's what you call fighting?" Nino drawled as he walked in, a sport bag slung over his shoulder. His attentive gaze stopped on Leona. Every muscle in me tensed.

I lowered Leona then put my hand on her back.

Nino followed the gesture. His expression didn't change. Unlike Remo, he wasn't prone to emotional outbursts. It made him harder to read, but definitely not less dangerous. Tall, lean, immaculate beard, and dark hair pulled into a short ponytail, Nino looked like a runway model. Women fell hard for him . . . until they realized that his emotionless expression wasn't a mask. Nino didn't have to hide his emotions. He had none.

"We're done here," I said. I nudged Leona toward the cage door, opened it, then climbed out first before I lifted Leona down. She stood close beside me. She was wary of Nino, as she should be. Her instincts couldn't be completely off if she recognized him as a threat.

I greeted him with a short embrace and a clap on the shoulder. "Who are you training with?"

"Adamo, if he decides to show up."

I rolled my eyes. "Good luck." His eyes slid behind me to Leona. And something protective and fierce swelled in my chest. He didn't say anymore. I doubted he was really interested in her. He was curious because I showed interest in her.

I led Leona toward the changing room but only grabbed our bags.

"Aren't we going to change?" she asked.

I shook my head. I wanted to get her away from Nino. It was safer if Remo and his brothers didn't see Leona too often. I led her outside toward my car. Some of the tension dissipated as we added some distance between us and Nino. Remo and his brothers were like family to me, but I knew better than to trust them with Leona.

Leona gave me a sideways glance. "Who was he?"

"Nino. One of Remo's brothers."

"You didn't like being around him," she said.

If she'd picked up on it, Nino would have too. That wasn't good. "I practically grew up with him. He's like my brother, but I don't like you around him. It's better if you don't get involved in that part of my life."

"Okay," she said simply.

When we arrived in front of her apartment, I turned toward her, wanting to fucking kiss her again. I played it cool since our first kiss, but I was tired of holding back, especially after what happened in the cage.

"Are you celebrating Christmas with Remo and his brothers?" she asked.

I stiffened. I hadn't expected that question. "I don't really celebrate Christmas." I hadn't in several years. Not since my sisters left for New York.

I didn't care for the holidays, but now that she'd mentioned it, I realized that Christmas was only a week away.

"Me neither. I'll probably work," she said with a small shrug.

"You won't celebrate with your father or your mother?"

She stared out of the windshield, fidgeting with her shorts. "I used to. A long time ago. When I was little, we managed two or three nice Christmas evenings. The rest were a mess." She sighed. "After my dad abandoned us, my mother was busy working all the time to get money for meth. She forgot things like Christmas and my birthday. They weren't important to her. And my dad..." she shrugged "...I suppose he was glad to be away from us and the responsibility."

She still hadn't mentioned her mother being a whore, but I allowed her that small reprieve. "That's why you shouldn't feel responsible for your father. He isn't an honorable man. He should protect his own flesh and blood and not offer it to someone in exchange for a debt."

She flushed. "You know about that?"

"Soto told me."

"It's not easy to abandon him. I still love him, despite his flaws. I can't help it."

I grimaced. "Love is a weakness, a sickness. You'll see where it gets you."

Her blue eyes searched mine, still looking, still hoping. "You can't mean that. Love is what makes us human, what makes life worth living. Love is unconditional."

She said it with so much fervor that I knew she was trying to convince herself as much as me. "Do you really believe that? Do you think it turned you into the person you are today? Because love definitely didn't make me who I am. Blood and hate and thirst for revenge kept me going. They still do, and so do honor, pride, and loyalty. So tell me, Leona, did love form you?"

Leona clutched her backpack against her chest. "Not me. But nobody ever loved me like that," she said quietly. "My parents always loved their addiction more than me, and there was never anyone else. So I suppose love didn't form me." She looked me square in the eyes, a challenge. Did she expect pity? She needn't worry. Pity was an emotion I'd given up a long time ago. I was furious. Furious on her behalf.

"Then what did?" I asked.

CHAPTER 12

LEONA

"Then what did?"

That question threatened to unravel me. "I don't know," I admitted. I looked down at the scars on Fabiano's chest, at the tattoo on his wrist, appraised the confident way he held himself. Pride and honor. He oozed it. His body was a testament to his convictions ... to how far he'd come. And me?

I let out a small, empty laugh. "Hope for the future kept me going. I was a good student, and I worked hard. I thought I'd have a bright future after high school. I thought I'd go to college, get a law degree, and become something more than the daughter of a..." I swallowed the word whore, not able to admit the truth to Fabiano "...drug addict, but I'm failing."

Fabiano's face still showed no pity, and I was glad for it. There was something dark and fierce in his eyes. "If you don't fight for what you want, you won't get it. People like us don't get their wishes handed to them on a platter."

How could he compare us? He was strong and successful, admittedly not in the conventional sense, but he had what he longed for. The Camorra was his passion. "You are a born fighter. I am not."

"I wasn't born a fighter. I was formed into one by the shit thrown my way over the years, Leona."

I wanted to ask him about his past, but he was always so cautious when he mentioned anything related to it. I let out a breath. He leaned over, cupped the back of my head, and kissed me. I sank into the kiss. I needed it now, needed to feel something other than desperation. His tongue danced with mine, and his scent engulfed me. I closed my eyes, allowing my body to relax.

He pulled back. "I will fight your battles for you now, Leona. I told you I'd protect you."

I nodded, as if my approval meant anything. Fabiano's overwhelming presence, his unrelenting possessiveness, they were something I never encountered before. My parents had never displayed any kind of emotion toward me. I had been an afterthought for them—sometimes useful, sometimes bothersome, never something to waste too much energy on.

Deep down, I knew Fabiano's attention would come with a price. I'd pay for surrendering to him in one way or another. But right in this moment I couldn't care less.

I got out of the car, my legs shaky. I could feel Fabiano's gaze on me all the way into the apartment. I leaned back against the door and released a breath. It felt as if he'd laid me bare without touching me, as if he knew my deepest desires, my darkest fears.

I functioned on autopilot that day. Cheryl didn't say anything, but I could tell that she wanted to.

Fabiano was waiting for me when I got off at two-thirty. He didn't start the car right away. His eyes darted down to the modest black heels I was wearing then over the blue dress. Both weren't anything special and had been on sale, but they were new. I bought them this afternoon before work to cheer myself up.

"I want to show you where I live," Fabiano said simply.

The tiredness melted away. "Okay."

I wasn't sure what else to say. This seemed like a very personal thing, like another level in our ... what? Relationship? It was difficult to put a label on it. I had a feeling Fabiano didn't take many people to his apartment. He seemed like someone who kept his private space well protected. Like he'd said, he didn't like to share, and that he wanted to share his apartment with me, if only for a few hours, made me happy. At the same time, however, I knew that being alone in his apartment, with a bedroom at our disposal, opened up new possibilities I wasn't sure I was ready for ... mentally. My body was a different matter.

His blue eyes regarded me for a few heartbeats, perhaps reconsidering his decision.

As we drove, we passed familiar sites like the Venitian and the Bellagio, and I wondered if I'd ever manage to get a job in a place that was even half as good. Maybe Fabiano could help me. He knew more than enough people in Las Vegas, and I didn't even want to know how many good hotels and restaurants were owned or controlled by the Camorra. I also didn't want to ask him for that kind of favor. I could only imagine how many people tried to gain something just from knowing him. I didn't want to be like that.

Silence filled the space between us. The soft hum of the engine lulled me to sleep, and I wondered if agreeing to go to his apartment this late at night was a mistake. Did Fabiano expect me to spend the night with him?

My thoughts were cut short when we pulled up in front of a sleek skyscraper and drove down into an underground parking garage.

"No villa in the suburbs with a park-like garden for you?" I asked, hoping my voice didn't give away my nerves.

He grimaced. "I prefer to live in the center of life. The suburbs are for families."

We got out of his car. The clean, new smell of the parking garage filled with dozens of luxury cars already made me feel out of place. Even new clothes wouldn't change that. My heels clicked on the white marble of the elevator as we got in. Fabiano's hand on my lower back was already oddly familiar. He pressed the button for the top floor, and the elevator began its silent ascension. Fabiano didn't say anything. Perhaps he was having second thoughts about bringing me to his home.

The elevator came to a stop, and the doors glided open without a sound. A long corridor with a plush beige carpet and cream-colored walls with golden accents stretched before us. Fabiano led me toward a dark wooden door at the end of it, which seemed to be the only door on this floor, except for the emergency exit.

My stomach fluttered with nerves when he opened the door wide for me. I stepped past him into his apartment, and the moment the light came on, I froze.

I'd never seen luxury like this before. We stood in the entrance area, which was on a higher level than the living area. Vaulted ceilings were supported by marble columns. I stepped down the three steps, my heels clacking loudly on the smooth marble. I wished I'd worn the shoes Fabiano had bought for me and not the ones I got for half-price at Target today.

The marble floor was black and white and laid out in geometrical design. Four white couches surrounded an enormous low, black marble table. Above the seating area, a huge lamp that looked like a ginormous silver ball of wool hung from the two-story-high ceiling. To the left was a dining table that could seat at least sixteen people. Like the floor, it was also made of black marble. Further to the left was the open kitchen with its white appliances. My eyes were drawn back to the living area and the floor-to-ceiling windows. A huge terrace with white columns overlooked the Strip with its illuminated skyscrapers and flashing lights.

I hesitated, not sure if I was allowed to wander around.

Fabiano made an inviting gesture, and I walked toward the windows and looked out. Now I could see that the white columns surrounded a long square pool that glowed with turquoise light in the dark.

Fabiano opened the terrace door for me, and I stepped out. Walking past the pool, I stopped at the balustrade. Down below, I could see the Strip with the Eiffel Tower. I breathed in deeply, stunned by the sight and the apartment. I didn't dare ask what it had cost. Crime paid off, if done right. My parents had never figured the right way to do it, though.

Fabiano came up behind me, his arms wrapping around my waist. He kissed my shoulder then up to my ear. A familiar tingling filled my body as I leaned into him. I didn't want to push him back, didn't want to consider how it looked being alone in an apartment with him at night. I just wanted to be, wanted to relish in the most beautiful sight I'd ever seen.

"This is incredible," I whispered. I could imagine living here, could easily imagine enjoying it. I never considered myself a girl who longed for these kinds of things, but I'd never been surrounded by it before.

He hummed his approval then nudged my hair away from my throat. He kissed the skin over my pulse point then gently bit down. I shivered at the possessive gesture. His mouth moved lower, and he licked my collarbone. His hands moved from my waist up to my ribcage, the pressure light and yet almost overwhelming. His presence, our surroundings, the possibilities of what might happen next were a tidal wave tossing me around.

"Fabiano," I said, uncertain, but my voice died in my throat when his hands cupped my breasts through the fabric of my dress. Only once had a guy groped at my breast, and it had been painful and disgusting; I had pushed him off and thrown up afterward.

Fabiano's touch was soft and yet sent spikes of pleasure through the rest of my body. I could feel my nipples harden, and I knew he would feel it against his palms. Embarrassment fought with need. I never wanted to be intimate with someone. Physical closeness had always been associated with bad things for me. Watching my mother sell her body had made me wary of allowing a man to get physical with me. I dreamed of falling in love and eventually making love with a man someday, but Fabiano didn't believe in love, and I wasn't sure if I did anymore either. Perhaps I'd have to settle for less. It wasn't the first time in my life. Being with Fabiano made me feel seen and protected. That was more than I'd had in a long time. And God did it scare me, because I knew how easily it could be taken from me.

His palms slid up to my shoulders, and he began pushing my dress down. My stomach tightened with anticipation and fear when the fabric gave way pooled around my waist. The cool breeze touched my skin, and my thin bra didn't protect me—neither from the night's cold nor from Fabiano's hungry gaze. No one had ever looked at me like that. I closed my eyes.

FABIANO

Goose bumps flashed across Leona's smooth skin, and the outline of her erect nipples strained against the thin fabric of her bra. My cock hardened at the tantalizing sight. Fuck. I wanted her, wanted to possess her. I ran my fingers over her ribcage then up to the edge of her bra. It wasn't spectacular, nothing pricy like lace or silk, and yet she made it seem like the sexiest garment in the world. Her body tensed under my touch, but not with eagerness. I regarded her face, her closed eyes, the way she was biting down on her lower lip and her lashes that fluttered. She was nervous and scared. I wondered what had her feeling that way. I definitely hadn't given her reason to be scared of me, which was surprising in itself.

I leaned down to her ear. "Have you ever been with a man?"

I knew the answer. I was too good at reading body language and people in general not to know, but I wanted to hear it from her lips. I was fucking eager to have her admit it.

She shuddered and gave a small shake of her head.

"Say it," I ordered.

Her eyelashes fluttered open. "No, I haven't been with a man."

I kissed her throat. "So I will be your first." My cock twitched with eagerness.

"I won't sleep with you tonight, Fabiano," she whispered.

I straightened, stunned by the words. Her expression showed mostly resolve, but there was a flicker of uncertainty as well. "I'm not used to waiting. For anything."

She didn't move away from me, her back still pressed against my chest, my fingers still on her ribcage. It heaved under my touch. One deep breath and her spine straightened. "Some things are worth waiting for."

"And you are one of them?" I asked.

She looked away, out toward the city lights. Her lashes fluttered again, but this time it was to keep the tears contained. "I don't know."

The words were so quiet, the wind almost carried them off before they reached my ears.

For a moment I felt like smashing the world, like burning down everything. I wanted to go after her father and see the life drain from his eyes slowly. I wanted to find her mother and cut her throat, see her sputter on her own blood. These emotions were foreign, not because of their brutality or fierceness, but because they were on behalf of a woman. I'd had bouts of protectiveness when I was younger, over my sisters—before they left me and before I became the man I was today.

I traced my fingers down her ribs then slid my arms around her stomach. She shivered. "Let's go inside. You're cold."

Her eyes searched mine, curiously, hopefully. When she didn't find what she was looking for, she nodded slowly and let me lead her inside. The wonder returned to her expression as she took in the living area. I'd spent most of my life in luxury, had taken it for granted most of the time until it had been ripped from me. Leona had never had anything close to it. I pulled her against me, her hard nipples pressing up against my ribs.

"Stay with me tonight."

Her eyes widened. Then she gave one frantic shake of her head. "I told you, I won't sleep with you."

Not tonight, but soon. Leona might still believe she could evade me, but she was mine.

"I know," I said in a low voice then slid my hands over her back.

She relaxed then tensed as if remembering herself. "Then why? Why have me spend the night if there's nothing in it for you?"

Fuck, if I knew.

"Stay," I said again, an order this time. She looked up at me, fearful for all the wrong reasons.

"Okay," she breathed, resigned and tired.

She'd had a long day. Working at Roger's Arena wasn't easy. I lifted her into my arms. She didn't protest, as if she realized it was a losing battle. I carried her toward the stairs.

Leaning her cheek against my chest, she whispered, "Please don't hurt me. I don't think I can handle it."

I paused with my foot on the first step, glancing down at her crown of amber curls. It wasn't meant the way people usually meant it when they begged me not to hurt them. It would have been easier if it were. I wasn't sure I could stop myself from hurting her. I was dragging her into a world where the things she longed for were even less attainable than in the hopeless life she was used to.

Her breathing had flattened. Had she fallen asleep?

She shouldn't have, not in the arms of a man like me. Her trust was foolish and completely unfounded. I ascended the stairs and entered my bedroom. I never brought anyone here. I put Leona down on my bed, and she didn't wake. I allowed myself to regard her. Her narrow hips, her round breasts barely hidden from view by the sheer fabric of her bra, the outline of her pussy underneath her panties. I raked a hand through my hair. Women were supposed to be entertainment and a pleasant distraction. So far Leona was neither of those things, but I couldn't allow her to be anything else. My life was dedicated to the Camorra, my loyalties belonged only to them. It couldn't be any other way. I got out of my clothes and stretched out beside Leona in my briefs. I watched her as she slept beside me peacefully. Never had a woman slept in my bed. I never saw the appeal. I still thought of many more entertaining things to do with Leona than sleep, but watching her peaceful expression gave me a sense of calm I hadn't felt in a long time, perhaps if ever.

I curled my arm over her hip protectively and allowed myself to close my eyes. As I listened to her rhythmic breathing, I began to drift off.

I woke with Leona's body curled into me, one of her legs intertwined with mine, her breathing fluttering against my bare chest. I'd never woken up beside a woman, let alone allowed that kind of physical closeness. Sex was a different kind of closeness and all I would permit.

I carefully untangled myself from her. She turned onto her back, the blankets pooling at her hips. Her face was relaxed, no sign that she was going to wake any time soon.

She was supposed to be fun.

That was all Remo would ever allow.

Fun.

I brushed my thumb over the small nub straining against her bra. It pebbled under my touch. Leona's lips parted, but she didn't wake. I wasn't a good man, nothing close to it, and it was time I stopped acting like I was … like I could be. The bracelet Aria had given me was stuffed inside my sock drawer and it would stay there.

I trapped her nipple between my thumb and forefinger and began moving it back and forth slowly, feeling it harden even more. Leona shifted her legs. Was she feeling it between her perfect thighs? I tugged, and she let out a low moan. Her eyelids fluttered then opened sleepily before finding me. Surprise and shock flashed across her face. I tugged at her nipple once more, and her lips fell open with a gasp. My eyes on her face, daring her to stop me, I lowered my mouth to her breast and tugged her nipple with my lips, sucking it lightly through the fabric. That stopped any protest she might have had in mind. I watched her hooded eyes as I sucked harder.

I slid a finger over the edge of her bra and tugged it down, revealing the pink nub. "Fabiano," she said hesitantly, but I didn't allow her time for more words. I swirled my tongue around her nipple then pulled back to watch Leona press her legs together. She tasted amazing, like clean sweat and something sweeter.

I lowered my mouth again, traced the tip of my tongue around the edge of her nipple, then slid to the peak and flicked it, licking her with languid strokes of my tongue. I sucked the small pink nipple into my mouth, relishing in the taste and Leona's shivers. She moaned again.

If playing with her tits made her come undone, I couldn't wait to dip my tongue between her silky folds.

I took my time with her nipple, wanting her to beg me for release. She ground her hips into the mattress in obvious need but didn't say the words I wanted to hear. My erection was rubbing painfully against the fabric of my briefs, driving me insane.

Done with being patient, I brushed my palm up her inner thigh. Her muscles tensed under my touch, but she didn't stop me. I held her gaze as my fingers brushed the crook between her thigh and pussy. Still no sign of protest. Instead, she opened her legs a bit wider, trust in her eyes.

Damn it, Leona.

I claimed her mouth for a fierce kiss and slipped my fingers under her panties and over her soft folds. She was so fucking aroused, so fucking ready to have me take her. Her body was practically begging for it, but that fucking trusting look in her eyes ruined it all. I ran my thumb up slowly until I brushed her clit. She bit her lip, hips rising up from the bed. I kept my eyes on her face, relishing in the twitches of pleasure, the wonder at how I could make her feel with just a simple touch of my thumb. The trust in her eyes anchored me, and I needed it to, because my body wanted more than she was willing to give, and the darkest parts of me knew nothing would stop me. And those dark parts were almost all that was left of me. Those parts of me had run the show for years. My thumb moved in slow circles over her wet flesh, and her gasps and moans were less controlled. She clutched my arm, and I kissed her hard, swallowing her cry as she tumbled over the edge. Her eyes fell shut as she shuddered, and for the briefest moment, I considered breaking my promise and breaking whatever dangerous bond was forming between us. Then she looked up at me, shy and embarrassed and guilty, and I knew it was too fucking late for that.

CHAPTER 13

LEONA

My heart raced in my chest as the last waves of pleasure ebbed away. Embarrassment slowly banished the thrilling euphoria. Fabiano didn't say anything, and I wasn't really sure what to say either. I hadn't meant for things to progress this fast. To sleep in Fabiano's bed, to have him touch me. The sensations had been wondrous, unlike anything I'd ever been capable of eliciting with my own fingers.

He peered down at me, a dark expression on his face, as if what had just happened was a mistake. I felt self-conscious under his scrutiny. It didn't make sense why he'd be unhappy about it. He hadn't gone against his own convictions, but perhaps he had come to the realization that I wasn't worth his attention. Maybe I did something wrong, though I couldn't really see how that was possible seeing as I hadn't done anything but let him touch me.

Worry filled me. Perhaps that was the problem.

I sat up. Sunlight filtered through the gap in the white curtains and past it I caught a glimpse of the Strip. I didn't belong here. I wasn't an Italian girl from noble upbringing.

"I should get going," I said lightly.

Fabiano didn't say anything, but behind his blue eyes was some kind of inner conflict raging on.

I was about to slip out of bed, when he placed his hand on my shoulder, stopping me. He leaned over to me for a gentle kiss that left me breathless then pulled back. "This is only the beginning."

This is only the beginning. I couldn't decide if it was promise or threat.

I slipped into Dad's apartment, closing the door with a soft click, not wanting to wake him. Seconds after the roar of Fabiano's engine had faded, Dad slunk out of the kitchen. He looked worse than the last time I'd seen him, like he needed a long shower and a few days of sleep.

His bloodshot eyes regarded me with silent judgment. They lingered on a spot above my pulse point, and the memory of Fabiano leaving his mark resurfaced. I placed my palm over the tender spot.

Dad shook his head. "You should have stayed with your mother." I didn't argue. Part of me knew he was right. I walked past him toward my bedroom. The space felt even less like home after my night in Fabiano's apartment. I knew I couldn't allow myself to grow accustomed to the luxury he had at his disposal. It wasn't something I could ever hope to have, and until now it never had been, but it was hard not to want something that beautiful once you experienced it firsthand. And his tenderness, his closeness … that was the most beautiful thing of all. Something I needed, something I was scared to lose.

The memory of Fabiano's mouth and hands on me sent a pleasant shiver through my body. That, too, was an experience I never thought I would want and now I worried I wouldn't stop wanting it.

I changed out of yesterday's clothes and into shorts and a shirt, swung my backpack over my shoulder, and left. Until I had to start work, I stayed elsewhere. And I already had an idea where. Now that things with Fabiano were getting more serious, I needed to find out more about his past.

The library was quiet as I took my seat at one of the computers. I typed Fabiano Scuderi into the search engine and hit enter. There were a few entries about Remo Falcone from recent years, especially regarding his fighting, which included the occasional photo of Fabiano with beautiful girls that sent my stomach plummeting. Over all, he seemed to keep out of the public eye. Then I found older articles, from more than eight years ago, which surprised me.

The articles weren't from Las Vegas. They were from Chicago. Some of them mentioned a man called Rocco Scuderi, who was Fabiano's father and supposedly the Consigliere of the Chicago Outfit. I still wasn't very well informed about the mob and its terms, but even I knew that Fabiano's father was a big deal in Chicago. From what I'd gathered, the Las Vegas Camorra wasn't getting along with the other mob families in the country. Why was Fabiano here and not in Chicago? One photo of him and his family caught my eye. It showed Fabiano with his parents and three older sisters, all three of them so beautiful and elegant it hurt looking at them. This was what Cheryl meant when she said Italian virgins from noble upbringing.

I was nothing like them.

Only one of them, the youngest, shared his dark blond hair, while the eldest was almost golden and the one in the middle a redhead. They were a striking family. I kept scrolling for more results and soon found articles about his sisters as well, especially the oldest sister, Aria, with her husband, the head of the New

York mafia.

I wondered why he never talked about them. Of course, I didn't talk about my mother either, but she was a crystal meth addict and a whore. The only thing that was remotely embarrassing about his family was that they were gangsters, and that definitely wasn't the reason why Fabiano had kept them a secret. If I had siblings, I'd want to stay in contact with them. I'd always wanted a brother or sister at my side for support during the many nights I was left alone when my mother was out looking for johns or other ways to get money.

At last, there was one article from a small Las Vegas newspaper about Fabiano titled "The Renegade son," which speculated about him joining the Las Vegas Camorra to become Capo. Apparently there had been a falling-out with his father that made him leave Chicago and help Remo Falcone. Overall, the information was sparse. It didn't give me what I really wanted, a glimpse behind the mask Fabiano displayed to the public.

The next day was Christmas Eve, and I went to work as if it was a day like any other. I tried to call the rehab center but hadn't reached anyone. Dad hadn't left his room before I had to leave the bar. Merry Christmas to me. Not that I had any intention of celebrating. The bar was deserted, only a few lonely souls crouched over their drinks.

"Why don't you go early?" Cheryl asked around eight o'clock. "I can handle our two customers."

I shook my head. "Don't you have family to celebrate with?"

Her lips tightened. "No. Roger will grab me around midnight for a Christmas quickie though."

I tried to hide my pity. I knew how it infuriated me when people gave me pitying looks. And it wasn't as if my Christmas was much better. "Where is he anyway? This is the first time he isn't in the bar."

"He's at home, celebrating Christmas with his daughter."

"Daughter?" I echoed in disbelief.

Cheryl nodded. "His wife died a few years ago and he's raising her alone."

"Oh." For some reason I had thought Roger didn't have a life outside of the bar.

"Just go, chick."

I sighed. Dad probably wasn't home. He'd mentioned an important race he had to watch. I grabbed my backpack then took out the cell phone Fabiano had given me yesterday so I could contact him. The only person I could think of calling was Fabiano, but would he even want to spend Christmas Eve with me? He was busy yesterday and only dropped me off at home after work … without mentioning Christmas at all. I clicked his name and quickly typed a message.

Got off early. You don't have to pick me up if you're busy. It's not too late for me to walk home.

I wasn't even out of the bar when Fabiano replied.

Wait for me.

I couldn't help the smile.

Cheryl watched me from across the room, shaking her head, and I quickly walked out into the parking lot. I knew she wouldn't be happy if she knew how much time I was spending with Fabiano. I was happy, despite everything.

Ten minutes later, his Mercedes pulled to a stop beside me.

I got in and took my seat beside him as if it had always been like this. He didn't move to kiss me, never had while we could be watched, but he put a hand on my knee.

"I didn't think you'd really go through with driving me home every night," I said, trying to ignore the way my body warmed at his touch.

Fabiano steered the car with one hand. "I'm a man of honor. I keep my promises."

Honor. A word that had played little to no role in my life so far. My parents were unfamiliar with the concept. Honor would have gotten in the way of their addiction.

My eyes traveled to the Camorra tattoo again. It scared people. Fabiano scared people. I hadn't realized it at first, but now that I looked for the little details in people's demeanor around him, it was impossible to miss.

Perhaps I didn't know enough about the Camorra and Fabiano to be scared. Maybe I was foolish not to be scared.

"I thought perhaps tonight you wanted to celebrate Christmas Eve with the Falcones." They were like his family, after all.

His fingers on my knee tightened. "Remo and his brothers don't celebrate Christmas Eve."

"But what about your real family? You never mention them."

Fabiano's lips thinned for the briefest instant before he schooled his expression into one of usual calm. "The Camorra is my family. Remo is like my brother. I don't need any other family than that."

I'd hoped he'd tell me more about his real family. I hesitated, unsure if I should mention that I'd found articles about them. I didn't want to appear as if I stalked him, even though that was the case.

"Ask," Fabiano said with a shrug, as usual able to read my face and the questions there.

"I found something about your family on the internet. There was a picture of you with them and a few articles about your sisters. One of them called you 'the renegade son.'"

His lips pulled into a sardonic smile. "Interesting twist on events they construed in that article," he said.

"So, you didn't leave for Las Vegas because you wanted to become Capo here?"

"I would have been happy becoming Consigliere for Dante Cavallaro and the Outfit. Back when I didn't know anything, I thought it was the ultimate honor to follow in my father's footsteps. Now I know that there's no honor in inheriting your position. The only way to deserve a position of power is if you fight for it, if you bleed and suffer for it."

"And you did," I said. I'd seen the scars. And even without them, you didn't become like Fabiano if life hadn't forged you in fire.

"I did, and so did Remo. He tore his position as Capo from the bleeding hands of the man who deemed himself capable of the job."

"And his brothers? What about them? Is that why they all have to fight? To prove their worth."

"That's one reason, yes."

It was strange that humankind thought it had come so far that humans considered themselves superior to animals, when we, too, still followed our base instincts. We looked up to the strong for a true leader, an alpha to guide our way, to take away the difficult decisions. The thrill of power struggles still captivated us. Why else were sports like cage fighting or boxing so popular?

I realized we weren't heading for my father's apartment nor to Fabiano's place.

"Hungry?" he asked, nodding toward the KFC drive-thru, the corner of his mouth twitching.

I nodded, wondering what he was up to.

"How about chicken for dinner and Las Vegas to ourselves?" he asked.

I smiled. "Sounds perfect."

The car smelled of the fried chicken and fries as Fabiano drove us up to the hill he had taken me for our first date. We were probably the only people who celebrated Christmas Eve with a KFC meal, but I didn't care. It wasn't like I'd had better Christmas dinners in the previous years. I was glad that Fabiano wasn't trying to imitate a traditional celebration. We parked at the very edge of the hill and stared out toward the bright city lights as we ate. "I think this is the best Christmas of my life," I said between bites of chicken.

"I wished it weren't," Fabiano murmured.

I shrugged. "So you had good Christmases with your family?"

His walls came up, but he gave me a reply. "When I was young, five or six, before my oldest sister left. After that, things quickly went downhill."

He fell silent and put down his half-eaten drumstick.

I licked sauce off my fingers then dropped them self-consciously when I noticed Fabiano watching me. He reached for my throat and brushed over my pulse point where he'd left a mark two days ago, his blue eyes possessive and ... something gentler.

"Let's go out for a bit. I have a blanket in the trunk."

Fabiano got out of the car and picked up the blanket. I walked up to the hood of the car and let my eyes take in the skyline. Las Vegas looked like it always did. It was flashy and colorful and bright. It could have been any evening other than Christmas, and I was glad for it. Fabiano came up beside me and handed me the wool blanket. I wrapped it around myself. It was soft and smelled of lavender. Fabiano's body was taut with tension, and he was looking—no, *glaring*—down at a small package in his hands.

A dark blue box with a silver ribbon. Oh, no. Was this for me? My stomach plummeted. I didn't have anything for him. I hadn't even thought about it. It had been so long since I'd celebrated Christmas that I hadn't even considered buying him a present. And what could I have gotten him anyway? He had every luxury possible.

I looked up from the box to find Fabiano now regarding me as if he was trying to make up his mind. Eventually he held out his hand with the present.

I didn't take it. "You don't have to give me anything."

His grip on the parcel tightened. "I want it gone."

Okay. I blinked.

I took the box hesitantly. "I don't have anything for you."

He didn't look surprised. "You don't have to, Leona. It's nothing."

"No, it's not. Nobody has given me a Christmas present in years," I admitted and felt raw because of it.

Fabiano's expression softened for the briefest moment. I opened the box with shaking fingers. Inside was a gold bracelet with small blue stones decorating it. "It's beautiful."

"Put it on," he said as he sank down on the hood of his car. He had a very strange look in his eyes as he regarded the bracelet, almost as if the piece of jewelry had come to haunt him.

I held my arm out for him, and he fastened the bracelet around my wrist. The stones flashed in the headlights. I'd have to keep it hidden from my father and in the bar as well. It was pathetic to think that I would rarely have an opportunity to wear it openly.

I searched Fabiano's eyes. They gave nothing away. Part of me was scared of what I wanted. Part of me was scared he'd grow tired of me the moment I gave him what he *wanted*. I knew how things could turn out.

His hand found mine, linking our fingers, and I stared down at our hands then slowly back up because I wasn't sure if he was doing this because he knew how it affected me or if he was being real. If this … whatever it was … was even real.

He cupped my face and pulled me toward him. My knees hit the bumper between his legs as our bodies molded together. He kissed me, slow and languid. I pressed my palms against his firm chest, feeling his calm heartbeat. His lips trailed over my cheek then brushed my ear.

"I can think of something you could give me as a present."

I stilled against him, my gaze seeking his. In the near dark it was difficult to read him. Sometimes it felt like he was doing it on purpose, saying something to break the moment, to destroy what could amount to something beautiful.

I cleared my throat. "I told you—"

"You won't sleep with me, I know."

I raised the wrist with the bracelet. "Is that why you bought this?"

His eyes narrowed. "So you would sleep with me?" He let out a dark laugh. "To be honest, I'd hoped you would want to do it without the help of fancy jewelry."

I flushed. "I do."

His eyes became eager, his body alert. "You do?" he asked in a low voice.

"But not today and not tomorrow. I need to get to know you better."

His face was very close to mine, and he shook his head. "You know everything there is to know. And everything you don't know yet is for your own good."

"I want to know everything, not just the good things."

"There are no good things, Leona. You know the bad things, and there are only worse things lurking behind that."

"I don't believe you," I whispered, leaning close and kissing him lightly.

"You should. I'm everything people warn you about. I'm every despicable thing they tell you and worse."

"Then why do I feel safe when I'm with you?"

He shook his head, his face almost angry. "Because you don't know what's good for you, and because you only see what you want to see."

"You are kind to me."

That seemed to be the last straw. He stood, his hands clutching my upper arms. "I'm not kind, Leona. Never have been. To anyone."

"To me you are," I said stubbornly. Why couldn't he see it?

He glared down at me then raised his eyes to the city behind my back. His grip on my arms loosened. What was he thinking?

He sank back down on the hood before he turned me around and pulled me against him so my back was pressed up against his chest.

"Tell me something about your family," I whispered. "Anything."

For a long time he didn't react. "My sisters raised me more than my mother or father did."

I held my breath, hoping he'd say more. Eventually, I risked another question. "How were they?"

Fabiano rested his head lightly on the top of my head. "Aria was protective and caring. Gianna loyal and fierce. Lily hopeful and lighthearted." I tried to picture them together, trying to bring together Fabiano's description with the press photo I'd found with their fake smiles.

"And you? How were you as a boy?"

His grip on my hips became painful, and I knew he was slipping away. "I was weak."

"You were a child." I felt him shake his head. Then he pulled back. I didn't want him to and put my hands over his to keep them in place. "What happened?"

"They left. Because they left, my father wanted me dead. And the boy he wanted dead ... *died*."

What? His father had wanted him dead?

His breath was hot against my throat when he murmured, "I want to see you naked."

I tensed then tried to turn around to look at him, but he wouldn't let me see his face. His hands on my waist kept me in place. His sudden change of topic *and mood* disturbed me.

"You said you felt safe with me. Then prove it. I want to see every inch of you."

"It's not fair that you're using it against me," I said quietly. My mind was whirring with what he'd told me.

"If you feel safe, then you trust me."

Did I trust him? I wasn't sure. I hadn't trusted anyone in a very long time, if ever. I didn't even trust myself half the time.

"Or perhaps deep down you know that you can't trust a man like me. Perhaps deep down you know I'm not safe." He sounded triumphant.

I reached for the zipper on the side of my dress and slowly began moving it down. Fabiano released me so I could stand and lower the zipper completely. I reached for the hem of the dress, but Fabiano's hands were there to stop me.

"Let me."

I raised my arms despite my nerves, and he pulled the garment over my head. I shivered against the cold. He had seen me in my underwear before, yet this felt different, more exposing. I met his gaze. He sat on the edge of the hood, body taut with anticipation, like a jaguar on the verge of jumping its prey.

"Come," he said quietly, and I stepped between his legs. He unhooked my bra and let it drop to the ground between us. Then his fingers hooked in the hem of my panties. Slowly, he raked them down my hips until they pooled at my feet. His eyes took in my body unabashedly. His gaze lingered on my most private part, and I had to fight the urge to cover myself. He regarded me as if I was special and it made my breath catch in my throat. "See," I said eventually. "I do feel safe with you."

He wrapped his arms around me, pulling me close. My nipples rubbed against his dress shirt and a sweet tingle formed in my belly. "You shouldn't." His voice was rough and deep. His hands came down on my hips, then one began its slow ascend until he cupped my breast. The coldness of my surroundings became a distant memory as he tugged at my nipple, rolling it between his thumb and forefinger. I could feel myself growing wet from his touch. Slowly, his other hand slid down from my waist to my butt. He cupped my cheek and squeezed then moved lower, to the back of my upper thigh, before he slid his fingers between my legs. His fingertips brushed over me, and I released a long shuddering breath. In the dim light, I caught sight of his erection straining against his pants.

What was I doing?

Whenever I lay awake at night, listening to my mother with her customers, I imagined my future with a straight-laced husband. A man who worked nine-to-five, a man who was safe and boring, yet here I was with Fabiano, a man who was anything but. He didn't fit with the future I imagined, didn't fit into the life I'd so carefully planned out for myself. But who ever said he'd be a part of my future? He definitely never gave any indication that he wanted a forever, that he even wanted a relationship. And what did I want? I wasn't sure anymore. As his fingers worked my heated flesh and I clung to him, I decided to let go of my worries for now. My body surrendered to the feelings coiling in the pit of my stomach, and I gasped as his fingers stroked me. It was exhilarating. Alive. I felt alive. He moved faster, and I cried out, my head falling back as currents of pleasure shot through me.

The sky above us was infinite, filled with possibilities and hope. Foolish hope.

Oh God. I was falling for him.

I pressed my forehead against Fabiano's shoulder, trying to catch my breath. He took my hand and rested it against the bulge in his pants. "That's what you do to me, Leona," he growled.

Was that all I did to him?

A mix of triumph and need filled me. Need for more than what his body could give, but I reached for his zipper and pulled it down. *Settle for what you can get, Leona.*

My fingers halted. I raised my eyes to his and there was that same flicker of need. Did he feel it too? Fabiano rose from the hood, breaking the moment, and freed his erection from his pants. His eyes made me shiver, cold and hungry.

"I want you on your knees, Leona. I want my cock in your mouth."

I froze, my defenses shooting up. Another moment ruined. He was so damn good at it.

Me on my knees? That was something I swore I'd never do. Not with anyone. My mother's johns had always wanted her mouth on them, had felt powerful when she knelt before them, had enjoyed degrading her like that. Sometimes when she was high, she told me about it, about her revulsion, about the disgusting taste, about choking when they fucked her mouth without mercy. I would never allow that to happen to me. Least of all like this. I wasn't sure what Fabiano saw in me, if he cared for me or if him wanting to be in my mouth was his way of possessing me a bit more.

I took a step back, shaking my head. "No," I said. Fabiano's eyes flashed with an emotion I couldn't read.

"I'm not your whore, Fabiano. I don't like you ordering me around."

He smiled darkly. "That wasn't an order, Leona. Believe me, it sounds very different when I give an order."

Dangerous. That was what he was. Sometimes I caught glimpses of it beneath his mask, and I always tried to forget.

"And I don't like you teasing me. You keep flirting with me, letting me touch you, and you think I won't want more? Even a normal guy would want to get in your pants, and I'm a fucking *killer*. You expect me to sit back and wait patiently for you to make your mind up."

A killer. He never admitted it, but I never asked him—because deep down I didn't want to know. Even still, the concept of him ending someone's life was too abstract to grasp. It seemed like something distant, something not of this world.

A sharp comment died on my lips when I caught the hint of wariness in Fabiano's eyes. He was wary of me, thought I was playing with him, perhaps using him like the other women who'd only seen his power and the possibilities it meant for them. Fabiano and I had a hard time trusting others.

"I'm not teasing you," I said quietly. I touched his chest, feeling his heat even through the shirt. His muscles flexed under my touch, but he didn't soften, his body nor expression. He regarded me like a snake does a mouse. I sighed, not wanting to explain my reaction to him because I couldn't tell him about my mother, not without him looking at me differently. "I want to touch you," I said, and it was true. "But I won't put my mouth on you. I think it's degrading. My mother always had bad taste in men, and they all liked to put her down like that."

His eyes were too assertive, like he knew more than I was willing to share. I looked away, worried he knew exactly what I was hiding, not only about my mother.

"I have no intention of degrading you," he said. I tentatively reached for him, my fingers brushing over his silkiness. He hardened immediately, but no sound left his lips as he watched me. For once, I didn't want to know what was going on in his head, too frightened that it would tell me more about myself than about him. His hand closed around my fingers, showing me exactly how he liked to be touched.

My own breathing quickened as I stroked him harder and faster. He never took his eyes off me, and there it was again … that flicker of emotion. I tightened my grip even more, made him growl low in his throat and replaced the tender emotion in his eyes with lust. Better. *Safer.* I could break the moment too—had to break it if I wanted to come out of this unscathed.

Fabiano tensed, control finally slipping, and he released himself with a shudder. The revulsion I expected never came. I wanted to touch him, and it felt amazing to watch him like that. I wanted more of it and more than just that.

When our breathing finally calmed, Fabiano took the wool blanket from the ground and wrapped it around us, his body warm against mine. I leaned back, closing my eyes. Despite the beauty of the city below, nothing could compare to the feel of our bodies pressed against each other. I'd been alone for so long. Perhaps all my life. And now there was someone whose closeness gave me a sense of belonging I hadn't thought possible. Fabiano was a danger to anyone around him, but to my heart he posed the greatest danger of all.

CHAPTER 14

LEONA

Christmas morning. My father wolfed down the French toast I prepared then got up. "One of the biggest races of the year goes down on Christmas. I need to place my bet."

Of course he had to. It was always about betting and gambling. About races and fights. How could I expect my father to want to spend Christmas with me? I nodded, swallowing the bitter words that wanted to spill from my mouth. He left the kitchen, leaving me alone with the dirty dishes. I waited for him to leave the apartment before I took the folded piece of paper with the number of the rehab center from my backpack and dialed it with my new phone. After two rings, a clipped female voice answered. "I'm calling for Melissa Hall, I'm her daughter." Guilt filled me. This was only the second time I'd tried to call since I was in Las Vegas, but the doctors had told me that it was better to give my mother time to settle in before she was confronted with influences from the outside world. And secretly I'd been relieved to be away from her troubles for a while.

There was silence on the other end except for the click-click of someone typing something into a keyboard. "She left two days ago."

"Left?" I repeated, my stomach clenching tightly.

"Relapse." The woman was silent on the other end, waiting for me to say something. When I didn't, she added, "Do you want me to get one of her attending doctors so he can explain the details to you?"

"No," I said angrily then hung up. I knew everything. My mother had given up again. I wasn't sure why I had expected anything else from her. And now she was out there alone, without me. Fear jabbed at my insides. This had been her last chance. She'd overdosed twice in the past, and I had been the one to save her, but now I was too far away. She couldn't be on her own. She forgot to eat and she got sad after the stimulating effect of meth wore off, too sad, especially after a john treated her like shit. She needed me.

I stared bleakly at the plates in front of me, listened to the deafening silence of the apartment. Tears blurred my vision. I needed to find her before it was too late. I had always been the caretaker in our relationship. My mother was like a child in so many ways. I should have never listened to the doctors. I'd known from the start that my mother was a lost cause. There was only one person I could turn to.

I typed **'I need your help, Fabiano. Please.'** into my mobile and pressed send.

FABIANO

"Today is going to bring us millions," Nino said.

I tore my gaze away from the TV screen that showed the warm-up race.

Nino was staring down at the iPad in his lap.

Remo shook his head at his brother, annoyed. "Watch the race for fuck's sake. We have a bookie for the numbers. Enjoy yourself for once. Stop acting like a fucking math nerd."

Nino shrugged. "I don't trust our bookies to do a better job than I can. Why settle for a lesser option?"

Savio snorted. "You are so fucking full of yourself."

If Nino wasn't Remo's brother, he would have studied math or some shit like that. He was a genius, which made him twice as lethal.

Remo slid his knife out of the holster across his chest then threw it with a flick of his wrist. The sharp blade pierced the soft brown leather beside Nino's left thigh. Nino glanced up from the iPad then down at the knife protruding from the sofa. "Good thing the races bring us so much money … You keep destroying our furniture," he drawled.

Remo waved him off.

Nino put the iPad down on the table beside him then pulled out the knife. He began twisting it between his fingers.

"So how's it going with your waitress?" Remo asked. "Not bored of her yet?"

I shrugged. "She's entertaining enough."

Nino's assertive eyes regarded me above his toying with the knife. I wasn't sure what his twisted brain had gathered from the one time he saw me with Leona. He didn't understand emotions. That was my salvation.

"Good fuck?" Savio asked, grinning.

I wasn't happy about the turn our conversation had taken.

"What the fuck?" Savio exclaimed, pointing at the TV. "Adamo is driving one of the race cars."

We all turned to the screen. Adamo was overtaking two cars at once; their drivers hadn't seen him coming up behind them. "Good driving skills for a thirteen-year-old," I said.

Remo scowled. "One of these days I'm going to kill him, brother or not."

My mobile vibrated in my jeans pocket. I took it out then glanced at the screen. Leona.

I need your help, Fabiano. Please.

Feeling Remo's eyes on me, I slid the phone back into my pocket.

"Your waitress," he said.

I crossed my arms behind my head. "She can wait."

"Why would you waste your day with us if you can have a nice fuck?" Savio asked before standing. "Actually, why didn't you organize some kind of entertainment, Remo?"

Remo reached for his mobile. "Obviously family time is over." Then he laughed at his own joke before his eyes slid over to me. "Go to her. Then we won't have to share the girls with you."

I got up with a shrug, as if I couldn't care less if I stayed or left, but my mind was reeling. What was going on? Leona sounded desperate.

"Don't overexert yourself with that girl of yours," Remo said with a shark smile. "It wouldn't look good if my Enforcer lost a fight."

I rolled my eyes. My next fight was in six days, on New Year's Eve. "Don't worry."

The streets were deserted as I drove to Leona's. People were celebrating Christmas with their families. I caught the occasional glimpse through windows where people exchanged presents or shared a family meal. I knew most of it was a façade. My family had always made a big show out of celebrating Christmas together as well, but behind closed doors we had been as far from a happy family as you could get. Our father had always made sure that we were miserable.

Last night was the first Christmas Eve I'd enjoyed in a long time. Because of Leona. My hands clenched. I shouldn't have given her the bracelet. I wasn't sure what had gotten into me.

Nothing. I wanted to get rid of the fucking thing. That was all. And why not give it to Leona?

I parked in Leona's street and got out of the car. I hadn't bothered texting her.

I rang the bell and moments later Leona opened the door, looking surprised and relieved. Her eyes were red from crying. I chose not to comment. Consoling others wasn't my forte, and I had a feeling she preferred me ignoring her emotionality.

Behind her I saw the small apartment she and her father shared, with the worn-out carpet and the smoke-yellowed wallpaper. She followed my gaze and flushed. "I didn't think you'd come," she said quietly.

"I'm here."

She nodded slowly then opened the door wide. "Do you want to come in?"

The apartment was a far cry from being inviting, but I stepped inside. Leona closed the door and then her arms were around my waist in a tight grip. She shuddered. I hesitated then raised my hand to her head and touched her lightly.

"Leona, what's going on?" Had someone hurt her? When could that have happened? I brought her home around four in the morning. It was only twelve now.

She raised her head. "Please help me find my mother."

"Your mother?"

"She left rehab. She can't take care of herself without me. I have always been the one who made sure she ate and didn't overdose. I should have never left her, but I thought she was safe in rehab."

"Shhh," I said, touching her cheek. She was shaking. "I'm sure your mother is fine."

"No, she isn't. She can't deal with life." She closed her eyes, and I knew what was coming. "She sells her body for crystal meth. And sometimes it makes her feel so dirty and horrible that she just wants to give up. I won't be there to stop her next time that happens."

After all the neglect Leona had suffered, she shouldn't be worrying about her mother like that. That she did stirred some part of me I thought was dead. "I will find her for you," I told her. "Where was she last seen?"

"Austin."

That was a bit of a problem. The Mexican cartels and local MCs were in control of Texas. Remo wanted to change it, eventually, but right now the Camorra had little power there. Remo had his contacts, of course—people who'd rather see us in power than the Mexicans. Perhaps one of them could help. But that would require that *I ask* Remo for help.

"Are you sure your mother won't come to find you?"

Leona gave a miserable shrug. "I don't know. She might. If she remembers where I went. She doesn't always remember. Her brain is a mess because of all the drugs." She closed her eyes. "If something happens to her, I'll never forgive myself."

"Nothing will happen to her," I said firmly. I stroked her cheek, and she gave me a teary smile. "Thank you, Fabiano." I lowered my head and kissed her lips. The kiss was sweet. I'd never had a fucking sweet kiss in my life.

When I returned to the Falcone mansion, I heard the moans. I made my way into the entertainment room with the pool tables, couches, TVs, and boxing ring. Savio was bent over a naked woman sprawled out on the pool table, thrusting into her. Another woman fingered herself on the same table.

She sat up when she spotted me then hopped off. I fucked her before, but I didn't remember her name. She sauntered over to me, but I shook my head, narrowing my eyes at her. She froze, eyes darting with unease.

"Where is he?" I asked.

Remo never took these women into his bedroom.

"Outside," Savio muttered then kept fucking the whore.

I strode out toward the living area and onto the terrace. Remo was there, naked, his hand fisting a woman's hair while fucking her mouth hard. He was glaring down at her as if he'd rather slice her open than shoot his cum down her throat.

His eyes shot up to meet mine, and he stopped thrusting but held the woman in place with his fist, his cock deep inside her mouth.

"I need your help," I said. He had already gathered information about Leona's mother, so I knew he'd find her.

Remo's black brows drew together. He shoved the woman away, and she landed on her ass then quickly scurried off. He didn't bother covering himself.

"I need to find someone. Leona's mother."

"You do?" he said quietly, suspicion tightening his eyes. "Why do *you* need to find the crack-whore?"

If he thought Leona was becoming too important to me, which she wasn't, he might take actions into his hands and get rid of her. "Because Leona got it in her head that the crack-whore will die without her help."

Remo came closer. I couldn't tell his mood. He was … tense. "And you are helping her because …?"

That was the fucking question, wasn't it?

"Because I want to." It was a dangerous admittance. I had to hope that the years we'd spent like brothers protected me.

"That got something to do with your sisters and how you were abandoned and that shit?"

"You saved me when I needed saving."

"I wasn't being heroic, Fabiano. I did it because I knew you were worthy to become what you are today."

"I'm not being heroic either. Will you help me?"

Remo shook his head. "Don't start going soft on me, Fabiano." He didn't sound angry or threatening.

I relaxed my stance. "I'm not, trust me."

Remo ran a hand through his hair. "You are a cock-blocking asshole."

"You probably would have killed her before you shot your cum down her throat."

"I would have killed her while shooting my cum down her throat," Remo said with a twisted grin. He grabbed his pants and pulled them on. "I assume the whore is somewhere in Texas, selling her worn-out pussy to any asshole with a few bucks?"

"Probably."

"Good opportunity to piss off the Mexicans, I suppose. Perhaps I can call in a favor with the Tartarus MC."

I didn't thank him. He wouldn't appreciate it.

CHAPTER 15

FABIANO

Something had Remo excited. I checked his face occasionally, knowing things that excited Remo usually involved blood and destruction.

Soto entered the room, dragging a woman in by her arm.

I stifled a sigh. Women weren't in my scope of work. Remo knew I preferred to handle men, and in the last couple of years, he allowed me that leniency. I doubted he understood, nor approved of my reluctance to deal with women, but hurting them had never given me the same thrill punishing men did. Soto, on the other hand. got off on degrading the weaker sex … in more than just the literal sense.

Degrading. Leona's expression when I'd asked her to give me a blow job flashed in my mind, but I banished any thought of her.

I threw Remo a questioning look. Why was I supposed to watch him dish out punishment to some run-down crack-whore?

Soto shoved the woman in our direction. She teetered on her too-high, red patent leather heels and eventually tumbled to her knees. She got back up, revealing ripped fishnet stockings. The tight red pleather dress hung off her emaciated body. When she lifted her face to stare fearfully at us, a jolt of recognition went through me. I masked my shock before Remo could pick up on it. He had been watching me closely in the last few days since I'd asked him for help.

Dazed eyes, cornflower blue like Leona's, darted from me to Remo to Soto. There was a distant resemblance. Perhaps in younger years, Leona's mother looked even more like her daughter—before the drugs and the alcohol and the constant beatings from johns.

She wobbled on her high heels, fingers trembling, and there was a fine sheen of sweat on her leathery skin. She needed her next fix.

"Found her," Remo said, an excited gleam in his eyes that told me this was about more than just helping me. More than once, I'd regretted my decision of approaching him. Leona was no longer one among many to him. She was someone with a name and a face, someone to be wary of.

"Had to hand over a few thousand in cash to the *president* of the fucking MC for this worthless whore because she worked his streets. I wonder what part of her is supposed to be worth five thousand dollars. Just look at her."

I didn't have to. She wasn't worth that much money.

Five thousand dollars.

Fuck.

Tartarus had ripped us off. And Remo let them. Not good.

"What do you say, whore? Are you worth that much money?" His voice was dangerously pleasant. People who didn't know him might have mistaken it for kindness.

She quickly shook her head, obviously knowing how to handle dangerous men.

With a past like hers, it shouldn't have come as a surprise. "Wh-where am I?"

"Las Vegas, *my property*, and now you are too."

She nodded slowly, dazed, then her expression shifted. "My daughter Leona is here."

Shut the fuck up. I didn't want Leona's name spoken in this room. I needed to figure out a way to get my girl out of Remo's head.

"That she is," Remo said, eyes slithering over to me, his lips tightening. "Now back to that five thousand dollars you owe me."

Damn it. It would have been easy for me to pay the money, but I wasn't out of my mind.

She smiled crookedly. "I earn good money. I know what men want."

Remo's dark eyes traveled over her body. "I doubt any man would want to get his cock dirty like that."

She didn't even flinch at his words. She'd heard worse. Whatever pride she once had was gone. She had no honor. She had nothing. That was why Leona clung to her virginity like it was her only salvation. And even knowing that, I still wanted to take it from her.

From his pocket, Remo pulled out a small see-through bag with two meth cubes and let it dangle from his fingertips. Leona's mother sucked in her breath, a sharp, raspy sound. Her body became taut, eyes keen and eager. For him it was nothing. Our storage was full of meth and heroin and ecstasy, full of money too.

She took a step toward him, licking her cracked lips.

"You want this, hmm?" he asked in a low voice. She gave a jerky nod.

"What would you do to get it?"

"Anything," she said quickly. "I'll suck your cock and you can have my ass. No condom."

As if Remo would settle for someone like her. He *was* Las Vegas. He could have anyone. Remo's mouth tightened with disgust. "There isn't enough bleach in the world to clean you."

"Then perhaps him?" she nodded toward me.

Remo's eyes turned on me. "I think he prefers a younger version of you. Less used up."

Leona wasn't used up in any way. She was pure and innocent. She was *mine*.

Leona's mother looked at Soto. Even he didn't look remotely close to being excited about the prospect of fucking her. He usually wasn't choosy over where he put his ugly cock, but that woman was too wasted even for him.

"I'm good, Boss," he said, waving her off like a bothersome fly.

Remo closed his fingers around the bag. "Perhaps you have something else you can offer us. Or perhaps someone else?" He tilted his head with a dangerous smile. "Perhaps that daughter of yours will take it up her ass in your stead. She might even be worth five thousand dollars."

My fingers twitched for my gun, but I stilled. This was crazy. I'd sworn loyalty to Remo and the Camorra. This wasn't about the woman in front of us. Remo was testing me. That he felt the need to do so unsettled me. Leona was a distraction. She wasn't a threat to the Camorra in any way.

"She's not like that. Do not touch her," Leona's mother said fiercely. I regarded her anew. Little was left of her. She had no pride, no honor, nothing, but despite her need for the drugs in Remo's hands, the part of her that cared for her daughter—no matter how little was left of it—won out. That was more than one could say about Leona's father.

Remo threw the bag on the ground. "You're not worth my time."

She scrambled forward and took the bag, cradling it like a child. "You are my property as long you owe me money. Hit the streets. You're too used up, even for our whorehouses." She wasn't listening. She was rummaging in her purse. Eventually her hand emerged with a syringe crusted with old blood. Of course, she didn't snort or smoke the shit. Shooting it into a vein boosted its stimulating effects.

Remo's face contorted with rage. "Not here!"

She reared back. I moved over to her, gripped her upper arm, and hoisted her to her feet. I dragged her out, Remo's eyes burning through my back as I did. "Five thousand plus interest, Fabiano. Tell Leona too."

I shoved Leona's mother onto the backseat of my Mercedes then got behind the wheel. "Don't even think about shooting up in my car," I snarled, angry at her, at Leona, and most of all myself.

Leona's mother cowered against the seat. She didn't move the entire ride, except for her eyes, which watched me like I was about to pounce on her. She was already broken. I sighed and left her in the car as I set out toward Roger's Arena.

The moment Leona saw me, she dropped everything and rushed toward me.

"I found her. She's in my car."

Leona's eyes widened, and she hugged me. Fucking hugged me in the middle of Roger's Arena, under the eyes of dozens of customers. I gripped her arms and pushed her away.

LEONA

My arms fell, realizing what I'd done. Fabiano looked pissed. And I got it. Not only did he have to keep up appearances, but people weren't supposed to know about us.

"How is she?" I asked as I followed him outside. I could barely keep up with his pace. He seemed desperate to get away.

He yanked open the door and Mom stumbled out. She looked a mess, as if she'd been found with a john and didn't have time to clean herself properly. I'd seen her worse off, so I moved forward and wrapped my arms around her.

She hugged me back briefly then dropped her arms, trembling. When I saw the syringe and plastic bag in her left hand, I knew why. "I need . . ." she whispered.

I nodded. I knew she needed a hit. I stepped back and she fell to her knees, nervously fumbling with the plastic bag.

Fabiano stood close behind me. I could feel his presence like a disapproving shadow. The smell of melting crystal meth filled my nose as Mom held the spoon over her lighter. She let out a small moan when the needle finally pierced her bruised skin.

I cast a glance over my shoulder. Fabiano's expression was stone. Hard, unrelenting, cold. "Thank you."

Blue eyes narrowed a fraction. "Five thousand, that's what Remo had to pay for her. Until she can pay it off, she belongs to the Camorra."

"That's too much money. She'll never be able to pay it off. She was barely able to pay for meth and food before."

He looked away and headed for the driver's side. "She's sold her body for years, she'll have to keep doing it. We'll send her the johns who don't have enough money for the whorehouses and she'll give them what they want."

I stared at his back because he wouldn't show me his face. "But those men are always the worst. They like to beat and humiliate women."

He stopped with his hand on the car door. His shoulders sagged. His eyes were cold as a glacial lake as he turned his head. "I can't do anything. I did too much already. You don't know how much I'm risking for you. Your mother is lost, Leona. She has been for a long time. Save yourself and let her handle her shit alone."

"I can't," I told him. He got into the car and drove off without another word.

You don't know how much I'm risking for you.

"Why? Why are you risking so much," I wanted to ask, but he was gone. And he wouldn't reply anyway.

Mom curled into herself, a blissful expression on her face. It wouldn't last long. Her breathing quickened and she rolled on her back, chest heaving, eyes wide, pupils dilated.

"Who's that?" Cheryl's voice made me jump. She appeared beside me.

"My mother," I admitted.

Cheryl didn't say anything as we both watched my mother get lost in her drug haze. Over the years it got worse. Meth destroyed her piece by piece. "She can't stay here. Roger will lose his shit if he sees a junky in his parking lot."

"I know," I said. "But I don't have a car, and there's no way a cab will give us a ride with her like that."

Cheryl sighed. "I hate to say it, chick, but you are more trouble than you look." She pulled car keys from her back pocket then pointed at an old, rusty Toyota. "Get in. I'll give you a quick ride. Mel can handle the bar."

"Thank you," I whispered.

She waved me off and helped me lead my mother to her car, positioning her on the backseat. She also helped me get my mother into the apartment, even as my father raged around us. I had paid for food and had given him more than enough money in the last few weeks. He would have to deal with Mom sleeping on the couch for now.

"You will end up just like her!" he shouted as he stormed out. Cheryl was already gone.

I perched on the edge of the couch beside my mother, who was mumbling in her drug-induced daze. Her eyes twitched around as she trembled with nervous energy. Mom being in Vegas meant more trouble for me. I didn't want her to work the streets again, but I didn't have nearly enough money to pay off her debt to the Camorra.

My mobile beeped. I removed it from my backpack.

It was a message from Fabiano.

Do you need me to pick you up from work tonight?

Even though he was pissed about the situation, he honored his promise to protect me. I smiled down at my phone.

No. I'm home with my mother. Thank you.

"That look," Mom croaked, startling me. "Who is he?"

"No one. There's no one, Mom. Sleep."

She rocked back and forth, the drugs beckoning to her. "I hope he's good to you."

"He's good to me," I said. Good *for* me ... that was a different matter.

"Does he love you like you him?"

My throat closed. "Sleep, Mom." I knew her body was torn between the stimulating effect of the meth and utter exhaustion from lack of sleep and food. And finally her eyes closed but she didn't lie down. Soon she'd go looking for johns.

Love broke people. It had broken Mom before, and the drugs did the rest.

I didn't love Fabiano. I ... I was falling for him. Falling deeper and deeper every day. Into his darkness and what lay beneath it.

Fabiano didn't want love. He didn't believe in it.

I couldn't love him.

CHAPTER 16

LEONA

My stomach fluttered with nerves, as if I was the one who had to fight in a cage. I glanced at the changing room doors, waiting for Fabiano to emerge. This was his second fight that I got to watch, but this time I was worried. Worried for Fabiano, worried he'd get hurt ... or worse. In the last few weeks of me working in Roger's Arena, I'd seen how brutal cage fighting could be. Several men had died in the hospital afterward. What if something happened to Fabiano?

I hadn't seen him since he'd dropped off my mother in the parking lot yesterday. I was in the storage area when he came in, and it drove me crazy that I couldn't tell him again how much I appreciated his help. Mom had been sleeping when I left, and I made her promise me she wouldn't leave the apartment alone. We'd figure out a way to get the money she owed later, until then my savings would have to do. My father wasn't going to help, that much was clear.

The door of the changing room opened, and Fabiano stepped out, tall and muscled. I smiled. He looked invincible. Fabiano was grace and fierceness and power as he strode toward the center of the room under the cheers of the crowd. His eyes were the scariest thing I'd ever seen. He was furious. Because of me, because of my mother. Perhaps his opponent, who waiting for him, saw it too, because for a moment he looked like he wanted to cancel the fight.

Fabiano leaped into the cage, catlike and breathtaking. His eyes sought mine and for a split second he looked at peace.

I had stopped washing the glasses, stopped listening to the customers. There was only him. The crowd erupted with a new wave of cheers. That *man*. He was mine. I had never been worth anything, but one look from him made me feel like the center of the world.

His opponent hopped from one foot to the other, balled fists raised, trying to goad Fabiano into action. One last glance at me, and Fabiano leaped toward his opponent.

His punches were hard. There was no hesitation in his hits and kicks. His eyes were keen and attentive, reading his opponent and using his weakness. Everything about this sport was brutal and hard. Relentless. But Fabiano's movements boasted grace and control. The crowd yowled and applauded every time he landed a hit. Blood soon covered Fabiano's hands and arms. He was harder and crueler on this opponent than last time.

Cheryl leaned in close as she put dirty glasses in the wash water. "I hope that puts some sense in you. If that doesn't scare you shitless, nothing will."

Fear was the last thing on my mind as I watched Fabiano. Cheryl regarded me then shook her head. "Oh, chick, and here I thought Stefano was the Camorra's romancer. Who would have thought that their monster would break your heart?"

"He isn't a monster. And he's not breaking anything," I murmured.

She loaded her tray with beer bottles for the next table. "He will break *something*. If it's only your heart, you're lucky. And if you haven't seen his monster until now, you might be in more trouble than I thought. Don't come running to me when you encounter it."

She knew nothing. "Don't worry."

Soon the man was lying on the ground. Fabiano crouched over him, punching him over and over again.

I shivered and felt relieved when the man finally patted the ground in surrender. The referee entered the cage and raised Fabiano's arm into the air. Fabiano looked my way, his body covered in blood.

He looked magnificent. His words about alpha males and their appeal from our first meeting came back to me, and I had to admit that he had been right as far as I was concerned. Fighting never mesmerized me before but watching Fabiano was something else entirely.

He climbed out of the cage and accepted the congratulating hands of several customers, but his eyes kept returning to me. I put down the dishtowel then grabbed a bottle of water.

"Where are you going, chick? Right into the lion's den?" Cheryl shook her head and took my place behind the bar. "Go ahead. Everyone has to dig their own grave, I suppose."

I sent her a grateful smile despite her annoying words and slunk toward the changing room. People were still too focused on the fighting cage, where the Camorra's bookie was stationed.

I didn't bother knocking before I entered the changing room. Fabiano saw me following him. I doubted anyone ever managed to sneak up on him. My clothes stuck to my skin from working all day and it should have made me self-conscious. I needed a shower, but my need for something else was even stronger. Fabiano wiped the remaining traces of blood from his body. Now his chest only glistened with sweat, the sheen accentuating every hard ridge of his perfect body. I wanted to trace my tongue along the dip between his pecs, down to the fine hair disappearing under the hem of his boxers. I'd never felt want like this. He was risking his position for me, and I wanted to risk something too.

I quickly tore my gaze from Fabiano and stepped into the changing room then closed the door before someone saw me. I needed to stop thinking like that about Fabiano. Touching him and having him touch me was okay, but if I allowed more, he'd stop respecting me. He'd lose interest. I *knew* it. Especially now that he knew what my mother was. The cool door under my palms grounded me. I didn't hear him approach but felt him close behind me, his heat pressing up against my back.

"You kept distracting me today," he murmured close to my ear. I shuddered at his proximity. Seeing him fight today had turned me on. There was no use denying it. The sport was brutal and hard, and Fabiano showed no mercy when he beat up his opponents, but my body responded to the sight of him. He'd looked invincible. Powerful.

The image of his hungry stare after he'd won sent a sweet tingling to the spot between my legs. "I can't stay here forever. People will start to wonder what we're doing."

I doubted no one had noticed me going into the changing room with Fabiano. I cringed at what they might think about me now.

"Let them wonder," Fabiano growled then licked my shoulder blade. "You taste perfect."

I shivered. "I'm sweaty."

He gripped my hips and whirled me around to face him, his head coming down and his lips claiming mine. I opened up, my tongue darting out to meet his. I ran my hand over his slick chest, my fingers trailing over the ridges. Perfection. He hissed when I slid over a cut.

"Sorry," I mumbled quickly but he quieted me with his tongue.

He backed me up until my legs collided with something hard. His arm wrapped around my lower back, and he lowered me until I lay on the narrow wooden bench. One knee between my legs, he bent over me, his mouth conquering mine, stealing my breath and making me dizzy with emotions and need. He didn't let up, and I could feel myself getting more and more aroused with every second. His tongue was so wonderfully skillful as it caressed mine. The scent of fresh sweat and Fabiano's own muskiness engulfed me.

He moved his knee up until it pressed against my crotch, and I moaned into his mouth at the sensation. I had to stop myself from rubbing myself shamelessly against his knee for some release.

"Stay like that," he ordered. Then he moved back, and only when he knelt on the floor between my legs did it dawn on me what he had in mind.

My eyes darted to the door. "Fabiano, please. What if someone comes in?"

"They won't."

"I'm sweaty. You *can't*." I shoved at his head, but he didn't let himself be deterred from what he was doing. He slid my skirt up then hooked a finger under my panties and shifted them to the side. Cool air hit my wet flesh, and my muscles tightened with need.

"Oh, Leona," he whispered darkly. "I thought you didn't like to see me fighting." He leaned his head against my inner thigh, his eyes darting from my most private area, wet and throbbing for him, to my face. I flushed with embarrassment but didn't say anything.

"But your pussy seems to enjoy it a lot."

Why did he have to use that word?

He blew against me and I quivered. I needed him to touch me. Shoving him away took a backseat in my mind as I watched him lower his hungry gaze between my legs again. And then he leaned forward, and I held my breath, every

201

muscle in my body taut with tension. His tongue darted out, licking over my heated flesh, sending a torrent of sensations through my lower body. I squeezed my eyes shut and bit down on my lip to stop myself from making a sound. Outside music still blared, but I didn't want to risk anything. He took his time, exploring with his tongue. Good Lord.

I gasped and arched off the bench as he kept up his ministrations, mouth and tongue sure of every twitch and turn they did, driving me up toward a point I'd never imagined.

"You are perfect," he rumbled against me, and the sound of his voice was like a hot shower after hours in the cold.

I curled my fingers around the edge of the bench, clinging to it desperately as my legs began trembling. My breath came in short bursts. Fabiano closed his mouth over me and began sucking. I whimpered but he pressed on, tongue circling and flicking. I was falling. A different kind of falling than before. I let out a small cry, one hand darting out to grab his blond hair. He hummed his approval as I kept him in place. I needed this. He pulled a few inches back, and I huffed in protest. I was so close.

"Don't stop," I pleaded, not caring how desperate I sounded. I was so close to the edge with raw need.

A need so strong it *hurt*. I wanted to tumble over this cliff, and fall and fall. I needed that fall.

"But what if someone comes in," he asked in a low voice, his tongue sliding along my inner thigh. He was taunting me now.

"Fabiano, please. I don't care!"

He chuckled, holding my gaze as he lowered his head so very slowly. When his lips brushed my flesh, I almost cried from relief. He flicked his tongue over my clit, eyes possessing me, *owning* every inch of me, and I gasped as my body exploded with heat. I shook against the bench. If Fabiano's hands on my hips hadn't kept me in place, I would have tumbled onto the floor in a heap. Blackness seeped into my vision as the waves of pleasure raced through me.

My limbs felt heavy and sluggish. Gradually, the throbbing between my legs started to fade. Fabiano crouched over me, eyes full of possessiveness. I breathed heavily.

"That was perfect," I managed to get out.

He shook his head. "It's only the beginning."

There it was again. That promise sounding like a threat. Where was he taking me? Down a path I'd never chosen for myself, a path farther away from the mundane life I'd imagined for myself. He kissed my throat. "And happy New Year."

New Year. I'd almost forgotten. Would this finally be a good year?

Fabiano straightened, all flexed muscles and dark hunger as he towered over me. Even the loose fighting boxers couldn't hide his arousal. I pushed myself into a sitting position, knowing what he wanted, and wanting it too … but unsure if it was wise. We'd been in the changing room for too long already. But I stopped being wise a long time ago.

I peered up at him, my eyes locked with his. I reached out and pressed my palm against the bulge in his pants. His abs flexed, but he didn't make a sound. Still so full of control. I wanted to see him give it up, wanted him to fall like I had. Both in body and heart.

Rubbing him through the thin fabric, I felt him grow even bigger. I tugged at his waistband, wanting to see him in all his naked glory.

And for the first time I didn't care how it would make me look, wanting a man. I felt lust and acted upon it. I curled my fingers around his shaft, feeling it throb. It was hard and hot and yet smooth. Marvelous. Every inch of him.

I ran my fingers up and down slowly, but Fabiano gave a thrust of his hips. I peered up at him. "Leona, I'm in no state of mind for the soft approach."

Tightening my hold, I moved faster but eventually let him take control as he closed his hand over mine and thrust his hips in rhythm with his strokes. New blood dripped from the wound over his ribs, but he didn't seem to mind. I raised my gaze from our hands moving together to his face. Hunger and need. And that gentler emotion that scared me shitless, but it scared him even more. I knew that now.

When he tensed and his release took over, I watched his face in wonder, hoping for a revelation. He looked marvelous but not unhinged. Still in control, even now.

I think I love you.

His eyes peeled open, and his emotionless mask slid over his features as we stared at each other. He took my hand and led me toward the shower.

I followed even as I said, "Fabiano, we can't."

He ignored my protest and pulled my dress up over my head then removed my underwear. "You said you needed a shower."

I gave up on protesting and slipped under the warm stream with him. His hands slid over my slick skin and his lips found mine. Blood tinged the ground pink. He peered down at me as the water plastered his hair against his head.

"Do you still think I want to degrade you?"

I flushed, wanting to forget my words from that night. He had given me pleasure with his mouth, but it was different. "No," I said quietly.

"Good." And then his lips were back on mine, and I let him pull me out of reality as his warmth surrounded me. I placed my palm over his heart, feeling it beat. I wanted it to beat only for me. His fingers curled around my hand, and he pulled it away—away from his heart—and raised it to his lips for a kiss. I pressed my forehead against his shoulder.

This was enough.

CHAPTER 17

LEONA

When a knock sounded at my door, I stifled a sigh. I had to leave for work in a few minutes and had no time for a talk to my father. Mom had moved in with us two days ago, so our already strained relationship took a nosedive toward worse. He only wanted money from me anyway. That was the only reason he even let me and Mom stay with him. I didn't have much money left. I'd given almost all of my savings to my mother, so she could pay part of her debt to the Camorra. And it still wasn't enough, which was why she was out on the street selling her body again.

I begrudgingly opened the door.

Dad was deathly pale, sweat coating his forehead.

"What's wrong?" I asked, even though I had a sinking feeling that I knew. It was always the same thing.

"I'm in trouble, Leona."

"You always are," I said, reaching for my backpack, ready to leave, but Dad gripped my arm. "Leona, please. They will kill me. He will."

I froze. "Why would they do that?"

"I owe too much. I can't pay them. I'm a dead man if you don't help me, Leo, please."

He used to call me Leo when I was a little girl, when he was occasionally a decent father.

He's not your business. That's what Fabiano had told me, and after these last few days of my father treating my mother like shit, I started to agree with him.

"How much do you owe them?"

"I don't know. Two thousand? I don't know! I lost track."

How could he lose track? I closed my eyes for a moment. The remaining money was supposed to get me into college, buy me a future, and again my father ruined it. I turned and took the money from its hiding place beneath the carpet and held it out to my father. He didn't take it.

"I can't bring them the money. They will kill me before I have a chance to hand it over. Leona, you must go for me."

I could go to Fabiano and give him the money, but he wouldn't take it. He would gladly kill my father. He had done enough for me already. "Where do I need to bring it?"

"It's called the Sugar Trap. That's where Falcone and his Enforcers hang around most days." He gave me the address then clutched my hand. "You have to hurry. Perhaps they already sent someone out for me."

I grabbed my backpack and headed for this Sugar Trap, wherever that was. I wasn't just handing over my hard-earned money for him, I was also going to be late for work. If Roger threw me out, I was screwed. I doubted I'd get a job on the Strip or anywhere else any time soon. We needed every cent I earned, with both my mother and father in Vegas.

When the red and yellow neon sign of the Sugar Trap caught my eye, I halted. The word was wedged between two open legs wearing high heels. The windows were tinted black so you couldn't look inside. I knew what kind of place this was, and it wasn't a place I ever wanted to set foot in.

There was a ginormous black man guarding the door. I approached him slowly. He didn't budge.

"I'm here to see Remo Falcone." Even as I said it, I realized how foolish I must have sounded. Remo Falcone was the Capo of the Camorra. He owned everything that mattered . . . if Fabiano was to be believed. Why on earth would he waste his time with me?

The bouncer seemed to think the same because he snorted. "Mr. Falcone doesn't choose the girls who work here. Go away."

Choose the girls? "I'm not here to work," I said indignantly. "I'm here because I have money for him."

The man tilted his head to the side but still didn't let me pass. I tried to catch a glimpse at his watch to see how late I was for work. I pulled the money from my backpack and held it out to the bouncer. He reached for it, but I snatched it back. I didn't trust him to hand it over to Falcone. "Go away," he muttered.

"Let her through," came a cold drawl from behind me. I whirled around to look up at a tall man. Nino Falcone. He nodded for me to step into the gloomy light of the Sugar Trap. And I did, because *really* no one could refuse those cold eyes.

"Straight ahead," he said. I kept walking, even though having him behind me gave me the creeps.

The corridor opened up to a bar area of red velvet and black lacquer. There were poles and booths with velvet curtains and several doors that branched off the main room.

"Go ahead. First door on the right."

I peered at him over my shoulder. He walked two steps behind me, watching me with those cold, unreadable eyes. I showed him the money. "Perhaps you can give your brother the money. It's from my father. His name is Greg Hall."

"I know who he is," Nino Falcone said with absolutely no hint of emotion in his eyes. "Go ahead."

I shivered and moved toward the door he indicated. I pushed down the handle and stepped through into another long corridor with black walls and a red carpet. I kept walking to the end, where another door waited. The hairs on my neck rose at the proximity of Nino Falcone and at his quiet scrutiny.

"Let me," he drawled and stepped past me to open that door. He entered a long room without windows. There was a desk on the left side that looked untouched. To the left was a heavy bag and some couches. Remo sat on one of them, laptop on his lap. His eyes moved up when his brother entered. Then they slid over to me, and I knew it had been a huge mistake to come here. The man, Soto, who had attacked my father, stood off to the side as if he were reporting to his Capo.

Remo Falcone put aside his laptop and rose from the sofa. Where Fabiano was grace and control, this man was unhinged power and barely contained aggression. My fingers crumpled the money.

"She's here to pay her father's debts," Nino said. I wasn't sure he was talking about money.

"Is she now?" Remo asked curiously. He came around the sofa, closer to me, and I wished he didn't. A smile curled his lips, and I took a step back, but Nino's arm stopped my movement. He wasn't looking at me, only at his brother. Some silent understanding passed between them I wasn't in on. "I'll let you handle it, then. I'll be back later," Nino said and just left, closing the door in my face.

I stood there, feeling small and shaking but trying to look determined and strong. My eyes flitted over to where Remo propped his hip against the backrest of the sofa. Soto, behind him, had something eager and gleeful in his expression.

I held up the money uncertainly. "I have the money my father owes you."

Remo regarded me with unsettling intensity. "I doubt that."

I frowned. He couldn't possibly see how much money I held in my hands. It was a bundle of ten and twenty dollar notes. "It's one thousand dollars."

"One thousand?" Remo asked with a laugh. "How much do you think he owes us?"

I shivered. My eyes darted to Soto again then back to Remo.

I licked my lips nervously. "He said a couple of thousand."

Remo shook his head once and pushed away from the sofa. He came closer, and I fought the urge to run. There was no way I could have outrun him anyway. He scared me more than anything ever had, and *I* had been stupid enough to face him because my father couldn't get a grip on his addiction.

"Ten thousand, and that's without interest. In total he owes us close to fourteen thousand."

My stomach plummeted. "Four thousand in interest?" I gasped. "That's usury!"

"We're the mob, Leona," Remo Falcone said, amused. He knew my name? Had Fabiano talked to him about me? *Because of my mother.*

"Every day he doesn't pay us, another five hundred of interest gets added on top."

I couldn't believe it. My father must have known he owed much more than just a couple of thousands. Did he set me up? "But . . . but I don't have that much, and there's no way I can earn enough money unless you stop adding interest."

Remo shook his head. "This isn't a negotiation, girl. Your father owes us money, and perhaps you forgot, but your mother does too. Your father was supposed to pay at midnight yesterday. He didn't." By now, Remo was only two steps away from me, and it set my body into flight mode.

"I have this." I held up my wrist with the bracelet Fabiano had given me for

Christmas. Guilt filled me. How could I even consider giving his present away?

Something in Remo's eyes shifted, and he bridged the remaining distance between us. I bumped against the door, trying to evade him, but he gripped my arm tightly and regarded the bracelet. A fire simmered in his eyes when he looked up at me. "That would settle your father's debt. An expensive piece of jewelry for someone like you."

It would settle fourteen thousand dollars? I stared down at the bracelet. Remo released my wrist. His lips twisted cruelly. "Sadly, it's too late. Your father will pay his debt in blood."

"Please," I begged. "He won't ever owe you money again."

"Are you willing to swear on it?" Remo hissed.

I knew how much an oath meant to the Camorra. And I knew it would have been a lie. I averted my eyes from Remo's cruel ones. "Please. There has to be something I can do. Don't kill him."

Remo tilted his head. My begging did nothing. "It's not me who will kill him. It's Fabiano, but you must know that ..." His voice was low and threatening.

"Isn't there something I can do?" I whispered desperately. Something flickered in his dark eyes. God, I wanted to swallow every syllable I'd just uttered. What did I say? My father sent me here to pay for his debts and I was risking my life for him.

For a long time, Remo didn't say anything.

I gave a jerky nod. "Okay. I'll just go."

Remo put a hand on the door. I sucked in a breath and backed away from him. I fumbled for my cell phone. Maybe Fabiano could help me. I didn't get far. Remo took it from my hand and glanced down at it.

"Just let me leave."

He shut off my cell with a thunderous expression. "It's too late for that, I fear." He nodded toward Soto, who came our way at once. "I think we need to set an example."

Soto gripped my arm. The excited gleam in his expression made terror soar through my veins. "The basement?" he asked with barely hidden eagerness.

Bile traveled up my throat. Remo gave a nod, his eyes slipping down to my bracelet again, recognition filling his eyes like he'd seen it before. "And, Soto, you'll wait until I give you an order before you begin. If you lay a finger on her before, I'll cut it off."

Soto pulled me down a flight of stairs and into a small room with only a mattress in one corner and a chair in the other.

"I can't wait to start, bitch. Fabiano will be fucking furious," Soto muttered then let go of me. I stumbled back against the wall. There was no escaping him.

I wasn't sure how much time passed as he undressed me with his eyes, but a low buzzing sound made me jump. Soto pulled out his mobile. Then he looked back at me with a leer. "Time to play."

CHAPTER 18

FABIANO

cursed when Griffin handed me the list of people who hadn't paid their betting debts. Greg Hall. This time he owed more than he'd be able to pay back. He was third on the list. Leona would hopefully be gone by the time I paid him a visit.

Why did this fucker have to borrow money from us?

When it was finally his turn, I parked at the curb, pissed off. I got out, but the purr of my engine had caught Hall's attention.

He spotted me through the windows. He'd probably been watching the street all day. He knew the rules. He knew the consequences. This wasn't his first time, after all. But today he'd suffer more than a few broken bones. His life would end today.

He disappeared from view, probably trying to escape. As if that was going to happen. I jogged around the building and saw him rushing out of the back door of the apartment complex. Sighing, I ran after him. His legs were shorter, and he was too out of shape to evade me.

When I caught up with him, I grabbed him by the cuff of his stupid Hawaii shirt and slammed him to the ground. He cried out as he landed hard on his back, bloodshot eyes staring up at me with trepidation. The impact already made him cry out like a pussy, so I'd have to stuff his mouth with something or else he'd alert the entire neighborhood with his screaming. I punched him hard in the ribs, making him gasp for breath. That would silence him for a while. Then I dragged him after me, hearing his desperate attempts to speak past the lack of oxygen in his lungs. "Don't. Please," he managed when we reached the apartment door.

I ignored him. If I stopped whenever someone begged me, the Camorra would have no money. And a big part of me was looking forward to torturing him for his behavior toward Leona. He caused her nothing but trouble, and he would continue to do so.

I shoved him into the apartment that he hadn't bothered locking when he ran from me. He hit the ground, and I pulled my knife. Perhaps I'd finish my work on his back first.

His eyes zeroed in on the blade in terror. "I sent Leona to settle my debt! You don't have to do this."

I froze. "What did you just say?" I stalked toward him. If he'd agreed to let his daughter handle this, he was the worst scum on Earth. He nodded and disgust washed over me. I really wanted to plunge my knife into his cowardly eyes.

"I sent Leona—"

I crouched over him, lifting him by his collar. "Where did you send her?"

"To Falcone."

I thrust my fist into his face, breaking his nose and jaw. I would have beaten him to death if I thought there was time. If Leona was on her way to Remo,

I couldn't waste a single second. "Where exactly?" Leona wouldn't walk into Remo's mansion after all.

"I told her to go to the Sugar Trap," he got out, blood dripping out of his mouth. I punched him again then jumped to my feet and gripped his collar. I dragged him toward my car.

"I told you I sent Leona! My debt will be settled!"

"Shut up!" I snarled.

I knew how much he owed us, and he knew it too. There was no way Leona had enough money.

The Sugar Trap was the worst place to send her, and I suspected he knew that. He sacrificed his own daughter to save his sorry ass. I opened the trunk and flung him inside, glaring at his terrified face in disgust as I closed it.

I raced down the Strip, only slowing when I came closer to the Sugar Trap, one of our whorehouses and the place where Remo dealt with women who gave the Camorra trouble. It wouldn't do any good if someone saw me hurrying. Remo would wonder why and put things together. Perhaps he had already.

I parked in my usual spot. Remo's Aston Martin was already parked in front and so was Soto's Buick. I hauled Leona's father out of the trunk then dragged him after me as I stalked past the guard without a greeting and crossed the public part of the whorehouse, to the back wing. He kept pleading and groveling. I found Remo in his office, as usual, not behind his desk but on the sofa, browsing through a car magazine. He didn't look up when I stepped in, but he knew it was me. He was waiting for me. I'd known him for years and knew the games he played. I'd been one of his best players for a long time. It took all of my self-control not to ask him about Leona right away. I needed to play this right or it would all be in vain.

"You're done early," he said, and when he met my gaze, there was something snake-like in his expression. I shoved Leona's father to the ground. He landed hard, his fucking beady eyes darting between Remo and me.

"The asshole told me he sent his daughter to handle his debt. I needed to check with you before I proceeded with him."

"Of course," Remo said with a cold smile. He didn't look at Hall. This was about me, about us. "It's the third time Hall is behind. His daughter offered to pay his debt."

I knew all that and didn't give a fuck. All I cared about was Leona not getting hurt.

"So you took her money?"

"I didn't ask her for money. She wouldn't be able to pay that much. But she was determined to save her father."

"Where is she?" I asked carefully. Every muscle in my body was tense because I knew if something happened to Leona, I'd fucking lose it.

"She's in the basement. Paying his debt the only way she can."

My blood ran cold. "Soto?" was all I managed.

Remo nodded but his eyes bored into my skull. "He went down with her a couple of minutes ago."

Two minutes. I didn't have much time. Leona didn't have much time. "I'm your Enforcer. Let me handle her."

Remo came up to me, steps slow and measured. And for the first time, I tried to imagine what I'd have to do to beat him, to kill him. He was like my brother, and I hated that it had gotten this far. "You never deal with women. You asked me to let Soto handle that part of the business, and I granted you your wish, Fabiano."

He was right. He never understood, but because I was like his brother he accepted my reluctance. And Remo wasn't the accepting type.

"It's different with her," I said, letting my desire show but not my protectiveness. If Remo thought this was anything but fun for me, nothing would save Leona.

Her father was still crouched on the floor, and I made a silent vow to let him suffer before I granted him death.

"I don't think you handling her will have the desired effect," Remo said. "You have been seeing her for weeks. You fucking her in my dungeon won't really send a message."

"I haven't fucked her yet. She refused me."

"Refused you?" Remo asked, as if the word meant nothing to him. His eyes became calculating. "And you let her?"

Oh, Leona, I hope you are worth it. Remo was on the hunt.

I didn't say anything. I had a feeling it would make things worse. "Let me handle her," I said calmly. I put my hand on his shoulder, and that he let it happen gave me hope. Still like brothers. "You won't regret it."

"I know I won't," he said. "But perhaps you will." He paused. "Then handle her, Fabiano." I was about to turn around and storm into the cellar to get Leona, but his hand clamped down on my forearm. He turned it so the tattoo of the Camorra was facing up. "You are my enforcer, Fabiano. You have been at my side since the beginning. You never disappoint me. Don't start now."

"And I won't," I said fiercely. "I will take care of her."

Remo gave me a warning look. "Don't disappoint me, Fabiano. She is just one woman. Remember where your loyalties lie."

I barely listened. I hurried out of the room and down the stairs. I knew I had to make it there before Soto sank his claws in her. I took the stairs two at a time. I couldn't be late.

I knew where to go. Soto always chose the same room. I didn't bother knocking. Instead, I pushed open the door to our interrogation room. "I can't wait to have you suck my cock," Soto drawled. "Fucking choice be damned."

Leona was pressed up against the wall, looking terrified, while Soto was pulling down his pants, revealing his hairy ass. Terror filled Leona's beautiful face, and for a moment I considered putting a knife in Soto's back.

"Get out," I snarled. "I'm taking over."

Soto whirled around, showing me his pitiful cock. He gave me a stunned look. "I thought you didn't like to handle women," he said mockingly. "That's why Remo gave me the job."

"I changed my mind," I growled. "Now get out before I lose my patience."

Soto shot Leona another hungry look, but then he pulled up his pants and stalked past me, muttering curses.

The door slammed shut. I knew the camera was pointed at us, recording everything. Perhaps Remo was watching. This had nothing to do with Greg Hall and everything to do with me. Remo was testing me. Remo trusted me as much as a man like him could trust anyone, like he trusted his brothers, and now he felt the need to test me.

A small part of me felt fury toward Leona for being the reason for it.

Remo had never doubted me. *Never*. And I had sworn with my own blood to never give him reason to.

Leona pushed away from the wall, looking confused and hopeful and scared all at once. "Oh, Fabiano," she whispered, relieved. "I'm so glad you came. I was so scared."

I didn't go over to her.

I wasn't the savior she'd hoped for. She took another step in my direction then stopped, looking at me with fucking hopeful eyes. Slowly, the hope disappeared. "Fabiano?" she asked in the barest whisper.

I shut off my fucking useless feelings. I would be dead without Remo. Everything I was today was thanks to him. He saved me. I couldn't try to kill him, not even for Leona. And trying would be all it was. Remo was as strong as me, and he still had his brothers at his side.

I stalked toward Leona, and for the first time she backed off. When her back hit the wall, I was in front of her. I pressed my body against hers, caging her in, and sank my nose into her hair. The camera would make it look like I was cornering her. Her sweet flowery scent reached my nose.

"Fabiano?" she murmured. Hesitantly, she put her hands on my waist as if she wasn't sure if she should hug me. That would have been the end of everything. Fuck, but I wanted to wrap my arms around her.

Fuck me. Fuck us.

"I told you I'm not good," I said quietly.

She peered up into my eyes, and I knew what she would see, exactly what I needed her to see to be convincing. Leona started trembling against me, fear eating away at what little hope was left. I pulled her arms away from my waist, grabbed her wrists, and pinned them on top her head resting against the wall. I cornered her with my body, and she allowed it. She let out a choked whimper, a confused expression on her face. She should have fought by now. This brokenhearted surrender was something I couldn't handle. There was still that stupid fucking hope there. It was worse than begging and crying. Worse than anything had ever been … because it meant she still believed there was more to me than the coldhearted killer.

Perhaps she still didn't understand what I was supposed to do to her.

I pressed my lips against her ear. "I can't spare you. We're being watched. If I don't do it, Soto will … and I can't allow that."

Fear widened her eyes as she stared up at me. "Because you don't share, right?" she whispered miserably.

I wished it were only that. "Because Soto will *break* you."

"And you won't?"

We'd been talking for too long already. Every second that passed could seal both our fates.

"As a woman, you are granted a choice, unlike men. You can pay with your blood as a man would have to or with your body," I said sharply. I'd only spoken those damn words once before and never again after that. Remo had handed over the task to Soto because I couldn't fucking do it. He allowed me that one fucking weakness.

She raised her chin, and I knew she considered choosing the first option because she'd rather suffer through pain than become like her mother. Damn it. "Leona," I whispered, leaning into her again, surprised by the despair in my voice. Careful, Fabiano.

You are my enforcer.

"Number two. I can fake that one, but not the other."

Confusion filled her face.

"Choose the second option," I murmured again.

"Two," she said, resigned but still not understanding what I had offered.

She started crying softly. I watched the tears make their silent descent over her soft freckles. Her eyes held mine, and then just like that, she nodded. "Do what you have to do."

I'd wanted her from the first second I'd laid eyes on her, had wanted to be the one to rip her innocence from her, wanted to possess her in every way possible. But not like this, not in front of a fucking camera, not hard and fast and brutally as Remo expected. Was she worth the risk?

The Camorra was my family. *My life.*

In my darkest hour, Remo had been there to pick me up. He had showed me my worth. He could have killed me. He was a monster, but so was I.

Leona held my gaze. And I made my own decision. Fuck it. "I'll try not to hurt you. Fight me and cry. It has to look real," I whispered harshly.

Confusion filled her eyes.

I shook her wrists and tightened my hold. "Play your part or we are both dead."

I gave her a warning look then gripped her hips and threw her down on the mattress in the corner. She let out a terrified scream that bounced off the walls. I didn't give her time to recover. This needed to be convincing. I hoped the long wait in the beginning hadn't raised Remo's suspicions, because I *knew* he was watching. I climbed on top off her, pinning her down with my taller body. My mouth was back on her ear. "Trust me. Because from now on, I'll have to look the monster I am with everyone else. Now fight me with all you have."

I didn't wait for her reply because it didn't matter if she agreed or not. We were past that point. I grabbed her wrists in one hand and began pushing them up when Leona finally sprang into action.

She screamed, "No," and fought against my hold, her hips bucking, legs kicking, but it was no use. I shoved her wrists hard against the floor. She gasped in pain. Damn it. Playing rough was difficult without *actually hurting* someone. I loosened my hold, knowing it wouldn't be noticeable on camera. I squeezed her breasts through her dress then moved lower and pushed my hand below her skirt. I was glad she'd allowed me to touch and see her before so this wouldn't be her first experience.

"No, please don't! Please!" she cried, so convincing that something ugly and heavy settled in my stomach. This was why Soto had been responsible for that part of the job.

"Shut up, you whore!" I snarled.

Hurt settled in her eyes. I breathed heavily. I could not take my eyes off her face, off those cornflower blue eyes, off those damn freckles. She held my gaze and I hers. One second. Two seconds. I couldn't do this, not even pretending. I felt fucking sick to my stomach. Fuck. I'd cut men into tiny pieces, had done so many horrible things that had never bothered me, but this … this I could not do. Not for real. Not for show. Never.

I let go of her wrists. Her brows furrowed. I lowered my head until my forehead rested against hers, and she released a small breath then lifted her hand and touched my cheek.

I wasn't sure how much of it the camera recorded. I didn't care.

"Fabiano?"

I wasn't sure if I could save her, save us, after this. I pulled away and straightened before I helped her to her feet. She clutched my arm, still shaking.

"What's going to happen now?" she whispered.

Remo wanted blood. He wanted confirmation that I was his soldier, that I was capable of doing what had to be done. He wanted to see my monster. And he would.

Leona would hate me for it.

CHAPTER 19

FABIANO

We headed upstairs. Remo was waiting for us. Nino was there too, and at his feet cowered Leona's father, tape over his mouth but still very much alive. Leona stiffened, but my grip on her arm kept her at my side. I wasn't sure if she'd try to run toward him otherwise.

Remo regarded Leona from head to toe. He knew, had known before he laid eyes on her. Leona trembled against me.

That Nino was here told me two things: one, Remo thought he needed reinforcement and that reinforcement wasn't going to be me and two, that reinforcement wasn't going to be me because he thought he needed reinforcement *against me.*

I released Leona but gave her a look that made it clear she needed to stay where she was. She understood.

I walked toward Remo. He didn't rise from where he was perched on the desk, but the look he gave me was one he only ever leveled at his opponents in the cage.

"So," he said tightly, "you didn't handle her."

"I didn't handle her because he is the one I should handle." I nodded toward her father. "Since when do we let out debtors get away with this shit? Since when do we let their daughters or wives pay for their crimes? Since when, Remo?" I was very close to him now, and finally he stood, bringing us to eyelevel.

"Since the moment I decided she was going to pay for her father. My word is the law."

"It is the law," I confirmed fiercely. "Because you are Capo. *My Capo*, and I've always followed your command, because you taught me the true meaning of honor and loyalty and pride." I took another step toward him so we were almost touching. "But there's nothing honorable about making an innocent woman pay for her father's debts, Remo."

His dark eyes pierced mine. I knew Nino was watching, probably with a hand on his gun. "We don't spare women."

"No, we don't spare women who are indebted to us, because they brought it upon themselves. They knew what they were getting themselves into when they asked for money. But this is different and you know it. I don't know why you feel the need to test my loyalty like that, but I ask you to reconsider. There's no reason for you to doubt me. Leona is only one woman. She means nothing to me. You are like my brother."

"Are you sure about that?" he asked in a low murmur. "Because when you look at her, she isn't just one woman."

My chest constricted. "I'm loyal to you, to the Camorra, to our cause."

"Someone will have to bleed for this," he said, and he settled back on the desk. Relief washed over me.

"And I will make *him* bleed for you."

"I know you will," he said quietly, challengingly.

I turned to her father. His eyes widened then darted over to Leona. She stood frozen. I wanted her to leave, but that wasn't what Remo wanted, and I couldn't ask for more than he'd already given. I nodded at Nino, and he understood. He moved to Leona, who took a step back. When his fingers closed around her upper arm to keep her from interfering, it took all my willpower not to snarl at him.

I prowled toward her father, who tried to scramble back but hit the couch. I yanked the tape off his mouth, and he cried out in pain.

"Fabiano, please," Leona begged.

It was either her father or her. Someone had to pay.

"When you sent your daughter to Remo to pay your debt, did you know what would happen to her? Did you know that she would bleed for you?"

His eyes darted to Leona again, looking for help.

I grabbed him by the shirt and hauled him up. "Did you know what would happen to Leona?"

"Yes!" he cried.

"And you didn't care?"

"I didn't want to die!"

"So you sent her so she could bleed and die for you?"

He gaped at me. *Oh, I would make him bleed.*

And I would enjoy every second of it. I didn't risk a look at Leona. Maybe someday she could forgive me. But I didn't think she'd ever look at me the same again. Not after what I had to do now. After what I *wanted* to do.

I extracted my knife. Her father tried to run, but I shoved him down and climbed on top of him. He struggled and I punched him. His head snapped back, but I needed to be careful not to knock him out. That just wouldn't do.

Remo's legs appeared beside me, and then he held down Hall. He gave me his twisted grin, and I felt my own lips curl. We would do this together. Together like in the beginning. I brought my knife down, and when the tip of the blade slid into Hall's stomach, parting flesh and muscle, everything else faded to black.

Remo and I did what we did best.

I wasn't sure if I'd been a monster before him, if I'd always had it in me and he only awakened that part, or if he turned me into one. It didn't matter.

When Hall's cries died and his heart stopped beating, I came back to myself. Remo and I knelt on the ground beside the body, in its blood. My hands were covered in it, and so was the knife still clutched in my hand.

Remo leaned forward, voice calm. "That's what you really are. What we both are. Do you think she can accept it?"

I didn't say anything. I was fucking scared to face Leona, to see the disgust and terror in her expression.

Remo nodded. "That's what I thought. She will leave. They all do. She's not worth the trouble. People like us are always alone." He touched my shoulder. "We are brothers."

"We are," I confirmed then finally dared to glance back at her. Leona and Nino were gone. I jerked to my feet, knife clattering to the ground.

"Where is she?"

"Nino dragged her out when she threw up because things got too rough."

I stared at the spot where she had been.

"Go clean up," Remo said. "I'll have Nino drop the body somewhere it will be found quickly."

I nodded but didn't move.

"And, Fabiano..." Remo waited until I met his gaze "...I let you refuse my order once. I let you spare her once. Remember your oath. The Camorra is our family."

I nodded again then went to change clothes before I went to search for Leona. I found her in the main room of the Sugar Trap, perched on a barstool at the bar, clutching a glass filled with a dark liquid in her hands. Nino leaned against the counter like a sentinel. She kept staring at her hands when I stopped beside her. Nino left without a word.

I reached for the glass, and she flinched away from me. There it was. Finally she reacted to my closeness the way she should have. And I fucking hated it. I took the glass and downed the burning liquid. Brandy.

"I thought you didn't drink," I said quietly.

She raised those cornflower blue eyes to me. Against her deathly pale skin, her freckles stood out even more. "Today is a good day to start, I think." She swallowed, lowering her gaze as if she couldn't bear looking at me. She was still in shock.

"No, it's not. Don't let it happen."

"Let what happen?" she echoed.

"Don't let my darkness drag you down."

Those fucking blue eyes filled with tears. I curled my hand around her wrist, ignoring her shiver, and tugged lightly. "Come on, Leona. We should leave."

For a long time, her eyes rested on my fingers. Then she finally slipped off the stool and followed.

I was a hypocrite because even as I'd warned her about my darkness, I knew I would never let her go.

LEONA

My hands shook as I wedged them between my legs. Fabiano was silent beside me as he steered his Mercedes through traffic. He was clean now.

His fingers, his hands, his clothes.

The blood was gone.

My father's blood.

A new wave of sickness washed over me, but there was nothing left in my stomach.

Things had taken a turn for the worse that I hadn't expected.

You didn't choose your family. That was what people always said. And it didn't have to define who you became, but my mother and father had managed to steer me so far off the path I planned for myself, I wasn't sure I'd ever find my way back.

And now my father was dead. Killed by the man I loved.

God help me, I still loved him.

Still?

Still. After what I'd seen, after what he'd done.

And that was the worst. I could still feel something for him after I saw what he truly was. A monster.

My father was a horrible human being—had been a horrible human being. He drove my mother to selling her body, even offered my body to Soto for his debts, and he pretty much admitted he'd let me die just so he could live. Perhaps he'd deserved death, but he didn't deserve what happened today. Nobody did.

I closed my eyes against the images of Fabiano with the knife, of the twisted look he shared with Remo. They had done this before. They *enjoyed* it.

Nino dragged me away after Fabiano began cutting my father. But the screams followed us until they were no more. I was relieved because it was over. Over for my father and over for my mother and me. No more betting debts or drunken fits. And that realization shattered me completely. I didn't miss my own father.

He set me up. I knew he was scared of the Camorra, but so was I.

Fabiano killed him.

My eyes shifted to the man beside me. His gaze was focused on the road ahead. In the past few weeks, we'd gotten to know each other—or I thought I'd gotten to know him, thought we'd built a connection. Now I wasn't sure that was real anymore.

Enforcer. The word held no meaning for me until now. I shuddered when I remembered the basement. How much horrors had those walls seen? And for how many of them was Fabiano responsible? How many people had he killed? Had he made bleed?

So much blood on his hands.

I pushed the thought aside. It led down a dark path I couldn't stomach right now. I had already dug myself into a deep hole I couldn't possibly ever get out of. Could I really love someone like him? And could someone like him *love at all?*

Love is a sickness, a weakness.

Leona is only one woman. She means nothing to me.

Those words had threatened to break me, but then Remo had said, *"Are you sure about that? Because when you look at her she isn't just one woman."*

And those words still haunted me, after everything. Tears prickled my eyes. Fabiano was a murderer.

He did it for me, so he didn't have to hurt me. He protected me. And part of me was consoled by that fact. What did that say about me?

I closed my eyes again. I had to end this, had to leave. I couldn't stay, even though I loved him, or maybe I had to leave because I did. I had to break this twisted bond, had to do it as long as the memories of today were still fresh.

"Where are you taking me?" I asked as I realized we were heading to the better parts of Vegas.

"To my apartment."

I stared blankly. Did he really think I'd spend the night in the same bed with him after what he did today?

228

You want his closeness.

Still.

After everything.

Fear filled my veins. Not of him. I pushed through it, let it feed my next words. "Have you lost your mind? I'm not going home with you after what you did."

Fabiano jerked the car to the side and hit the brakes, making me gasp from the impact of the belt. I didn't get the chance to catch my breath. He wasn't strapped in so he leaned over me, eyes furious. "Don't you realize in what kind of trouble we are? I went against Remo's orders for you. I showed weakness. He will watch my every move now. He will watch us."

"You killed my father."

"I did, so I wouldn't have to hurt you, so Remo didn't feel the need to hurt you."

"Maybe I would have preferred if you let him hurt me."

Fabiano laughed darkly, blue eyes searching my face. "You can't still believe that after today. Remo has made grown men beg for mercy, for death even."

"So have you," I whispered. "You and him, you are the same. You both enjoyed this. I saw it in your eyes." I swallowed hard.

His eyes flickered with emotion and my heart broke seeing it. "You don't even realize what I'm risking for you. You made me go against everything I ever cared about."

Everything I ever cared about.

Cared. Past tense. As in not anymore?

Deep down, I knew the answer, and it terrified me because if he felt what I felt ... if he was capable of it, leaving him would destroy not only me.

"You should just have let Soto have his way with me."

His expression was blank. He was too good at this. Too good at all things dark and dangerous. "Perhaps I should have," he said simply. "It would have spared me a lot of trouble." He twisted a strand of my hair around his finger with a strange expression on his face. "After all, who says you are worth it?"

His words didn't hurt me because I'd seen the look in his eyes down in the basement—even if I hadn't dared believe it. Remo confirmed it wasn't my imagination.

Fabiano needed to push me way. And I knew I needed to let him so I could do what had to be done. "Don't pretend you acted out of the goodness of your heart. You saved me because you wanted to be the first one *to fuck* me."

The word left a bitter taste in my mouth, but it got a reaction from Fabiano. His lips curled into a cold smile. "You are right. I will be the first to fuck you."

"Not if I have a say in the matter."

He let out a joyless laugh before he pulled the car back onto the street.

"You are a monster," I said harshly.

"I know."

Fifteen minutes later, we entered the underground parking garage. He was really taking me to his apartment. Fabiano opened the car door and held out his hand for me. I stared at it then up at his face. "Come on, Leona," he said quietly. "Don't make me carry you."

I took his hand and let him pull me to my feet. He didn't let go of me as he tugged me along toward the elevator that would take us up to his apartment.

Once we were inside the elevator, my emotions began to bubble over. Anger and terror and sadness and everything in between. "Why did you have to choose me?" I asked miserably. And *why, why, why* had my heart chosen him?

He didn't say anything, only gave me that impenetrable look. The elevator doors slid open, and he guided me into his apartment. He pulled me against his chest and kissed me fiercely, and for a second I kissed him back, kissed him with every twisted, horrid part of me that loved him.

My palms came up against his chest. "No," I said firmly and tore away from him. My pulse raced in my veins. Fabiano came around, never allowing me to pull away. Why couldn't he just let me be?

"You know," he said quietly. "I never meant for any of this to happen. You were just a poor, lonely girl. I didn't choose this, didn't choose you."

"Then stop this. Whatever it is between us, stop it. Now," I whispered, peering up at his cold, beautiful face.

He cupped my face. "Don't you think I would if I could?" His lips brushed mine. "But I can't. I won't. You are mine, and I will protect you no matter the price."

"Protect me?" I echoed.

Fabiano was a destroyer, not a protector. He was no knight in shining armor.

"And who will protect me from you?"

"You don't need protection from me. Today should have proven that."

"Today proved that you have done horrendous crimes in your past and that you are still committing atrocious acts every day ... and that you enjoy doing them."

"Leona," he said darkly. "I never lied to you. I am the Camorra's enforcer. I am pain and death. I never pretended to be anything else. Don't pretend you were ignorant to make yourself feel better."

I lowered my gaze, feeling guilty and furious because he was right.

Death. Blood. Pain.

That was what being with Fabiano meant.

And love.

I couldn't get one without the other.

That wasn't the life I'd imagined. And did he love me? Whatever he felt, whatever I had seen, whatever Remo had seen ... it wasn't love.

"Come on," Fabiano said, tugging me toward the stairs. "Let's talk in the morning. You've gone through a lot today."

What was there left to talk about in the morning? Yet I still followed.

I took a shower and Fabiano didn't join me. Perhaps he finally understood that his closeness was too much right now. I put on the T-shirt he'd laid out for me then walked into the bedroom.

Fabiano was already in bed, the covers pulled up to his waist, revealing his chest. Falling asleep against his chest had been the best thing about being with him these last few weeks. One last time, I promised myself. I slipped under the covers with him and rested my cheek against his chest, right over his heart. It beat a calm rhythm. If today's events didn't increase his heart rate, what could? His fingers stroked my upper arm, and I ran my fingertips over all the scars on his chest and stomach.

"This can't end well. It will get us killed, you know that."

Fabiano pulled me on top of his body. "Do you think I'd ever allow it? I will do anything to protect you."

"Even kill Remo?"

He grew tense. "Remo is like my brother. If he goes down, so will I."

I searched his eyes. He was serious. "You could leave Las Vegas. Start somewhere new."

Leona, stop this. End this.

He shook his head like I couldn't understand. "The Camorra is in my blood."

Blood. Screams.

I glanced at the tattoo on his forearm. The Camorra was the love of his life. Nothing could compete with that, least of all me. "Blood," I murmured.

Fabiano's eyes were like a stormy summer sky. "I will handle Remo. Don't worry about it. Now that your father is gone, things will settle down. You can continue with your life."

Gone.

Killed. Murdered. Tortured.

"Do you really believe that?" I asked. What life was I supposed to continue?

232

FABIANO

The look she gave me now was the one I'd expected in the beginning. It was a look I hated seeing now. I was risking my reputation, my life, and Remo's trust for her. All for her.

I kissed Leona hard. For a moment she froze, then she returned the kiss with the same force.

Deepening it, my hands moved down on her hips, and I rolled us over, stretching out over her. I supported my weight with my elbows as I kissed her harder. She returned the kiss with just as much need. I slid my hand under her shirt, my fingers trailing over her smooth thigh. I wanted her, never wanted anything as much in my life. She pulled away from my mouth, growing tense beneath me. "No, Fabiano," she got out from under me. "I can't do this now, not after everything that has happened."

I sucked in a deep breath. Who said there would be another chance for us? My cock was so hard it threatened to tear through my boxers. I had half a mind of ignoring her plea and just keep going. I could imagine how tight and warm she'd be, how her channel would squeeze down on my cock. Fuck. I wanted her. I wanted to have her before I faced Remo tomorrow, before I risked my life *again*. What if he changed his mind?

Her blue eyes met mine. I hated that the trusting innocence was gone from them, hated that I was the reason for it.

Fuck. What had I become?

I pressed my forehead against hers, breathing in deeply. "You'll be the end of me, Leona."

She didn't say anything. I rolled away, because staying between her legs gave me ideas I didn't need. I pulled her into my arms, and she didn't resist.

She held me just as tightly. "I won't," she murmured sleepily.

"Won't?"

"Be the end of you."

Her body went slack. I propped myself up on my elbow, trailing my fingertips over her throat, watching her sleep. I was glad she finally drifted off, glad her eyes weren't looking at me with that broken expression anymore.

She didn't understand what I'd risked for her today. She couldn't possibly understand.

I would do it again, would save her again, even if it meant risking Remo's wrath.

CHAPTER 20

LEONA

I woke to silence and an empty bed. I rolled over, staring at the rumpled sheets beside me. Burying my nose in the pillow, I inhaled Fabiano's familiar scent, letting it take me back to the time I was able to pretend I didn't know what he was.

Regret came over me. Last night when he'd wanted me, I should have let him. I should have allowed us that one night, that one moment to cherish. Too late now.

I allowed myself to lie in the feather soft bed for a few more minutes before I sat up, my legs dangling over the edge of the bed. Everything smelled fresh and clean, and the room was flooded with light. This was nothing like the places I'd grown up in. It almost seemed like a dream at times, Fabiano's attention, that someone like him could want me. I should have realized it wasn't meant to last. For girls like me, dreams always came with a price. The time for dreaming was over now.

I quickly gathered my clothes and got dressed, allowing myself a couple of seconds to admire the Las Vegas strip stretching out below the apartment. I felt uneasy about this luxury the first time I saw it. I'd seldom had more than a few bucks, and here I was standing in an apartment that had cost more than I'd make my whole life as a waitress. *"Beautiful things are always taken from you."* That was what my mother used to say. I hadn't wanted to believe her, even though this thing between Fabiano and me seemed too good to be true ... especially in a city ruled by someone like Remo Falcone. And now her warning was true.

Once in the elevator, I closed my eyes, reliving everything that had happened since I set foot in Las Vegas. I wasn't that girl anymore. Fabiano had changed me, but I couldn't change him, and I wasn't sure I wanted to.

Fabiano. He was on his way to Remo again, on his way to do the man's bidding. I was grateful that he'd protected me—that he'd saved me—but the only reason why I needed saving was because of the one thing he gave his life to: the Camorra.

My father was responsible for his debts. My father had set me up. I knew all that. But my father, at least, had his addiction as an excuse. Fabiano, however, was in control of his own actions. He chose to be Remo's enforcer. He chose the Camorra every day. He chose darkness and violence. He chose this life. And now it was my turn to make a choice.

I could admit that I was scared of what I felt for him and had been from the start. Over the years, I watched my mother fall for one horrible guy after the other, dragging her deeper and deeper into her drug addiction. Everything had started with her first bad choice: my father, who had turned her into a whore.

Fabiano was a man people always warned me about, and yet I couldn't stay away from him. His family had shaped him just like mine had shaped me. We were two sides of the same coin. Perhaps that was why I knew I needed to leave as long as it was still a possibility. Part of me didn't want to go. There was nothing out there waiting for me. I was turning my back on something I'd longed for all my life: love.

I took a bus back home, even though Fabiano always urged me to take a taxi. I was out of cash, except for the few coins I'd found on the kitchen counter in Fabiano's apartment. Yesterday, I handed Remo everything I had. Now I had to start from zero. If things kept progressing the way they were, I'd never be able to pay tuition for college.

Maybe I wanted too much out of life.

I hesitated in front of the door to our apartment. He was dead. And in some way it was my fault.

I took a deep breath before I moved inside. The smell of fresh coffee wafted over to me and relief filled me. At least Mom was there. I quickly rushed into the kitchen to find my mother hunched over a cup of coffee. She looked up. There was a dark bruise on her cheek. I touched the spot. "What happened?"

"Your father and I got in an argument yesterday morning. He wanted money, but I told him I didn't have any."

I dropped my hand. And to think that I had risked my life for him. That because of him I'd been forced to see Fabiano's darkest side.

He paid for his crimes. Fabiano made him pay.

Her glassy eyes scanned me from head to top. "Where is your father?"

"Gone," I said hoarsely. "Dad is gone."

"Gone?"

"He killed him because of me," I admitted, and it felt good to voice the truth.

I put a hand down on my mother's frail shoulder. She didn't look sad. Relief filled her eyes. "He got himself killed. Bets. Always bets and gambling. I told him it would kill him."

"Yes, but in the end Fabiano killed him because of me. For me. To protect me."

Mom's bloodshot eyes were too knowing, and for once I wanted her in a drug haze. "That the one you love? The one with the cold blue eyes?"

"Yes," I whispered.

"I thought he treated you well."

"He did," I said.

"Men like him usually don't."

"I have to leave."

"Because of him?"

Because I loved him, despite what he was.

"Because if I stay I won't get the future I've always wanted," I tell her.

"Sometimes the future we thought we wanted isn't the future we need."

I shake my head. "He isn't a man I should love. That's why I need to leave."

Mom tilted her head. "Can't run from love."

It made no sense talking to her about this. Every life choice of hers had been a mistake. We both knew it. "You have to come with me, Mom. You can't stay here alone."

She shook her head. "I've got to pay off my debts to the Camorra. And I like it here. This apartment is better than the last one we had."

"It's Dad's apartment."

"Now it's mine," Mom said.

"Mom…" I gripped both of her shoulders, trying to make her see reason "…if you stay here, I can't protect you."

She smiled. "You have no business protecting me, Leona. I am your mother."

"Mom—"

She stood. "No, for once, let me be the mother. If you have to leave, then do it. But I can't run again."

"The Camorra will hurt you if you don't pay them. You should come with me, Mom. We can start over."

"Leona, it's too late for me to start over. And what can they do to hurt me that hasn't been done to me before? I've lived through it all, and I'm still here."

I stared at her. She was still here, but only because she numbed everything with drugs.

"Has he hurt you?"

It took a moment before I understood whom she meant. "Fabiano? He hasn't hurt me. But he hurts other people."

"If he's good to you, why leave?"

Fabiano had been the first person to take care of me, but he was also the man taking me down a path I shouldn't follow.

I reached for the cup of coffee. My hands shook as I brought the cup up to my mouth and took a long sip.

I had to leave. I closed my eyes against the sense of hopelessness that washed over me. I'd never really thought Las Vegas was my final destination, but I'd hoped I could use it as my starting point for something new and better.

Now I was even worse off than when I arrived in this damned city with my backpack and flip-flops. I didn't have any savings and not only that, now I lost my heart to a man whose own heart only beat for the Camorra. A man who was brutal and dangerous. A man who would eventually be my death because he couldn't possibly keep me safe and not betray his oath.

Still a small, stupid voice asked the same question my mother had: *Why leave?* That was probably the same voice my mother listened to every time she'd gone back to a pimp after he apologized for beating her to a bloody pulp. Perhaps Fabiano had been right on the night of our first encounter, that our DNA determined most of our decisions. Perhaps my mother's genes would always prevent me from living a normal life.

My eyes were drawn back to her wiry form hunched over the table again. She wasn't looking at me anymore. Instead, she was peeling off more of red her nail polish. Her hands were shaking. She needed a fix. She raised her eyes.

"You don't have any money for me before you leave?"

No. This wasn't my future. "I'm sorry, Mom."

She nodded. "It's okay. Just leave and be happy."

Be happy.

I didn't say anything. I grabbed a quick shower, feeling a bone-deep tiredness that didn't have anything to do with sleepless nights. I was leaving Las Vegas behind. I was leaving Fabiano behind and all that he stood for: blood and darkness and sin.

I leaned in the doorway to the kitchen. "I'm leaving," I told my mother.

She looked up. "And you won't come back?"

"I can't."

She nodded as if she understood, and perhaps she did. After all, we moved after each one of her breakups and never returned.

"I have to go now," I said. I went over to her and kissed her cheek. She smelled of smoke and faintly of alcohol. I didn't know if I'd ever see her again.

Thirty minutes later I arrived at Roger's arena. I headed directly for Cheryl, who was as usual early. Her affair with Roger kept her busy until the early mornings most days. Sometimes I thought she lived at the bar. The moment she spotted me stark relief filled her face, and she rushed over to me, grabbed my arm, and dragged me toward a booth.

"Are you alright, chick?" she asked in a worried tone. I was startled by her concern. She pulled back. "Heard what happened to your father."

I stiffened, doubting she had heard what really happened.

"It was Fabiano, wasn't it?"

I looked away.

"I told you he was dangerous, chick. But don't blame yourself for what happened to your father. He had it coming for a long time. It's a miracle he lasted that long with all the gambling."

"Can you give me some money?"

She narrowed her eyes. "What happened to the money you earned? Did your no-good bastard of a father spend it on bets?" She crossed her arms over her chest as if that would make her insulting a dead man any better.

"Please, Cheryl." I didn't tell her I'd pay her back because I didn't think I could. I was never returning to Las Vegas, and if I sent her money, Fabiano would trace it back to me.

"You wanna run, right?"

I nodded. "I have to."

She pressed her lips together. "He won't be happy about it."

"It's my life. My choice."

Cheryl touched my cheek in an almost motherly gesture. "Chick, it stopped being your choice the moment he first laid eyes on you and decided he wanted to have a piece. He won't let you go unless he loses interest."

"I have to leave," I said again.

"What happened to your father finally made you see what kind of man he is?" She must have seen something on my face because her expression softened. "Did he hurt you too?"

I bit my lip with a small shake of my head. I couldn't trust her. What happened between Fabiano and me had to remain my secret. How could I explain to her that I'd fallen for someone like him?

"If I give you money and he finds out …" She trailed off.

I hadn't even considered that. I pulled away and nodded. "You're right. I can't drag you into this. You warned me from the start. I didn't want to listen.

Now I have to deal with the consequences."

She sighed then grabbed her purse and pulled out a few bills. "One hundred enough for you?"

I searched her face. Did she really want to do this?

She thrust the money at me. "Don't give me that puppy dog look, chick. Just take the money and run as fast as you can ... and don't you dare come back."

I took it hesitantly then pulled Cheryl into a tight hug. After a moment of surprise, she squeezed me back. "Can you keep an eye on my mother? I know it's a lot to ask, but—"

"I will," she said firmly then pushed me away. "Now go."

And I did. I turned around and didn't look back.

CHAPTER 21

FABIANO

'd texted Leona twice, but she didn't reply. I wanted nothing more than to go to her at once, but I couldn't disappoint Remo again. This morning he acted as if everything was okay between us, but I was wary.

Still, I needed to see her, needed to see if that broken look from yesterday was gone. I couldn't think about anything else. I stood up from crouching over the men on the floor. "Today's your lucky day. I can't spare any more time for you," I said as I sheathed my knife. I went over to the washbasin and began cleaning my hands. It took a while before the water was clear.

The man lifted his bloody face from the ground. "I swear I'll pay tomorrow. I swear. I'll go to my brother …"

"I don't give a fuck where you get your money. Tomorrow we get our money or you'll spend more quality time with my knife."

He blanched.

I left him in his pitiful state and jogged to my car. I tried calling Leona again, but it went directly to her voicemail. What if Remo had changed his mind after all?

I called him as I headed toward Roger's Arena.

He answered after the second ring. "Done?"

"Yes, done. Is there anything else you need me to handle?"

There was a pause. "Come over later. Nino, Adamo, and Savio will be there. I'll order pizza and we can watch some old fights."

"Salami and peppers for me," I said then hung up. Remo didn't have Leona. He was willing to forget yesterday.

Then why was she ignoring me?

I knew why. After she had fallen asleep in my arms last night, I thought she could forgive me for what I'd done, for what I had to do because her asshole father didn't leave me a choice.

I pulled up in front of Roger's arena. Her shift began about one hour ago. I entered the bar. There were only few customers at the tables. They looked my way before whispering among themselves. Everyone knew about the bloody message Remo had left for our other debtors. Hall's corpse was a good warning. Most of them had paid their debts in the morning.

My eyes scanned the bar area, but instead of Leona's amber curls, I spotted horribly dyed black hair behind the counter. Cheryl, if I remembered correctly.

I stalked over to her. She straightened and put on a fake smile, but the fear in her eyes screamed at me. "Where is Leona?" I demanded.

"Leona?" she asked, puzzled, like she didn't know who I was talking about. One look from me, and she quickly said, "She didn't show up. I had to take over her shift. Roger is pissed."

"I don't give a fuck what Roger is," I snarled, making her recoil.

I stared at her for a few heartbeats. She squirmed under my gaze. "You sure you don't know where she could be?"

"She's a colleague, not a friend. I keep my nose out of other people's business. It's safer."

I whirled around and left. Where the hell was Leona?

I raced toward the apartment complex she lived in and hammered my fist against the door. The moment Leona's mother opened it a gap, I pushed inside. She stumbled back on her heels, colliding with the wall. She was only wearing a thong, revealing too much of her used-up body, and a moment later I realized why. A fat guy emerged from another room, only in white briefs, sporting a fucking boner.

"Where is she?" I growled.

Leona's mother blinked. She was fucking drugged out.

Her john stared at me with an open mouth. It annoyed the fucking crap out of me. I gripped his throat and smashed him against the wall, making him sputter. Then I looked up at Leona's mother again. "I'll give you ten seconds to tell me where she is, or by God, I will make you watch me skin this asshole alive."

Terror shook his frame.

Leona's mother didn't seem to care. Her lipstick was smeared across her left cheek as if she'd wiped her mouth. I looked from her to her john, my lips curling with disgust. She probably wouldn't mind me cutting him to pieces. I shoved him away then advanced on her. I didn't like hurting women, and Leona would definitely never forgive me if I hurt her mother, but I needed to find her. That left me at an impasse. I tried to calm the fuck down and focus. Tried to read her as if we were facing off in the cage.

I softened my expression. "I protected your daughter. Your husband—"

"Ex-husband," she corrected.

"I got rid of him so he couldn't hurt you or Leona again."

I could tell that her resolve was slipping away, but it still wasn't enough to tell me what I wanted to know. I reached into my back pocket and pulled out two hundred dollars. I held it out to her. "Take it." She did, but she still hesitated. "I could give you some drugs every now and then ... for free."

Her eyes lit up. And I knew I won. Drugs won over her need to protect her daughter. "She left," she said in that raspy voice. "She packed her things and left about two hours ago. I don't know where. I didn't ask her."

"Are you sure you don't know?" I asked in a low voice.

"The stupid whore barely remembers her name or how to suck a cock," her john muttered, trying to side with me to save his ass. He was trying to get back up, but I shoved him to the ground and unsheathed my knife, cold fury burning in my stomach. "Did I ask for your opinion? Next time you interrupt us, I'll have to give you a taste of my knife, got it?"

Leona's mother met my gaze. "Leona went to the bus station. That's all I know. I swear." I searched her face. She was telling the truth. "So will you give me meth?"

"I will," I said, disgusted.

"What do you even want with her?" Leona's mother asked.

"She is *mine*," I told her.

"Don't hurt her. She loves you."

Shock shot through me. "You don't know what you're talking about."

She didn't say anything, and I stormed out of the apartment. I hurried into my car and hit the gas. Was she running from me? Did she really think I would let her?

She loves you.

If she did, she wouldn't run. I remembered Remo's words after we'd killed Hall. That people always left. Leona had left too.

I stopped the car at the bus station. One of the bus drivers honked because I was barring his way. When he spotted me as I got out, he quickly swerved the bus around my car and almost hit another bus.

I went to the ticket office.

"What can I do for you?" an older woman drawled in a bored voice.

I slid my mobile with a photo of Leona on the screen over to her. "Where did she go?"

The woman looked down at the screen then shook her head. "I can't tell you—"

"Where?" I repeated slowly.

She raised her eyes to mine. She didn't recognize me. I pushed back my shirt and showed her the tattoo on my forearm. If she lived in Vegas for more than a few weeks, she knew exactly what it meant.

"I . . . I think she took the bus to San Francisco. It left ten minutes ago."

"Are you certain? I'd hate to waste my time." I took my phone back and stashed it in my pocket.

She nodded.

It took me ten more minutes to find the bus. I positioned myself in front of it and hit the breaks. The bus driver honked at me and tried to pass me on the left. I mirrored his move, so he had no choice but to come to a halt behind me.

I jumped out of the car at the same time as the driver opened the bus door. He was pulling his trousers that were way too big up over his paunch as he walked down the steps, shouting, "Have you lost your fucking mind? I'm calling the police!"

I ignored him and tried walking past him into the bus. His hand shot out, and he grabbed me by the arm. Then he swung his fist at me.

Wrong move, buddy. I brought my forearm up, dodging his punch, then rammed my elbow into his face, hearing and feeling the bones break. He sagged to his knees with a muffled cry. "Stay there. One more move, and you'll never see your family again."

He gave me a sideways glance, but after catching sight of my tattoo, he was too clever to act on his anger. This time he didn't stop me as I took the steps up into the bus. My eyes wandered the rows of seats until they came to rest on familiar amber curls in the second to last row.

I ignored the staring crowd and headed toward Leona, who watched me like I was a demon risen from hell. I stopped in front of her and held my hand out. "Come."

"I'm leaving Las Vegas," she said, but her words lacked conviction. Her blue eyes seemed to see into the deepest, darkest parts of my soul, and I knew she hated what she saw. Love. No, she couldn't love me.

"No, you are not. We have to talk. You are leaving the bus with me *now.*"

"Hey, listen, dude, if the lady doesn't want to be with you, you have to grow a pair and accept it," said a guy who looked like he had no fucking care in the world. Some backpacker kid who looked like he came from a nice family and had had a sheltered childhood but was now out for some adventure. I could give him more than that.

Some of the bravado slipped from his face. He swallowed.

Leona practically jumped from her chair, gripping my arm, fingernails digging in. I averted my eyes from backpacker kid and turned to her.

"I'm coming with you. Just … just let's go now," she whispered.

I took her backpack from her and gestured for her to walk ahead of me. She did without protest. Nobody else tried to stop me, especially backpacker kid.

Outside, a police car had pulled up beside the bus. The police officers were standing with the bus driver, beside my car, talking into their radio set. Probably checking my license.

Leona paused and gave me a questioning look. "You seem to be in trouble."

I put my hand on her lower back, ignoring the way she shied away from my touch. She stared stubbornly ahead, not giving me a chance to read her face. I could tell that the only reason why she was cooperating at all was that there were too many people around that I could potentially hurt.

The police officer lowered his radio set when he noticed me. He said something to his colleague. Then they gestured at the bus driver to follow them. He looked stunned as he pointed in my direction. The older police officer yanked down the man's arm and said something angrily then nodded back toward the bus.

Leona followed the scene with an incredulous expression. "Even the police?" she asked horrified.

I opened the car door for her. She hesitated.

"Las Vegas is ours."

And you are *mine*.

She sank down on the leather seat, and I closed the door. After I'd thrown her backpack in my trunk, I slipped behind the steering wheel and started the engine.

"Where are you taking me?" she asked.

"Home."

"Home?"

"To your mother. That's your home for now, right?"

She frowned. "I'm not going back there. I'm leaving Las Vegas."

"I told you you're not."

"Stop the car." She began shaking beside me. "Stop the car!" she screamed. If anyone except for Remo had taken that tone with me, they would have regretted it thoroughly.

I pulled into a parking lot and shut the engine off before turning to face her.

She was glaring at the windshield, and her fingers clutched her knees so hard her knuckles were turning white. "You can't make me stay," she got out.

"I can and I am," I told her. I knew I should have let her leave, should have given her the chance to move on, to find a better life, but I couldn't.

"Haven't you done enough already?" she asked in an angry whisper.

I raised my eyebrows. "I've never done anything to you."

"Do you really believe that?"

"I found your mother for you. I saved your life."

"You killed my father," she hissed.

"Don't tell me you miss him. Your mother definitely doesn't."

She paled as if I hit too close to home. "You dragged me into your darkness."

"I didn't *drag* you into anything. I didn't force you to go on that first date. I didn't force you to kiss me or to let me lick and finger you. You were a willing participant, and we both know you enjoyed it. My darkness turned you on."

Her eyes grew wide, but she didn't deny it. She couldn't. I leaned very close to her, relishing in that sweet scent of hers. Was she making me out to be the bad guy in this? Really? Did she not realize what I was putting on the line? Remo was going to be even more suspicious in the future. I was risking my status and what was I getting in return?

She pushed me away from her. "I will try to leave again and again. You can't always be there to stop me."

"Perhaps you should remember that your mother still owes us four thousand dollars."

She froze. "Are you threatening to kill her too?"

"No," I said. "Just reminding you that she needs someone who makes sure she pays us back." I was a fucking bastard for using her mother against her, but I'd do anything to stop Leona from leaving, even this.

"Just tell me what you want from me. You want me to sleep with you? Would that settle my mother's debt?" She said it with so much disgust that it set my veins aflame with fury.

"Do you really think fucking you once is worth that much? Leona, believe me, it's not. For you to pay off four grand, you'll have to let me have your pussy for a long time."

She slapped me hard, catching me by surprise. I grabbed her hand, my fingers tight around her thin wrist. I jerked her toward me, so our faces were inches apart. "This once. Only this once," I said in a low voice. "Never raise your hand against me again."

She glared at me with tear-filled eyes. "I hate you."

Those words weren't new to me, but coming from her . . .

"I can deal with hate. The sex is so much better when hate's involved."

"I'm never going to sleep with you, Fabiano. If that means I'm breaking some Camorra rule, then so be it. Torture me if you must, but I won't be yours. Not now, not ever."

I could tell that she was serious, but she knew nothing of torture. I leaned close to her ear. "We'll see about that."

She jerked open the door and fled the car.

"Don't forget your backpack," I called through the open window, popping the trunk. She went to the back and picked it up. "And, Leona," I said in warning. "Don't ever try to run from me again. I won't let you go, and I'll find you wherever you go."

She watched me, shoulders slumping, her expression desperate. "Why?" she murmured. "Why won't you let me leave? I'm not worth the bother."

Remo had said the same. And I knew they were right. She was nothing. I'd fucked so many women and could have many more. Leona was nothing to write home about.

"You're right. You aren't."

She flinched as if I'd gutted her. Those hurt blue eyes were what gutted me. She nodded then turned toward the apartment complex.

I almost called out to her, but what would I have said?

I'm sorry. The idea of you leaving me is the worst torture I can imagine. Be the woman Aria gave me that bracelet for.

Stay, even if I'm not worth it.

CHAPTER 22

LEONA

I practically ran back home, my heart beating in my throat from anger and hurt. I couldn't believe what he said to me. Did he really mean it?

I was breathless when I arrived at the apartment. I unlocked the door and froze, on my way to my bedroom. Grunting and moans were coming from my father's bedroom. Was my mother already using it for work? He hadn't been dead for more than twenty-four hours, and she had moved on.

I hammered against the bedroom door until she finally opened it, dressed in a bathrobe with nothing beneath it.

"Leona?"

A hairy man, at least seventy, was sprawled on the bed, completely naked. I whirled around and stormed into the kitchen, holding on to the counter in a death grip.

Tears burned my eyes.

I could hear Mom's shuffling behind me. "Did you return because of that man? He seemed really intent on finding you. Looks like you really got under his skin," Mom said as she stopped beside me. I had a hard time ignoring her skinny nakedness.

The only way to get under Fabiano's skin was with a knife. It shouldn't have come as a surprise that my mother took Fabiano's possessiveness as a sign of him caring for me. She had a habit of making that mistake with her past boyfriends. "He didn't let me leave. I didn't want to return."

"Perhaps it's for the best."

I searched her face. "You told him I went to the bus station?"

She finally closed her bathrobe. "I think he really cares about you."

"What did he do? Did he threaten you?"

She looked embarrassed.

"He gave you what? Money? Drugs?"

"He promised to give me meth every now and then. For free, Leona. But I wouldn't have told him anything if I didn't think he meant well." Mom touched my hand. "It's not a bad thing to be with someone like him, especially if he is good to you. He holds power. He can protect you. What's so bad about being with him?"

"Mom, Fabiano killed Dad. Don't you remember?"

Mom's hand tightened on mine. "I do remember, but I also remember the first time I had to sell my body, back when we lived in San Antonio and your father owed one of the local MCs money. He asked me to help him, but behind my back he had already told their president I would spread my legs to pay off his debt. You were only a baby, and I was still recovering from giving birth to you. Five of them. I had to sleep with five of them, had to endure their filthy hands touching me everywhere. They took more than was agreed upon. And it was fucking painful, but you know what? Afterward, your father asked if I would fuck him too. I hated him. But he promised it was only this once. It wasn't. Next time he owed money, I had to do it again, and that time they gave me meth, and I took it because it made me forget. So yes, I remember that Fabiano killed your father ... and I am thankful. While I was working the street, they told me what happened to him. All I could think was that I wished I could have been there to see it because he destroyed me. And I was never there for you because of it. I was a horrible mother."

I was speechless. I just stared at her with my mouth gaping.

"Your father only protected himself. That's all he cared about, saving his own ugly ass. So if you tell me that Fabiano kills someone to *protect you*, I'll tell you it could be worse. Would Fabiano ever make you pay off his debts with your body?"

"No," I said with conviction. "He would kill anyone who dared to touch me."

"Good."

"Hey, are you coming back? I paid you forty dollars!" my mother's john shouted.

Mom sighed. "I have to get back to *him*."

I watched her scurry back into the bedroom. Slowly, I loosened my death grip on the counter. I needed to figure out a way to get the money my mother owed the Camorra so she could stop selling her body. If I kept working in Roger's Arena, I would make enough money to pay for the apartment, food, and her drugs. She'd never have to bear anyone's touch again. I didn't want to think about what she said about Fabiano. Even before her words, back when I sat in the bus, I wondered if I should really leave him. If I should give up the chance of love. But Fabiano's harsh words today had taken that decision off my chest. This wasn't about love, not for him at least.

I pulled the rest of the money Cheryl had loaned me from my pocket. I still had fifty dollars left. Not much. But it could turn into more.

I grabbed my backpack again and headed out, glad for the silence in the bedroom. If I had to listen to my mother doing that old bastard, I'd lose it.

Cheryl's face fell when I walked into the bar. She dropped what she was doing and staggered toward me, ignoring the few customers waving at her to serve them. Mel took over quickly. Cheryl gripped my arm and pulled me behind the bar. "What are you doing here? Shouldn't you be gone by now?"

"Fabiano caught me," I said quietly. I didn't need people to overhear. I could tell from the looks people were giving me that they were already talking about me because of what happened to my father.

"Oh fuck." She sighed. "I told you."

"I know."

"You know, if he doesn't let you leave, maybe you need to beat him with his own weapons. Go along, let him have fun, give him what he wants until he doesn't want it anymore. Can't be that hard?"

I looked away.

"Or is he some kind of sadistic bastard in the bedroom too?"

I didn't say anything. I knew Fabiano wouldn't appreciate me talking about these kinds of things. For some reason, I didn't want to betray his trust, and I was uncomfortable talking about it with her. Because no matter what he'd said during our last encounter, he showed a gentler side when he was with me, a side he didn't want people to know about.

Sleeping with Fabiano didn't scare me for the reasons Cheryl suspected. He had been a far cry from sadist in the bedroom.

"I'll give you your money back as soon as Roger pays me, okay?" I told her.

She shrugged. "I don't care about the money. I wish it would have helped you."

I smiled. I'd never forget she was willing to help me. "Where is Griffin?"

Her eyebrows shot up. "Don't go down that road. It's a slippery one. You saw where it got your father."

255

She didn't have to tell me. I remembered what had happened to my father, had relived it in vivid color … repeatedly. But after what Mom had told me today, I wasn't broken up over his death anymore. At least not because he was gone. I only wished I didn't have to see Fabiano do what he'd done. "I know what addiction does to people, and I have no intention of making betting a habit, believe me."

"Nobody ever does." She shrugged. "He's in the booth behind the cage."

"Thanks," I said then made my way to Griffin. He sat with his gaze glued to his iPad while he pushed fork after fork of fries into his mouth. I sat down on the bench across from him. He looked up then back down, muttering, "I don't need anything."

"I'm not here to serve you," I said quickly.

I pushed the fifty dollars over to him. "I want to bet against Boulder."

Griffin raised one grey eyebrow then nodded. Boulder had won every fight in the last couple of weeks. He was rumored to be Fabiano's next opponent if he won tonight. And everyone was certain he would win tonight.

"That's one to twenty," he said calmly.

So much money. "Can I bet money I don't have?"

"You can get a credit from us and use it for your bet," Griffin said then pointed at my wrist. "Or you could put that down for a bet. I'd give you five hundred."

"It's worth much more," I muttered.

He shrugged. "Then sell it somewhere else."

I fingered the delicate gold chain. "It's not for sale." Stupid. Stupid. Stupid. For some silly reason, I didn't have the heart to sell Fabiano's gift.

"Just give me two hundred as a credit." Indebting myself to the Camorra, what a day. If Boulder lost tonight, then Mom would be free … and Fabiano wouldn't be able to hold her debt against me anymore.

FABIANO

I had to look a second time, unable to believe my eyes. Leona was handing over money to Griffin, our bookie. I'd only come to Roger's arena to see if Leona already returned to work and to watch Boulder's fight. I stalked toward them. "What's going on here?"

Griffin nodded a greeting at me. "Earning money like I'm supposed to."

Leona gave me an indignant look.

"How much did she bet?"

"Fifty in cash and two hundred in advance against Boulder."

I shot her a look. Boulder was one of the best. He came directly after me and the Falcone brothers. He wouldn't lose his fight. "She's not betting," I ordered.

Griffin hesitated with his fingers against his iPad, finally looking up to me. A frown knitted his gray brows together.

"I am," Leona interrupted. "My money is as good as anyone's."

People around were starting to stare. I grabbed her by the arm and pulled her up from the leather booth, away from Griffin.

"Does that mean the bet is still on?" he shouted. That was why Remo liked him. He was always focused on the job at hand, never one to be distracted.

"Yes," Leona shouted in reply.

I dragged her toward the back and then downstairs into the storage room, seething. Only when the door shut behind us did I let go of her. "Have you lost your fucking mind?"

"I need money to pay my mother's debts off, remember?" she muttered. I staggered toward her, backing her into the wall. She was driving me insane. "And you think you can do that by making new debts? Boulder is going to win, and you'll lose not only the fifty you handed over but you'll be indebted with two hundred more. I don't think you have that, and soon it'll be twice as much."

She gave me a 'so what?' look. "I know what it means to be indebted to the Camorra." For the first time, she rolled the r's the same way I did. "I saw what it means to be indebted to *your Capo*."

I pressed my palms against the wall beside her head, glaring down at her. "You have seen what it means to be indebted to Remo, but you have never *felt* what it means to be indebted to us. There's a world of a difference between those two scenarios."

She smiled joylessly. No. So wrong on her freckled face. These fake smiles were for others to have, not for her. "And who's going to make me feel what it means? Who's going to remind me of my debts? Who's Falcone going to send to do his dirty work? Who will he send to break my fingers or take me back to that basement?"

I didn't say anything.

"Who will be the one to make me bleed and beg, Fabiano? Who?"

She shook her head, looking crushed. "You are his enforcer. His bloody hand. You are the one I have to fear, right?"

She straightened her spine and reached for the knife in my chest holster. I let her do it. She held my gaze as she pulled it out. "Who's going to pierce my skin with this knife? Who's going to draw my blood with this blade?"

She pressed the tip of the knife against my chest. "Who?" The word was a mere whisper.

I leaned closer, even as the blade cut through my shirt and skin. Leona drew it back, but I moved even closer. "I hope you'll never find out," I murmured. "Because it sure as hell won't be me, Leona."

She exhaled, and I crashed my lips against hers, my tongue demanding entrance. And she opened up, kissing me back almost angrily. The knife fell to the ground with a clatter as I slipped my hand between us, into her panties, until I found her hot center already wet. I stroked my fingers over her clit, making her gasp into my mouth. I slid my finger into her tight heat. So fucking hot.

She tensed at the foreign intrusion but softened around me as I pressed the heel of my palm against her bundle of nerves. I finger-fucked her slowly, allowing her to grow used to the sensation. "I don't want to see you placing a bet ever again. You hear me? And no other messed-up ways of earning money either. I won't always be able to protect you."

She huffed, her eyes glazed over with pleasure as I pumped into her slowly with my finger. "How am I supposed to pay back my mother's debt? Or perhaps you don't want me to so you can blackmail me with it?" Her voice was shaky with desire, the sexiest sound in the world.

I stroked my knuckles over her side up to her breast and brushed her nipple through her shirt, feeling her shiver against my touch. She was getting close. "This is a good start." I was *teasing* her.

She flinched, forcing me to pull my finger away. "No," she hissed like a wounded animal. "I told you no and that stands. You said it yourself: I'm not worth your time. I'm nothing, remember?"

I shook my head. "You aren't nothing." If she were, Remo wouldn't be breathing down my neck.

"What am I then, Fabiano?"

I leaned down and kissed her slowly, letting her scent and taste engulf my senses, before I drew back. Her cheeks were flushed. "You are mine."

I stepped away, turned around, and left her alone in the storage room.

LEONA

"You are mine."

I watched him leave, stunned. For a moment, he looked at me like I was inexplicably precious.

Was this about more than him wanting to own me?

Don't be stupid.

He was a killer. A monster. He was Falcone's right hand man. He was his *enforcer.*

I shuddered at the idea of what he did to people on Falcone's orders. He wasn't the cute guy I'd taken him for the first time I'd seen him. How could I have ever taken him for anything other than a killer? Fabiano was many things, but cute and kind weren't among them. And yet I had fallen for him. What did that say about me?

This city was rotten, corrupt, and brutal. The Devil had his claws sunk deeply into Vegas soil, and he wasn't letting go. If I wanted to survive in this city, I had to play dirty like anyone else. I glanced down at my watch. Three hours until the final match, until Boulder would have to earn me my money back. Fabiano had said it himself: he couldn't always protect me, and I didn't want him to. I needed to take things into my own hands. Something on the ground caught my eye. Fabiano's knife. I picked it up.

I quickly rushed back up the stairs, searching the bar for any sign of Fabiano but he was gone. Relieved, I hurried toward Cheryl. "I need to leave for a while. I'll be back soon."

"Hey!" she called after me, but I was already on my way out.

I returned one hour later with a few of my mother's pills in my pocket. They were the ones she took when she couldn't get her hands on meth. They made her dizzy and her heart beat like drums in her chest. I hoped they'd do the same to Boulder.

My nerves were frayed as the second to last fight started. I hadn't seen Boulder yet. And if he didn't show up early for his fight, I wouldn't be able to hand him the bottle of water I prepared for him.

"What's the matter with you tonight?" Cheryl took the glass filled with beer from my hand. The foam head had dwindled. She tossed it into the sink then poured a new one and gave it to the man at the end of the bar.

Then the barrel-chested, bald man known as Boulder finally entered the bar and made his way toward the changing room. I took the bottle from the backpack beneath the bar and another untouched one for his opponent before I followed him. I glanced around before knocking on the door. People were occupied with the fight.

No sound came from inside, but I pushed the handle down and stepped in.

Boulder was sitting on the bench, staring down at the floor in concentration. He looked up, and I held the bottle out for him. He didn't take it, only nodded to the bench beside him. I was about to put it there when I noticed the white substance that had gathered at the bottom of the bottle. I gave it a quick shake then set it down beside him.

I waited a moment, but he didn't move to take it. His opponent came out of the toilet, and I handed him the other bottle.

I turned around and left. I always brought the fighters water, but I didn't hover to see them drink it. When I slipped out, I released a nervous breath then quickly went behind the bar before someone noticed something was off.

When Boulder emerged for his fight, he was holding the bottle in his hand. If he didn't drink it, I'd be digging myself a deeper hole. He climbed into the ring and raised the bottle then spilled some of the liquid over his head.

I held my breath, releasing it when finally he lifted the bottle to his lips and emptied it.

It took a while for the pills to take affect and the change was subtle. Hopefully subtle enough that no one would suspect anything. It merely looked as if he was lacking concentration, as if he was dazed, which could be explained by the hits his opponent landed against his head.

When Boulder went down and eventually surrendered, I could have died from relief. I waited for the uproar to settle down and most of the guests to leave before I approached Griffin. He handed me five thousand dollars, and the feel of the crisp bills soothed my nerves.

"This is your lucky day, I suppose," he said.

I nodded, suddenly terrified that he might be suspicious. I turned and left before someone else saw me with Griffin.

Grabbing my backpack, I stuffed the money inside and headed for the backdoor. What if this had been a huge mistake? If someone found out, I'd be dead.

Fabiano would be waiting for me in the parking lot, and I didn't want to face him now, not until I was sure I could convincingly lie about today. I stepped through the backdoor and breathed in the cold night air, trying to stifle my panic.

"Funny coincidence," said someone behind me.

I whirled around to find Soto a few steps behind me.

"You won quite a bit of money today."

I tightened my grip on my backpack. I still had Fabiano's knife buried inside there somewhere, but I remembered how little it had helped me against Fabiano. Soto wasn't Fabiano. I never saw him fight, but I suspected he had more practice handling knives than I did.

He moved closer. "Makes me wonder how you got so lucky. I'm sure Remo will wonder about it too … if I tell him."

I reached inside my backpack then drew the knife.

He laughed. "Ever since the basement, I couldn't stop imagining how it would be to bury my cock in your pussy. It's a pity that Fabiano got the honor of handling you."

"Don't come closer, or I'm going to—"

"Kill me?" He leered.

"Soto." Fabiano's voice sliced through the dim light of the back alley. I turned slowly. Fabiano was stalking toward us. Dressed in a black shirt and black slacks, his tall form blended in with the darkness.

Soto had his hand on the gun in the holster around his waist, his narrowed eyes on Fabiano. "I saw her bring Boulder water before the fight, and then he loses."

"She's a waitress, Soto. She serves everyone drinks. She served me water before my fights too," Fabiano said condescendingly as he positioned himself between Soto and me.

"She served you more than that from what I hear. She bet money against him and he lost. Remo won't believe it's a coincidence. Remo will love that. Apparently, you didn't do a good job in the basement, fucking some sense into her. This time I'll make sure Remo lets me handle it. And he will after your fuck up."

"You are probably right," Fabiano said slowly, eyes on me. I couldn't look away. His eyes were burning with emotion. "He will let you handle her." He held his gun in his hand, but Soto couldn't see it.

I didn't say anything.

He put a silencer on the barrel with practiced ease.

Heaven help me. I'd let him kill a man for me. Again. But this time I could have stopped him.

Fabiano held my gaze as if he waited for me to protest. I didn't.

Then he whirled around and pulled the trigger. Soto's head was shoved backwards by the force, and then he tumbled to the ground. I stared at his unmoving form. I didn't feel anything. No regret. No relief. No triumph. Nothing.

Fabiano dismantled the silencer from the gun and returned both to the holster around his chest. Then he walked up to me, took the knife from my shaking hands before touching a palm to my cheek. I looked up at him. "You killed him."

He killed one of Remo's men. Another Camorrista. For me.

"I promised I'd protect you, and I will honor my promise no matter the price."

The words hung between us.

"Leave. Go to my apartment and wait there for me. Take a taxi."

He held out his keys. I took them without a word of protest. He released me and I moved back slowly. "What are you going to do?"

"I'll handle this," he said, frowning at the dead body.

I swallowed then turned on my heel, hurrying toward the main road to catch a cab. I had to trust in Fabiano to handle this, to get us out of the mess I'd caused.

It felt strange entering his apartment without him. My body shook with adrenaline as I walked up the stairs to the bedroom. Fabiano had killed for me. And I had let him. I could have warned Soto. A word of warning was all it would have taken, but I had remained silent. And there was no guilt on my part.

Why wasn't there any guilt?

You're finally playing by their rules, Leona. That's why.

I took a long, hot shower to calm my frayed nerves. When I returned to the bedroom, dressed in one of Fabiano's crisp white shirts, almost one hour had passed. I'd hoped Fabiano would be here by now.

Worry twisted my stomach. What if something had gone wrong? What if someone had seen us and alerted Remo?

I felt dizzy with anxiety as I sank down on the bed. My eyes remained on the clock on the nightstand, watching one minute after the other pass, wondering why I needed Fabiano to return safely to me.

FABIANO

Betrayal.

I broke Omertà by killing a fellow Camorrista.

For Leona.

I considered my options as I stared down at Soto's body. I could, of course, make him disappear. Nobody would miss him, least of all his cowering wife. But Remo might be reluctant to believe that Soto deserted us. After all, the man had been loyal.

"Damn it," I muttered. *Loyalty.*

Loyalty to the Camorra and to Remo … That was what I'd sworn, an oath that meant everything to me, but protecting Leona made keeping my oath impossible.

Remo didn't give a fuck about Soto or that I'd killed him, but he would care about me going around killing made men without his direct orders.

And then there was Boulder's miserable fight tonight. It was a big possibility that Remo was suspicious about that as well. God, Leona. Why did she have to bet money? Why did she have to meddle with things she had no clue about?

Because I backed her in a corner, and cornered dogs tried to bite. Fuck!

I could try to blame Boulder's failure on Soto. Tell Remo he had drugged the man and that I had killed him because of it, but Soto had no interest in changing the outcome of the fight. He hadn't placed a bet … No, Camorrista never did if they knew what was good for them. But Leona had, and Griffin would tell Remo if he asked. I grabbed Soto and dragged him toward my car. The parking lot was deserted, but if I wasted more time standing around looking for a solution to the mess I was in, that might change. I put Soto's body in my trunk and drove off, out of the city and into the desert. I had a shovel in my trunk, next to the spare tire.

When I found a promising spot, I parked the car, took the shovel from the trunk, and shoved it violently into the dry ground. It would take me hours to dig deep enough to hide the body. And all that hard work might be for nothing in the end.

I was covered in dirt and sweat when I finally unlocked my apartment door with my spare key. It was quiet inside. I closed the door and headed for the liquor cabinet. I didn't bother with a glass. Instead, I took a long swig of whiskey from the bottle. The burn of the alcohol cleared the fog of exhaustion.

Leona appeared at the top of the stairs, backlit by the soft glow from the bedroom. She was dressed in one of my shirts. She looked small in it. Vulnerable.

"Fabiano? Is that you?" she asked hesitantly.

I took another swig. I set the bottle down on the counter and moved toward the stairs, then took them one after the other. Leona's eyes took in my rumpled appearance.

"I was worried," she said as I stopped two steps below her, bringing us on eye level.

"It takes a while to bury a body in dry desert soil," I said, my voice raspy from the whisky.

She nodded as if she knew what I was talking about. "I'm sorry."

"I'm sorry too," I ground out.

Her mouth parted. "You are?"

"For making you think you had no choice but to do something that foolish, for making you think you couldn't come to me to ask for help. Not for killing your father. I would do it again if it meant protecting you."

She averted her gaze, her chest heaving. "You look like you could use a shower."

I smiled wryly. "I could use a lot of things right now."

She tilted her head toward me, searched my eyes but didn't say anything. I walked past her into the bedroom and continued into the bathroom. I got out of my clothes. They were covered in dust and Soto's blood. I'd have to burn them tomorrow. Not that it would matter. I stepped into the shower. Leona stood in the doorway, watching me. I kept my eyes on her as hot water rained down on me. I liked the sight of her in my shirt. I would have preferred her naked.

Tonight everything had changed. I had made a choice, and I had chosen Leona. Over the Camorra. Over Remo.

What had happened in the basement was something Remo had been able to overlook, but today, me killing one of his men to protect a woman? No. That was something he'd never forgive nor comprehend. He wasn't the forgiving type. I wouldn't forgive me if I were him.

I shut the water off. Leona picked up a towel and handed it to me. Her eyes moved down my body then back up to my face. I wanted her. I wanted, I *needed* some small sign that I had chosen right. Fuck.

I dried myself off halfheartedly then thrust the towel on to the ground.

Leona didn't move as I advanced on her, gripped her hips and lowered my mouth to hers for a hard kiss. My fingers on her waist tightened when she kissed me back.

I began guiding her backwards, out of the bathroom and toward my bed. She didn't resist. Her legs hit the bedframe, and she fell backwards. My shirt rode up her thighs, revealing that she wasn't wearing panties. I breathed out harshly. My cock was already hard. I wanted to finally be inside her.

She must have seen it too, but there was only need in her eyes, not fear. I climbed on the bed and moved between her legs then pushed them apart and lowered my body on top of hers.

She sucked in a tense breath but didn't push me away or protest. I kissed her again, my tongue tasting her mouth. My cock was pressed up against her inner thigh. A small shift of my hips and I'd be buried in her tight heat.

Leona brought her hand up, the one with the bracelet, and raked her fingers through my wet hair, which dripped water down onto our faces.

I pulled back a couple of inches. "Why didn't you pawn it for your bet?"

She followed my gaze. "I couldn't do it. Because you gave it to me."

Fuck. The look in her eyes. "I thought you hated me. That's what you said."

"I was trying to. But …" She trailed off. "You saved me again. You are the only one who cares enough to risk anything at all for me. It's pathetic, but there's only you."

I couldn't say anything in response to her emotional words. Nothing that would have done them justice. "I want you," I rasped into her ear, then added in an even lower voice, "I *need* you."

Her eyes searched mine. She couldn't stop looking for something even after everything that had happened. She lifted her hips slightly, making the tip of my cock slide over her slick folds. I hissed in response to the silent invitation. It was too enticing to take her right now, no more waiting. But she was worth the wait.

I sat back on my haunches and unbuttoned her shirt then helped her pull it off, allowing my eyes to take in her flawless skin. I was tired and still riled up. My control was at its limit, but I forced myself to lower my mouth to her pussy. Surprise flashed across her face and then her lips parted in a soft moan as I dipped my tongue between her folds. After a few strokes along her heated flesh,

I closed my lips around her clit. I was too impatient for the slow approach.

She rewarded me with a gasp and opened her legs even wider. My mouth on her bundle of nerves quickly had her panting and slick with arousal. I pushed a finger into her, fucking loving the way her walls clamped around me. I couldn't wait for them to do that to my cock. She bucked her hips, crying out, and I pushed a second finger into her. She shuddered as I guided her through her orgasm with slow strokes of my fingers and tongue. But my own need was too urgent now. My cock was close to exploding.

I straightened and reached for the drawer. I took a condom from it before I covered my cock with it. Leona watched me with a mix of trepidation and anticipation. I stretched out above her and guided my cock to her entrance. For a moment, I considered saying something, words she wanted to hear, loving words, gentle words, but I couldn't. I was filled with so much darkness and despair because I knew this was the only night we'd ever have. I felt it deep down.

I held her gaze as I pushed forward. My tip slid in, tightly gripped by her heat. She tensed, her breath stilling in her throat. Her eyes were soft and fucking emotional. I could not hold back. I didn't want to. I captured her mouth, my eyes boring into hers as I claimed her fully. Her resistance fell away under the pressure, and she gasped against my lips, her body taut under me.

"I betrayed for you, I killed for you," I said roughly, pulling out of her slowly until only my tip remained inside her. "I'll bleed and I'll die for you." I thrust back into her, trying to hold back.

Her eyes widened. From my words and pain. She clung to me. Those fucking cornflower blue eyes never leaving my face.

I'll bleed and I'll die for you.

It wasn't a promise, not a sappy declaration of my feelings. It was a prediction.

I pushed deeper and harder with every thrust, and she held on to me, eyes boring into mine. And I claimed her with every thrust, trying to convince myself that this was worth it, that Leona was worth the trouble I was willing to take on for her. That she was worth dying for.

Because Remo would kill me.

She sucked in her breath a few times. I knew I needed to be more careful, to go slower, but I couldn't stop. It felt like our time was falling through our fingers, and I needed to make every moment count. She made me betray Remo, something I never considered before. She made me break my oath of putting the Camorra first.

Was she worth it?

As our sweat-covered bodies moved against each other, as her tightness squeezed down on me, as her eyes clung onto mine with trust and something stronger and more dangerous, I decided she was worth it. I wasn't sure how it had come to this. How could I have let it get so far? How could she still look at me with those fucking caring eyes after everything? She was messed up and so was I.

I held her tightly as I came inside her. She gasped again, her breathing labored, cheeks flushed. She blinked at me slowly as if she was dazed and only just waking from a dream. Her lips brushed mine softly, and I could tell from the look in her eyes that she was about to say words I couldn't say back. Words she shouldn't even consider saying, not after what I'd done, not after what she knew about me. Not when I was a dead man walking. No words would change that. Nothing could.

"Don't say anything," I whispered harshly, and she listened.

I rolled us over and pulled her close. She winced but then pressed up against me; her body against mine felt like it was supposed to be like that. But I knew it might be the only time I could hold her like that.

LEONA

270

I woke to Fabiano's fingers tracing my spine. The touch was gentle, almost reverent.

I peered over my shoulder. He was propped up on his arm and followed the movement of his hand on my back. Hands that could kill without remorse, hands that were inexplicably gentle with me. His gaze found me, and I rolled over. Neither of us said anything. I kissed him.

I was sore from last night, but I wouldn't let that stop me, not only because he looked like he needed this more than air but also because I needed him. Last night, Fabiano, above me, in me, I felt like things had finally fallen into place. I never had a place to call home, but with him I felt anchored.

Things were complicated between us; they couldn't be anything else, given our pasts and lives, but I knew no matter what he was, nobody would ever make me feel more cared for than he did. We were twisted and broken and fucked up. Both of us. Why did I ever think I could be with someone straitlaced, someone with a normal past? That kind of man would never get me, not the same way Fabiano did. Reaching for his neck, I pulled him toward me. He didn't resist. Our lips glided over each other as he reached between us and found my opening to test my readiness. He shifted and his tip pressed against me. My fingers on his neck tightened as he claimed me with a slow push. My walls quivered in a mix of pain and pleasure. I exhaled sharply. He moved slowly, gently. Last night had been despair and possessiveness, and perhaps even fear and anger. This was different. It felt like … lovemaking. In a twisted way. Perhaps twisted was all I'd ever get.

His mouth found mine as his chest rubbed over my breasts. I moaned as he hit a spot deep within, lifted my butt, needing more. His fingers slipped between my legs, finding my bundle of nerves, and began their soft play. I gasped against his lips, and his tongue slipped in, meeting mine for a slow dance. My toes curled and my fingers scratched over the bed sheet as he sped up. Sparks of pleasure traveled from my core into every nerve ending.

I cried out, my hips bucking, and Fabiano pushed hard into me as he, too, lost control. We gasped, shaking against each other. Too many sensations, too many feelings. For a moment he didn't move, his hot mouth against my throat. Then he rolled over and pulled me with him so my cheek rested against his chest. It was almost as if he was trying to hide his face from me.

Our breathing was ragged.

"My sister gave it to me," he said. His words dragged me back to reality.

I followed his gaze toward the bracelet dangling around my wrist. I twisted my head to catch a glimpse at his expression, but he tightened his hold so I couldn't move.

"Your sister?"

"Aria, my oldest sister. Last time I saw her, she gave it to me."

That his sister had given it to him made it somehow even more precious. "When you were younger?"

"No," he said quietly. "Shortly before I met you. I was on a mission in New York." He fell silent. He didn't want to talk about the mission, and I wouldn't push.

"So she gave it to you so you'd remember her?"

He laughed, a raw sound. "She gave it to me so I would give it someone who would help me remember the brother she used to know."

"So you haven't always been like this." It was a stupid thing to say. Nobody was born a killer. They were turned into one by society and their upbringing. He finally allowed me to lift my face.

There was a strange smile on his face. "Like this?"

"You know," I said quietly, because what else was there to say. He knew what he was.

"I know," he murmured. "That's all I'll ever be. You know that, right?"

Part of me wanted to contradict him, but I couldn't. "I know," I said, and he smiled wryly.

"I gave the bracelet to you because I wanted it gone. It annoyed the crap out of me that my sister was trying to manipulate me somehow. But I think she got it right in the end."

I wondered what he meant by that, but his phone rang that moment. We both looked toward the nightstand and my heart skipped a beat when I saw who was calling.

FABIANO

I glanced down at the screen. Remo. I untangled myself from Leona and reached for my mobile.

Leona's eyes pleaded with me to ignore the call, but I needed to find out if Remo was on our trail. I picked up. "What's up?"

"I need you to kill Adamo for me," he muttered.

I sat up, shocked.

Leona threw me a worried look. I shook my head, trying to show her that we weren't in trouble. Yet.

"What do you mean?" I asked carefully. He couldn't possibly be serious. Adamo was a pain in the ass, but how could he be any other way. He was only thirteen and was only five when his father had been killed. Remo and his brothers had to go into hiding after that because their own family was fighting for the position of Capo and wanted them dead. They'd seen too much already.

"Cane told me he got word that Adamo did cocaine. Twice."

I grimaced. "You sure?"

"Apparently he's hanging with one of our errand boys. The fucker gave him the stuff." Remo paused. "Last night, he stole my Bugatti and drove it into a building."

Adamo had managed to steal another car?

"One day he's going to get himself killed. He doesn't seem to care about his life."

Remo was worried. Or as worried as Remo was capable of being. "What do you want me to do?"

"Give him a good scare. One that keeps him from doing shit like this. And kill all the other fuckers. Make him watch. Don't be lenient. Hurt him, Fabiano. If he gets addicted to the shit, he's fucking lost. A bullet to the head will be his end."

"Got it. I'll handle him."

Leona worried her lower lip. "That doesn't sound good."

"It's not, but it's got nothing to do with us," I said with a sigh. It was a good sign that Remo trusted me with Adamo. That meant perhaps I'd live to spend another night with Leona in my arms. "I have to deal with one of Remo's brothers."

Surprise filled her face, but she didn't ask for more details.

"Why don't you stay here and have breakfast? I should still have eggs in the fridge." I slid out of bed and dressed quickly. With a kiss and last glance at Leona's worried face, I headed out and went in search of Adamo.

I found the Bugatti on the side of the street, completely trashed. A tow truck from the company we worked with for the races was parked behind it, and Marcos, one of the other organizers of the races—and the driver of the tow truck—were walking around the car. I got out of my own car and strode toward them.

Marcos raised his palms. "I don't know how he managed to sneak into the qualification race. That boy is like fucking David Copperfield."

"Where is he?" I asked.

He shrugged. "He went off with two guys. That Rodriguez kid and the Pruitt kid, the one that sells snuff around here."

I asked around until I finally found one of our dealers who knew where Pruitt spent his days. It was an abandoned repair shop. I peered through the half-open gate.

Adamo and the two older boys were gathered around the hood of an old red Chevy. Adamo's long hair was matted to his head with blood, and yet he was laughing at something Pruitt said. The fucker shoved a piece of mirror with white powder on it over to Adamo, who looked fucking eager to get his nose down to business.

"Best nose candy, I'll tell ya," Pruitt said as he leaned down to sniff his own stuff.

I slid in. Adamo was the first to see me, and he opened his mouth for a warning. I gripped the back of Pruitt's head and shoved it down hard, smashing his face into the hood. "Enjoy your nose candy," I growled then ripped his head back. Blood was shooting out of his nose, and his face was covered in it and cocaine. His wide, dazed eyes settled on my face. I gave him a cold smile but released him when Rodriguez leaped toward me with an iron bar. Pruitt crumbled to my feet, and Rodriguez swept the bar at my head. I dropped to my knees. The bar crashed down on the hood. I pulled my knife and slashed it upwards, cutting him open. He dropped the iron bar then sank to his knees across from me, clutching his stomach. I rose to my feet then turned to Adamo. His shock was replaced by defiance when he met my eyes. He lifted his chin in challenge.

Oh, kiddo.

He took a step back from the hood and lifted his balled hands, one of them was clutching a knife, just like I'd taught him. "You think you are tough, don't you? That's what I thought when I was your age."

I approached and pointed toward the cocaine on the hood. "So that's how you want to end your life?"

"It doesn't matter. Remo sent you to kill me anyway!" he shouted. He glared, but there were tears in his eyes. "I crashed his favorite car. And I know

Cane told him about the snuff."

"If you plan on using that knife any time soon, do it."

He ran toward me and slashed the knife sideways, as if he intended to cut my throat, but the attempt was halfhearted and his aim way too low. He wasn't into it. I grabbed his shoulder, thrust him down on the hood, then brought my elbow down on his wrist. He dropped the knife with a cry of pain. I released him and stepped back. He cradled his wrist, tears finally falling as he sank to the dirty floor. Still only a boy. Remo liked to forget. Since Remo had become Capo, Adamo had been alone too often. "Don't raise a knife against me again unless it's for training or you really mean to kill," I told him.

"Just do it," he muttered, but there was fear in his voice.

I crouched in front of him. "Do what?"

"Kill me."

"Remo doesn't want you dead, Adamo. And I think you know that. And you know I won't kill you. If all this shit is your way to get his attention, it's not working the way you want it to. You're only pissing him off."

"He's always pissed off since he's become Capo," Adamo said quietly. "Perhaps he needs to get laid more often."

I laughed because he was too young to pull it off. "You're the one who needs to get laid, but if you keep this shit up, you'll die a virgin."

He flushed and looked away.

"I'm sure Remo can ask a few pretty girls to take care of it for you."

"No," he said fiercely. "I don't like those girls."

I straightened and held out my hand for him to take. "Easy, tiger." He took my hand after a moment of hesitation, and I pulled him to his feet. He moaned in pain and cradled his wrist again. "I'll take you to Nino. He'll set it for you." Nino, being the fucking genius that he was, knew more about medicine than most doctors.

"Come on," I told Adamo. He swayed slightly—whether from the wound on his head from the car crash or because of the pain in his wrist, I couldn't say. I gripped his arm and steadied him. He only reached my shoulders, so it was no trouble keeping him upright. Pruitt was crawling away, off to another door. I pulled my gun out of my holster and put a bullet through his head.

Adamo winced beside me. "You didn't have to do that."

"You are right. I could have taken him to Remo." We both knew how that would have ended.

Adamo didn't say anymore as I led him toward my car and helped him into the passenger seat. "They were my friends," he muttered when I started the car.

"Friends wouldn't have given you cocaine."

"We are selling the stuff. Every junkie in Vegas is a customer of the Camorra."

"Yes. And because we know what it does to people, we don't take the shit."

Adamo rolled his eyes before he leaned his head against the window, smearing it with blood. "What's with you and that girl?"

I jerked. "What are you talking about?"

"The one with the freckles."

I narrowed my eyes in warning.

Adamo gave me a triumphant smile. "You like her."

"Careful," I warned.

He shrugged. "I won't tell Remo. At least she has her own free will. The girls Remo always brings home kiss the ground he walks on because they fear him. It's disgusting."

"Adamo, you are a kid. You need to grow up and learn when to keep your fucking mouth shut. Remo is your brother, but he is still … Remo."

Adamo did keep his mouth shut when we walked into the Falcone mansion. Remo, Savio, and Nino were sitting on the couches in the living room. Savio got up with a grin and punched his brother's shoulder. "You are screwed." Then he sauntered off. Sixteen and almost as intolerable as Adamo most days; Nino, on the other hand, he looked almost bored, but that didn't mean he wouldn't be able to recite every fucking word tomorrow.

Remo gave me a nod. Perhaps Remo hadn't lost his trust in me. Perhaps things would turn out okay after all. Remo turned to his brother. "Broken wrist?"

Adamo glared at the ground. I let go of him and took a step back. That was between Remo and him. Remo pushed off the couch and came toward Adamo. "You won't take drugs again. No cocaine, heroin, grass, crack, you name it. Next time, I won't send Fabiano. Next time, I will deal with you." If anyone ever killed one of his brothers, it would be Remo.

Adamo raised his head, the same fucking challenge back in his eyes.

I wanted to slap him.

"Like you dealt with our mother?"

Remo's face became still.

Nino slowly rose from the couch. "You shouldn't speak of things you don't understand."

"Because nobody explains them to me," Adamo hissed. "I'm sick of you treating me like a stupid child."

Nino positioned himself between Adamo and Remo, who still hadn't said anything. "Then stop acting like one." He gripped Adamo's arm and pulled him along. "Let me treat your wounds."

Remo hadn't moved yet. His eyes were like black hellfire.

Great. And I was left to deal with him like that.

"Set up a fight for me. Tonight. Someone who can hold his own against me."

The only people who could hold their own against him were Nino and me. Savio was on his way to getting there.

Remo's eyes settled on me, and for a moment I was certain he'd ask me to fight him. We hadn't ever fought in an official match. For good reason. There were no ties in the fighting cage. One of us would have to give up.

"Or better two. Alert Griffin. He should hurry with the bets."

I sighed, but it was no use arguing with Remo when he was in a mood like that. Perhaps this would distract him for a while. The longer it took for him to notice that Soto had disappeared, the better. I was about to set everything up when Remo's voice made me stop.

"Fabiano, have you seen Soto recently? I can't contact him and nobody seems to know where he is."

I forced my expression into one of mild curiosity. "Perhaps one of his clients gave him trouble today?"

"Perhaps," he said quietly, but his eyes said something else.

CHAPTER 23

LEONA

had considered calling in sick at the bar and staying at Fabiano's apartment, snuggled in the soft blankets that smelled of him, of us, but eventually the worrying in my head got too loud. I needed to distract myself.

And it worked. The bar was busy that day. People were overexcited about something. They drank and ate more than usual, and Griffin had a hard time taking their bets. I heard the name Falcone being mentioned a few times but wasn't sure which of them was going to go into the cage.

"Did you hear Remo Falcone is going to fight again tonight?" Cheryl said when I stepped up to her behind the bar.

Hearing his name turned my insides to ice. "And?"

"It's a big deal. He hasn't fought in almost a year. He's Capo, after all."

"Then why now?" I asked, suddenly worried.

"I hear his youngest brother wrecked his favorite car," she said. Good. Was that what Fabiano had to deal with?

Roger came up behind us with a crate of beer and set it down beside us with a resounding thud. "And I hear it's because one of his men disappeared, probably defected," he said. "And now stop gossiping. Falcone doesn't like it."

"Who was it?" Cheryl asked.

"A guy called Soto."

Coldness washed over me. "What do you mean he defected?"

Roger gave me a strange look. "He disappeared without a word. If the Russians or someone else got him, they'd have left a bloody message behind." He went past us toward Griffin and two fighters already dressed in shorts. I had seen them in the cage in the last few days. Both of them had won their fights.

"You look pale. What's wrong? You should be used to all this. It's daily business around here."

I nodded distractedly.

"When one speaks of the Devil," Cheryl whispered.

I followed her gaze toward the entrance. Falcone and Fabiano had entered the room. My eyes found Fabiano's. His were fierce and worried.

I clutched the edges of the counter.

I'd come to Las Vegas for a better life, for a future away from the misery that was my mother's existence. Away from the darkness that was her constant companion. And now I was caught up in something far darker than anything I ever knew existed.

Remo's eyes wandered from Fabiano to me, and something cold and frightened curled up in the pit of my stomach. If he found out that Fabiano had killed one of his men because of me, he'd not only end Fabiano's life but also mine. And it wouldn't be quick.

Remo finally averted his eyes from me, and I could breathe again. I quickly turned around and busied myself sorting the clean glasses Cheryl had brought in from the kitchen earlier. I kept my head down as I served beer to customers. I didn't want to risk catching Fabiano's eyes again.

Griffin climbed up on the platform of the cage, and I stopped what I was doing. He had never done that before. He raised his hands to quiet the crowd. "Death match," he announced simply and a hush went through the crowd, followed by thunderous applause.

"What does that mean?" I whispered.

Cheryl gave me a pointed look. "It's going to be ugly, chick."

Fabiano leaned against the side of a booth, where two of the Falcone brothers sat. He hadn't looked my way since he'd first come in with Remo. It was probably better that way. Deep down, I wished he'd give me a small signal of reassurance ... even if it was only show.

When Remo stalked toward the cage, a lump formed in my throat. This was going to get ugly ... just like Cheryl had said.

Remo's fight outmatched all the previous fights in its brutality. Remo was out to hurt. To break. To kill. This wasn't about winning.

This was madness and cruelty and bloodlust.

He faced two opponents, but the first was dead within two minutes. Falcone broke his neck with a hard kick. After that, he was more careful. The second opponent was the one I felt sorry for. His death wasn't quick. It was like watching a cat toy with a mouse.

Eventually, I had to turn my back on the scene. I pressed my palm against my mouth, breathing through my nose. When the crowd erupted with cheers, I dared to look back and wished I hadn't. Remo was completely covered in blood. The man at his feet was the source of it. I sucked in a deep breath, trying to fight my rising nausea.

"I think you should go outside and catch some air," Cheryl said. "If you throw up, it means only more work for both of us."

I gave a shake of my head. "I'm fine," I bit out. I forced a smile at a customer who was waving at me for more beer. I quickly loaded a tray and headed over to him. Perhaps work would keep me distracted from the cage. I never looked toward it or Remo. If I wanted to keep my composure, I had to pretend none of this had happened.

Roger was cursing as he cleaned the cage. Neither Cheryl nor Mel, and least of all I would agree to get in there.

Fabiano had disappeared with Remo and his brothers almost one hour ago, and I wondered if he would pick me up tonight. I suspected he might not risk us being seen together today. My suspicions were confirmed when I walked out to the parking lot and found it empty except for Roger's car.

I hesitated. Should I wait for him? What if Remo required his presence? Fabiano couldn't risk anything right now. Lifting my backpack on my shoulder, I decided to head home. I wrapped my arms around myself for warmth. I wasn't sure if my teeth were chattering because I was cold or because of what I had witnessed. I still had the money I won from my bet against Boulder in the backpack. I hadn't found time to give it to my mother yet. I wanted to get rid of the money as quickly as possible.

A new wave of panic washed over me. We needed to leave Las Vegas before Remo found out. And when had *I* become *we*? When I watched Fabiano commit the ultimate sin for me? He'd done it before, but this time I let him.

The familiar purr of an engine caught my attention. I stopped and turned to see Fabiano's Mercedes driving down the street toward me. Of course he would make sure I was safe.

I got in the moment he stopped beside me. He hit the gas and did a U-turn, taking us back to his apartment. After what had happened in the last twenty-four hours, it was difficult to form the right words ... or any words, really. Fabiano didn't speak either. He was tense, his fingers clutching the wheel, eyes glaring out into the darkness.

"Does he know? Is that why he went berserk today?"

"That wasn't Remo going berserk, trust me. That was him trying not to go berserk."

So much blood and the sick excitement in Remo's eyes when he broke the neck of the first man, and then what came after ... If that wasn't going berserk I didn't know what was. "Fabiano," I began, but he shook his head.

"At home. I need to think."

I gave him space and quiet, even if my own mind was whirring so loudly with thoughts I couldn't believe he didn't hear it.

He didn't say anything, but he took my hand as he led me toward his apartment. I squeezed to show him that I wasn't going to break, that I could handle things too. The moment the door closed, he cupped my cheeks and kissed me. He pulled back after a moment. "You should leave Las Vegas."

FABIANO

"What? You stopped me from leaving not too long ago," she said incredulously, stepping away from me.

I was equally surprised by my words. I didn't want Leona to leave. I didn't want to lose her, but if she stayed, I'd lose her too.

"I know, but things are different now. I can't protect you if Remo finds out about Soto."

"What about you? Don't tell me he'll forgive you."

I shook my head. "He won't." Forgiveness? No, that wasn't something Remo ever dished out. Leona squeezed my hand again as if I was the one in need of comforting. I couldn't remember the last time someone had tried to comfort me.

"Then come with me. We can leave Las Vegas together."

I glanced down at my tattoo, at the words that still filled me with pride when I read them. "I took an oath."

Leona shook her head in disbelief. "You took an oath for a man who will kill you."

"Yes, because I broke my oath by killing a fellow Camorrista. I can hardly blame Remo for that."

She shook her head again, only harder. "Fabiano, please. Can't we just go to New York … where your sister lives? She will take you in, won't she?"

Aria would take me in, but Luca … He would put a bullet in my head as he should. "Perhaps. She's stupid like that. Because she still thinks I can return to being the brother she knew, but I'm not him anymore, and I don't want to be." That boy had wanted to please his father so he'd deign him worthy enough to inherit his rank. I had learned to fight for it.

"She will learn to accept the person you are now."

"I doubt it."

"Why? I do." Her eyes had become soft and something in my chest tightened.

"Sometimes you actually remind me of Aria with your stubborn insistence on taking care of your mother, even if she doesn't deserve it."

"That's because I love her. I can't help it."

"Then maybe love isn't the right choice for you."

She regarded me with a strange expression, one I couldn't place. "Yes, very likely. My mother always loved the wrong people and things. I guess I got that from her."

She didn't say anything for a while, and I wasn't sure what to say.

I cleared my throat. "I won't leave Las Vegas, or the Camorra, or Remo and his brothers. I'll risk his wrath, but I'll keep my oath."

"Why does this mean so much to you? I don't get it." Her fingers clutched my shirt. "Explain it to me. Why would you risk so much for them?"

"My sisters and I we were a unit. We stuck together against our father and our mother. I thought it would always be like that. I was just a boy. Then, one after the other left until I was left in a huge house with my choleric father and his child bride. They thought I could handle myself, but back then I was still weak. And when my father decided he didn't need me anymore, I was lost. I didn't want to run to New York with my tail between my legs, like a fucking failure, and beg Luca to take me in. He would have done so only because of Aria."

I ran my hand down Leona's throat and shoulder, relishing in the softness of her skin. I could tell she was trying to follow my words, but for her, my world—the mafia—was foreign. If you didn't grow up like me or my sisters, you wouldn't understand exactly what it meant to be born into our world.

"I would have died without Remo. I was incapable of taking care of myself, of fighting, of pretty much anything, but Remo knew how to survive and he taught me. He took me in like I was another one of his brothers. Remo is a cruel fucker, but over all the years he fought to claim Las Vegas, and in the years that followed, he kept his brothers close. They were more of a burden than help in the beginning, especially Savio and Adamo who were too young. He could have controlled Las Vegas sooner, but he stayed in hiding to keep them safe. He protected them and me. I don't always know what's going on in his twisted mind, but he's loyal and a good brother."

I could tell that she didn't believe it, and from what she'd seen of Remo, her disbelief was understandable. "So you'll leave Las Vegas and take your mother with you, if you must, and move to the East Coast. Remo won't risk an attack on Luca's territory right now." I lifted her arm with the bracelet. "And if you don't know what to do, if you need help, then go to New York, to a club called the Sphere and show them your bracelet. Tell them Aria will recognize it. And tell Aria that you are the one."

"The one?" she asked with a frown.

"Aria will understand."

CHAPTER 24

LEONA

washed a few glasses that nobody had taken care of last night. This morning I'd finally given Mom the money I won. I hoped she'd use it to pay her debt. I warned her to not pay everything at once so it wouldn't raise eyebrows. She'd probably spend most of it on a supply of drugs anyway.

Cheryl was rolling cigarettes beside me. When things got busy later she would hardly find the time. Her fingertips had a slight yellow tinge. She'd been smoking a lot in the last few days. Considering my frayed nerves, I wished I had something to calm them.

She hadn't asked me about Fabiano in a while, and I knew better than to offer any kind of information to her. It was too complicated to involve more people.

The door swung open. "We're closed," she shouted without even looking up.

My eyes slid over to the entrance and my hands stilled. Nino Falcone and one of his younger brothers entered. Cheryl followed my gaze and set down her cigarettes. Her eyes darted to me.

They came over to us. They didn't hurry and seemed almost relaxed as if this were a friendly visit. But Nino's cold gray eyes settled on me, and I just knew that they were here for me. Iciness clawed at my chest. I quickly dried my hands, my right hand reaching for the mobile I'd put down on the counter beside me. I needed to tell Fabiano about this. Perhaps he could at least escape, but I knew he wouldn't.

Nino shook his head, an empty expression on his face, eyes hard. "I wouldn't touch that if I were you."

I snatched my hand back from my mobile. Cheryl took a step back from me, from them. Her eyes held worry and fear—whether for herself or for me, I couldn't say.

Nino propped his elbows up on the bar. He was wearing a black turtleneck, and he looked like an Ivy League student, not a mobster. One look at his eyes and nobody would have taken him for anything but dangerous. And I had seen him fight, had seen the many disturbing tattoos on his body, always covered by clothing when he wasn't in the cage. He pointed at the Johnie Walker Blue Label. "Give me a glass."

My hands were shaking when I filled the glass with scotch. He took a sip. "My brother and I are going to take you with us now. We have some matters to discuss." He scanned my face. "You won't fight us, I assume."

I swallowed. The younger brother came around. He was still a teenager, definitely a couple of years younger than me, but there was no sign of boyish innocence on his face. He didn't touch me as he stopped beside me. Cheryl's eyes filled with pity.

I gave her a small smile then nodded toward Nino in agreement. There was no other option. Fighting them would have been ridiculous. I heard Fabiano talk about their fighting skills. I saw Nino in the cage with my own eyes. They would have me on the ground in a heartbeat, and unlike Fabiano, they wouldn't take care not to hurt me. Quite the contrary. I grabbed my backpack and mobile.

"Savio," Nino said simply.

Savio held out his hands, and I gave him both without resistance. Then he jerked his head. I walked ahead of him, even if having him at my back raised the little hairs on my neck. Nino appeared at my side. Neither of us spoke as they led me outside toward their car, a black Mercedes SUV. Savio opened the backdoor, and I climbed in. They sat in the front, not bothering to tie me up. There was no running. Nino sat behind the steering wheel and we drove off.

My hands shook badly as I curled my fingers around my knees in an attempt to calm myself. This didn't mean we were in trouble. Perhaps something else was up. But I couldn't come up with an explanation that set my mind at ease. I caught Savio watching me through the rearview mirror on occasion, while his older brother was completely focused on the windshield.

The drive passed in utter silence. Eventually a high wall came into view, and we drove through the gates and up the driveway toward a mansion. It was a beautiful sprawling estate. White and regal.

The Falcone brothers got out. Then a moment later, Nino held open my door. I hopped out of the car, glad my legs managed to hold me up despite their shaking.

"Where's Fabiano?" I asked, trying to mask my fear and failing on a grand scale.

Nino nodded toward the entrance, ignoring my question ... or perhaps answering it. I wasn't sure. Together, we walked inside the beautiful house. They led me into another wing and then into a large room with a pool table and boxing ring. In it, Remo was kicking and punching a heavy bag.

He wasn't wearing a shirt, and for some reason that sight more than anything else sent a wave terror through my body. His upper body was covered in scars, most of them not as faded as the one on his face, and like Fabiano, he was all muscle. A tattoo of a kneeling angel surrounded by broken wings covered his back. I'd never seen it up close. He jumped over the rope and landed gracefully on the other side, his eyes never leaving me as he approached me. My entire body seized.

"Where's Fabiano?" I asked again, hating how shaky my voice came out.

He tilted his head to the side. "He will be here soon, don't worry." His words weren't meant to be consoling. The menace in them prevented that.

FABIANO

I stared down at Remo's text: **Come over.**

Nothing more.

I paused, knowing immediately that something was up. I tried calling Leona, but I got her voicemail, and that was when a stab of worry went through me. I raced toward Roger's Arena.

Cheryl was having a smoke in front of the entrance, fingers trembling as she held the cigarette to her mouth. Fuck.

She shook her head at me. "She's not here. They took her." She took a drag. "I hope you're happy … now that you've ruined her life."

That was the first time she'd given me anything but fake friendliness. I had no time to waste on a reply. Instead, I slipped back inside my car and raced off.

Would Remo do the honors himself? Or would he ask Nino to put a bullet in my head?

That was assuming he'd allow me the privilege of dying a quick death at all, which I doubted. And what about Leona? I could handle his torture, but Leona … What if he hurt her in front of me and made me watch her die? My hands clawed at the steering wheel.

I pulled up in Remo's driveway and jumped out of the car, not bothering to close the door. A few of Remo's soldiers watched me like the dead man that I was. We all knew I wasn't getting out of here alive. I didn't have to ask where Leona was. I knew where Remo held these kinds of conversations. I didn't bother knocking and instead stepped right into the sparring hall.

Remo, Nino, and Savio were there. And Leona stood in the center. Her eyes darted to me and relief flashed in them. Her hope was misguided. This time I couldn't save her. We'd both die. I'd die trying to defend her, but it wouldn't help. Not against Remo, Nino, and Savio ... and all the men gathered in other areas of the house.

Remo perched on the edge of the pool table. He looked controlled, which worried me. He wasn't a man that usually bothered controlling himself or his anger.

"Remo," I said quietly with a nod. I walked up to Leona. I needed to be close to her when things escalated.

Remo's eyes flashed with suppressed rage. I had to fight the urge to reach for my gun. Remo, Nino, and Savio appeared relaxed enough, but I wasn't stupid enough to think that they hadn't taken all necessary precautions to guarantee we didn't get out of here alive.

"What's the meaning of all this, Remo?" I asked carefully.

He gritted his teeth and pushed himself away from the table. "Still not admitting to it?"

My muscles tensed. "Admitting to what?"

I didn't know what exactly Remo had found out. Admitting to killing Soto for Leona would be suicide.

"When you started pursuing her, I thought it was a brief adventure, but you got yourself in over your head."

"I've been doing my job as always, Remo."

He stopped across from me. Too close. "I don't recall asking you to kill Soto."

There it was. The thing that sealed our fate.

I considered pretending I didn't know what he was talking about but that would have made things worse. I pushed Leona a step back so my body was shielding her completely.

Remo saw. "All this because of that girl," he snarled. "You betrayed me for the daughter of a cheap crack-whore and a gambling addict. After everything I've done for you, you stab me in the back."

I held Leona's hand in a crushing grip, shielding her with my body, even if it drove Remo into madness. My eyes did a quick scan of the room. Remo alone was a dangerous opponent, but I would have tried my luck. With his two brothers in the room with us, I stood no chance. Nino, too, was impossible to beat.

I would still fight them, but it was only postponing the inevitable. I allowed myself a glance down at Leona, who was watching me with trust in her eyes. She thought I could get us out. Slowly, fear replaced her trust. I squeezed her hand once. She rewarded me with a shaky smile, and I released her hand. I needed both of my hands if I wanted to stand the slightest chance at all.

I considered denying I had killed Soto, but while I could withstand torture, Leona wouldn't be able to keep our secret if Remo or Nino turned their special talents on her. "I never meant to betray you. And I never did. Soto was a rat. He wasn't a good soldier."

"It's not your place to decide who is a good soldier. I am Capo, and I decide who lives and dies," he said in his quietest voice.

Remo was never quiet like that. He wasn't just furious. He was fucking crushed because I betrayed him and that was so much worse to him.

"I shouldn't have. I have always been a good soldier and I will always be your loyal soldier if you let me."

"Are you asking for forgiveness? For mercy?" He laughed.

I smiled coldly. "No. I won't."

Leona looked at me like I'd lost my mind, but she didn't know Remo. I'd seen him laugh into the faces of the begging and dying for years and knew he didn't have a heart to melt.

"Do with me whatever you want. But as a favor for years of loyal service, I ask you to let Leona go."

Remo laughed again. The way his eyes wandered over Leona, he was probably already thinking about all the things he could do to her. Raw protectiveness crushed me.

"Let me fight for her life. I'll fight as many men as you want."

Remo walked toward me. I fought the urge to pull a weapon. He stopped right in front of me. Our eyes locked. Years of loyalty, of brotherhood, passed in that one moment, and deep regret settled in my bones.

"You will fight me to the death," Remo said.

I stared at him uncomprehendingly. Since my sisters had left, since my mother had died and my father had wanted me dead, he was the only family I had. He and his brothers. Fuck, we spent every day together for the last five years. Had bled together, laughed together, killed together. I swore loyalty to him. I would have put my life down for him.

I turned my gaze to Leona, who was watching me and Remo with her innocent doe eyes. For her . . . I would kill him. I would kill them all.

"If you win, she will be free," Remo said to Nino, who would become Capo if Remo died. "And you, Fabiano, will put your life down without another fight."

"I will."

He nodded. "Perhaps Nino will feel lenient enough to grant you life afterward." Nino's expression left me little hope for that. Not that it mattered. If I killed Remo, the Camorra would be in uproar. Nino would have his hands full with that. He would prevail, of course, but perhaps it would give me the chance to . . . to what? Run away with Leona? From Vegas, from the Camorra?

Join the fucking Famiglia? Fuck. I wasn't sure I could do it. But it wasn't something I had to decide now, probably never.

"To the death," I told Remo, holding out my hand for him. He gripped it, and we shook hands. Then he stepped back, fixing his cold stare on Leona. "I hope you can live with yourself now that Fabiano's signed his death note for you."

Leona opened her mouth in what looked like protest, but I gripped her hand hard. She pressed her lips together.

"Tomorrow," Remo said then turned to Nino. "Set everything up. Call Griffin."

He fought two men only yesterday, but I knew the advantage that gave me was balanced out by the fury Remo felt.

His eyes found me again. "You will spend the night here, where I can keep an eye on you."

"You know I won't run," I told him.

"Once I *knew* you were loyal," he said.

He nodded at Nino and Savio, and they led Leona and me toward a panic room without windows and locked the door.

Leona gripped my shirt. "This is suicide. He wants to kill you."

"That he's giving me the chance to fight for your life is more than he would have given anyone else. That he fights me himself is the greatest proof of respect I can think of."

She didn't look like she understood. I didn't expected her to. "You will win, right? You are the best."

"I've never won against Remo."

Leona's eyes grew wide. "Never?"

I pulled her against me, my hands slipping under her shirt. I brushed my nose along her throat. "Never."

Her hands tightened on my shirt then she slid under the fabric, her fingers raking over my skin. Her need met my own as we tore and tugged at each other's clothes until we were finally naked. I tried to memorize every inch of her body, her smell, her softness, her moans.

Later, when we lay in each other's arms, I murmured, "I don't mind dying for you."

"Don't," she whispered. "Don't say that. You won't die."

I kissed the top of her head. "Love only gets you killed. That's what my father said. I suppose he got one thing right."

Leona stopped breathing. She raised her head. One look at her cornflower blue eyes and I knew she was worth it. "Did you just …?"

"Sleep," I said softly.

CHAPTER 25

FABIANO

"**Y**ou are lucky my brother does this for you," Nino said. "I'd have cut your throat."

He said it in a clinical voice. For him this was about logic and pragmatism. For Remo, this was personal. For Remo, I was like a brother … and I had gone against him. Nino moved across the room to his brothers.

Every last seat was occupied. Even more spectators stood against the walls, eyes eager for the fight of a lifetime. Leona wrung her hands beside me, eyes sliding from me to Remo, who was surrounded by his three brothers. Even Adamo would be watching the fight for once. They knew it might be their last chance to say goodbye to him.

The excitement of the crowd slowly crept into my bones. The thrill of the fight took hold of me. Remo looked at me. Tonight we'd both die. We knew it. Every other outcome would be a miracle. Leona was reluctant to let me go when Griffin called my name. Before I loosened her grip, I kissed her in front of everyone, because it didn't matter anymore. I pulled back and climbed into the cage where Remo was already waiting for me.

Griffin was saying something to the crowd or to us ... I wasn't sure.

Remo approached and only stopped when his chest almost touched mine. "I loved you like a brother. Tonight is where it all ends." He held out his hand.

I wasn't sure if Remo could love. Before Leona, I was sure I wasn't capable of it either. I gripped his forearm, my palm covering the tattoo on his forearm, and he mirrored the gesture. Then we let go and took a few steps back.

Griffin climbed out of the cage and locked the door before he shouted, "To the death!"

The bar erupted with applause, but it all faded to the background. This was about Remo and me. I charged forward and so did he. After that, our world narrowed to this fight, to this moment. Remo was fast and angry. He landed a few good hits before my fist collided with his abdomen for the first time. There was blood in my mouth and my right side ached fiercely, but I ignored both, focused on Remo, on his heaving chest, his narrowed eyes. He lunged and I tried to duck, but then he was upon me. We fell to the floor, his forearm pressed against my throat.

Remo tightened his hold until stars danced in front of my eyes. "And do you still think she's worth it?" he muttered into my ear.

I sought Leona's fear-stricken face in the crowd.

"Yes," I gritted out. Never had anything been more worth dying for.

LEONA

Fabiano's face was turning increasingly red in Remo's chokehold. I couldn't breathe. The crowd around me cheered like madmen, as if this wasn't about life or death. For them it was pure entertainment, something to distract them from their miserable lives.

Fabiano's blue eyes fixed on me, fierce and determined.

I tried to give him strength with my expression, even though I'd never felt more helpless and desperate in my life. The man I loved was fighting for both of our lives. Love. When had it happened? I wasn't sure. It was creeping up on me. I didn't even tell him outright. Perhaps I'd never get the chance to tell him.

And even if he won, Nino might still end his life.

Suddenly, Fabiano arched his back and thrust his elbow into Remo's side, but Remo didn't budge. Fabiano bowed forward as much as Remo's hold allowed, and then he thrust his head back with full force, crashing against Remo's face. The crowd exploded with cheers and yowls.

And suddenly, Fabiano wound himself out of Remo's grip and staggered to his feet before aiming a kick at Remo, hitting him square in the ribs. Remo jerked but quickly rolled away and pushed to his own feet. Then they were facing off again. They were circling each other, both covered in blood from head to toe, littered with bruises and cuts. Two predators waiting for a flicker of weakness.

"Perhaps now you realize what you've done," Nino said from close behind me. I jumped and took a step away from him. I didn't take my eyes off the fight. What had I done? I allowed myself to get close to a man who should have been out of reach. I had proven that I was more like my mother than I wanted to admit. But I didn't regret it. And I wouldn't allow Nino Falcone to scare me. I was past that point.

Remo landed three hard punches against Fabiano's stomach before he got hit in the face, and then they were kicking and punching so fast I lost count. They thrust each other to ground, got up, hit and kicked some more.

Fabiano's face wasn't even recognizable anymore from all the blood covering it, but neither was Remo's. I shivered.

I lost track of time; their fighting grew more erratic and less cautious. There was no holding back. Even to someone who wasn't in on the rules, it would have been clear that these two men were fighting for their life.

Remo grabbed Fabiano and thrust him full force into the fence. Fabiano bounced off and fell to his knees. I gasped and took a step forward.

Remo gripped Fabiano's head, but somehow Fabiano managed to push off the ground and thrust his knee into Remo's groin. Both of them toppled to the mat, panting and spitting blood. For a split second Fabiano allowed himself another look at me. Why did it feel like saying goodbye?

I began walking toward the cage, needing to stop this madness. Nino stepped in my way, tall and cold. "You stay where you are unless you want to die."

"How can you watch your brother die?" I asked incredulously.

Nino's unrelenting eyes took in the fight in the cage where both men were beating each other with elbows and fists, half kneeling on the floor, too weak to get up from almost one hour of non-stop fighting.

"We all have to die. We can choose to die standing up or on our knees begging for mercy. Remo's laughing death in the face like any self-respecting man should."

FABIANO

With every breath I took, it felt like a knife was slicing into my lungs. I pressed my palm against my right side, feeling my ribs. They were broken. I spit blood on the ground.

Remo was watching me closely as I knelt across from him. He'd make sure to aim his next hits on my right side. His left arm was hanging limply after I had managed to dislocate it with my elbow. This time I wouldn't give him the time to set it in place.

I pressed my palm against the ground, trying to push myself back into a standing position. The floor was slippery with blood. The room shook with roars and clapping when both Remo and I had managed to get to our feet. We were both swaying. We wouldn't be able to last long. Every bone in my body felt like it was broken. Remo winced, not bothering to hide it. We were past the point of pretending we weren't in pain. This was coming to a close.

"Thinking about giving up?" I asked.

Remo pulled back his lips in a bloody smile. "Never. And you?"

He could have had me killed without getting his hands dirty. He could have put a bullet through my skull and would have been done with it. Instead, he chose to give me a fair chance. Remo was hated. He deserved that hate like few other men in this world, but for what he did today, I'd respect him till my last breath.

"Never."

I barreled toward Remo under the thunderous applause of the crowd. The money the Camorra would win with bets tonight would set new standards. My body exploded with pain as I collided with Remo. We both fell to the ground and began wrestling. We had no strength for kick boxing anymore. This would be settled on the ground, with one of us choking the other or breaking his neck.

Something exploded. Remo and I fell apart, disoriented. The door to the fight arena went down, and men stormed in. They shouted at each other in Italian and English. Not the Russians.

The Outfit or the Famiglia attacking Las Vegas on their own?

They flooded the room like wildfire, lighting it up with gunshots.

And Remo and I sat in the middle of the room, in an illuminated fighting cage, like goldfish in a bowl.

From the corner of my eye, I saw Nino pushing Leona to the side so she fell to the ground, out of the line of fire. He began firing at the intruders as he rushed toward us. Remo and I pressed to the floor, trying not to be hit by stray bullets. It wasn't an honorable death to die kneeling on the ground, unable to fight back.

I could see one tall masked intruder heading our way, already reloading his gun. This wasn't the end I'd imagined. Being shot in the head by some Outfit or Famiglia asshole.

Nino reached the cage when two men began firing at him. Before he dove under a table, he threw a gun over the top of the cage. It landed with a soft thud in the blood puddle between Remo and me.

Remo had only one good arm, though, so I dove forward and grabbed the gun with my right hand while I used my left one to punch Remo's dislocated shoulder, stopping a grappling match before it could even start. He growled as he fell back. I knelt immediately, gun pointed straight ahead.

Remo smiled crookedly and opened his arms in invitation. "Do it. Better you than them."

Sorry, Remo, not like that.

I took aim, trying to stop my bruised arms from shaking, and then I pulled the trigger. The bullet hit its target right between the eyes.

Remo whirled around to what was behind him and could only watch the attacker, who had been pointing a gun at his head, tumble to the ground. I stumbled toward Remo, ignoring my body's screams of pain. I didn't waste time nor warned Remo. Instead, I grabbed his dislocated arm and pushed it back in place with one practiced move. Remo groaned then stumbled to his own feet. I threw my arm over his shoulder and steered him toward the door of the cage, shooting at anyone who looked like they might be a threat. I hammered against the locked cage door, but people were busy saving their own asses. And Remo's men and brothers were having a shooting match with five attackers hiding behind the bar.

My eyes searched our surroundings. Where was Leona? Was she safe? She knew this place and would be hiding somewhere safe. She was clever. I tried to calm myself. It wasn't fucking working. I ripped at the door, but the thing was built to last. "Fuck!" I screamed.

Remo tried his luck as well, but that thing was too strong. It rattled but apart from that nothing.

Suddenly, Leona's head popped up before us. Her eyes wandered between Remo and me, but she didn't say anything. She'd probably given up understanding me and this world a long time ago. She fumbled with the key in the lock until finally the door swung open, releasing us. I let go of Remo and jumped out of the cage, gasping at the impact. I'd be bruised for weeks.

If Remo let me live that long ... I was still supposed to die for my betrayal. Remo landed beside me and picked up a gun from a fallen man on the ground. "I go ahead, you have my back," he ordered like in old times. I pressed a kiss to Leona's lips. He watched with an unmoving expression.

"Let's leave," she begged. "This isn't our fight."

I smiled apologetically. "This will always be my fight as long as Remo lets me." I pushed her under the side of the cage where she wouldn't be spotted easily. "Stay there. It's too dangerous."

She nodded like she understood why I had to do this as she pressed herself against the side of the cage.

Remo and I turned around, and then we did what we did best. It took another hour to break the attack. The last two men raised their guns to their heads to end their own lives before we could get our hands on them. I shot one of them in the hand before he could pull the trigger. Then I was on him. "You'll regret the day you decided to enter our territory."

He spat onto my naked feet. "Fuck off."

Remo chuckled then coughed and spit blood on the ground. "That's how your spit is going to look soon too," he murmured.

We let Nino and Savio bring the man down to the soundproof storage room. Adamo stood back against one of the booths, looking shaken. He held a gun in his hand and stared down at one of the attackers. Was this the day of his first kill?

I could feel Leona's eyes on me as I followed after Remo to force information out of the attacker. I knew she was appalled by what I was doing. But she knew what I could do, and yet she was still here.

It took forty minutes to get the information we needed. Remo and I both were bruised and tired and needed medical treatment. We couldn't waste time on elaborate torture methods. Luckily, Nino did most of the work. The man was lying on the ground, wheezing. Remo knelt beside him. "So let me get this straight," he said calmly. "The Outfit sent you to my territory. For what?"

The man shook his head. "I don't know. I'm following orders. Your territory is bigger than ours. We want a piece. This was a good time."

Remo nodded. "Playing dirty. I like it."

He stood and gave me a look. I shoved my knife up the sucker's throat.

"This means war. If the Outfit thinks they can play, we'll show them what we are capable of."

I wiped my knife on my bloody shorts. "I bet that would be interesting."

Remo raised his dark eyebrows. "Would be?"

I straightened, despite the pain in my ribs. "I'm supposed to die, remember?"

Remo and I stared at each other for a long time. Nino and Savio exchanged looks as well. I wondered what they wanted. Me dead? I couldn't say, and they weren't the ones to decide anyway.

Remo put his hand on my shoulder, eyes fierce and full of warning. "This once I will let you live. You proved your loyalty by putting a fucking bullet into the head of my enemy when you could have killed me instead. Don't go behind my back again, Fabiano. That time there won't be a death match. I'll just put a bullet through your skull."

"As you should," I told him then pressed my palm again my side again. "Leona must be safe. She must be mine. I want her at my side. I want to spend my life with her."

"If that's what you want."

I nodded. "She's seen me at my worst, and she's still here."

Remo waved a hand at me. He couldn't comprehend. "She is yours, no worries. Now go to her and get a nice long blowjob as a reward for your troubles."

I rolled my eyes and dragged myself up the staircase. I doubted I'd get it up today. Every part of my body was aching, but I was willing to give it a try.

The moment I stepped back into the bar, Leona hopped off the barstool she had been waiting on and rushed toward me, throwing her arms around my waist. I gasped from the stab of pain in my ribs, my shoulder—fuck, my entire body. She loosened her hold, worried eyes peering up at me. Her hair was all over the place, and there was a small cut over her cheekbone. I ran the back of my index finger over it.

"You're hurt."

She choked out a laugh. "I'm hurt? You are bleeding and bruised. I thought you would die in that cage, and when you disappeared with Remo down into the storage room, I feared you wouldn't come out again," she whispered.

"I'm fine," I told her, and she gave me a look. "I'm alive," I amended.

For my fucking body to get anywhere close to being fine again, that would take a while.

"But what about Remo? Won't he kill you?"

Wasn't she worried about her own life as well? Perhaps she'd forgotten, but my fight would have decided her fate too.

"We came to an understanding. He gave me another chance." Fuck, to think that I would see that day.

"He did?" Leona voiced the disbelief still anchored in my body.

I nudged her in the direction of the entrance. "Come. I want to go home."

She froze. "We're not going home. You need to go to the hospital. Remo must have broken every bone in your body."

"I broke just as many of his," I said immediately.

Leona shook her head, unbelieving. "I don't care about him. But you need treatment."

I leaned down, my mouth curling into a smile despite the fucking cut in my lower lip. "I know just the right treatment."

She angled her head away. "You can't be serious."

I brushed my hand over her side. "I am dead serious. Won't you honor the wish of a dying man?"

She shoved me, angry and half amused. I winced because my body fucking ached. "Sorry!" she blurted, fingers ghosting over my chest in silent apology.

"I almost lost you and my fucking life. Don't you think I deserve a reward?"

She shook her head again, but her resolve was melting. Her fingers lingered on my abs, the touch a mix of pain and promise. "I really don't think ..."

"I won't go to the hospital," I interrupted her then buried my nose against her throat. "I want to feel you. Want to feel something else other than this fucking pain."

She opened the passenger door of my Mercedes for me. I raised my eyebrows. "You can't drive."

I handed her the keys without protest, enjoying her surprise. "Then you will."

I could tell she was terrified of wrecking my car. As if I gave a fucking damn about the thing. "Take us to our hill," I ordered when she pulled out of the parking lot.

Her brows pinched together again, but she did as I asked. After she parked, I pushed myself out of the car and carried myself toward the hood. I sank down and let my eyes take in my city. Leona stepped up beside me.

"And now?" she whispered.

I pulled her between my legs and kissed her softly, then harder but had to pull away when my vision began spinning. I tried to mask my dizziness, but Leona's eyes narrowed.

"Your body is a mess, Fabiano. Let's go to the hospital. There's no way you can do anything right now anyway."

I guided her hand to my dick, which was growing hard under her touch.

Her blue eyes met mine. "So every part of your body is hurting except for him," she said, squeezing my cock through the fabric. I chuckled and regretted it at once. "Seems so."

"Sure," she murmured doubtfully. "You should really go see a doctor."

"I will, later," I said quietly. "Now I want to remember why life is better than fucking death."

She leaned forward once more, kissing me sweetly and almost shyly, as if something in her mind was distracting her. When she pulled away, her uncertainty had been replaced by resolve. She slid down my shorts, grazing several wounds on the way, and got down on her knees before me. My cock jolted at the tantalizing sight. I hadn't expected her to do it after what she'd said about cock sucking being degrading and all, but I wasn't going to remind her. She wrapped her fingers around the base of my cock, opened her mouth, and slowly took me in inch by inch.

Holy Fuck.

I'd been with so many women, but every experience with Leona outshined my past. She gagged when my tip hit the back of her throat, and she quickly moved back. I had to resist the urge to grab her hair and hold her in place so I could fuck her sweet mouth. Instead, I forced my body to relax under her soft tongue, allowed her to explore and taste me. But eventually I needed more, so I took control. I began moving my hips, sliding my cock in and out of her warm mouth harder and faster every time.

Leona and I could have been dead by now. But we weren't. I jerked my hips upwards, and she let me. She struggled to take as much of me into her mouth as possible, and the sight fucking undid me. My balls tightened, and I called out a warning, but Leona didn't pull away. I released into her mouth.

It was the most painful orgasm I'd ever had, and yet as I watched Leona lick her lips with uncertainty, I decided it was also the fucking best. She ran a hand over her mouth, looking up at me. I could see the vulnerability in her eyes.

I pulled her up to me despite the agony that shot through my ribs, needing her to get it out of her head that anything I did was to degrade her. I needed her to understand what I felt for her, even if I had a hard time understanding it myself. "Leona, nothing I do will be to degrade you. And no one else will ever dare degrade you either." I softened my voice. "Are you okay?" I ran my thumb over her soft lips.

She ran a hand through my sweaty, blood-streaked hair. "Can we be together now? I mean for real?"

"We can and we will. I want you to move in with me. I want to bind you to me. I want to stop you from getting away ever again."

It wasn't romantic, it wasn't nice, but I wasn't either of those things.

"Then I'm okay."

I let out a small laugh, followed by a wince. She lightly traced my ribs but even that hurt.

"Why did you want me in the first place? I've been wondering about that from the start, but I knew you'd never tell me the truth anyway," she said.

"And now you think I will?"

She traced the cut below my cheekbone. "You are pretty rattled. I think now is my best chance."

"You are becoming more cunning."

She shrugged. "Survival of the fittest and all that. Or what did you call it?"

I slipped my hand under her shirt and bra and ran my forefinger over her nipple. It puckered immediately under the ministration. Leona licked her lips as her eyes glazed over. "Why?" she repeated her earlier question. I tugged at her nipple. She smiled. "Stop distracting me."

I slid my other hand up her thigh and into the leg of her shorts. My thumb brushed aside her thong and slid into her wet heat. She was still tight, but there was no resistance. Her walls squeezed around my finger as I slid it in and out slowly. She moaned and began bucking her hips.

"Why," she ground out again as she rocked her pussy against my hand. I exchanged my thumb for two fingers and moved faster. I stood and lifted her shirt then closed my lips around that perfect pink nipple. I tasted sweat on her skin. She'd been afraid for me, for us. I sucked her nipple harder. She gasped, slowly coming undone. I added a third finger, and she clawed at my shoulders, her expression a mix of ecstasy and discomfort. Pain shot through me when her fingers dug into bruised skin, but it felt fucking good. I thrust my fingers harder and faster into her, enjoying her tightness, her wetness, her whimpers. Fuck, those breathless sounds were music to my ears. Her walls clamped down on my fingers, and she threw her head back, letting out a long moan. I released her nipple and watched my fingers slide in and out of her. Her grip on my shoulders loosened. Slowly, her eyes peeled open and she watched me. I kept moving my fingers in and out of her, letting her ride out the last gentle waves of pleasure. "Because you didn't judge me. You didn't know me. You didn't go into our conversation hoping to get something out of it."

Leona smiled. "But I got something out of it. I got you."

I shook my head at her. I slid my fingers out of her. "You don't know what's good for you."

She released a small breath then lifted one shoulder. "Good's overrated."

I kissed her again, tasting myself on her.

"You almost died today … for me," she whispered. "Nobody has ever done something like that for me. People can keep telling me to stay away from you if they want, but it won't make me love you any less."

My body grew taut at her admission. Love was a dangerous thing, something that had brought the hardest fighters to their knees. Weakness was something I couldn't afford, not if I wanted to stay on Remo's good side. But love wasn't a choice. It was like fucking torture. Something that happened to you and you were unable to stop it. It was the only form of torture I was unable to endure.

I brushed a sweaty curl out of her face, wondering how she could have put a hole in the impenetrable façade I'd built since my father had abandoned me. Leona, with her infuriating naivety, her shy smile … I'd watched the people I cared about leave me one after the other. I swore to myself to never allow anyone else into my heart. And now Leona had changed everything.

"Your expression is a bit on the unsettling side. What's going on?"

I shook my head in exasperation. I hadn't been afraid of anyone or anything in a while, and here I was being a fucking pussy about this. "Fuck," I breathed. "I love you."

She took a small step back, astonishment reflecting on her beautiful face. "I didn't think you'd say it."

"You didn't think I loved you?"

She laughed then wedged herself between my legs again, bringing us closer and sending a stab of pain through my body from the movement, but I couldn't care less. If I didn't think it might shove one of my broken ribs into my lungs, I'd have fucked her right then. No, *made love to her*. God help me.

"After you agreed to a death match, I was fairly certain you did," she said with a small smile, "but I didn't think you'd admit it."

Sometimes I forgot how well she'd come to know me. That she still wanted to be with me filled my heart with a strange sense of comfort but also with a bone-deep fear I hadn't felt in a long time. The idea of a death match with Remo hadn't scared me, death and pain certainly didn't, but Leona's love and my love for her scared me shitless. It was something I'd just have to deal with because Leona wasn't going anywhere, and I wouldn't stop loving her.

CHAPTER 26

LEONA

Fabiano's bruises and cuts had healed. Roger's Arena had been renovated, but I was no longer working for him. Fabiano didn't want me to. After all, now I was officially his girl. Even my mother stopped selling her body because she didn't have to do it anymore. She got her meth from Fabiano. The Camorra had more than enough of the toxic stuff. It wasn't what I'd wanted for her, and I still wished she'd stop taking the shit altogether, but it was her choice; I'd done what I could for her.

Suddenly people treated me differently. With respect. Not because of who I was but because of who I belonged to: The Enforcer of the Camorra.

It was nice in some regard, but I still preferred people respect me for my own accomplishments. One day perhaps.

I sat quietly beside Fabiano, watching Nino Falcone destroy his opponent in the fighting cage. Remo sat at the same table, but I ignored him. He was being civil toward me since the fight to the death, and I treated him with the respect he expected as Capo. I did it for Fabiano and because I wasn't suicidal. But I'd never like him. Too little humanity remained in him—if it had ever been there in the first place. His two brothers were at the table too. Savio, who whistled whenever his brother landed a hit, and Adamo, who seemed drawn into himself, not once glancing toward the cage.

Fabiano traced a hand up my thigh, startling me. My eyes met his then quickly did a scan of our surroundings. People were mesmerized by the fight and didn't pay attention to what was going on underneath our table.

Fabiano turned his attention back to the fight as well, but he kept stroking the inside of my thigh. Nino threw his opponent into the cage, and the room exploded with applause. Fabiano slipped his hand beneath my panties, finding me aroused, which was usually the case when he touched me. He leaned over, his breath hot against my ear. "I hope this isn't because of Nino," he said huskily.

I rolled my eyes.

"Tonight I'm going to fuck you in that cage."

He dipped a finger between my folds, and I had to stifle a groan. Remo's eyes slid over to me, and I quickly closed my legs, forcing Fabiano to pull his hand away. He smirked then commented on a move Nino did with his leg as if nothing had happened.

With an audible crack, Nino broke his opponent's arm. Adamo jerked back his chair and stood, eyes wild, then he turned and hurried off toward the exit. I wasn't sure why, but I pushed my own chair back and followed him. He was a Falcone, Remo's brother, but he was also only thirteen. And he obviously wasn't coping with what happened the last couple of weeks. I caught up with him in the parking lot, his hand on the door of a sleek red Ford Mustang.

"Your car?" I asked jokingly.

"Remo's," Adamo said, twisting car keys between his fingers.

"He lets you drive it?" I doubted anyone would let a thirteen-year-old drive a car around Vegas, but Remo didn't exactly play by the rules.

Adamo turned angry eyes toward me. "No, he'll probably kick my ass. I stole the key."

"Oh." He was still watching me, still twisting the key as if he needed the smallest reason to stay. I took a step closer. "I don't enjoy the cage fighting. Too brutal."

"Not as brutal as real life."

Mob life. His life ... and now mine as well. "I dream about the attack." And about the hours before it, the fear of the death match.

He looked down at the key in his hand. "I shot someone."

"I know," I said quietly and took another step forward. I put my hand on his forearm lightly. His eyes met mine. Only thirteen and they looked jaded. "It was self-defense."

"It won't always be. I'm a Falcone. Soon, I'll be a Camorrista."

"True. But who says you'll have to hurt people. You could do street races. It's a big part of the business, right? So it would be good to have a Falcone showing off what he can do. I hear you are quite good already."

His lips twitched. "Yeah. But Remo thinks I'm too young."

"Once you're inducted, I'm sure he'll change his mind. If you can handle a gun, you can race a car, don't you think?"

He shook his head slowly. "Remo will attack the Outfit in retribution. He will need a fighter, not a race driver."

I'd figured as much from Fabiano's cryptic comments these last few days. Things would get rough pretty soon. "Why don't you come back inside? Stealing your brother's car won't get you any favors."

His eyes shifted between the car and the bar. Then he closed the door. We turned and headed back toward the entrance, where Fabiano was waiting with his arms crossed over his chest.

Adamo winced.

"Have you been spying on us?" I asked.

He pushed off the wall. "You both have a penchant for getting into trouble."

I huffed.

Fabiano caught Adamo's gaze and put a hand on his shoulder. "Running won't help." He poked his index finger against Adamo's forehead. "Can't run from what's in there. Regret and guilt, they follow." Fabiano touched Adamo's forearm, and the boy gave a small nod as if he understood.

Fabiano tousled his hair. Adamo pulled back in protest. Then Fabiano feigned an attack and a grappling match ensued. After a moment, Fabiano pushed a smiling Adamo toward the door. "Inside."

Adamo entered the bar, and we followed. Remo's eyes zeroed in on us at once. His brother put the key down in front of him then slumped back in his chair.

Fabiano and I took our seats, and he took my hand under the table, linking our fingers.

Remo leaned over to me, and I tensed. Fabiano squeezed my hand in support, but his eyes were on the fight. "What did you do to stop him from driving off?"

It took effort to hold Remo's fierce dark eyes. "Tried to make him see light in the dark."

"Like you did for him," he said with a tilt of his head. It wasn't a question.

I glanced at Fabiano, but his eyes followed Nino's movements in the cage … at least it appeared that way. Before Remo turned away, a flicker of acknowledgement passed over his expression.

I didn't think he was serious, but Fabiano and I were the last guests in the bar. Cheryl cleaned the counter, eying us wearily. "We should leave too."

"I told you I'd have you against that cage tonight." He turned to Cheryl and raised his voice. "You can leave. I have the keys. I will lock up later."

Cheryl put down the cloth, picked up her purse, and walked past us. She'd been distant since I was officially at Fabiano's side.

He took my hand and pulled me to my feet then led me toward the cage in the center. My core tightened in anticipation as he leaped onto the platform and pulled me along. I climbed into the cage then heard the familiar click of the door closing. A pleasant shiver raced down my spine. Fabiano pressed up against my body from behind, his erection digging into my lower back. I arched my butt against him, needing his hands on me. After his teasing during the fight, it had been difficult to grasp a straight thought. He pulled my dress over my head and dropped it onto the ground then pulled down my panties.

Fabiano urged me forward with his body until I had no choice but to brace myself against the cage. He ran his hands over my shoulders and down my arms, then gripped my hands, lifting them above my head. I linked my fingers in the mesh of the cage as Fabiano pressed my body against the cold metal. My nipples hardened immediately. The feel of the unrelenting steel against my breasts and Fabiano's equally unrelenting muscles was oddly erotic. He stepped back and I huffed in protest, but when I looked over my shoulder, I saw him pull down his briefs. His cock was already hard for me. I shivered in anticipation. There was hunger in his eyes and the warmer emotion that he didn't try to hide anymore. His movements were lithe and dangerous as he stalked toward me. Fighter and killer and mine. I turned back to the cage and leaned my forehead against it. Not able to see him approach heightened my senses, made me even more aroused.

He slid a hand between my thighs and urged them apart. I complied eagerly then waited for his fingers to send me to Heaven. Instead, I felt his tip press against my opening. Surprise filled me, but then I arched my butt to show him I didn't mind him skipping foreplay. Being in a cage with him was all the foreplay I needed. But he didn't push into me. Instead, he ran his tip up from my opening to my clit and back again. I moaned, arching against him for more friction. My nipples rubbed against the metal deliciously.

And then he pushed into me with one hard thrust. I cried out, my fingers clinging painfully to the wire mesh. He slid in and out. His hand glided over my stomach and lower until his fingers brushed my clit. I cried out again, and he thrust even harder into me. His fingers established a slow rhythm while he fucked me fast. My fingers on the mesh tightened painfully as a wave of pleasure swept through me. I cried out his name, half delirious from the force of my orgasm. I had trouble staying upright. My fingers loosened their grip on the mesh fence, and Fabiano's hands covered mine, linking our fingers and holding me up.

His pelvis hit my butt again. I whimpered. The sensations were almost too much, but Fabiano knew no mercy. His pelvis slammed against my butt over and over again as he drove himself even deeper into me. Dots danced before my vision. "Oh God," I gasped. His next thrust catapulted me into sweet oblivion, a darkness of heightened senses and overwhelming pleasure. He turned me around and lowered me to the ground then lifted my feet to his shoulders, raising my butt. His tip rested against my sensitive flesh. His blue eyes looked unhinged. Out of control for once. He slid into me slowly then back out. The way he was holding my hips, I could see his erection sliding between my folds as I felt my walls yielding to him. Fabiano's muscles flexed as he took his time sliding in and out of me. I didn't think I was capable of another orgasm after my last, but seeing Fabiano's cock bury itself in me aroused me even more.

I began quivering. Fabiano smiled darkly and parted my folds with his thumbs, revealing my clit. If he touched me there, I'd fall apart. But he didn't. He only watched his cock slide in and out, his thumbs so very close to where I needed his touch the most.

I reached out, too desperate for my next release to wait for him to make a move, but he caught my wrist. He raised my palm to his mouth and pressed an open-mouthed kiss to my flesh, his tongue darting out and licking off sweat. I groaned at the sensation as it traveled all the way down to my clit. "Fabiano," I begged. "Stop torturing me."

A predator grin. "But it's what I do best."

Good God. There was no way I wasn't going to Hell for this. And I couldn't even pretend I cared. He slid into me again and then mercifully, he captured my clit between his fingers and twirled it between them. I came apart. My shoulder blades arched painfully against the floor, my nails searching for leverage. And then Fabiano followed after me with a curse and groan. I forced my eyes open, needing to see him. He had his head thrown back, eyes closed. The most amazing sight ever.

Slowly, he lowered his head and looked at me, his lips twisting wryly. "I truly corrupted you. You weren't even worried someone could walk in on us."

I turned my head to the side. The bar was deserted, but of course he had a point. We hadn't locked the doors, and it wouldn't be the first time Roger spent the night in his office.

I covered my eyes with my hand, trying to catch my breath. Fabiano took my wrist and pulled my shield away, then stood me up so I straddled his legs. I wrapped my arms around his neck, searching his eyes for confirmation that he was okay with me enjoying this so much. "

You were worth it, you know?" He nuzzled my neck and I smiled to myself.

"What exactly?" I whispered.

"The pain, the wait, Remo's wrath. Everything."

This was where it all started. Where my dreams of an ordinary life ended and something else, something equally good I realized now, had begun.

"I love you," I breathed.

"And I love you," he said. The words still sounded foreign from his lips.

I touched the tattoo on his forearm. "More than this."

"More than this." But because I knew he loved the Camorra, loved Remo as a brother—for whatever inexplicable reason—I would never ask him to choose.

He brushed my hair back from my sweaty forehead. "You should start looking into applying to college. University of Nevada is a good place to start."

I pulled back. "I don't have the money."

Fabiano smiled. "I might as well put all the blood money in my account to good use. The Camorra still needs a good lawyer. Why not you?"

I couldn't believe it. "You mean it?" I didn't dare hope I was hearing him right.

He nodded. "But I have to tell you that it has to be in Vegas. I can't let you go, being a possessive bastard and all."

I kissed him, excitement surging through me.

"My possessiveness never excited you that much before," he said wryly.

I shook my head, having a hard time forming words to express my gratitude. "I don't want to leave Las Vegas. Because Las Vegas is your home and you are mine."

He pulled me into a painful embrace and I sank into him. My protector.

THE END

BORN IN BLOOD MAFIA CHRONICLES

Bound By Honor
Aria & Luca

Bound By Duty
Dante & Valentina

Bound By Hatred
Gianna & Matteo

Bound By Temptation
Liliana & Romero

Bound By Vengeance
Cara & Growl

Bound By Love
Aria & Luca

Read Fabiano's story in the first book of the Camorra Chronicles,
a new spin-off series to the Born in Blood Mafia Chronicles:

Twisted Loyalties
Fabiano & Leona

ABOUT THE AUTHOR

Cora Reilly is the author of the Born in Blood Mafia Series, the Camorra Chronicles and many other books, most of them featuring dangerously sexy bad boys. Before she found her passion in romance books, she was a traditionally published author of young adult literature.

Cora lives in Germany with a cute but crazy Bearded Collie, as well as the cute but crazy man at her side. When she doesn't spend her days dreaming up sexy books, she plans her next travel adventure or cooks too spicy dishes from all over the world.

Despite her law degree, Cora prefers to talk books to laws any day.